Lord
of
the
World

Lord of the World

ROBERT HUGH BENSON

TAN Books
Charlotte, North Carolina

First Published in 1907

TAN edition © 2016 TAN Books

Retypeset by TAN Books in 2016. The type in this book is the property of TAN Books and may not be reproduced, in whole or in part, without written permission from the publisher.

Foreword by James V. Schall, S.J., copyright © 2016 TAN Books.

Cover design by David Ferris
www.davidferrisdesigns.com

ISBN: 978-1-5051-0925-2

Published in the United States by
TAN Books
P. O. Box 410487
Charlotte, NC 28241
www.TANBooks.com

Printed in the United States of America

Dedication
CLAVI DOMUS DAVID

CONTENTS

Foreword. ix

Preface xiii

Prologue xv

BOOK I—The Advent

Chapter I. 1

Chapter II 21

Chapter III. 43

Chapter IV. 61

Chapter V 75

BOOK II—The Encounter

Chapter I. 87

Chapter II 107

Chapter III. 131

Chapter IV. 155

Chapter V 173

Chapter VI. 191

Chapter VII 209

Chapter VIII. 223

BOOK III—The Victory

Chapter I. 241

Chapter II 259

Chapter III. 275

Chapter IV. 289

Chapter V 305

Chapter VI. 321

FOREWORD

In 2001 (surely not on 9/11!), St. Augustine's Press published a new edition of Robert Hugh Benson's 1907 novel, *The Lord of the World*. I had never read it. A friend of mine in Vermont urged me to read it, and so I did. And, now, I have the pleasure to introduce a new generation of readers to this wonderful book.

The late Ralph McInerny, in a brief introduction to that edition, writes: "The novel wonderfully conveys the flatness and boredom of a world without God. Boredom becomes a condition for recognizing our need for something more than this—a few more decades of life and then a total void."

This novel is remarkably similar in theme to Benedict's encyclical *Spe Salvi*, one of the very great encyclicals. That is, the novel is about the futility of a this-worldly utopia with the instruments of death (abortion, euthanasia) and endless "life" (prolongation of life, cloning) that are designed to make it come about. Indeed, in a lecture he gave at the Catholic University in Milan on February 6, 1992, Joseph Ratzinger cited *The Lord of the World* and the deadly Universalist, inner-world atmosphere it depicted.

My father had this Benson novel around the house when I was a boy in Iowa. I remember reading it. What I remember most about it was how frightening it was to me with its vivid end-of-the world description. Indeed, I have often said that this novel and C. S. Lewis' *That Hideous Strength* are the most frightening books that I have ever read. Now, no longer a youth and then some, when I ask myself why this fright, it is because both books make the this-worldly triumph of evil so plausible, so intellectual, so logical.

Both books seem to exemplify the validity of a remark of Herbert Deane in his book on Augustine: "As history draws to its close, the number of true Christians in the world will decline rather than increase. His (Augustine's) words give no support to the hope that the world will gradually be brought to belief in Christ and that earthly society can be transformed, step by step, into the kingdom of God". The anti-Christ figure in *The Lord of the World* becomes the "Man-God," the "Lord of the World," precisely by promising universal brotherhood, peace, and love, but no transcendence.

The hero of the book is an English priest, Percy Franklin, who looks almost exactly like the mysterious Julian Felsenburgh, who is an American senator from, yes, Vermont. Felsenburgh suddenly appears as a lone and dramatic figure promising the world goodness if it but follow him. No one quite knows who he is or where he is from, but his voice mesmerizes. Under his leadership, East and West join. War is abolished. Felsenburgh becomes the President of Europe, then of the World, by popular acclaim. Everyone is fascinated by him. Still no one knows much about him. People are both riveted and frightened by the way he demands attention. Most follow without question.

The only people who oppose him in any way are the few loyal Catholics. These two adjectives beg the question. When and if times of persecution come, will you and I be counted among the few and the loyal? Can we be so counted today?

The last words of the novel are . . . well, you have it in

your hands. Continue reading and you will find out. Rest assured, however, that they could not be more dramatic, or more moving. Somehow, I no longer find those words so frightening. Rather, they are almost consoling.

James V. Schall, S.J.
Santa Clara, 2016

This foreword is an edited and adapted version of a longer essay which first appeared on the website www.insidecatholic.com on March 9, 2009.

PREFACE

I AM perfectly aware that this is a terribly sensational book, and open to innumerable criticisms on that account, as well as on many others. But I did not know how else to express the principles I desired (and which I passionately believe to be true) except by producing their lines to a sensational point. I have tried, however, not to scream unduly loud, and to retain, so far as possible, reverence and consideration for the opinions of other people. Whether I have succeeded in that attempt is quite another matter.

Robert Hugh Benson
Cambridge, 1907.

PERSONS WHO DO not like tiresome prologues, need not read this one. It is essential only to the situation, not to the story.

R.H.B.

PROLOGUE

"YOU MUST give me a moment," said the old man, leaning back.

Percy resettled himself in his chair and waited, chin on hand.

It was a very silent room in which the three men sat, furnished with the extreme common sense of the period. It had neither window nor door; for it was now sixty years since the world, recognising that space is not confined to the surface of the globe, had begun to burrow in earnest. Old Mr. Templeton's house stood some forty feet below the level of the Thames embankment, in what was considered a somewhat commodious position, for he had only a hundred yards to walk before he reached the station of the Second Central Motor-circle, and a quarter of a mile to the volor-station at Blackfriars. He was over ninety years old, however, and seldom left his house now. The room itself was lined throughout with the delicate green jade-enamel prescribed by the Board of Health, and was suffused with the artificial sunlight discovered by the great Reuter forty years before; it had the colour-tone of a spring wood, and was warmed and ventilated through the classical frieze grating to the exact temperature of 18° Centigrade. Mr. Templeton was a plain man, content to live as his father had lived before him. The furniture, too, was a little old-fashioned in make and design, constructed however according to the prevailing system of soft asbestos enamel welded over iron, indestructible, pleasant to the touch, and resembling mahogany. A couple of book-cases well filled ran on either side of the bronze pedestal electric fire before which sat the three men; and in the further corners stood the hydraulic lifts that gave entrance, the one to the bedroom, the other to the corridor fifty feet up which opened on to the Embankment.

Father Percy Franklin, the elder of the two priests, was rather a remarkable-looking man, not more than thirty-five years old, but with hair that was white throughout; his grey eyes, under black eyebrows, were peculiarly bright and almost passionate but his prominent nose and chin and the extreme decisiveness of his mouth reassured the observer as to his will. Strangers usually looked twice at him.

Father Francis, however, sitting in his upright chair on the other side of the hearth, brought down the average; for, though his brown eyes were pleasant and pathetic, there was no strength in his face; there was even a tendency to feminine melancholy in the corners of his mouth and the marked droop of his eyelids.

Mr. Templeton was just a very old man, with a strong face in folds, clean-shaven like the rest of the world, and was now lying back on his water-pillows with the quilt over his feet.

At last he spoke, glancing first at Percy, on his left.

"Well," he said, "it is a great business to remember exactly; but this is how I put it to myself."

"In England our party was first seriously alarmed at the Labour Parliament of 1917. That showed us how deeply Hervéism had impregnated the whole social atmosphere. There had been Socialists before, but none like Gustave Hervé in his old age—at least no one of the same power.

He, perhaps you have read, taught absolute Materialism and Socialism developed to their logical issues. Patriotism, he said, was a relic of barbarism; and sensual enjoyment was the only certain good. Of course, every one laughed at him. It was said that without religion there could be no adequate motive among the masses for even the simplest social order. But he was right, it seemed. After the fall of the French Church at the beginning of the century and the massacres of 1914, the *bourgeoisie* settled down to organise itself; and that extraordinary movement began in earnest, pushed through by the middle classes, with no patriotism, no class distinctions, practically no army. Of course, Freemasonry directed it all. This spread to Germany, where the influence of Karl Marx had already——"

"Yes, sir," put in Percy smoothly, "but what of England, if you don't mind——"

"Ah, yes; England. Well, in 1917 the Labour Party gathered up the reins, and Communism really began. That was long before I can remember, of course, but my father used to date it from then. The only wonder was that things did not go forward more quickly; but I suppose there was a good deal of Tory leaven left. Besides, centuries generally run slower than is expected, especially after beginning with an impulse. But the new order began then; and the Communists have never suffered a serious reverse since, except the little one in '25. Blenkin founded 'The New People' then; and the 'Times' dropped out; but it was not, strangely enough, till '35 that the House of Lords fell for the last time. The Established Church had gone finally in '29."

"And the religious effect of that?" asked Percy swiftly, as the old man paused to cough slightly, lifting his inhaler. The priest was anxious to keep to the point.

"It was an effect itself," said the other, "rather than a cause. You see, the Ritualists, as they used to call them, after a desperate attempt to get into the Labour swim, came into the Church after the Convocation of '19, when the Nicene Creed dropped out; and there was no real enthusiasm except among them. But, so far as there was an effect from the final Disestablishment, I think it was that what was left of the State Church melted into the Free Church, and the Free Church was, after all, nothing more than a little sentiment. The Bible was completely given up as an authority after the renewed German attacks in the twenties; and the Divinity of our Lord, some think, had gone all but in name by the beginning of the century. The Kenotic theory had provided for that. Then there was that strange little movement among the Free Churchmen even earlier; when ministers who did no more than follow the swim—who were sensitive to draughts, so to speak—broke off from their old positions. It is curious to read in the history of the time how they were hailed as independent thinkers. It was just exactly what they were not.... Where was I? Oh, yes.... Well, that cleared the ground for us, and the Church made extraordinary progress for a while—extraordinary, that is, under the circumstances, because you must remember, things were very different from twenty, or even ten, years before. I mean that, roughly speaking, the severing of the sheep and the goats had begun. The religious people were practically all Catholics and Individualists; the irreligious people rejected the supernatural altogether, and were, to a man, Materialists and Communists. But we made progress because we had a few exceptional men—Delaney the philosopher, McArthur and Largent, the philanthropists, and so on. It really seemed as if Delaney and his disciples might carry everything before them. You remember his 'Analogy'? Oh, yes, it is all in the text-books....

"Well, then, at the close of the Vatican Council, which had been called in the nineteenth century, and never dissolved, we lost a great number through the final definitions. The 'Exodus of the Intellectuals' the world called it——"

"The Biblical decisions," put in the younger priest.

"That partly; and the whole conflict that began with the rise of Modernism at the beginning of the century: but much more the condemnation of Delaney, and of the New Transcendentalism generally, as it was then understood. He died outside the Church, you know. Then there was the condemnation of Sciotti's book on Comparative Religion.... After that the Communists went on by strides, although by very slow ones. It seems extraordinary to you, I dare say, but you cannot imagine the excitement when the *Necessary Trades Bill* became law in '60. People thought that all enterprise would stop when so many professions were nationalised; but, you know, it didn't. Certainly the nation was behind it."

"What year was the *Two-Thirds Majority Bill* passed?" asked Percy.

"Oh! long before—within a year or two of the fall of the House of Lords. It was necessary, I think, or the Individualists would have gone raving mad.... Well, the *Necessary Trades Bill* was inevitable: people had begun to see that even so far back as the time when the railways were municipalised. For a while there was a burst of art; because all the Individualists who could went in for it (it was then that the Toller school was founded); but they soon drifted back into Government employment; after all, the six-percent limit for all individual enterprise was not much of a temptation; and Government paid well."

Percy shook his head.

"Yes; but I cannot understand the present state of affairs. You said just now that things went slowly?"

"Yes," said the old man, "but you must remember the Poor Laws. That established the Communists for ever. Certainly Braithwaite knew his business."

The younger priest looked up inquiringly.

"The abolition of the old workhouse system," said Mr. Templeton. "It is all ancient history to you, of course; but I remember as if it was yesterday. It was that which brought down what was still called Monarchy and the Universities."

"Ah," said Percy. "I should like to hear you talk about that, sir."

"Presently, father.... Well, this is what Braithwaite did. By the old system all paupers were treated alike, and resented it. By the new system there were the three grades that we have now, and the enfranchisement of the two higher grades. Only the absolutely worthless were assigned to the third grade, and treated more or less as criminals—of course after careful examination. Then there was the reorganisation of the Old Age Pensions. Well, don't you see how strong that made the Communists? The Individualists—they were still called Tories when I was a boy—the Individualists have had no chance since. They are no more than a worn-out drag now. The whole of the working classes—and that meant ninety-nine of a hundred—were all against them."

Percy looked up; but the other went on.

"Then there was the Prison Reform Bill under Macpherson, and the abolition of capital punishment; there was the final Education Act of '59, whereby dogmatic secularism was established; the practical abolition of inheritance under the reformation of the Death Duties—"

"I forgot what the old system was," said Percy.

"Why, it seems incredible, but the old system was that all paid alike. First came the *Heirloom Act*, and then the change by which inherited wealth paid three times the duty of earned wealth, leading up to the acceptance of Karl Marx's doctrines in '89—but the former came in '77.... Well, all these things kept England up to the level of the Continent; she had only been just in time to join in with the final scheme of Western Free Trade. That was the first effect, you remember, of the Socialists' victory in Germany."

"And how did we keep out of the Eastern War?" asked Percy anxiously.

"Oh! that's a long story; but, in a word, America stopped us; so we lost India and Australia. I think that was the nearest to the downfall of the Communists since '25. But Braithwaite got out of it very cleverly by getting us the protectorate of South Africa once and for all. He was an old man then, too."

Mr. Templeton stopped to cough again. Father Francis sighed and shifted in his chair.

"And America?" asked Percy.

"Ah! all that is very complicated. But she knew her strength and annexed Canada the same year. That was when we were at our weakest."

Percy stood up.

"Have you a Comparative Atlas, sir?" he asked.

The old man pointed to a shelf.

"There," he said.

Percy looked at the sheets a minute or two in silence, spreading them on his knee.

"It is all much simpler, certainly," he murmured, glancing first at the old complicated colouring of the beginning of the twentieth century, and then at the three great washes of the twenty-first.

He moved his finger along Asia. The words EASTERN EMPIRE ran across the pale yellow, from the Ural Mountains on the left to the Behring Straits on the right, curling round in giant letters through India, Australia, and New Zealand. He glanced at the red; it was considerably smaller, but still important enough, considering that it covered not only Europe proper, but all Russia up to the Ural Mountains, and Africa to the south. The blue-labelled AMERICAN REPUBLIC swept over the whole of that continent, and disappeared right round to the left of the Western Hemisphere in a shower of blue sparks on the white sea.

"Yes, it's simpler," said the old man drily.

Percy shut the book and set it by his chair.

"And what next, sir? What will happen?"

The old Tory statesman smiled.

"God knows," he said. "If the Eastern Empire chooses to move, we can do nothing. I don't know why they have not moved. I suppose it is because of religious differences."

"Europe will not split?" asked the priest.

"No, no. We know our danger now. And America would certainly help us. But, all the same, God help us—or you, I should rather say—if the Empire does move! She knows her strength at last."

There was silence for a moment or two. A faint vibration trembled through the deep-sunk room as some huge machine went past on the broad boulevard overhead.

"Prophesy, sir," said Percy suddenly. "I mean about religion."

Mr. Templeton inhaled another long breath from his instrument. Then again he took up his discourse.

"Briefly," he said, "there are three forces—Catholicism, Humanitarianism, and the Eastern religions. About the third I cannot prophesy, though I think the Sufis will be victorious. Anything may happen; Esotericism is making enormous strides—and that means Pantheism; and the blending of the Chinese and Japanese dynasties throws out all our calculations. But in Europe and America, there is no doubt that the struggle lies between the other two. We can neglect everything else. And, I think, if you wish me to say what I think, that, humanly speaking, Catholicism will decrease rapidly now. It is perfectly true that Protestantism is dead. Men do recognize at last that a supernatural Religion involves an absolute authority, and that Private Judgment in matters of faith is nothing else than the beginning of disintegration. And it is also true since the Catholic Church is the only institution that even claims supernatural authority, with all its merciless logic, she has again the allegiance of practically all Christians who have any supernatural belief left. There are a few faddists left, especially in America and here; but they are negligible. That is all very well; but, on the other hand, you must remember that Humanitarianism, contrary to all persons' expectations, is becoming an actual religion itself, though anti-supernatural. It is Pantheism; it is developing a ritual under Freemasonry; it has a creed, 'God is Man,' and the rest. It has therefore a real food of a sort to offer to religious cravings; it idealises, and yet it makes no demand upon the spiritual faculties. Then, they have the use of all the churches except ours, and all the Cathedrals; and they are beginning at last to encourage sentiment. Then, they may display their symbols and we may not: I think that they will be established legally in another ten years at the latest.

"Now, we Catholics, remember, are losing; we have lost steadily for more than fifty years. I suppose that we have, nominally, about one-fortieth of America now—and that is the result of the Catholic movement of the early twenties. In France and Spain we are nowhere; in Germany we are less. We hold our position in the East, certainly; but even there we have not more than one in two hundred—so the statistics say—and we are scattered. In Italy? Well, we have Rome again to ourselves, but nothing else; here, we have Ireland altogether and perhaps one in sixty of England, Wales and Scotland; but we had one in forty seventy years ago. Then there is the enormous progress of psychology—all clean against us for at least a century. First, you see, there was Materialism, pure and simple—that failed more or less—it was too crude—until psychology came to the rescue. Now psychology claims all the rest of the ground; and the supernatural sense seems accounted for. That's the claim. No, father, we are losing; and we shall go on losing, and I think we must even be ready for a catastrophe at any moment."

"But——" began Percy.

"You think that weak for an old man on the edge of the grave. Well, it is what I think. I see no hope. In fact, it seems to me that even now something may come on us quickly. No; I see no hope until——"

Percy looked up sharply.

"Until our Lord comes back," said the old statesman.

Father Francis sighed once more, and there fell a silence.

"And the fall of the Universities?" said Percy at last.

"My dear father, it was exactly like the fall of the Monasteries under Henry VIII—the same results, the same arguments, the same incidents. They were the strongholds of Individualism, as the Monasteries were the strongholds of Papalism; and they were regarded with the same kind of awe and envy. Then the usual sort of remarks began about the amount of port wine drunk; and suddenly people said that they had done their work, that the inmates were mistaking means for ends; and there was a great deal more reason for saying it. After all, granted the supernatural, Religious Houses are an obvious consequence; but the object of secular education is presumably the production of something visible—either character or competence; and it became quite impossible to prove that the Universities produced either—which was worth having. The distinction between ov and $\mu\acute{\eta}$ is not an end in itself; and the kind of person produced by its study was not one which appealed to England in the twentieth century. I am not sure that it appealed even to me much (and I was always a strong Individualist)—except by way of pathos——"

"Yes?" said Percy.

"Oh, it was pathetic enough. The Science Schools of Cambridge and the Colonial Department of Oxford were the last hope; and then those went. The old dons crept about with their books, but nobody wanted them—they were too purely theoretical; some drifted into the poorhouses, first or second grade; some were taken care of by charitable clergymen; there was that attempt to concentrate in Dublin; but it failed, and people soon forgot them. The buildings, as you know, were used for all kinds of things. Oxford became an engineering establishment for a while, and Cambridge a kind of Government laboratory. I was at King's College, you know. Of course it was all as horrible as it could be—though I am glad they kept the chapel open even as a museum. It was not nice to see the chantries filled with anatomical specimens. However, I don't think it was much worse than keeping stoves and surplices in them."

"What happened to you?"

"Oh! I was in Parliament very soon; and I had a little money of my own, too. But it was very hard on some of them; they had little pensions, at least all who were past work. And yet, I don't know: I suppose it had to come. They were very little more than picturesque survivals, you know; and had not even the grace of a religious faith about them."

Percy sighed again, looking at the humorously reminiscent face of the old man. Then he suddenly changed the subject again.

"What about this European parliament?" he said

The old man started.

"Oh! … I think it will pass," he said, "if a man can be found to push it. All this last century has been leading up to it, as you see. Patriotism has been dying fast; but it ought to have died, like slavery and so forth, under the influence of the Catholic Church. As it is, the work has been done without the Church; and the result is that the world is beginning to range itself against us: it is an organised antagonism—a kind of Catholic anti-Church. Democracy has done what the Divine Monarchy should have done. If the proposal passes I think we may expect something like persecution once more.… But, again, the Eastern invasion may save us, if it comes off.… I do not know.…"

Percy sat still yet a moment; then he stood up suddenly.

"I must go, sir," he said, relapsing into Esperanto. "It is past nineteen o'clock. Thank you so much. Are you coming, father?"

Father Francis stood up also, in the dark grey suit permitted to priests, and took up his hat.

"Well, father," said the old man again, "come again some day, if I haven't been too discursive. I suppose you have to write your letter yet?"

Percy nodded.

"I did half of it this morning," he said, "but I felt I wanted another bird's-eye view before I could understand properly: I am so grateful to you for giving it me. It is really a great labour, this daily letter to the Cardinal-Protector. I am thinking of resigning if I am allowed."

"My dear father, don't do that. If I may say so to your face, I think you have a very shrewd mind; and unless Rome has balanced information she can do nothing. I don't suppose your colleagues are as careful as yourself."

Percy smiled, lifting his dark eyebrows deprecatingly.

"Come, father," he said.

The two priests parted at the steps of the corridor, and Percy stood for a minute or two staring out at the familiar autumn scene, trying to understand what it all meant. What he had heard downstairs seemed strangely to illuminate that vision of splendid prosperity that lay before him.

The air was as bright as day; artificial sunlight had carried all before it, and London now knew no difference between dark and light. He stood in a kind of glazed cloister, heavily floored with a preparation of rubber on which footsteps made no sound. Beneath him, at the foot of the stairs, poured an endless double line of persons severed by a partition, going to right and left, noiselessly, except for the murmur of Esperanto talking that sounded ceaselessly as they went. Through the clear, hardened glass of the public passage showed a broad sleek black roadway, ribbed from side to side, and puckered in the centre, significantly empty, but even as he stood there a note sounded far away from Old Westminster, like the hum of a giant hive, rising as it came, and an instant later a transparent thing shot past, flashing from every angle, and the note died to a hum again and a silence as the great Government motor from the south whirled eastwards with the mails. This was a privileged roadway; nothing but state-vehicles were allowed to use it, and those at a speed not exceeding one hundred miles an hour.

Other noises were subdued in this city of rubber; the passenger-circles were a hundred yards away, and the subterranean traffic lay too deep for anything but a vibration to make itself felt. It was to remove this vibration, and silence the hum of the ordinary vehicles, that the Government experts had been working for the last twenty years.

Once again before he moved there came a long cry from overhead, startlingly beautiful and piercing, and, as he lifted his eyes from the glimpse of the steady river which alone had refused to be transformed, he saw high above him against the heavy illuminated clouds, a long slender object, glowing with soft light, slide northwards and vanish on outstretched wings. That musical cry, he told himself, was the voice of one of the European line of volors announcing its arrival in the capital of Great Britain.

"Until our Lord comes back," he thought to himself; and for an instant the old misery stabbed at his heart. How difficult it was to hold the eyes focussed on that far horizon when this world lay in the foreground so compelling in its splendour and its strength! Oh, he had argued with Father Francis an hour ago that size was not the same as greatness, and that an insistent external could not exclude a subtle internal and he had believed what he had then said; but the doubt yet remained till he silenced it by a fierce effort, crying in his heart to the Poor Man of Nazareth to keep his heart as the heart of a little child.

Then he set his lips, wondering how long Father Francis would bear the pressure, and went down the steps.

BOOK I — THE ADVENT

CHAPTER I

I

OLIVER BRAND, the new member for Croydon (4), sat in his study, looking out of the window over the top of his typewriter.

His house stood facing northwards at the extreme end of a spur of the Surrey Hills, now cut and tunnelled out of all recognition; only to a Communist the view was an inspiriting one. Immediately below the wide windows the embanked ground fell away rapidly for perhaps a hundred feet, ending in a high wall, and beyond that the world and works of men were triumphant as far as eye could see. Two vast tracks like streaked race-courses, each not less than a quarter of a mile in width, and sunk twenty feet below the surface of the ground, swept up to a meeting a mile ahead at the huge junction. Of those, that on his left was the First Trunk road to Brighton, inscribed in capital letters in the Railroad Guide, that to the right the Second Trunk to the Tunbridge and Hastings district. Each was divided lengthways by a cement wall, on one side of which, on steel rails, ran the electric trams, and on the other lay the motor-track itself again divided into three, on which ran, first the Government coaches at a speed of one hundred and fifty miles an hour, second the private motors at not more than sixty, third the cheap Government line at thirty, with stations every five miles. This was further bordered by a road confined to pedestrians, cyclists and ordinary cars on which no vehicle was allowed to move at more than twelve miles an hour.

Beyond these great tracks lay an immense plain of house-roofs, with short towers here and there marking public buildings, from the Caterham district on the left to Croydon in front, all clear and bright in smokeless air; and far away to the west and north showed the low suburban hills against the April sky.

There was surprisingly little sound, considering the pressure of the population; and, with the exception of the buzz of the steel rails as a train fled north or south, and the occasional sweet chord of the great motors as they neared or left the junction, there was little to be heard in this study except a smooth, soothing murmur that filled the air like the murmur of bees in a garden.

Oliver loved every hint of human life—all busy sights and sounds—and was listening now, smiling faintly to himself as he stared out into the clear air. Then he set his lips, laid his fingers on the keys once more, and went on speech-constructing.

He was very fortunate in the situation of his house. It stood in an angle of one of those huge spider-webs with which the country was covered, and for his purposes was all that he could expect. It was close enough to London to be extremely cheap, for all wealthy persons had retired at least a hundred miles from the throbbing heart of England; and yet it was as quiet as he could wish. He was within ten minutes of Westminster on the one side, and twenty minutes of the sea on the other; and his constituency lay before him like a raised map. Further, since the great London termini were but ten minutes away, there were at his disposal the First Trunk lines to every big town in England. For a politician of no great means, who was asked to speak at Edinburgh on one evening and in Marseilles on the next, he was as well placed as any man in Europe.

He was a pleasant-looking man, not much over thirty years old; black wire-haired, clean-shaven, thin, virile, magnetic, blue-eyed and white-skinned; and he appeared this day extremely content with himself and the world. His lips moved slightly as he worked, his eyes enlarged and diminished with excitement, and more than once he paused and stared out again, smiling and flushed.

Then a door opened; a middle-aged man came nervously in with a bundle of papers, laid them down on the table without a word, and turned to go out. Oliver lifted his hand for attention, snapped a lever, and spoke.

"Well, Mr. Phillips?" he said.

"There is news from the East, sir," said the secretary.

Oliver shot a glance sideways, and laid his hand on the bundle.

"Any complete message?" he asked.

"No, sir; it is interrupted again. Mr. Felsenburgh's name is mentioned."

Oliver did not seem to hear; he lifted the flimsy printed sheets with a sudden movement, and began turning them.

"The fourth from the top, Mr. Brand," said the secretary.

Oliver jerked his head impatiently, and the other went out as if at a signal.

The fourth sheet from the top, printed in red on green, seemed to absorb Oliver's attention altogether, for he read it through two or three times, leaning back motionless in his chair. Then he sighed, and stared again through the window.

Then once more the door opened, and a tall girl came in.

"Well, my dear?" she observed.

Oliver shook his head, with compressed lips.

"Nothing definite," he said. "Even less than usual. Listen."

He took up the green sheet and began to read aloud as the girl sat down in a window-seat on his left.

She was a very charming-looking creature, tall and slender, with serious, ardent grey eyes, firm red lips, and a beautiful carriage of head and shoulders. She had walked slowly across the room as Oliver took up the paper, and now sat back in her brown dress in a very graceful and stately attitude. She seemed to listen with a deliberate kind of patience; but her eyes flickered with interest.

" 'Irkutsk — April fourteen — Yesterday — as — usual — But — rumoured — defection — from — Sufi — party — Troops — continue — gathering — Felsenburgh — addressed — Buddhist — crowd — Attempt — on — Llama — last — Friday — work — of — Anarchists — Felsenburgh — leaving — for — Moscow — as — arranged — he....' There — that is absolutely all," ended Oliver dispiritedly.

"It's interrupted as usual."

The girl began to swing a foot.

"I don't understand in the least," she said. "Who is Felsenburgh, after all?"

"My dear child, that is what all the world is asking. Nothing is known except that he was included in the American deputation at the last moment. The *Herald* published his life last week; but it has been contradicted. It is certain that he is quite a young man, and that he has been quite obscure until now."

"Well, he is not obscure now," observed the girl.

"I know; it seems as if he were running the whole thing. One never hears a word of the others. It's lucky he's on the right side."

Oliver turned vacant eyes again out of the window.

"I think it is touch and go," he said. "The only remarkable thing is that here hardly anybody seems to realise it. It's too big for the imagination, I suppose. There is no doubt that the East has been preparing for a descent on Europe for these last five years. They have only been checked by America; and this is one last attempt to stop them. But why Felsenburgh should come to the front—" he broke off. "He must be a good linguist, at any rate. This is at least the fifth crowd he has addressed; perhaps he is just the American interpreter. Christ! I wonder who he is."

"Has he any other name?"

"Julian, I believe. One message said so."

"How did this come through?"

Oliver shook his head.

"Private enterprise," he said. "The European agencies have stopped work. Every telegraph station is guarded night and day. There are lines of volors strung out on every frontier. The Empire means to settle this business without us."

"And if it goes wrong?"

"My dear Mabel—if hell breaks loose—" he threw out his hands deprecatingly.

"And what is the Government doing?"

"Working night and day; so is the rest of Europe. It'll be Armageddon with a vengeance if it comes to war."

"What chance do you see?"

"I see two chances," said Oliver slowly: "one, that they may be afraid of America, and may hold their hands from sheer fear; the other that they may be induced to hold their hands from charity; if only they can be made to understand that co-operation is the one hope of the world. But those damned religions of theirs——"

The girl sighed, and looked out again on to the wide plain of house-roofs below the window.

The situation was indeed as serious as it could be. That huge Empire, consisting of a federalism of States under the Son of Heaven (made possible by the merging of the Japanese and Chinese dynasties and the fall of Russia), had been consolidating its forces and learning its own power during the last thirty-five years, ever since, in fact, it had laid its lean yellow hands upon Australia and India. While the rest of the world had learned the folly of war, ever since the fall of the Russian republic under the combined attack of the yellow races, the last had grasped its possibilities. It seemed now as if the civilisation of the last century was to be swept back once more into chaos. It was not that the mob of the East cared very greatly; it was their rulers who had begun to stretch themselves after an almost eternal lethargy, and it was hard to imagine how they could be checked at this point. There was a touch of grimness too in the rumour that religious fanaticism was behind the movement, and the patient East proposed at last to proselytise by the modern equivalents of fire and sword those who had laid aside for the most part all religious beliefs except that in Humanity. To Oliver it was simply maddening. As he looked from his window and saw that vast limit of London laid peaceably before him, as his imagination ran out over Europe and saw everywhere that steady triumph of common sense and fact over the wild fairy-stories of Christianity, it seemed intolerable that there should be even a possibility that all this should be swept back again into the barbarous turmoil of sects and dogmas; for no less than this would be the result if the East laid hands on Europe. Even Catholicism would revive, he told himself, that strange faith that had blazed so often as persecution had been dashed to quench it; and, of all forms of faith, to Oliver's mind Catholicism was the most grotesque and enslaving. And the prospect of all this honestly troubled him, far more than the thought of the physical catastrophe and bloodshed that would fall on Europe with the advent of the East. There was but one hope on the religious side, as he had told Mabel a dozen times, and that was that the Quietistic Pantheism which for the last century had made such giant strides in East and West alike, among Mohammedans, Buddhists, Hindus, Confucianists and the rest, should avail to check the supernatural frenzy that inspired their exoteric brethren. Pantheism, he understood, was what he held himself; for him "God" was the develop-ing sum of created life, and impersonal Unity was the essence of His being; competition then was the great heresy that set men one against another and delayed all progress; for, to his mind, progress lay in the merging of the individual in the family, of the family in the commonwealth, of the common-wealth in the continent, and of the continent in the world. Finally, the world itself at any moment was no more than the mood of impersonal life. It was, in fact, the Catholic idea with the supernatural left out, a union of earthly fortunes, and abandonment of individualism on the one side, and of supernaturalism on the other. It was treason to appeal from God Immanent to God Transcendent; there was no God tran-scendent; God, so far as He could be known, was man.

Yet these two, husband and wife after a fashion—for they had entered into that terminable contract now recognised explicitly by the State—these two were very far from sharing in the usual heavy dulness of mere materialists. The world, for them, beat with one ardent life blossoming in flower and beast and man, a torrent of beautiful vigour flowing from a deep source and irrigating all that moved or felt. Its romance was the more appreciable because it was comprehensible to the minds that sprang from it; there were mysteries in it, but mysteries that enticed rather than baffled, for they unfolded new glories with every discovery that man could make; even inanimate objects, the fossil, the electric current, the far-off stars, these were dust thrown off by the Spirit of the World— fragrant with His Presence and eloquent of His Nature. For example, the announcement made by Klein, the astronomer, twenty years before, that the inhabitation of certain planets had become a certified fact—how vastly this had altered men's views of themselves. But the one condition of progress and the building of Jerusalem, on the planet that happened to be men's dwelling place, was peace, not the sword which Christ brought or that which Mahomet wielded; but peace that arose from, not passed, understanding; the peace that sprang from knowledge that man was all and was able to develop himself only by sympathy with his fellows. To Oliver and his wife, then, the last century seemed like a revelation; little by little the old superstitions had died, and the new light broadened; the Spirit of the World had roused Himself, the sun had dawned in the west; and now with horror and loathing they had seen the clouds gather once more in the quarter whence all superstition had had its birth.

Mabel got up presently and came across to her husband.

"My dear," she said, "you must not be downhearted. It all may pass as it passed before. It is a great thing that they are listening to America at all. And this Mr. Felsenburgh seems to be on the right side."

Oliver took her hand and kissed it.

II

OLIVER seemed altogether depressed at breakfast, half an hour later. His mother, an old lady of nearly eighty, who never appeared till noon, seemed to see it at once, for after a look or two at him and a word, she subsided into silence behind her plate.

It was a pleasant little room in which they sat, immediately behind Oliver's own, and was furnished, according to universal custom, in light green. Its windows looked out upon a strip of garden at the back, and the high creeper-grown wall that separated that domain from the next. The furniture, too, was of the usual sort; a sensible round table stood in the middle, with three tall arm-chairs, with the proper angles and rests, drawn up to it; and the centre of it, resting apparently on a broad round column, held the dishes. It was thirty years now since the practice of placing the dining-room above the kitchen, and of raising and lowering the courses by hydraulic power into the centre of the dining-table, had become universal in the houses of the well-to-do. The floor consisted entirely of the asbestos cork preparation invented in America, noiseless, clean, and pleasant to both foot and eye.

Mabel broke the silence.

"And your speech to-morrow?" she asked, taking up her fork.

Oliver brightened a little, and began to discourse.

It seemed that Birmingham was beginning to fret. They were crying out once more for free trade with America: European facilities were not enough, and it was Oliver's business to keep them quiet. It was useless, he proposed to tell them, to agitate until the Eastern business was settled: they must not bother the Government with such details just now.

He was to tell them, too, that the Government was wholly on their side; that it was bound to come soon.

"They are pig-headed," he added fiercely; "pig-headed and selfish; they are like children who cry for food ten minutes before dinner-time: it is bound to come if they will wait a little."

"And you will tell them so?"

"That they are pig-headed? Certainly."

Mabel looked at her husband with a pleased twinkle in her eyes. She knew perfectly well that his popularity rested largely on his outspokenness: folks liked to be scolded and abused by a genial bold man who danced and gesticulated in a magnetic fury; she liked it herself.

"How shall you go?" she asked.

"Volor. I shall catch the eighteen o'clock at Blackfriars; the meeting is at nineteen, and I shall be back at twenty-one."

He addressed himself vigorously to his *entrée*, and his mother looked up with a patient, old-woman smile.

Mabel began to drum her fingers softly on the damask.

"Please make haste, my dear," she said; "I have to be at Brighton at three."

Oliver gulped his last mouthful, pushed his plate over the line, glanced to see if all plates were there, and then put his hand beneath the table.

Instantly, without a sound, the centre-piece vanished, and the three waited unconcernedly while the clink of dishes came from beneath.

Old Mrs. Brand was a hale-looking old lady, rosy and wrinkled, with the mantilla head-dress of fifty years ago; but she, too, looked a little depressed this morning. The *entrée* was not very successful, she thought; the new food-stuff was not up to the old, it was a trifle gritty: she would see about it afterwards. There was a clink, a soft sound like a push, and the centre-piece snapped into its place, bearing an admirable imitation of roasted fowl.

Oliver and his wife were alone again for a minute or two after breakfast before Mabel started down the path to catch the 14½ o'clock 4th grade sub-truck line to the junction.

"What's the matter with mother?" he said.

"Oh! it's the food-stuff again: she's never got accustomed to it; she says it doesn't suit her."

"Nothing else?"

"No, dear, I am sure of it. She hasn't said a word lately."

Oliver watched his wife go down the path, reassured. He had been a little troubled once or twice lately by an odd word or two that his mother had let fall. She had been brought up a Christian for a few years, and it seemed to him sometimes as if it had left a taint. There was an old "Garden of the Soul" that she liked to keep by her, though she always protested with an appearance of scorn that it was nothing but nonsense. Still, Oliver would have preferred that she had burned it; superstition was a desperate thing for retaining life, and, as the brain weakened, might conceivably reassert itself. Christianity was both wild and dull, he told himself, wild because of its obvious grotesqueness and impossibility, and dull because it was so utterly apart from the exhilarating stream of human life; it crept dustily about still, he knew, in little dark churches here and there; it screamed with hysterical sentimentality in Westminster Cathedral which he had once entered and looked upon with a kind of disgusted fury; it gabbled strange, false words to the incompetent and the old and the half-witted. But it would be too dreadful if his own mother ever looked upon it again with favour.

Oliver himself, ever since he could remember, had been violently opposed to the concessions to Rome and Ireland. It was intolerable that these two places should be definitely yielded up to this foolish, treacherous nonsense: they were hot-beds of sediton; plague-spots on the face of humanity. He had never agreed with those who said that it was better that all the poison of the West should be gathered rather than dispersed. But, at any rate, there it was. Rome had been given up wholly to that old man in white in exchange for all the parish churches and cathedrals of Italy, and it was understood that mediaeval darkness reigned there supreme; and Ireland, after receiving Home Rule thirty years before, had declared for Catholicism, and opened her arms to Individualism in its most virulent form. England had laughed and assented, for she was saved from a quantity of agitation by the immediate departure of half her Catholic population for that island, and had, consistently with her Communist-colonial policy, granted every facility for Individualism to reduce itself there *ad absurdum*. All kinds of funny things were happening there: Oliver had read with bitter amusement of new appearances there, of a Woman in Blue and shrines raised where her feet had rested; but he was scarcely amused at Rome, for the movement to Turin of the Italian Government had deprived the Republic of quite a quantity of sentimental prestige, and had haloed the old religious nonsense with all the meretriciousness of historical association. However, it obviously could not last much longer: the world was beginning to understand at last.

He stood a moment or two at the door after his wife had gone, drinking in reassurance from that glorious vision of solid sense that spread itself before his eyes: the endless house-roofs; the high glass vaults of the public baths and gymnasiums; the pinnacled schools where Citizenship was taught each morning; the spider-like cranes and scaffoldings that rose here and there; and even the few pricking spires did not disconcert him. There it stretched away into the grey haze of London, really beautiful, this vast hive of men and women who had learned at least the primary lesson of the gospel that there was no God but man, no priest but the politician, no prophet but the schoolmaster.

Then he went back once more to his speech-constructing.

Mabel, too, was a little thoughtful as she sat with her paper on her lap, spinning down the broad line to Brighton. This Eastern news was more disconcerting to her than she allowed her husband to see; yet it seemed incredible that there could be any real danger of invasion. This Western life was so sensible and peaceful; folks had their feet at last upon the rock, and it was unthinkable that they could ever be forced back on to the mud-flats: it was contrary to the whole law of development. Yet she could not but recognize that catastrophe seemed one of nature's methods....

She sat very quiet, glancing once or twice at the meagre little scrap of news, and read the leading article upon it: that too seemed significant of dismay. A couple of men were talking in the half-compartment beyond on the same subject; one described the Government engineering works that he had visited, the breathless haste that dominated them; the other put in interrogations and questions. There was not much comfort there. There were no windows through which she could look; on the main lines the speed was too great for the eyes; the long compartment flooded with soft light bounded her horizon. She stared at the moulded white ceiling, the delicious oak-framed paintings, the deep spring-seats, the mellow globes overhead that poured out radiance, at a mother and child diagonally opposite her. Then the great chord sounded; the faint vibration increased ever so slightly; and an instant later the automatic doors ran back, and she stepped out on to the platform of Brighton station.

As she went down the steps leading to the station square she noticed a priest going before her. He seemed a very upright and sturdy old man, for though his hair was white he walked steadily and strongly. At the foot of the steps he stopped and half turned, and then, to her surprise, she saw that his face was that of a young man, fine-featured and strong, with black eyebrows and very bright grey eyes. Then she passed on and began to cross the square in the direction of her aunt's house.

Then without the slightest warning, except one shrill hoot from overhead, a number of things happened.

A great shadow whirled across the sunlight at her feet, a sound of rending tore the air, and a noise like a giant's sigh; and, as she stopped bewildered, with a noise like ten thousand smashed kettles, a huge thing crashed on the rubber pavement before her, where it lay, filling half the square, writhing long wings on its upper side that beat and whirled like flappers of some ghastly extinct monster, pouring out human screams, and beginning almost instantly to crawl with broken life.

Mabel scarcely knew what happened next; but she found herself a moment later forced forward by some violent pressure from behind, till she stood shaking from head to foot with some kind of smashed body of a man moaning and stretching at her feet. There was a sort of articulate language coming from it; she caught distinctly the names of Jesus and Mary; then a voice hissed suddenly in her ears:

"Let me through. I am a priest."

She stood there a moment longer, dazed by the suddenness of the whole affair, and watched almost unintelligently the grey-haired young priest on his knees, with his coat torn open, and a crucifix out; she saw him bend close, wave his hand in a swift sign, and heard a murmur of a language she did not know. Then he was up again, holding the crucifix before him, and she saw him begin to move forward into the midst of the red-flooded pavement, looking this way and that as if for a signal. Down the steps of the great hospital on her right came figures running now, hatless, each carrying what looked like an old-fashioned camera. She knew what those men were, and her heart leaped in relief. They were the ministers of euthanasia. Then she felt herself taken by the shoulder and pulled back, and immediately found herself in the front rank of a crowd that was swaying and crying out, and behind a line of police and civilians who had formed themselves into a cordon to keep the pressure back.

III

Oliver was in a panic of terror as his mother, half an hour later, ran in with the news that one of the Government volors had fallen in the station square at Brighton just after the 14½ train had discharged its passengers. He knew quite well what that meant, for he remembered one such accident ten years before, just after the law forbidding private volors had been passed. It meant that every living creature in it was killed and probably many more in the place where it fell—and what then? The message was clear enough; she would certainly be in the square at that time.

He sent a desperate wire to her aunt asking for news; and sat, shaking in his chair, awaiting the answer. His mother sat by him.

"Please God—" she sobbed out once, and stopped confounded as he turned on her.

But Fate was merciful, and three minutes before Mr. Phillips toiled up the path with the answer, Mabel herself came into the room, rather pale and smiling.

"Christ!" cried Oliver, and gave one huge sob as he sprang up.

She had not a great deal to tell him. There was no explanation of the disaster published as yet; it seemed that the wings on one side had simply ceased to work.

She described the shadow, the hiss of sound, and the crash. Then she stopped.

"Well, my dear?" said her husband, still rather white beneath the eyes as he sat close to her patting her hand.

"There was a priest there," said Mabel. "I saw him before, at the station."

Oliver gave a little hysterical snort of laughter.

"He was on his knees at once," she said, "with his crucifix, even before the doctors came. My dear, do people really believe all that?"

"Why, they think they do," said her husband.

"It was all so—so sudden; and there he was, just as if he had been expecting it all. Oliver, how can they?"

"Why, people will believe anything if they begin early enough."

"And the man seemed to believe it, too—the dying man, I mean. I saw his eyes."

She stopped.

"Well, my dear?"

"Oliver, what do you say to people when they are dying?"

"Say! Why, nothing! What can I say? But I don't think I've ever seen any one die."

"Nor have I till to-day," said the girl, and shivered a little. "The euthanasia people were soon at work."

Oliver took her hand gently.

"My darling, it must have been frightful. Why, you're trembling still."

"No; but listen…. You know, if I had had anything to say I could have said it too. They were all just in front of me: I wondered; then I knew I hadn't. I couldn't possibly have talked about Humanity."

"My dear, it's all very sad; but you know it doesn't really matter. It's all over."

"And—and they've just stopped?"

"Why, yes."

Mabel compressed her lips a little; then she sighed. She had had an agitated sort of meditation in the train. She knew perfectly that it was sheer nerves; but she could not just yet shake them off. As she had said, it was the first time she had seen death.

"And that priest—that priest doesn't think so?"

"My dear, I'll tell you what he believes. He believes that that man whom he showed the crucifix to, and said those words over, is alive somewhere, in spite of his brain being dead: he is not quite sure where; but he is either in a kind of smelting works being slowly burned; or, if he is very lucky, and that piece of wood took effect, he is somewhere beyond the clouds, before Three Persons who are only One although They are Three; that there are quantities of other people there, a Woman in Blue, a great many others in white with their heads under their arms, and still more with their heads on one side; and that they've all got harps and go on singing for ever and ever, and walking about on the clouds, and liking it very much indeed. He thinks, too, that all these nice people are perpetually looking down upon the aforesaid smelting-works, and praising the Three Great Persons for making them. That's what the priest believes. Now you know it's not likely; that kind of thing may be very nice, but it isn't true."

Mabel smiled pleasantly. She had never heard it put so well.

"No, my dear, you're quite right. That sort of thing isn't true. How can he believe it? He looked quite intelligent!"

"My dear girl, if I had told you in your cradle that the moon was green cheese, and had hammered at you ever since, every day and all day, that it was, you'd very nearly believe it by now. Why, you know in your heart that the euthanatisers are the real priests. Of course you do."

Mabel sighed with satisfaction and stood up.

"Oliver, you're a most comforting person. I do like you! There! I must go to my room: I'm all shaky still."

Half across the room she stopped and put out a shoe.

"Why——" she began faintly.

There was a curious rusty-looking splash upon it; and her husband saw her turn white. He rose abruptly.

"My dear," he said, "don't be foolish."

She looked at him, smiled bravely, and went out.

When she was gone, he still sat on a moment where she had left him. Dear me! how pleased he was! He did not like to think of what life would have been without her. He had known her since she was twelve—that was seven years ago—and last year they had gone together to the district official to make their contract. She had really become very necessary to him. Of course the world could get on without her, and he supposed that he could too; but he did not want to have to try. He knew perfectly well, for it was his creed of human love, that there was between them a double affection, of mind as well as body;

and there was absolutely nothing else: but he loved her quick intuitions, and to hear his own thought echoed so perfectly. It was like two flames added together to make a third taller than either: of course one flame could burn without the other — in fact, one would have to, one day — but meantime the warmth and light were exhilarating. Yes, he was delighted that she happened to be clear of the falling volor.

He gave no more thought to his exposition of the Christian creed; it was a mere commonplace to him that Catholics believed that kind of thing; it was no more blasphemous to his mind so to describe it, than it would be to laugh at a Fijian idol with mother-of-pearl eyes, and a horse-hair wig; it was simply impossible to treat it seriously. He, too, had wondered once or twice in his life how human beings could believe such rubbish; but psychology had helped him, and he knew now well enough that suggestion will do almost anything. And it was this hateful thing that had so long restrained the euthanasia movement with all its splendid mercy.

His brows wrinkled a little as he remembered his mother's exclamation, "Please God"; then smiled at the poor old thing and her pathetic childishness, and turned once more to his table, thinking in spite of himself of his wife's hesitation as she had seen the splash of blood on her shoe. Blood! Yes; that was as much a fact as anything else. How was it to be dealt with? Why, by the glorious creed of Humanity—that splendid God who died and rose again ten thousand times a day, who had died daily like the old cracked fanatic Saul of Tarsus, ever since the world began, and who rose again, not once like the Carpenter's Son, but with every child that came into the world. That was the answer; and was it not overwhelmingly sufficient?

Mr. Phillips came in an hour later with another bundle of papers.

"No more news from the East, sir," he said.

CHAPTER II

I

PERCY FRANKLIN'S correspondence with the Cardinal Protector of England occupied him directly for at least two hours every day, and for nearly eight hours indirectly.

For the past eight years the methods of the Holy See had once more been revised with a view to modern needs, and now every important province throughout the world possessed not only an administrative metropolitan but a representative in Rome whose business it was to be in touch with the Pope on the one side and the people he represented on the other. In other words, centralisation had gone forward rapidly, in accordance with the laws of life; and, with the centralisation, freedom of method and expansion of power. England's Cardinal-Protector was one Abbot Martin, a Benedictine, and it was Percy's business, as of a dozen more bishops, priests and laymen (with whom, by the way, he was forbidden to hold any formal consultation), to write a long daily letter to him on affairs that came under his notice.

It was a curious life, therefore, that Percy led. He had a couple of rooms assigned to him in Archbishop's House at Westminster, and was attached loosely to the Cathedral staff, although with considerable liberty. He rose early, and went to meditation for an hour, after which he said his Mass. He took his coffee soon after, said a little office, and then settled down to map out his letter. At ten o'clock he was ready to receive callers, and till noon he was generally busy with both those who came to see him on their own responsibility and his staff of half-a-dozen reporters whose business it was to bring him marked paragraphs in the newspapers and their own comments. He then breakfasted with the other priests in the house, and set out soon after to call on people whose opinion was necessary, returning for a cup of tea soon after sixteen o'clock. Then he settled down, after the rest of his office and a visit to the Blessed Sacrament, to compose his letter, which though short, needed a great deal of care and sifting. After dinner he made a few notes for next day, received visitors again, and went to bed soon after twenty-two o'clock. Twice a week it was his business to assist at Vespers in the afternoon, and he usually sang High Mass on Saturdays.

It was, therefore, a curiously distracting life, with peculiar dangers.

It was one day, a week or two after his visit to Brighton, that he was just finishing his letter, when his servant looked in to tell him that Father Francis was below.

"In ten minutes," said Percy, without looking up.

He snapped off his last lines, drew out the sheet, and settled down to read it over translating it unconsciously from Latin to English.

"WESTMINSTER, May 14th.

"EMINENCE: Since yesterday I have a little more information. It appears certain that the Bill establishing Esperanto for all State purposes will be brought in in June. I have had this from Johnson. This, as I have pointed out before, is the very last stone in our consolidation with the continent, which, at present, is to be regretted.... A great access of Jews to Freemasonry is to be expected; hitherto they have held aloof to some extent, but the 'abolition of the Idea of God' is tending to draw in those Jews, now greatly on the increase once more, who repudiate all notion of a personal Messiah. It is 'Humanity' here, too, that is at work. To-day I heard the Rabbi Simeon speak to this effect in the City, and was impressed by the applause he received.... Yet among others an expectation is growing that a man will presently be found to lead the Communist movement and unite their forces more closely. I enclose a verbose cutting from the *New People* to that effect; and it is echoed everywhere. They say that the cause must give birth to one such soon; that they have had prophets and precursors for a hundred years past, and lately a cessation of them. It is strange how this coincides superficially with Christian ideas. Your Eminence will observe that a simile of the 'ninth wave' is used with some eloquence.... I hear to-day of the secession of an old Catholic family, the Wargraves of Norfolk, with their chaplain Micklem, who it seems has been busy in this direction for some while. The *Epoch* announces it with satisfaction, owing to the peculiar circumstances; but unhappily such events are not uncommon now.... There is much distrust among the laity. Seven priests in Westminster diocese have left us within the last three months; on the other hand, I have pleasure in telling your Eminence that his Grace received into Catholic Communion this morning the ex-Anglican Bishop of Carlisle, with half-a-dozen of his clergy. This has been expected for some weeks past. I append also cuttings from the *Tribune*, the *London Trumpet*, and the *Observer*, with my comments upon them. Your Eminence will see how great the excitement is with regard to the last.

"*Recommendation.* That formal excommunication of the Wargraves and these eight priests should be issued in Norfolk and Westminster respectively, and no further notice taken."

Percy laid down the sheet, gathered up the half dozen other papers that contained his extracts and running commentary, signed the last, and slipped the whole into the printed envelope that lay ready.

Then he took up his biretta and went to the lift.

The moment he came into the glass-doored parlour he saw that the crisis was come, if not passed already. Father Francis looked miserably ill, but there was a curious hardness, too, about his eyes and mouth, as he stood waiting. He shook his head abruptly.

"I have come to say good-bye, father. I can bear it no more."

Percy was careful to show no emotion at all. He made a little sign to a chair, and himself sat down too.

"It is an end of everything," said the other again in a perfectly steady voice. "I believe nothing. I have believed nothing for a year now."

"You have felt nothing, you mean," said Percy.

"That won't do, father," went on the other. "I tell you there is nothing left. I can't even argue now. It is just good-bye."

Percy had nothing to say. He had talked to this man during a period of over eight months, ever since Father Francis had first confided in him that his faith was going. He understood perfectly what a strain it had been; he felt bitterly compassionate towards this poor creature who had become caught up somehow into the dizzy triumphant whirl of the New Humanity. External facts were horribly strong just now; and faith, except to one who had learned that Will and Grace were all and emotion nothing, was as a child crawling about in the midst of some huge machinery: it might survive or it might not; but it required nerves of steel to keep steady. It was hard to know where blame could be assigned; yet Percy's faith told him that there was blame due. In the ages of faith a very inadequate grasp of religion would pass muster; in these searching days none but the humble and the pure could stand the test for long, unless indeed they were protected by a miracle of ignorance. The alliance of Psychology and Materialism did indeed seem, looked at from one angle, to account for everything; it needed a robust supernatural perception to understand their practical inadequacy. And as regards Father Francis's personal responsibility, he could not help feeling that the other had allowed ceremonial to play too great a part in his religion, and prayer too little. In him the external had absorbed the internal.

So he did not allow his sympathy to show itself in his bright eyes.

"You think it my fault, of course," said the other sharply.

"My dear father," said Percy, motionless in his chair, "I know it is your fault. Listen to me. You say Christianity is absurd and impossible. Now, you know, it cannot be that! It may be untrue—I am not speaking of that now, even though I am perfectly certain that it is absolutely true—but it cannot be absurd so long as educated and virtuous people continue to hold it. To say that it is absurd is simple pride; it is to dismiss all who believe in it as not merely mistaken, but unintelligent as well——"

"Very well, then," interrupted the other; "then suppose I withdraw that, and simply say that I do not believe it to be true."

"You do not withdraw it," continued Percy serenely; "you still really believe it to be absurd: you have told me so a dozen times. Well, I repeat, that is pride, and quite sufficient to account for it all. It is the moral attitude that matters. There may be other things too—"

Father Francis looked up sharply.

"Oh, the old story!" he said sneeringly.

"If you tell me on your word of honour that there is no woman in the case, or no particular programme of sin you propose to work out, I shall believe you. But it is an old story, as you say."

"I swear to you there is not," cried the other.

"Thank God then!" said Percy. "There are fewer obstacles to a return of faith."

There was silence for a moment after that. Percy had really no more to say. He had talked to him of the inner life again and again, in which verities are seen to be true, and acts of faith are ratified; he had urged prayer and humility till he was almost weary of the names; and had been met by the retort that this was to advise sheer self-hypnotism; and he had despaired of making clear to one who did not see it for himself that while Love and Faith may be called self-hypnotism from one angle, yet from another they are as much realities as, for example, artistic faculties, and need similar cultivation; that they produce a conviction that they are convictions, that they handle and taste things which when handled and tasted are overwhelmingly more real and objective than the things of sense. Evidences seemed to mean nothing to this man.

So he was silent now, chilled himself by the presence of this crisis, looking unseeingly out upon the plain, little old-world parlour, its tall window, its strip of matting, conscious chiefly of the dreary hopelessness of this human brother of his who had eyes but did not see, ears and was deaf. He wished he would say good-bye, and go. There was no more to be done.

Father Francis, who had been sitting in a lax kind of huddle, seemed to know his thoughts, and sat up suddenly.

"You are tired of me," he said. "I will go."

"I am not tired of you, my dear father," said Percy simply. "I am only terribly sorry. You see I know that it is all true."

The other looked at him heavily.

"And I know that it is not," he said. "It is very beautiful; I wish I could believe it. I don't think I shall be ever happy again—but—but there it is."

Percy sighed. He had told him so often that the heart is as divine a gift as the mind, and that to neglect it in the search for God is to seek ruin, but this priest had scarcely seen the application to himself. He had answered with the old psychological arguments that the suggestions of education accounted for everything.

"I suppose you will cast me off," said the other.

"It is you who are leaving me," said Percy. "I cannot follow, if you mean that."

"But—but cannot we be friends?"

A sudden heat touched the elder priest's heart.

"Friends?" he said. "Is sentimentality all you mean by friendship? What kind of friends can we be?"

The other's face became suddenly heavy.

"I thought so."

"John!" cried Percy. "You see that, do you not? How can we pretend anything when you do not believe in God? For I do you the honour of thinking that you do not."

Francis sprang up.

"Well—" he snapped. "I could not have believed—I am going."

He wheeled towards the door.

"John!" said Percy again. "Are you going like this? Can you not shake hands?"

The other wheeled again, with heavy anger in his face.

"Why, you said you could not be friends with me!"

Percy's mouth opened. Then he understood, and smiled.

"Oh! that is all you mean by friendship, is it?—I beg your pardon. Oh! we can be polite to one another, if you like."

He still stood holding out his hand. Father Francis looked at it a moment, his lips shook: then once more he turned, and went out without a word.

II

Percy stood motionless until he heard the automatic bell outside tell him that Father Francis was really gone, then he went out himself and turned towards the long passage leading to the Cathedral. As he passed out through the sacristy he heard far in front the murmur of an organ, and on coming through into the chapel used as a parish church he perceived that Vespers were not yet over in the great choir. He came straight down the aisle, turned to the right, crossed the centre and knelt down.

It was drawing on towards sunset, and the huge dark place was lighted here and there by patches of ruddy London light that lay on the gorgeous marble and gildings finished at last by a wealthy convert. In front of him rose up the choir, with a line of white surpliced and furred canons on either side, and the vast baldachino in the midst, beneath which burned the six lights as they had burned day by day for more than a century; behind that again lay the high line of the apse-choir with the dim, window-pierced vault above where Christ reigned in majesty. He let his eyes wander round for a few moments before beginning his deliberate prayer, drinking in the glory of the place, listening to the thunderous chorus, the peal of the organ, and the thin mellow voice of the priest. There on the left shone the refracted glow of the lamps that burned before the Lord in the Sacrament, on the right a dozen candles winked here and there at the foot of the gaunt images, high overhead hung the gigantic cross with that lean, emaciated Poor Man Who called all who looked on Him to the embraces of a God.

Then he hid his face in his hands, drew a couple of long breaths, and set to work.

He began, as his custom was in mental prayer, by a deliberate act of self-exclusion from the world of sense. Under the image of sinking beneath a surface he forced himself downwards and inwards, till the peal of the organ, the shuffle of footsteps, the rigidity of the chair-back beneath his wrists— all seemed apart and external, and he was left a single person with a beating heart, an intellect that suggested image after image, and emotions that were too languid to stir themselves. Then he made his second descent, renounced all that he possessed and was, and became conscious that even the body was left behind and that his mind and heart, awed by the Presence in which they found themselves, clung close and obedient to the will which was their lord and protector. He drew another long breath, or two, as he felt that Presence surge about him; he repeated a few mechanical words, and sank to that peace which follows the relinquishment of thought.

There he rested for a while. Far above him sounded the ecstatic music, the cry of trumpets and the shrilling of the flutes; but they were as insignificant street-noises to one who was falling asleep. He was within the veil of things now, beyond the barriers of sense and reflection, in that secret place to which he had learned the road by endless effort, in that strange region where realities are evident, where perceptions go to and fro with the swiftness of light, where the swaying will catches now this, now that act, moulds it and speeds it; where all things meet, where truth is known and handled and tasted, where God Immanent is one with God Transcendent, where the meaning of the external world is evident through its inner side, and the Church and its mysteries are seen from within a haze of glory.

So he lay a few moments, absorbing and resting.

Then he aroused himself to consciousness and began to speak.

"Lord, I am here, and Thou art here. I know Thee. There is nothing else but Thou and I.... I lay this all in Thy hands— Thy apostate priest, Thy people, the world, and myself. I spread it before Thee—I spread it before Thee."

He paused, poised in the act, till all of which he thought lay like a plain before a peak.

... "Myself, Lord—there but for Thy grace should I be going, in darkness and misery. It is Thou Who dost preserve me. Maintain and finish Thy work within my soul. Let me not falter for one instant. If Thou withdraw Thy hand I fall into utter nothingness."

So his soul stood a moment, with outstretched appealing hands, helpless and confident. Then the will flickered in self-consciousness, and he repeated acts of faith, hope and love to steady it. Then he drew another long breath, feeling the Presence tingle and shake about him, and began again.

"Lord; look on Thy people. Many are falling from Thee. *Ne in aeternum irascaris nobis. Ne in aeternum irascaris nobis....* I unite myself with all saints and angels and Mary Queen of Heaven; look on them and me, and hear us. *Emitte lucem tuam et veritatem tuam.* Thy light and Thy truth! Lay not on us heavier burdens than we can bear. Lord, why dost Thou not speak!"

He writhed himself forward in a passion of expectant

desire, hearing his muscles crack in the effort. Once more he relaxed himself; and the swift play of wordless acts began which he knew to be the very heart of prayer. The eyes of his soul flew hither and thither, from Calvary to heaven and back again to the tossing troubled earth. He saw Christ dying of desolation while the earth rocked and groaned; Christ reigning as a priest upon His Throne in robes of light, Christ patient and inexorably silent within the Sacramental species; and to each in turn he directed the eyes of the Eternal Father....

Then he waited for communications, and they came, so soft and delicate, passing like shadows, that his will sweated blood and tears in the effort to catch and fix them and correspond....

He saw the Body Mystical in its agony, strained over the world as on a cross, silent with pain; he saw this and that nerve wrenched and twisted, till pain presented it to himself as under the guise of flashes of colour; he saw the life-blood drop by drop run down from His head and hands and feet. The world was gathered mocking and good-humoured beneath. *"He saved others: Himself He cannot save.... Let Christ come down from the Cross and we will believe."* Far away behind bushes and in holes of the ground the friends of Jesus peeped and sobbed; Mary herself was silent, pierced by seven swords; the disciple whom He loved had no words of comfort.

He saw, too, how no word would be spoken from heaven; the angels themselves were bidden to put sword into sheath, and wait on the eternal patience of God, for the agony was hardly yet begun; there were a thousand horrors yet before the end could come, that final sum of crucifixion.... He must wait and watch, content to stand there and do nothing; and the Resurrection must seem to him no more than a dreamed-of hope. There was the Sabbath yet to come, while the Body Mystical must lie in its sepulchre cut off from light, and even the dignity of the Cross must be withdrawn and the knowledge that Jesus lived. That inner world, to which by long effort he had learned the way, was all alight with agony; it was bitter as brine, it was of that pale luminosity that is the utmost product of pain, it hummed in his ears with a note that rose to a scream ... it pressed upon him, penetrated him, stretched him as on a rack.... And with that his will grew sick and nerveless.

"Lord! I cannot bear it!" he moaned....

In an instant he was back again, drawing long breaths of misery. He passed his tongue over his lips, and opened his eyes on the darkening apse before him. The organ was silent now, and the choir was gone, and the lights out. The sunset colour, too, had faded from the walls, and grim cold faces looked down on him from wall and vault. He was back again on the surface of life; the vision had melted; he scarcely knew what it was that he had seen.

But he must gather up the threads, and by sheer effort absorb them. He must pay his duty, too, to the Lord that gave Himself to the senses as well as to the inner spirit. So he rose, stiff and constrained, and passed across to the Chapel of the Holy Sacrament.

As he came out from the block of chairs, very upright and tall, with his biretta once more on his white hair, he saw an old woman watching him very closely. He hesitated an instant, wondering whether she were a penitent, and as he hesitated she made a movement towards him.

"I beg your pardon, sir," she began.

She was not a Catholic then. He lifted his biretta.

"Can I do anything for you?" he asked.

"I beg your pardon, sir, but were you at Brighton, at the

accident two months ago?"

"I was."

"Ah! I thought so: my daughter-in-law saw you then."

Percy had a spasm of impatience: he was a little tired of being identified by his white hair and young face.

"Were you there, madam?"

She looked at him doubtfully and curiously, moving her old eyes up and down his figure. Then she recollected herself.

"No, sir; it was my daughter-in-law—I beg your pardon, sir, but——"

"Well?" asked Percy, trying to keep the impatience out of his voice.

"Are you the Archbishop, sir?"

The priest smiled, showing his white teeth.

"No, madam; I am just a poor priest. Dr. Cholmondeley is Archbishop. I am Father Percy Franklin."

She said nothing, but still looking at him made a little old-world movement of a bow; and Percy passed on to the dim, splendid chapel to pay his devotions.

III

There was great talk that night at dinner among the priests as to the extraordinary spread of Freemasonry. It had been going on for many years now, and Catholics perfectly recognised its dangers, for the profession of Masonry had been for some centuries rendered incompatible with religion through the Church's unswerving condemnation of it. A man must choose between that and his faith. Things had developed extraordinarily during the last century. First there had been the organised assault upon the Church in France; and what Catholics had always suspected then became a certainty in

the revelations of 1918, when P. Gerome, the Dominican and
ex-Mason, had made his disclosures with regard to the Mark-
Masons. It had become evident then that Catholics had been
right, and that Masonry, in its higher grades at least, had been
responsible throughout the world for the strange movement
against religion. But he had died in his bed, and the public had been impressed by that fact. Then came the splendid
donations in France and Italy—to hospitals, orphanages, and
the like; and once more suspicion began to disappear. After
all, it seemed—and continued to seem—for seventy years
and more that Masonry was nothing more than a vast phil-
anthropical society. Now once more men had their doubts.

"I hear that Felsenburgh is a Mason," observed Monsignor Macintosh, the Cathedral Administrator. "A Grand-
Master or something."

"But who is Felsenburgh?" put in a young priest.

Monsignor pursed his lips and shook his head. He was
one of those humble persons as proud of ignorance as others of knowledge. He boasted that he never read the papers
nor any book except those that had received the *imprimatur*;
it was a priest's business, he often remarked, to preserve the
faith, not to acquire worldly knowledge. Percy had occasionally rather envied his point of view.

"He's a mystery," said another priest, Father Blackmore;
"but he seems to be causing great excitement. They were sell-
ing his 'Life' to-day on the Embankment."

"I met an American senator," put in Percy, "three days
ago, who told me that even there they know nothing of him,
except his extraordinary eloquence. He only appeared last
year, and seems to have carried everything before him by
quite unusual methods. He is a great linguist, too. That is
why they took him to Irkutsk."

"Well, the Masons—" went on Monsignor. "It is very serious. In the last month four of my penitents have left me because of it."

"Their inclusion of women was their master-stroke," growled Father Blackmore, helping himself to claret.

"It is extraordinary that they hesitated so long about that," observed Percy.

A couple of others added their evidence. It appeared that they, too, had lost penitents lately through the spread of Masonry. It was rumoured that a Pastoral was a-preparing upstairs on the subject.

Monsignor shook his head ominously.

"More is wanted than that," he said.

Percy pointed out that the Church had said her last word several centuries ago. She had laid her excommunication on all members of secret societies, and there was really no more that she could do.

"Except bring it before her children again and again," put in Monsignor. "I shall preach on it next Sunday."

Percy jotted down a note when he reached his room, determining to say another word or two on the subject to the Cardinal-Protector. He had mentioned Freemasonry often before, but it seemed time for another remark. Then he opened his letters, first turning to one which he recognised as from the Cardinal.

It seemed a curious coincidence, as he read a series of questions that Cardinal Martin's letter contained, that one of them should be on this very subject. It ran as follows:

"What of Masonry? Felsenburgh is said to be one. Gather all the gossip you can about him. Send any English or

American biographies of him. Are you still losing Catholics through Masonry?"

He ran his eyes down the rest of the questions. They chiefly referred to previous remarks of his own, but twice, even in them, Felsenburgh's name appeared.

He laid the paper down and considered a little.

It was very curious, he thought, how this man's name was in every one's mouth, in spite of the fact that so little was known about him. He had bought in the streets, out of curiosity, three photographs that professed to represent this strange person, and though one of them might be genuine they all three could not be. He drew them out of a pigeon-hole, and spread them before him.

One represented a fierce, bearded creature like a Cossack, with round staring eyes. No; intrinsic evidence condemned this: it was exactly how a coarse imagination would have pictured a man who seemed to be having a great influence in the East.

The second showed a fat face with little eyes and a chin-beard. That might conceivably be genuine: he turned it over and saw the name of a New York firm on the back. Then he turned to the third. This presented a long, clean-shaven face with pince-nez, undeniably clever, but scarcely strong: and Felsenburgh was obviously a strong man.

Percy inclined to think the second was the most probable; but they were all unconvincing; and he shuffled them carelessly together and replaced them.

Then he put his elbows on the table, and began to think.

He tried to remember what Mr. Varhaus, the American senator, had told him of Felsenburgh; yet it did not seem sufficient to account for the facts. Felsenburgh, it seemed, had employed none of those methods common in modern politics. He controlled no newspapers, vituperated nobody, championed nobody: he had no picked underlings; he used no bribes; there were no monstrous crimes alleged against him. It seemed rather as if his originality lay in his clean hands and his stainless past—that, and his magnetic character. He was the kind of figure that belonged rather to the age of chivalry: a pure, clean, compelling personality, like a radiant child. He had taken people by surprise, then, rising out of the heaving dun-coloured waters of American socialism like a vision—from those waters so fiercely restrained from breaking into storm ever since the extraordinary social revolution under Mr. Hearst's disciples, a century ago. That had been the end of plutocracy; the famous old laws of 1914 had burst some of the stinking bubbles of the time; and the enactments of 1916 and 1917 had prevented their forming again in anything like their previous force. It had been the salvation of America, undoubtedly, even if that salvation were of a dreary and uninspiring description; and now out of the flat socialistic level had arisen this romantic figure utterly unlike any that had preceded it.... So the senator had hinted.... It was too complicated for Percy just now, and he gave it up.

It was a weary world, he told himself, turning his eyes homewards. Everything seemed so hopeless and ineffective. He tried not to reflect on his fellow-priests, but for the fiftieth time he could not help seeing that they were not the men for the present situation. It was not that he preferred himself; he knew perfectly well that he, too, was fully as incompetent: had he not proved to be so with poor Father Francis, and scores of others who had clutched at him in their agony during the last ten years? Even the Archbishop, holy man as he was, with all his childlike faith—was that the man to lead

English Catholics and confound their enemies? There seemed
no giants on the earth in these days. What in the world was to
be done? He buried his face in his hands....

Yes; what was wanted was a new Order in the Church;
the old ones were rule-bound through no fault of their own.
An Order was wanted without habit or tonsure, without traditions or customs, an Order with nothing but entire and
whole-hearted devotion, without pride even in their most
sacred privileges, without a past history in which they might
take complacent refuge. They must be *franc-tireurs* of Christ's
Army; like the Jesuits, but without their fatal reputation,
which, again, was no fault of their own.... But there must be
a Founder—Who, in God's Name?—a Founder *nudus sequens
Christum nudum....* Yes—*Franc-tireurs*—priests, bishops, laymen, and women—with the three vows of course, and a special clause forbidding utterly and for ever their ownership of
corporate wealth.—Every gift received must be handed to the
bishop of the diocese in which it was given, who must provide
them himself with necessaries of life and travel. Oh!—what
could they not do? ... He was off in a rhapsody.

Presently he recovered, and called himself a fool. Was
not that scheme as old as the eternal hills, and as useless for
practical purposes? Why, it had been the dream of every zeal-
ous man since the First Year of Salvation that such an Order
should be founded! ... He was a fool....

Then once more he began to think of it all over again.

Surely it was this which was wanted against the Masons;
and women, too.—Had not scheme after scheme broken
down because men had forgotten the power of women? It was
that lack that had ruined Napoleon: he had trusted Josephine,
and she had failed him; so he had trusted no other woman. In
the Catholic Church, too, woman had been given no active

work but either menial or connected with education: and was there not room for other activities than those? Well, it was useless to think of it. It was not his affair. If *Papa Angelicus* who now reigned in Rome had not thought of it, why should a foolish, conceited priest in Westminster set himself up to do so?

So he beat himself on the breast once more, and took up his office-book.

He finished in half an hour, and again sat thinking; but this time it was of poor Father Francis. He wondered what he was doing now; whether he had taken off the Roman collar of Christ's familiar slaves? The poor devil! And how far was he, Percy Franklin, responsible?

When a tap came at his door presently, and Father Blackmore looked in for a talk before going to bed, Percy told him what had happened.

Father Blackmore removed his pipe and sighed deliberately.

"I knew it was coming," he said. "Well, well."

"He has been honest enough," explained Percy. "He told me eight months ago he was in trouble."

Father Blackmore drew upon his pipe thoughtfully.

"Father Franklin," he said, "things are really very serious. There is the same story everywhere. What in the world is happening?"

Percy paused before answering.

"I think these things go in waves," he said.

"Waves, do you think?" said the other.

"What else?"

Father Blackmore looked at him intently.

"It is more like a dead calm, it seems to me," he said. "Have you ever been in a typhoon?"

Percy shook his head.

"Well," went on the other, "the most ominous thing is the calm. The sea is like oil; you feel half-dead: you can do nothing. Then comes the storm."

Percy looked at him, interested. He had not seen this mood in the priest before.

"Before every great crash there comes this calm. It is always so in history. It was so before the Eastern War; it was so before the French Revolution. It was so before the Reformation. There is a kind of oily heaving; and everything is languid. So everything has been in America, too, for over eighty years.... Father Franklin, I think something is going to happen."

"Tell me," said Percy, leaning forward.

"Well, I saw Templeton a week before he died, and he put the idea in my head.... Look here, father. It may be this Eastern affair that is coming on us; but somehow I don't think it is. It is in religion that something is going to happen. At least, so I think.... Father, who in God's name is Felsenburgh?"

Percy was so startled at the sudden introduction of this name again, that he stared a moment without speaking.

Outside, the summer night was very still. There was a faint vibration now and again from the underground track that ran twenty yards from the house where they sat; but the streets were quiet enough round the Cathedral. Once a hoot rang far away, as if some ominous bird of passage were crossing between London and the stars, and once the cry of a woman sounded thin and shrill from the direction of the river. For the rest there was no more than the solemn, subdued hum that never ceased now night or day.

"Yes; Felsenburgh," said Father Blackmore once more. "I cannot get that man out of my head. And yet, what do I know of him? What does anyone know of him?"

Percy licked his lips to answer, and drew a breath to still the beating of his heart. He could not imagine why he felt excited. After all, who was old Blackmore to frighten him? But old Blackmore went on before he could speak.

"See how people are leaving the Church! The Wargraves, the Hendersons, Sir James Bartlet, Lady Magnier, and then all the priests. Now they're not all knaves—I wish they were; it would be so much easier to talk of it. But Sir James Bartlet, last month! Now, there's a man who has spent half his fortune on the Church, and he doesn't resent it even now. He says that any religion is better than none, but that, for himself, he just can't believe any longer. Now what does all that mean? ... I tell you something is going to happen. God knows what! And I can't get Felsenburgh out of my head.... Father Franklin——"

"Yes?"

"Have you noticed how few great men we've got? It's not like fifty years ago, or even thirty. Then there were Mason, Selborne, Sherbrook, and half-a-dozen others. There was Brightman, too, as Archbishop: and now! Then the Communists, too. Braithwaite is dead fifteen years. Certainly he was big enough; but he was always speaking of the future, not of the present; and tell me what big man they have had since then! And now there's this new man, whom no one knows, who came forward in America a few months ago, and whose name is in every one's mouth. Very well, then!"

Percy knitted his forehead.

"I am not sure that I understand," he said.

Father Blackmore knocked his pipe out before answering.

"Well, this," he said, standing up. "I can't help thinking Felsenburgh is going to do something. I don't know what;

it may be for us or against us. But he is a Mason, remember that.... Well, well; I dare say I'm an old fool. Good-night."

"One moment, father," said Percy slowly. "Do you mean—? Good Lord! What do you mean?" He stopped, looking at the other.

The old priest stared back under his bushy eyebrows; it seemed to Percy as if he, too, were afraid of something in spite of his easy talk; but he made no sign.

Percy stood perfectly still a moment when the door was shut. Then he moved across to his *prie-dieu*.

CHAPTER III

I

OLD MRS. BRAND and Mabel were seated at a window of the new Admiralty Offices in Trafalgar Square to see Oliver deliver his speech on the fiftieth anniversary of the passing of the Poor Laws Reform.

It was an inspiriting sight, this bright June morning, to see the crowds gathering round Braithwaite's statue. That politician, dead fifteen years before, was represented in his famous attitude, with arms outstretched and down dropped, his head up and one foot slightly advanced, and to-day was decked, as was becoming more and more usual on such occasions, in his Masonic insignia. It was he who had given immense impetus to that secret movement by his declaration in the House that the key of future progress and brotherhood of nations was in the hands of the Order. It was through this alone that the false unity of the Church with its fantastic spiritual fraternity could be counteracted. St. Paul had been right, he declared, in his desire to break down the partition-walls between nations, and wrong only in his exaltation of Jesus Christ. Thus he had preluded his speech on the Poor Law question, pointing to the true charity that existed among Masons apart from religious motive, and appealing to the famous benefactions on the Continent; and in the enthusiasm of the Bill's success the Order had received a great accession of members.

Old Mrs. Brand was in her best to-day, and looked out with considerable excitement at the huge throng gathered to hear her son speak. A platform was erected round the bronze statue at such a height that the statesman appeared to be one of the speakers, though at a slightly higher elevation, and this platform was hung with roses, surmounted by a sounding-board, and set with a chair and table.

The whole square round about was paved with heads and resonant with sound, the murmurs of thousands of voices, overpowered now and again by the crash of brass and thunder of drums as the Benefit Societies and democratic Guilds, each headed by a banner, deployed from North, South, East and West, and converged towards the wide railed space about the platform where room was reserved for them. The windows on every side were packed with faces; tall stands were erected along the front of the National Gallery and St. Martin's Church, garden-beds of colour behind the mute, white statues that faced outwards round the square, from Braithwaite in front, past the Victorians—John Davidson, John Burns and the rest—round to Hampden and de Montfort towards the north. The old column was gone, with its lions. Nelson had not been found advantageous to the *Entente Cordiale*, nor the lions to the new art; and in their place stretched a wide pavement broken by slopes of steps that led up to the National Gallery. Overhead the roofs showed crowded friezes of heads against the blue summer sky. Not less than one hundred thousand persons, it was estimated in the evening papers, were collected within sight and sound of the platform by noon.

As the clock began to tell the hour, two figures appeared from behind the statue and came forward, and, in an instant, the murmurs of talk rose into cheering.

Old Lord Pemberton came first, a grey-haired, upright man, whose father had been active in denouncing the House of which he was a member on the occasion of its fall over seventy years ago, and his son had succeeded him worthily. This man was now a member of the Government, and sat for Manchester (3); and it was he who was to be chairman on this auspicious occasion. Behind him came Oliver, bareheaded, and spruce, and even at that distance his mother and wife could see his brisk movement, his sudden smile and nod as his name emerged from the storm of sound that surged round the platform. Lord Pemberton came forward, lifted his hand and made a signal; and in a moment the thin cheering died under the sudden roll of drums beneath that preluded the Masonic Hymn.

There was no doubt that these Londoners could sing. It was as if a giant voice hummed the sonorous melody, rising to enthusiasm till the music of massed bands followed it as a flag follows a flag-stick. The hymn was one composed ten years before, and all England was familiar with it. Old Mrs. Brand lifted the printed paper mechanically to her eyes, and saw the words that she knew so well:

> "*The Lord that dwells in earth and sea.*"...

She glanced down the verses, that from the Humanitarian point of view had been composed with both skill and ardour. They had a religious ring; the unintelligent Christian could sing them without a qualm; yet their sense was plain enough—the old human creed that man was all. Even Christ's words themselves were quoted. The kingdom of God, it was said, lay within the human heart, and the greatest of all graces was Charity.

She glanced at Mabel, and saw that the girl was singing with all her might, with her eyes fixed on her husband's dark figure a hundred yards away, and her soul pouring through them. So the mother, too, began to move her lips in chorus with that vast volume of sound.

As the hymn died away, and before the cheering could begin again, old Lord Pemberton was standing forward on the edge of the platform, and his thin metallic voice piped a sentence or two across the tinkling splash of the fountains behind him. Then he stepped back, and Oliver came forward.

It was too far for the two to hear what was said, but Mabel slipped a paper, smiling tremulously, into the old lady's hand, and herself bent forward to listen.

Old Mrs. Brand looked at that, too, knowing that it was an analysis of her son's speech, and aware that she would not be able to hear his words.

There was an exordium first, congratulating all who were present to do honour to the great man who presided from his pedestal on the occasion of this great anniversary. Then there came a retrospect, comparing the old state of England with the present. Fifty years ago, the speaker said, poverty was still a disgrace, now it was so no longer. It was in the causes that led to poverty that the disgrace or the merit lay. Who would not honour a man worn out in the service of his country, or overcome at last by circumstances against which his efforts could not prevail? ... He enumerated the reforms passed fifty years before on this very day, by which the nation once and for all declared the glory of poverty and man's sympathy with the unfortunate.

So he had told them he was to sing the praise of patient poverty and its reward, and that, he supposed, together with a few periods on the reform of the prison laws, would form the first half of his speech.

The second part was to be a panegyric of Braithwaite, treating him as the Precursor of a movement that even now had begun.

Old Mrs. Brand leaned back in her seat, and looked about her.

The window where they sat had been reserved for them; two arm-chairs filled the space, but immediately behind there were others, standing very silent now, craning forward, watching, too, with parted lips: a couple of women with an old man directly behind, and other faces visible again behind them. Their obvious absorption made the old lady a little ashamed of her distraction, and she turned resolutely once more to the square.

Ah! he was working up now to his panegyric! The tiny dark figure was back, a yard nearer the statue, and as she looked, his hand went up and he wheeled, pointing, as a murmur of applause drowned for an instant the minute, resonant voice. Then again he was forward, half crouching—for he was a born actor—and a storm of laughter rippled round the throng of heads. She heard an indrawn hiss behind her chair, and the next instant an exclamation from Mabel.... What was that?

There was a sharp crack, and the tiny gesticulating figure staggered back a step. The old man at the table was up in a moment, and simultaneously a violent commotion bubbled and heaved like water about a rock at a point in the crowd immediately outside the railed space where the bands were massed, and directly opposite the front of the platform.

Mrs. Brand, bewildered and dazed, found herself standing up, clutching the window rail, while the girl gripped her, crying out something she could not understand. A great roaring filled the square, the heads tossed this way and that, like corn under a squall of wind. Then Oliver was forward again, pointing and crying out, for she could see his gestures; and she sank back quickly, the blood racing through her old veins, and her heart hammering at the base of her throat.

"My dear, my dear, what is it?" she sobbed.

But Mabel was up, too, staring out at her husband; and a quick babble of talk and exclamations from behind made itself audible in spite of the roaring tumult of the square.

II

Oliver told them the explanation of the whole affair that evening at home, leaning back in his chair, with one arm bandaged and in a sling.

They had not been able to get near him at the time; the excitement in the square had been too fierce; but a messenger had come to his wife with the news that her husband was only slightly wounded, and was in the hands of the doctors.

"He was a Catholic," explained the drawn-faced Oliver. "He must have come ready, for his repeater was found loaded. Well, there was no chance for a priest this time."

Mabel nodded slowly: she had read of the man's fate on the placards.

"He was killed—trampled and strangled instantly," said Oliver. "I did what I could: you saw me. But—well, I dare say it was more merciful."

"But you did what you could, my dear?" said the old lady, anxiously, from her corner.

"I called out to them, mother, but they wouldn't hear me."

Mabel leaned forward——

"Oliver, I know this sounds stupid of me; but—but I wish they had not killed him."

Oliver smiled at her. He knew this tender trait in her.

"It would have been more perfect if they had not," she said. Then she broke off and sat back.

"Why did he shoot just then?" she asked.

Oliver turned his eyes for an instant towards his mother, but she was knitting tranquilly.

Then he answered with a curious deliberateness.

"I said that Braithwaite had done more for the world by one speech than Jesus and all His saints put together."

He was aware that the knitting-needles stopped for a second; then they went on again as before.

"But he must have meant to do it anyhow," continued Oliver.

"How did they know he was a Catholic?" asked the girl again.

"There was a rosary on him; and then he just had time to call on his God."

"And nothing more is known?"

"Nothing more. He was well dressed, though."

Oliver leaned back a little wearily and closed his eyes; his arm still throbbed intolerably. But he was happy at heart. It was true that he had been wounded by a fanatic, but he was not sorry to bear pain in such a cause, and it was obvious that the sympathy of England was with him. Mr. Phillips even now was busy in the next room, answering the telegrams that poured in every moment. Caldecott, the Prime Minister, Maxwell, Snowford and a dozen others had wired instantly their congratulations, and from every part of England streamed in message after message. It was an immense stroke for the Communists; their spokesman had been assaulted during the discharge of his duty, speaking in defence of his principles; it was an incalculable gain for them, and loss for the Individualists, that confessors were not all on one side after all. The huge electric placards over London had winked out the facts in Esperanto as Oliver stepped into the train at twilight.

> *"Oliver   Brand   wounded....   Catholic   assailant.... Indignation of the country.... Well-deserved fate of assassin."*

He was pleased, too, that he honestly had done his best to save the man. Even in that moment of sudden and acute pain he had cried out for a fair trial; but he had been too late. He had seen the starting eyes roll up in the crimson face, and the horrid grin come and go as the hands had clutched and torn at his throat. Then the face had vanished and a heavy trampling began where it had disappeared. Oh! there was some passion and loyalty left in England!

His mother got up presently and went out, still without a word; and Mabel turned to him, laying a hand on his knee.

"Are you too tired to talk, my dear?"

He opened his eyes.

"Of course not, my darling. What is it?"

"What do you think will be the effect?"

He raised himself a little, looking out as usual through the darkening windows on to that astonishing view. Everywhere now lights were glowing, a sea of mellow moons just above the houses, and above the mysterious heavy blue of a summer evening.

"The effect?" he said. "It can be nothing but good. It was time that something happened. My dear, I feel very downcast sometimes, as you know. Well, I do not think I shall be again. I have been afraid sometimes that we were losing all our spirit, and that the old Tories were partly right when they prophesied what Communism would do. But after this——"

"Well?"

"Well; we have shown that we can shed our blood too. It is in the nick of time, too, just at the crisis. I don't want to exaggerate; it is only a scratch—but it was so deliberate, and—and so dramatic. The poor devil could not have chosen a worse moment. People won't forget it."

Mabel's eyes shone with pleasure.

"You poor dear!" she said. "Are you in pain?"

"Not much. Besides, Christ! what do I care? If only this infernal Eastern affair would end!"

He knew he was feverish and irritable, and made a great effort to drive it down.

"Oh, my dear!" he went on, flushed a little. "If they would not be such heavy fools: they don't understand; they don't understand."

"Yes, Oliver?"

"They don't understand what a glorious thing it all is: Humanity, Life, Truth at last, and the death of Folly! But haven't I told them a hundred times?"

She looked at him with kindling eyes. She loved to see him like this, his confident, flushed face, the enthusiasm in his blue eyes; and the knowlege of his pain pricked her feeling with passion. She bent forward and kissed him suddenly.

"My dear, I am so proud of you. Oh, Oliver!"

He said nothing; but she could see what she loved to see, that response to her own heart; and so they sat in silence while the sky darkened yet more, and the click of the writer in the next room told them that the world was alive and that they had a share in its affairs.

Oliver stirred presently.

"Did you notice anything just now, sweetheart—when I said that about Jesus Christ?"

"She stopped knitting for a moment," said the girl.

He nodded.

"You saw that too, then…. Mabel, do you think she is falling back?"

"Oh, she is getting old," said the girl lightly. "Of course she looks back a little."

"But you don't think—it would be too awful!"

She shook her head.

"No, no, my dear; you're excited and tired. It's just a little sentiment…. Oliver, I don't think I would say that kind of thing before her."

"But she hears it everywhere now."

"No, she doesn't. Remember she hardly ever goes out. Besides, she hates it. After all, she was brought up a Catholic."

Oliver nodded, and lay back again, looking dreamily out.

"Isn't it astonishing the way in which suggestion lasts? She can't get it out of her head, even after fifty years. Well, watch her, won't you? … By the way …"

"Yes?"

"There's a little more news from the East. They say Felsenburgh's running the whole thing now. The Empire is sending him everywhere—Tobolsk, Benares, Yakutsk—everywhere; and he's been to Australia."

Mabel sat up briskly.

"Isn't that very hopeful?"

"I suppose so. There's no doubt that the Sufis are winning; but for how long is another question. Besides, the troops don't disperse."

"And Europe?"

"Europe is arming as fast as possible. I hear we are to meet the Powers next week at Paris. I must go."

"Your arm, my dear?"

"My arm must get well. It will have to go with me, anyhow."

"Tell me some more."

"There is no more. But it is just as certain as it can be that this is the crisis. If the East can be persuaded to hold its hand now, it will never be likely to raise it again. It will mean free trade all over the world, I suppose, and all that kind of thing. But if not——"

"Well?"

"If not, there will be a catastrophe such as never has been even imagined. The whole human race will be at war, and either East or West will be simply wiped out. These new Benninschein explosives will make certain of that."

"But is it absolutely certain that the East has got them?"

"Absolutely. Benninschein sold them simultaneously to East and West; then he died, luckily for him."

Mabel had heard this kind of talk before, but her imagination simply refused to grasp it. A duel of East and West under these new conditions was an unthinkable thing. There had been no European war within living memory, and the Eastern wars of the last century had been under the old conditions. Now, if tales were true, entire towns would be destroyed with a single shell. The new conditions were unimaginable. Military experts prophesied extravagantly, contradicting one another on vital points; the whole procedure of war was a matter of theory; there were no precedents with which to compare it. It was as if archers disputed as to the results of cordite. Only one thing was certain—that the East had every modern engine, and, as regards male population, half as much again as the rest of the world put together; and the conclusion to be drawn from these premises was not reassuring to England.

But imagination simply refused to speak. The daily papers had a short, careful leading article every day, founded upon the scraps of news that stole out from the conferences on the other side of the world; Felsenburgh's name appeared more frequently than ever; otherwise there seemed to be a kind of hush. Nothing suffered very much; trade went on; European stocks were not appreciably lower than usual; men still built houses, married wives, begat sons and daughters, did their business and went to the theatre, for the mere reason that there was no good in anything else. They could neither save nor precipitate the situation; it was on too large a scale. Occasionally people went mad— people who had succeeded in goading their imagination to a height whence a glimpse of reality could be obtained; and there was a diffused atmosphere of tenseness. But that was all. Not many speeches were made on the subject; it had been found inadvisable. After all, there was nothing to do but to wait.

III

Mabel remembered her husband's advice to watch, and for a few days did her best. But there was nothing that alarmed her. The old lady was a little quiet, perhaps, but went about her minute affairs as usual. She asked the girl to read to her sometimes, and listened unblenching to whatever was offered her; she attended in the kitchen daily, organised varieties of food, and appeared interested in all that concerned her son. She packed his bag with her own hands, set out his furs for the swift flight to Paris, and waved to him from the window as he went down the little path towards the junction. He would be gone three days, he said.

It was on the evening of the second day that she fell ill; and Mabel, running upstairs, in alarm at the message of the servant, found her rather flushed and agitated in her chair.

"It is nothing, my dear," said the old lady tremulously; and she added the description of a symptom or two.

Mabel got her to bed, sent for the doctor, and sat down to wait.

She was sincerely fond of the old lady, and had always found her presence in the house a quiet sort of delight. The effect of her upon the mind was as that of an easy-chair upon the body. The old lady was so tranquil and human, so absorbed in small external matters, so reminiscent now and then of the days of her youth, so utterly without resentment or peevishness. It seemed curiously pathetic to the girl to watch that quiet old spirit approach its extinction, or rather, as Mabel believed, its loss of personality in the reabsorption into the Spirit of Life which informed the world. She found less difficulty in contemplating the end of a vigorous soul, for in that case she imagined a kind of energetic rush of force back into the origin of things; but in this peaceful old lady there was so little energy; her whole point, so to speak, lay in the delicate little fabric of personality, built out of fragile things into an entity far more significant than the sum of its component parts: the death of a flower, reflected Mabel, is sadder than the death of a lion; the breaking of a piece of china more irreparable than the ruin of a palace.

"It is syncope," said the doctor when he came in. "She may die at any time; she may live ten years."

"There is no need to telegraph for Mr. Brand?"

He made a little deprecating movement with his hands.

"It is not certain that she will die—it is not imminent?" she asked.

"No, no; she may live ten years, I said."

He added a word or two of advice as to the use of the oxygen injector, and went away.

The old lady was lying quietly in bed, when the girl went up, and put out a wrinkled hand.

"Well, my dear?" she asked.

"It is just a little weakness, mother. You must lie quiet and do nothing. Shall I read to you?"

"No, my dear; I will think a little."

It was no part of Mabel's idea to duty to tell her that she was in danger, for there was no past to set straight, no Judge to be confronted. Death was an ending, not a beginning. It was a peaceful Gospel; at least, it became peaceful as soon as the end had come.

So the girl went downstairs once more, with a quiet little ache at her heart that refused to be still.

What a strange and beautiful thing death was, she told herself—this resolution of a chord that had hung suspended for thirty, fifty or seventy years—back again into the stillness of the huge Instrument that was all in all to itself. Those same notes would be struck again, were being struck again even now all over the world, though with an infinite delicacy of difference in the touch; but that particular emotion was gone: it was foolish to think that it was sounding eternally elsewhere, for there was no elsewhere. She, too, herself would cease one day, let her see to it that the tone was pure and lovely.

Mr. Phillips arrived the next morning as usual, just as Mabel had left the old lady's room, and asked news of her.

"She is a little better, I think," said Mabel. "She must be very quiet all day."

The secretary bowed and turned aside into Oliver's room, where a heap of letters lay to be answered.

A couple of hours later, as Mabel went upstairs once more, she met Mr. Phillips coming down. He looked a little flushed under his sallow skin.

"Mrs. Brand sent for me," he said. "She wished to know whether Mr. Oliver would be back to-night."

"He will, will he not? You have not heard?"

"Mr. Brand said he would be here for a late dinner. He will reach London at nineteen."

"And is there any other news?"

He compressed his lips.

"There are rumours," he said. "Mr. Brand wired to me an hour ago."

He seemed moved at something, and Mabel looked at him in astonishment.

"It is not Eastern news?" she asked.

His eyebrows wrinkled a little.

"You must forgive me, Mrs. Brand," he said. "I am not at liberty to say anything."

She was not offended, for she trusted her husband too well; but she went on into the sick-room with her heart beating.

The old lady, too, seemed excited. She lay in bed with a clear flush in her white cheeks, and hardly smiled at all to the girl's greeting.

"Well, you have seen Mr. Phillips, then?" said Mabel.

Old Mrs. Brand looked at her sharply an instant, but said nothing.

"Don't excite yourself, mother. Oliver will be back to-night."

The old lady drew a long breath.

"Don't trouble about me, my dear," she said. "I shall do very well now. He will be back to dinner, will he not?"

"If the volor is not late. Now, mother, are you ready for breakfast?"

Mabel passed an afternoon of considerable agitation. It

was certain that something had happened. The secretary, who breakfasted with her in the parlour looking on to the garden, had appeared strangely excited. He had told her that he would be away the rest of the day: Mr. Oliver had given him his instructions. He had refrained from all discussion of the Eastern question, and he had given her no news of the Paris Convention; he only repeated that Mr. Oliver would be back that night. Then he had gone off in a hurry half-an-hour later.

The old lady seemed asleep when the girl went up afterwards, and Mabel did not like to disturb her. Neither did she like to leave the house; so she walked by herself in the garden, thinking and hoping and fearing, till the long shadow lay across the path, and the tumbled platform of roofs was bathed in a dusty green haze from the west.

As she came in she took up the evening paper, but there was no news there except to the effect that the Convention would close that afternoon.

Twenty o'clock came, but there was no sign of Oliver. The Paris volor should have arrived an hour before, but Mabel, staring out into the darkening heavens had seen the stars come out like jewels one by one, but no slender winged fish pass overhead. Of course she might have missed it; there was no depending on its exact course; but she had seen it a hundred times before, and wondered unreasonably why she had not seen it now. But she would not sit down to dinner, and paced up and down in her white dress, turning again and again to the window, listening to the soft rush of the trains, the faint hoots from the track, and the musical chords from the junction a mile away. The lights were up by now, and the vast sweep of the towns looked like fairyland between the earthly light and the heavenly darkness. Why did not Oliver come, or at least let her know why he did not?

Once she went upstairs, miserably anxious herself, to reassure the old lady, and found her again very drowsy.

"He is not come," she said. "I dare say he may be kept in Paris."

The old face on the pillow nodded and murmured, and Mabel went down again. It was now an hour after dinner-time.

Oh! there were a hundred things that might have kept him. He had often been later than this: he might have missed the volor he meant to catch; the Convention might have been prolonged; he might be exhausted, and think it better to sleep in Paris after all, and have forgotten to wire. He might even have wired to Mr. Phillips, and the secretary have forgotten to pass on the message.

She went at last, hopelessly, to the telephone, and looked at it. There it was, that round silent mouth, that little row of labelled buttons. She half decided to touch them one by one, and inquire whether anything had been heard of her husband: there was his club, his office in Whitehall, Mr. Phillip's house, Parliament-house, and the rest. But she hesitated, telling herself to be patient. Oliver hated interference, and he would surely soon remember and relieve her anxiety.

Then, even as she turned away, the bell rang sharply, and a white label flashed into sight.——WHITEHALL.

She pressed the corresponding button, and, her hand shaking so much that she could scarcely hold the receiver to her ear, she listened.

"Who is there?"

Her heart leaped at the sound of her husband's voice, tiny and minute across the miles of wire.

"I—Mabel," she said. "Alone here."

"Oh! Mabel. Very well. I am back: all is well. Now listen. Can you hear?"

"Yes, yes."

"The best has happened. It is all over in the East. Felsenburgh has done it. Now listen. I cannot come home to-night. It will be announced in Paul's House in two hours from now. We are communicating with the Press. Come up here to me at once. You must be present.... Can you hear?"

"Oh, yes."

"Come then at once. It will be the greatest thing in history. Tell no one. Come before the rush begins. In half-an-hour the way will be stopped."

"Oliver."

"Yes? Quick."

"Mother is ill. Shall I leave her?"

"How ill?"

"Oh, no immediate danger. The doctor has seen her."

There was silence for a moment.

"Yes; come then. We will go back to-night anyhow, then. Tell her we shall be late."

"Very well."

"... Yes, you must come. Felsenburgh will be there."

CHAPTER IV

I

ON THE same afternoon Percy received a visitor. There was nothing exceptional about him; and Percy, as he came downstairs in his walking-dress and looked at him in the light from the tall parlour-window, came to no conclusion at all as to his business and person, except that he was not a Catholic.

"You wished to see me," said the priest, indicating a chair. "I fear I must not stop long."

"I shall not keep you long," said the stranger eagerly. "My business is done in five minutes."

Percy waited with his eyes cast down.

"A—a certain person has sent me to you. She was a Catholic once; she wishes to return to the Church."

Percy made a little movement with his head. It was a message he did not very often receive in these days.

"You will come, sir, will you not? You will promise me?"

The man seemed greatly agitated; his sallow face showed a little shining with sweat, and his eyes were piteous.

"Of course I will come," said Percy, smiling.

"Yes, sir; but you do not know who she is. It—it would make a great stir, sir, if it was known. It must not be known, sir; you will promise me that, too?"

"I must not make any promise of that kind," said the

61

priest gently. "I do not know the circumstances yet."

The stranger licked his lips nervously.

"Well, sir," he said hastily, "you will say nothing till you have seen her? You can promise me that."

"Oh, certainly," said the priest.

"Well, sir, you had better not know my name. It—it may make it easier for you and for me. And—and, if you please, sir, the lady is ill; you must come to-day, if you please, but not until the evening. Will twenty-two o'clock be convenient, sir?"

"Where is it?" asked Percy abruptly.

"It—it is near Croydon junction. I will write down the address presently. And you will not come until twenty-two o'clock, sir?"

"Why not now?"

"Because the—the others may be there. They will be away then; I know that."

This was rather suspicious, Percy thought: discreditable plots had been known before. But he could not refuse outright.

"Why does she not send for her parish-priest?" he asked.

"She—she does not know who he is, sir; she saw you once in the Cathedral, sir, and asked you for your name. Do you remember, sir?—an old lady?"

Percy did dimly remember something of the kind a month or two before; but he could not be certain, and said so.

"Well, sir, you will come, will you not?"

"I must communicate with Father Dolan," said the priest. "If he gives me permission——"

"If you please, sir, Father—Father Dolan must not know her name. You will not tell him?"

"I do not know it myself yet," said the priest, smiling.

The stranger sat back abruptly at that, and his face worked.

"Well, sir, let me tell you this first. This old lady's son is my employer, and a very prominent Communist. She lives with him and his wife. The other two will be away to-night. That is why I am asking you all this. And now, you will come, sir?"

Percy looked at him steadily for a moment or two. Certainly, if this was a conspiracy, the conspirators were feeble folk. Then he answered:

"I will come, sir; I promise. Now the name."

The stranger again licked his lips nervously, and glanced timidly from side to side. Then he seemed to gather his resolution; he leaned forward and whispered sharply.

"The old lady's name is Brand, sir—the mother of Mr. Oliver Brand."

For a moment Percy was bewildered. It was too extraordinary to be true. He knew Mr. Oliver Brand's name only too well; it was he who, by God's permission, was doing more in England at this moment against the Catholic cause than any other man alive; and it was he whom the Trafalgar Square incident had raised into such eminent popularity. And now, here was his mother—

He turned fiercely upon the man.

"I do not know what you are, sir—whether you believe in God or not; but will you swear to me on your religion and your honour that all this is true?"

The timid eyes met his, and wavered; but it was the wavering of weakness, not of treachery.

"I—I swear it, sir; by God Almighty."

"Are you a Catholic?"

The man shook his head.

"But I believe in God," he said. "At least, I think so."

Percy leaned back, trying to realize exactly what it all meant. There was no triumph in his mind—that kind of emotion was not his weakness; there was fear of a kind, excitement, bewilderment, and under all a satisfaction that God's grace was so sovereign. If it could reach this woman, who could be too far removed for it to take effect? Presently he noticed the other looking at him anxiously.

"You are afraid, sir? You are not going back from your promise?"

That dispersed the cloud a little, and Percy smiled.

"Oh! no," he said. "I will be there at twenty-two o'clock.... Is death imminent?"

"No, sir; it is syncope. She is recovered a little this morning."

The priest passed his hand over his eyes and stood up.

"Well, I will be there," he said. "Shall you be there, sir?"

The other shook his head, standing up too.

"I must be with Mr. Brand, sir; there is to be a meeting to-night; but I must not speak of that.... No, sir; ask for Mrs. Brand, and say that she is expecting you. They will take you upstairs at once."

"I must not say I am a priest, I suppose?"

"No, sir; if you please."

He drew out a pocket-book, scribbled in it a moment, tore out the sheet, and handed it to the priest.

"The address, sir. Will you kindly destroy that when you have copied it? I—I do not wish to lose my place, sir, if it can be helped."

Percy stood twisting the paper in his fingers a moment.

"Why are you not a Catholic yourself?" he asked.

The man shook his head mutely. Then he took up his hat, and went towards the door.

Percy passed a very emotional afternoon.

For the last month or two little had happened to encourage him. He had been obliged to report half-a-dozen more significant secessions, and hardly a conversion of any kind. There was no doubt at all that the tide was setting steadily against the Church. The mad act in Trafalgar Square, too, had done incalculable harm last week: men were saying more than ever, and the papers storming, that the Church's reliance on the supernatural was belied by every one of her public acts. "Scratch a Catholic and find an assassin" had been the text of a leading article in the *New People*, and Percy himself was dismayed at the folly of the attempt. It was true that the Archbishop had formally repudiated both the act and the motive from the Cathedral pulpit, but that too had only served as an opportunity hastily taken up by the principal papers, to recall the continual policy of the Church to avail herself of violence while she repudiated the violent. The horrible death of the man had in no way appeased popular indignation; there were not even wanting suggestions that the man had been seen coming out of Archbishop's House an hour before the attempt at assassination had taken place.

And now here, with dramatic swiftness, had come a message that the hero's own mother desired reconciliation with the Church that had attempted to murder her son.

Again and again that afternoon, as Percy sped northwards on his visit to a priest in Worcester, and southwards once more as the lights began to shine towards evening, he wondered whether this were not a plot after all—some kind of retaliation, an attempt to trap him. Yet he had promised to say nothing, and to go.

He finished his daily letter after dinner as usual, with a curious sense of fatality; addressed and stamped it. Then he went downstairs, in his walking-dress, to Father Blackmore's room.

"Will you hear my confession, father?" he said abruptly.

II

Victoria Station, still named after the great nineteenth-century Queen, was neither more nor less busy than usual as he came into it half-an-hour later. The vast platform, sunk now nearly two hundred feet below the ground level showed the double crowd of passengers entering and leaving town. Those on the extreme left, towards whom Percy began to descend in the open glazed lift, were by far the most numerous, and the stream at the lift-entrance made it necessary for him to move slowly.

He arrived at last, walking in the soft light on the noiseless ribbed rubber, and stood by the door of the long car that ran straight through to the Junction. It was the last of a series of a dozen or more, each of which slid off minute by minute. Then, still watching the endless movement of the lifts ascending and descending between the entrances of the upper end of the station, he stepped in and sat down.

He felt quiet now that he had actually started. He had made his confession, just in order to make certain of his own soul, though scarcely expecting any definite danger, and sat now, his grey suit and straw hat in no way distinguishing him as a priest (for a general leave was given by the authorities to dress so for any adequate reason). Since the case was not imminent, he had not brought stocks or pyx—Father Dolan had wired to him that he might fetch them if he wished from St. Joseph's, near the Junction. He had only the violet thread in his pocket, such as was customary for sick calls.

He was sliding along peaceably enough, fixing his eyes on the empty seat opposite, and trying to preserve complete collectedness when the car abruptly stopped. He looked out, astonished, and saw by the white enamelled walks twenty feet from the window that they were already in the tunnel. The stoppage might arise from many causes, and he was not greatly excited, nor did it seem that others in the carriage took it very seriously; he could hear, after a moment's silence, the talking recommence beyond the partition.

Then there came, echoed by the walls, the sound of shouting from far away, mingled with hoots and chords; it grew louder. The talking in the carriage stopped. He heard a window thrown up, and the next instant a car tore past, going back to the station although on the down line. This must be looked into, thought Percy: something certainly was happening; so he got up and went across the empty compartment to the further window. Again came the crying of voices, again the signals, and once more a car whirled past, followed almost immediately by another. There was a jerk—a smooth movement. Percy staggered and fell into a seat, as the carriage in which he was seated itself began to move backwards.

There was a clamour now in the next compartment, and Percy made his way there through the door, only to find half-a-dozen men with their heads thrust from the windows, who paid absolutely no attention to his inquiries. So he stood there, aware that they knew no more than himself, waiting for an explanation from some one. It was disgraceful, he told himself, that any misadventure should so disorganise the line.

Twice the car stopped; each time it moved on again after a hoot or two, and at last drew up at the platform whence it had started, although a hundred yards further out.

Ah! there was no doubt that something had happened! The instant he opened the door a great roar met his ears, and as he sprang on to the platform and looked up at the end of the station, he began to understand.

From right to left of the huge interior, across the platforms, swelling every instant, surged an enormous swaying, roaring crowd. The flight of steps, twenty yards broad, used only in cases of emergency, resembled a gigantic black cataract nearly two hundred feet in height. Each car as it drew up discharged more and more men and women, who ran like ants towards the assembly of their fellows. The noise was indescribable, the shouting of men, the screaming of women, the clang and hoot of the huge machines, and three or four times the brazen cry of a trumpet, as an emergency door was flung open overhead, and a small swirl of crowd poured through it towards the streets beyond. But after one look Percy looked no more at the people; for there high up beneath the clock, on the Government signal board, glared out monstrous letters of fire, telling in Esperanto and English, the message for which England had grown sick. He read it a dozen times before he moved, staring, as at a supernatural sight which might denote the triumph of either heaven or hell.

"EASTERN CONVENTION DISPERSED.

PEACE, NOT WAR.

UNIVERSAL BROTHERHOOD ESTABLISHED.

FELSENBURGH IN LONDON TO—NIGHT."

*   *   *   *   *

III

It was not until nearly two hours later that Percy was standing at the house beyond the Junction.

He had argued, expostulated, threatened, but the officials were like men possessed. Half of them had disappeared in the rush to the City, for it had leaked out, in spite of the Government's precautions, that Paul's House, known once as St. Paul's Cathedral, was to be the scene of Felsenburgh's reception. The others seemed demented; one man on the platform had dropped dead from nervous exhaustion, but no one appeared to care; and the body lay huddled beneath a seat. Again and again Percy had been swept away by a rush, as he struggled from platform to platform in his search for a car that would take him to Croydon. It seemed that there was none to be had, and the useless carriages collected like drift-wood between the platforms, as others whirled up from the country bringing loads of frantic, delirious men, who vanished like smoke from the white rubber-boards. The platforms were continually crowded, and as continually emptied, and it was not until half-an-hour before midnight that the block began to move outwards again.

Well, he was here at last, dishevelled, hatless and exhausted, looking up at the dark windows.

He scarcely knew what he thought of the whole matter. War, of course, was terrible. And such a war as this would have been too terrible for the imagination to visualise; but to the priest's mind there were other things even worse. What of universal peace—peace, that is to say, established by other than Christ's method? Or was God behind even this? The questions were hopeless.

Felsenburgh—it was he then who had done this thing—this thing undoubtedly greater than any secular event hitherto known in civilisation. What manner of man was he? What was his character, his motive, his method? How would he use his success? … So the points flew before him like a stream of sparks, each, it might be, harmless; each, equally, capable of setting a world on fire. Meanwhile here was an old woman who desired to be reconciled with God before she died.…

He touched the button again, three or four times, and waited. Then a light sprang out overhead, and he knew that he was heard.

"I was sent for," he exclaimed to the bewildered maid. "I should have been here at twenty-two: I was prevented by the rush."

She babbled out a question at him.

"Yes, it is true, I believe," he said. "It is peace, not war. Kindly take me upstairs."

He went through the hall with a curious sense of guilt. This was Brand's house then—that vivid orator, so bitterly eloquent against God; and here was he, a priest, slinking in under cover of night. Well, well, it was not of his appointment.

At the door of an upstairs room the maid turned to him.

"A doctor, sir?" she said.

"That is my affair," said Percy briefly, and opened the door.

A little wailing cry broke from the corner, before he had time to close the door again.

"Oh! thank God! I thought He had forgotten me. You are a priest, father?"

"I am a priest. Do you not remember seeing me in the Cathedral?"

"Yes, yes, sir; I saw you praying, father. Oh! thank God, thank God!"

Percy stood looking down at her a moment, seeing her flushed old face in the nightcap, her bright sunken eyes and her tremulous hands. Yes; this was genuine enough.

"Now, my child," he said, "tell me."

"My confession, father."

Percy drew out the purple thread, slipped it over his shoulders, and sat down by the bed.

*   *   *   *   *

But she would not let him go for a while after that.

"Tell me, father. When will you bring me Holy Communion?"

He hesitated.

"I understand that Mr. Brand and his wife know nothing of all this?"

"No, father."

"Tell me, are you very ill?"

"I don't know, father. They will not tell me. I thought I was gone last night."

"When would you wish me to bring you Holy Communion? I will do as you say."

"Shall I send to you in a day or two? Father, ought I to tell him?"

"You are not obliged."

"I will if I ought."

"Well, think about it, and let me know.… You have heard what has happened?"

She nodded, but almost uninterestedly; and Percy was conscious of a tiny prick of compunction at his own heart.

After all, the reconciling of a soul to God was a greater thing than the reconciling of East to West.

"It may make a difference to Mr. Brand," he said. "He will be a great man, now, you know."

She still looked at him in silence, smiling a little. Percy was astonished at the youthfulness of that old face. Then her face changed.

"Father, I must not keep you; but tell me this—Who is this man?"

"Felsenburgh?"

"Yes."

"No one knows. We shall know more to-morrow. He is in town to-night."

She looked so strange that Percy for an instant thought it was a seizure. Her face seemed to fall away in a kind of emotion, half cunning, half fear.

"Well, my child?"

"Father, I am a little afraid when I think of that man. He cannot harm me, can he? I am safe now? I am a Catholic——?"

"My child, of course you are safe. What is the matter? How can this man injure you?"

But the look of terror was still there, and Percy came a step nearer.

"You must not give way to fancies," he said. "Just commit yourself to our Blessed Lord. This man can do you no harm."

He was speaking now as to a child; but it was of no use. Her old mouth was still sucked in, and her eyes wandered past him into the gloom of the room behind.

"My child, tell me what is the matter. What do you know of Felsenburgh? You have been dreaming."

She nodded suddenly and energetically, and Percy for the first time felt his heart give a little leap of apprehension.

Was this old woman out of her mind, then? Or why was it that that name seemed to him sinister? Then he remembered that Father Blackmore had once talked like this. He made an effort, and sat down once more.

"Now tell me plainly," he said. "You have been dreaming. What have you dreamt?"

She raised herself a little in bed, again glancing round the room; then she put out her old ringed hand for one of his, and he gave it, wondering.

"The door is shut, father? There is no one listening?"

"No, no, my child. Why are you trembling? You must not be superstitious."

"Father, I will tell you. Dreams are nonsense, are they not? Well, at least, this is what I dreamt.

"I was somewhere in a great house; I do not know where it was. It was a house I have never seen. It was one of the old houses, and it was very dark. I was a child, I thought, and I was … I was afraid of something. The passages were all dark, and I went crying in the dark, looking for a light, and there was none. Then I heard a voice talking, a great way off. Father——"

Her hand gripped his more tightly, and again her eyes went round the room.

With great difficulty Percy repressed a sigh. Yet he dared not leave her just now. The house was very still; only from outside now and again sounded the clang of the cars, as they sped countrywards again from the congested town, and once the sound of great shouting. He wondered what time it was.

"Had you better tell me now?" he asked, still talking with a patient simplicity. "What time will they be back?"

"Not yet," she whispered. "Mabel said not till two o' clock. What time is it now, father?"

He pulled out his watch with his disengaged hand.

"It is not yet one," he said.

"Very well, listen, father.... I was in this house; and I heard that talking; and I ran along the passages, till I saw a light below a door; and then I stopped.... Nearer, father."

Percy was a little awed in spite of himself. Her voice had suddenly dropped to a whisper, and her old eyes seemed to hold him strangely.

"I stopped, father; I dared not go in. I could hear the talking, and I could see the light; and I dared not go in. Father, it was Felsenburgh in that room."

From beneath came the sudden snap of a door; then the sound of footsteps. Percy turned his head abruptly, and at the same moment heard a swift indrawn breath from the old woman.

"Hush!" he said. "Who is that?"

Two voices were talking in the hall below now, and at the sound the old woman relaxed her hold.

"I—I thought it to be him," she murmured.

Percy stood up; he could see that she did not understand the situation.

"Yes, my child," he said quietly, "but who is it?"

"My son and his wife," she said; then her face changed once more. "Why—why, father——"

Her voice died in her throat, as a step vibrated outside. For a moment there was complete silence; then a whisper, plainly audible, in a girl's voice.

"Why, her light is burning. Come in, Oliver, but softly."

Then the handle turned.

CHAPTER V

I

THERE WAS an exclamation, then silence, as a tall, beautiful girl with flushed face and shining grey eyes came forward and stopped, followed by a man whom Percy knew at once from his pictures. A little whimpering sounded from the bed, and the priest lifted his hand instinctively to silence it.

"Why," said Mabel; and then stared at the man with the young face and the white hair.

Oliver opened his lips and closed them again. He, too, had a strange excitement in his face. Then he spoke.

"Who is this?" he said deliberately.

"Oliver," cried the girl, turning to him abruptly, "this is the priest I saw——"

"A priest!" said the other, and came forward a step. "Why I thought——"

Percy drew a breath to steady that maddening vibration in his throat.

"Yes, I am a priest," he said.

Again the whimpering broke out from the bed; and Percy, half turning again to silence it, saw the girl mechanically loosen the clasp of the thin dust cloak over her white dress.

"You sent for him, mother?" snapped the man, with a tremble in his voice, and with a sudden jerk forward of his whole body. But the girl put out her hand.

"Quietly, my dear," she said. "Now sir——"

"Yes, I am a priest," said Percy again, strung up now to a desperate resistance of will, hardly knowing what he said.

"And you come to my house!" exclaimed the man. He came a step nearer, and half recoiled. "You swear you are a priest?" he said. "You have been here all this evening?"

"Since midnight."

"And you are not——" he stopped again.

Mabel stepped straight between them.

"Oliver," she said, still with that air of suppressed excitement, "we must not have a scene here. The poor dear is too ill. Will you come downstairs, sir?"

Percy took a step towards the door, and Oliver moved slightly aside. Then the priest stopped, turned and lifted his hand.

"God bless you!" he said simply, to the muttering figure in the bed. Then he went out, and waited outside the door.

He could hear a low talking within; then a compassionate murmur from the girl's voice; then Oliver was beside him, trembling all over, as white as ashes, and made a silent gesture as he went past him down the stairs.

The whole thing seemed to Percy like some incredible dream; it was all so unexpected, so untrue to life. He felt conscious of an enormous shame at the sordidness of the affair, and at the same time of a kind of hopeless recklessness. The worst had happened and the best—that was his sole comfort.

Oliver pushed a door open, touched a button, and went through into the suddenly lit room, followed by Percy. Still in silence, he pointed to a chair, Percy sat down, and Oliver stood before the fireplace, his hands deep in the pockets of his jacket, slightly turned away.

Percy's concentrated senses became aware of every detail of the room—the deep springy green carpet, smooth under his feet, the straight hanging thin silk curtains, the half-dozen low tables with a wealth of flowers upon them, and the books that lined the walls. The whole room was heavy with the scent of roses, although the windows were wide, and the night-breeze stirred the curtains continually. It was a woman's room, he told himself. Then he looked at the man's figure, lithe, tense, upright; the dark grey suit not unlike his own, the beautiful curve of the jaw, the clear pale complexion, the thin nose, the protruding curve of idealism over the eyes, and the dark hair. It was a poet's face, he told himself, and the whole personality was a living and vivid one. Then he turned a little and rose as the door opened, and Mabel came in, closing it behind her.

She came straight across to her husband, and put a hand on his shoulder.

"Sit down, my dear," she said. "We must talk a little. Please sit down, sir."

The three sat down, Percy on one side, and the husband and wife on a straight-backed settle opposite.

The girl began again.

"This must be arranged at once," she said, "but we must have no tragedy. Oliver, do you understand? You must not make a scene. Leave this to me."

She spoke with a curious gaiety; and Percy to his astonishment saw that she was quite sincere: there was not the hint of cynicism.

"Oliver, my dear," she said again, "don't mouth like that! It is all perfectly right. I am going to manage this."

Percy saw a venomous look directed at him by the man; the girl saw it too, moving her strong humorous eyes from one to the other. She put her hand on his knee.

"Oliver, attend! Don't look at this gentleman so bitterly. He has done no harm."

"No harm!" whispered the other.

"No—no harm in the world. What does it matter what that poor dear upstairs thinks? Now, sir, would you mind telling us why you came here?"

Percy drew another breath. He had not expected this line.

"I came here to receive Mrs. Brand back into the Church," he said.

"And you have done so?"

"I have done so."

"Would you mind telling us your name? It makes it so much more convenient."

Percy hesitated. Then he determined to meet her on her own ground.

"Certainly. My name is Franklin."

"Father Franklin?" asked the girl, with just the faintest tinge of mocking emphasis on the first word.

"Yes. Father Percy Franklin, from Archbishop's House, Westminster," said the priest steadily.

"Well, then, Father Percy Franklin; can you tell us why you came here? I mean, who sent for you?"

"Mrs. Brand sent for me."

"Yes, but by what means?"

"That I must not say."

"Oh, very good.... May we know what good comes of being 'received into the Church?' "

"By being received into the Church, the soul is reconciled to God."

"Oh! (Oliver, be quiet.) And how do you do it, Father Franklin?"

Percy stood up abruptly.

"This is no good, madam," he said. "What is the use of these questions?"

The girl looked at him in open-eyed astonishment, still with her hand on her husband's knee.

"The use, Father Franklin! Why, we want to know. There is no church law against your telling us, is there?"

Percy hesitated again. He did not understand in the least what she was after. Then he saw that he would give them an advantage if he lost his head at all: so he sat down again.

"Certainly not. I will tell you if you wish to know. I heard Mrs. Brand's confession, and gave her absolution."

"Oh! yes; that does it, then? And what next?"

"She ought to receive Holy Communion, and Anointing, if she is in danger of death."

Oliver twitched suddenly.

"Christ!" he said softly.

"Oliver!" cried the girl entreatingly. "Please leave this to me. It is much better so.—And then, I suppose, Father Franklin, you want to give those other things to my mother, too?"

"They are not absolutely necessary," said the priest, feeling, he did not know why, that he was somehow playing a losing game.

"Oh! they are not necessary? But you would like to?"

"I shall do so if possible. But I have done what is necessary."

It required all his will to keep quiet. He was as a man who had armed himself in steel, only to find that his enemy was in the form of a subtle vapour. He simply had not an idea what to do next. He would have given anything for the man to have risen and flown at his throat, for this girl was too much for them both.

"Yes," she said softly. "Well, it is hardly to be expected that my husband should give you leave to come here again.

But I am very glad that you have done what you think necessary. No doubt it will be a satisfaction to you, Father Franklin,
and to the poor old thing upstairs, too. While we—*we*—" she
pressed her husband's knee— "we do not mind at all. Oh!—
but there is one thing more."

"If you please," said Percy, wondering what on earth was
coming.

"You Christians—forgive me if I say anything rude—
but, you know, you Christians have a reputation for counting
heads, and making the most of converts. We shall be so much
obliged, Father Franklin, if you will give us your word not to
advertise this—this incident. It would distress my husband,
and give him a great deal of trouble."

"Mrs. Brand—" began the priest.

"One moment.... You see, we have not treated you badly.
There has been no violence. We will promise not to make
scenes with my mother. Will you promise us that?"

Percy had had time to consider, and he answered instantly.

"Certainly, I will promise that."

Mabel sighed contentedly.

"Well, that is all right. We are so much obliged.... And
I think we may say this, that perhaps after consideration my
husband may see his way to letting you come here again to do
Communion and—and the other thing——"

Again that spasm shook the man beside her.

"Well, we will see about that. At any rate, we know your
address, and can let you know.... By the way, Father Franklin,
are you going back to Westminster to-night?"

He bowed.

"Ah! I hope you will get through. You will find London
very much excited. Perhaps you heard——"

"Felsenburgh?" said Percy.

"Yes. Julian Felsenburgh," said the girl softly, again with that strange excitement suddenly alight in her eyes. "Julian Felsenburgh," she repeated. "He is there, you know. He will stay in England for the present."

Again Percy was conscious of that slight touch of fear at the mention of that name.

"I understand there is to be peace," he said.

The girl rose and her husband with her.

"Yes," she said, almost compassionately, "there is to be peace. Peace at last." (She moved half a step towards him, and her face glowed like a rose of fire. Her hand rose a little.) "Go back to London, Father Franklin, and use your eyes. You will see him, I dare say, and you will see more besides." (Her voice began to vibrate.) "And you will understand, perhaps, why we have treated you like this—why we are no longer afraid of you—why we are willing that my mother should do as she pleases. Oh! you will understand, Father Franklin—if not to-night, to-morrow; or if not to-morrow, at least in a very short time."

"Mabel!" cried her husband.

The girl wheeled, and threw her arms round him, and kissed him on the mouth.

"Oh! I am not ashamed, Oliver, my dear. Let him go and see for himself. Good-night, Father Franklin."

As he went towards the door, hearing the ping of the bell that some one touched in the room behind him, he turned once more, dazed and bewildered; and there were the two, husband and wife, standing in the soft, sunny light, as if transfigured. The girl had her arm round the man's shoulder, and stood upright and radiant as a pillar of fire; and even on the man's face there was no anger now—nothing but an almost supernatural pride and confidence. They were both smiling.

Then Percy passed out into the soft, summer night.

II

Percy understood nothing except that he was afraid, as he sat in the crowded car that whirled him up to London. He scarcely even heard the talk round him, although it was loud and continuous; and what he heard meant little to him. He understood only that there had been strange scenes, that London was said to have gone suddenly mad, that Felsenburgh had spoken that night in Paul's House.

He was afraid at the way in which he had been treated, and he asked himself dully again and again what it was that had inspired that treatment; it seemed that he had been in the presence of the supernatural; he was conscious of shivering a little, and of the symptoms of an intolerable sleepiness. It was scarcely strange to him that he should be sitting in a crowded car at two o' clock of a summer dawn.

Thrice the car stopped, and he stared out at the signs of confusion that were everywhere; at the figures that ran in the twilight between the tracks, at a couple of wrecked carriages, a tumble of tarpaulins; he listened mechanically to the hoots and cries that sounded everywhere.

As he stepped out at last on to the platform, he found it very much as he had left it two hours before. There was the same desperate rush as the car discharged its load, the same dead body beneath the seat; and above all, as he ran helplessly behind the crowd, scarcely knowing whither he ran or why, above him burned the same stupendous message beneath the clock. Then he found himself in the lift, and a minute later he was out on the steps behind the station.

There, too, was an astonishing sight. The lamps still burned overhead, but beyond them lay the first pale streaks of the false dawn. The street that ran now straight to the old royal palace, uniting there, as at the centre of a web, with those that came from Westminster, the Mall and Hyde Park, was one solid pavement of heads. On this side and that rose up the hotels and "Houses of Joy" the windows all ablaze with light, solemn and triumphant as if to welcome a king; while far ahead against the sky stood the monstrous palace outlined in fire, and alight from within like all other houses within view. The noise was bewildering. It was impossible to distinguish one sound from another. Voices, horns, drums, the tramp of a thousand footsteps on the rubber pavements, the sombre roll of wheels from the station behind—all united in one overwhelmingly solemn booming, overscored by shriller notes.

It was impossible to move.

He found himself standing in a position of extraordinary advantage, at the very top of the broad flight of steps that led down into the old station yard, now a wide space that united, on the left the broad road to the palace, and on the right Victoria Street, that showed like all else one vivid perspective of lights and heads. Against the sky on his right rose up the illuminated head of the Cathedral Campanile. It appeared to him as if he had known that in some previous existence.

He edged himself mechanically a foot or two to his left, till he clasped a pillar; then he waited, trying not to analyse his emotions, but to absorb them.

Gradually he became aware that this crowd was as no other that he had ever seen. To his psychical sense it seemed to him that it possessed a unity unlike any other. There was magnetism in the air. There was a sensation as if a creative act were in process, whereby thousands of individual cells were being welded more and more perfectly every instant into one huge sentient being with one will, one emotion, and one head. The crying of voices seemed significant only as the stirrings of this creative power which so expressed itself. Here rested this giant humanity, stretching to his sight in living limbs so far as he could see on every side, waiting, waiting for some consummation—stretching, too, as his tired brain began to guess, down every thoroughfare of the vast city.

He did not even ask himself for what they waited. He knew, yet he did not know. He knew it was for a revelation—for something that should crown their aspirations, and fix them so for ever.

He had a sense that he had seen all this before; and, like a child, he began to ask himself where it could have happened, until he remembered that it was so that he had once dreamt of the Judgment Day—of humanity gathered to meet Jesus Christ—Jesus Christ! Ah! how tiny that Figure seemed to him now—how far away—real indeed, but insignificant to himself—how hopelessly apart from this tremendous life! He glanced up at the Campanile. Yes; there was a piece of the True Cross there, was there not?—a little piece of the wood on which a Poor Man had died twenty centuries ago.... Well, well. It was a long way off....

He did not quite understand what was happening to him. "Sweet Jesus, be to me not a Judge but a Saviour," he whispered beneath his breath, gripping the granite of the pillar; and a moment later knew how futile was that prayer. It was gone like a breath in this vast, vivid atmosphere of man. He had said Mass, had he not? this morning—in white vestments.—Yes; he had believed it all then—desperately, but truly; and now....

To look into the future was as useless as to look into the past. There was no future, and no past: it was all one eternal instant, present and final....

Then he let go of effort, and again began to see with his bodily eyes.

The dawn was coming up the sky now, a steady soft brightening that appeared in spite of its sovereignty to be as nothing compared with the brilliant light of the streets. "We need no sun," he whispered, smiling piteously; "no sun or light of a candle. We have our light on earth—the light that lighteneth every man...."

The Campanile seemed further away than ever now, in that ghostly glimmer of dawn—more and more helpless every moment, compared with the beautiful vivid shining of the streets.

Then he listened to the sounds, and it seemed to him as if somewhere, far down eastwards, there was a silence beginning. He jerked his head impatiently, as a man behind him began to talk rapidly and confusedly. Why would he not be silent, and let silence be heard? ... The man stopped presently, and out of the distance there swelled up a roar, as soft as the roll of a summer tide; it passed up towards him from the right; it was about him, dinning in his ears. There was no longer any individual voice: it was the breathing of the giant that had been born; he was crying out too; he did not know what he said, but he could not be silent. His veins and nerves seemed alight with wine; and as he stared down the long street, hearing the huge cry ebb from him and move toward the palace, he knew why he had cried, and why he was now silent.

A slender, fish-shaped thing, as white as milk, as ghostly as a shadow, and as beautiful as the dawn, slid into sight half-a-mile away, turned and came towards him, floating, as it seemed, on the very wave of silence that it created, up, up the long curving street on outstretched wings, not twenty feet above the heads of the crowd. There was one great sigh, and then silence once more.

When Percy could think consciously again—for his will was only capable of efforts as a clock of ticks—the strange white thing was nearer. He told himself that he had seen a hundred such before; and at the same instant that this was different from all others.

Then it was nearer still, floating slowly, slowly, like a gull over the sea; he could make out its smooth nose, its low parapet beyond, the steersman's head motionless; he could even hear now the soft winnowing of the screw—and then he saw that for which he had waited.

High on the central deck there stood a chair, draped, too, in white, with some insignia visible above its back; and in the chair sat the figure of a man, motionless and lonely. He made no sign as he came; his dark dress showed vividly against the whiteness; his head was raised, and he turned it gently now and again from side to side.

It came nearer still, in the profound stillness; the head turned, and for an instant the face was plainly visible in the soft, radiant light.

It was a pale face, strongly marked, as of a young man, with arched, black eyebrows, thin lips, and white hair.

Then the face turned once more, the steersman shifted his head, and the beautiful shape, wheeling a little, passed the corner, and moved up towards the palace.

There was an hysterical yelp somewhere, a cry, and again the tempestuous groan broke out.

BOOK II—THE ENCOUNTER

CHAPTER I

I

OLIVER BRAND was seated at his desk, on the evening of the next day, reading the leading article of the *New People*, evening edition.

"We have had time," he read, "to recover ourselves a little from the intoxication of last night. Before embarking on prophecy, it will be as well to recall the facts. Up to yesterday evening our anxiety with regard to the Eastern crisis continued; and when twenty-one o'clock struck there were not more than forty persons in London—the English delegates, that is to say—who knew positively that the danger was over. Between that moment and half-an-hour later the Government took a few discreet steps: a select number of persons were informed; the police were called out, with half-a-dozen regiments, to preserve order; Paul's House was cleared; the railroad companies were warned; and at the half hour precisely the announcement was made by means of electric placards in every quarter of London, as well as in all large provincial towns. We have not space now to adequately describe the admirable manner in which the public authorities did their duty; it is enough to say that not more than seventy fatalities took place in the whole of London; nor is it our business to criticise the action of the Government, in choosing this mode of making the announcement.

"By twenty-two o'clock Paul's House was filled in every corner, the Old Choir was reserved for members of Parliament and public officials, the quarter-dome galleries were filled with ladies, and to the rest of the floor the public was freely admitted. The volor-police also inform us now that for about the distance of one mile in every direction round this centre every thoroughfare was blocked with pedestrians, and, two hours later, as we all know, practically all the main streets of the whole of London were in the same condition.

"It was an excellent choice by which Mr. OLIVER BRAND was selected as the first speaker. His arm was still in bandages; and the appeal of his figure as well as his passionate words struck the first explicit note of the evening. A report of his words will be found in another column. In their turns, the PRIME MINISTER, Mr. SNOWFORD, the FIRST MINISTER OF THE ADMIRALTY, the SECRETARY FOR EASTERN AFFAIRS, and LORD PEMBERTON, all spoke a few words, corroborating the extraordinary news. At a quarter before twenty-three, the noise of cheering outside announced the arrival of the American delegates from Paris, and one by one these ascended the platform by the south gates of the Old Choir. Each spoke in turn. It is impossible to appreciate words spoken at such a moment as this; but perhaps it is not invidious to name Mr. MARKHAM as the orator who above all others appealed to those who were privileged to hear him. It was he, too, who told us explicitly what others had merely mentioned, to the effect that the success of the American efforts was entirely due to Mr. JULIAN FELSENBURGH. As yet Mr. FELSENBURGH had not arrived; but in answer to a roar of inquiry, Mr. MARKHAM announced that this gentleman would be amongst them in a few minutes. He then proceeded to describe to us, so far as was possible in a few sentences, the methods by which Mr. FELSENBURGH had accomplished what is probably the most astonishing task known to history. It seems from his words that Mr. FELSENBURGH (whose biography, so far as it is known, we give in another column) is probably the greatest orator that the world has ever known—we use these words deliberately. All languages seem the same to him; he delivered speeches during the eight months through which the Eastern Convention lasted, in no less than fifteen tongues. Of his manner in speaking we shall have a few remarks to make presently. He showed also, Mr. MARKHAM told us, the most astonishing knowledge, not only of human nature, but of every trait under which that divine thing manifests itself. He appeared acquainted with the history, the prejudices, the fears, the hopes, the expectations of all the innumerable sects and castes of the East to whom it was his business to speak. In fact, as Mr. MARKHAM said, he is probably the first perfect product of that new cosmopolitan creation to which the world has laboured throughout its history. In no less than nine places—Damascus, Irkutsk, Constantinople, Calcutta, Benares, Nanking, among them—he was hailed as Messiah by a Mohammedan mob. Finally, in America, where this extraordinary figure has arisen, all speak well of him. He has been guilty of none of those crimes—there is not one that convicts him of sin—those crimes of the Yellow Press, of corruption, of commercial or political bullying which have so stained the past of all those old politicians who made the sister continent what she has become. Mr. FELSENBURGH has not even formed a party. He, and not his underlings, have conquered. Those who were present in Paul's House on this occasion will understand us when we say that the effect of those words was indescribable.

"When Mr. MARKHAM sat down, there was a silence; then in order to quiet the rising excitement, the organist struck the first chords of the Masonic Hymn; the words were taken up, and presently not only the whole interior of the building rang with it, but outside, too, the people responded, and the city of London for a few moments became indeed a temple of the Lord.

"Now indeed we come to the most difficult part of our task, and it is better to confess at once that anything resembling journalistic descriptiveness must be resolutely laid aside. The greatest things are best told in the simplest words.

"Towards the close of the fourth verse, a figure in a plain dark suit was observed ascending the steps of the platform. For a moment this attracted no attention, but when it was seen that a sudden movement had broken out among the delegates, the singing began to falter; and it ceased altogether as the figure, after a slight inclination to right and left, passed up the further steps that led to the rostrum. Then occurred a curious incident. The organist aloft at first did not seem to understand, and continued playing, but a sound broke out from the crowd resembling a kind of groan, and instantly he ceased. But no cheering followed. Instead a profound silence dominated in an instant the huge throng; this, by some strange magnetism, communicated itself to those without the building, and when Mr. FELSENBURGH uttered his first words, it was in a stillness that was like a living thing. We leave the explanation of this phenomenon to the expert in psychology.

"Of his actual words we have nothing to say. So far as we are aware no reporter made notes at the moment; but the speech, delivered in Esperanto, was a very simple one, and very short. It consisted of a brief announcement of the great fact of Universal Brotherhood, a congratulation to all who were yet alive to witness this consummation of history; and, at the end, an ascription of praise to that Spirit of the World whose incarnation was now accomplished.

"So much we can say; but we can say nothing as to the impression of the personality who stood there. In appearance the man seemed to be about thirty-three years of age, clean-shaven, upright, with white hair and dark eyes and brows; he stood motionless with his hands on the rail, he made but one gesture that drew a kind of sob from the crowd, he spoke these words slowly, distinctly, and in a clear voice; then he stood waiting.

"There was no response but a sigh which sounded in the ears of at least one who heard it as if the whole world drew breath for the first time; and then that strange heart-shaking silence fell again. Many were weeping silently, the lips of thousands moved without a sound, and all faces were turned to that simple figure, as if the hope of every soul were centred there. So, if we may believe it, the eyes of many, centuries ago, were turned on one known now to history as JESUS OF NAZARETH.

"Mr. FELSENBURGH stood so a moment longer, then he turned down the steps, passed across the platform and disappeared.

"Of what took place outside we have received the following account from an eye-witness. The white volor, so well known now to all who were in London that night, had remained stationary outside the little south door of the Old Choir aisle, poised about twenty feet above the ground. Gradually it became known to the crowd, in those few minutes, who it was who had arrived in it, and upon Mr. FELSENBURGH's reappearance that same strange groan sounded through the whole length of Paul's Churchyard, followed by the same silence. The volor descended; the master stepped on board, and once more the vessel rose to a height of twenty feet. It was thought at first that some speech would be made, but none was necessary; and after a moment's pause, the volor began that wonderful parade which London will never forget. Four times during the night Mr. Felsenburgh went round the enormous metropolis, speaking no word; and everywhere the groan preceded and followed him, while silence accompanied his actual passage. Two hours after sunrise the white ship rose over Hampstead and disappeared towards the North; and since then he, whom we call, in truth, the Saviour of the world, has not been seen.

"And now what remains to be said?

"Comment is useless. It is enough to say in one short sentence that the new era has begun, to which prophets and kings, and the suffering, the dying, all who labour and are heavy-laden, have aspired in vain. Not only has intercontinental rivalry ceased to exist, but the strife of home dissensions has ceased also. Of him who has been the herald of its inauguration we have nothing more to say. Time alone can show what is yet left for him to do.

"But what has been done is as follows. The Eastern peril has been for ever dissipated. It is understood now, by fanatic barbarians as well as by civilized nations, that the reign of War is ended. 'Not peace but a sword,' said Christ; and bitterly true have those words proved to be. 'Not a sword but peace' is the retort, articulate at last, from those who have renounced Christ's claims or have never accepted them. The principle of love and union learned however falteringly in the West during the last century, has been taken up in the East as well. There shall be no more an appeal to arms, but to justice; no longer a crying after a God Who hides Himself, but to Man who has learned his own Divinity. The Supernatural is dead; rather, we know now that it never yet has been alive. What remains is to work out this new lesson, to bring every action, word and thought to the bar of Love and Justice; and this will be, no doubt, the task of years. Every code must be reversed; every barrier thrown down; party must unite with party, country with country, and continent with continent. There is no longer the fear of fear, the dread of the page hereafter, or the paralysis of strife. Man has groaned long enough in the travails of birth; his blood has been poured out like water through his own foolishness; but at length he understands himself and is at peace.

"Let it be seen at least that England is not behind the nations in this work of reformation; let no national isolation, pride of race, or drunkenness of wealth hold her hands back from this enormous work. The responsibility is incalculable, but the victory certain. Let us go softly, humbled by the knowledge of our crimes in the past, confident in the hope of our achievements in the future, towards that reward which is in sight at last—the reward hidden so long by the selfishness of men, the darkness of religion, and the strife of tongues—the reward promised by one who knew not what he said and denied what he asserted—Blessed are the meek, the peacemakers, the merciful, for they shall inherit the earth, be named the children of God, and find mercy."

Oliver, white to the lips, with his wife kneeling now beside him, turned the page and read one more short paragraph, marked as being the latest news.

"It is understood that the Government is in communication with Mr. Felsenburgh."

II

"Ah! it is journalese," said Oliver, at last, leaning back. "Tawdry stuff! But—but the thing!"

Mabel got up, passed across to the window-seat, and sat down. Her lips opened once or twice, but she said nothing.

"My darling," cried the man, "have you nothing to say?"

She looked at him tremulously a moment.

"Say!" she said. "As you said, what is the use of words?"

"Tell me again," said Oliver. "How do I know it is not a dream?"

"A dream," she said. "Was there ever a dream like this?"

Again she got up restlessly, came across the floor, and knelt down by her husband once more, taking his hands in hers.

"My dear," she said, "I tell you it is not a dream. It is reality at last. I was there too—do you not remember? You waited for me when all was over—when He was gone out— we saw Him together, you and I. We heard Him—you on the platform and I in the gallery. We saw Him again pass up the Embankment as we stood in the crowd. Then we came home—and we found the priest."

Her face was transfigured as she spoke. It was as of one who saw a Divine Vision. She spoke very quietly, without excitement or hysteria. Oliver stared at her a moment; then he bent forward and kissed her gently.

"Yes, my darling; it is true. But I want to hear it again and again. Tell me again what you saw."

"I saw the Son of Man," she said. "Oh! there is no other phrase. The Saviour of the world, as that paper says. I knew Him in my heart as soon as I saw Him—as we all did—as soon as He stood there holding the rail. It was like a glory round his head. I understand it all now. It was He for whom we have waited so long; and He has come, bringing Peace and Goodwill in His hands. When He spoke, I knew it again. His voice was as—as the sound of the sea—as simple as that—as—as lamentable—as strong as that.—Did you not hear it?"

Oliver bowed his head.

"I can trust Him for all the rest," went on the girl softly. "I do not know where He is, nor when He will come back, nor what He will do. I suppose there is a great deal for Him to do, before He is fully known—laws, reforms—that will be your business, my dear. And the rest of us must wait, and love, and be content."

Oliver again lifted his face and looked at her.

"Mabel, my dear——"

"Oh! I knew it even last night," she said, "but I did not know that I knew it till I awoke to-day and remembered. I dreamed of Him all night.… Oliver, where is He?"

He shook his head.

"Yes, I know where He is, but I am under oath——"

She nodded quickly, and stood up.

"Yes. I should not have asked that. Well, we are content to wait."

There was silence for a moment or two. Oliver broke it.

"My dear, what do you mean when you say that He is not yet known?"

"I mean just that," she said. "The rest only know what He has done—not what He is; but that, too, will come in time."

"And meanwhile——"

"Meanwhile, you must work; the rest will come by and bye. Oh! Oliver, be strong and faithful."

She kissed him quickly, and went out.

Oliver sat on without moving, staring, as his habit was, out at the wide view beyond his windows. This time yesterday he was leaving Paris, knowing the fact indeed—for the delegates had arrived an hour before—but ignorant of the Man. Now he knew the Man as well—at least he had seen Him, heard Him, and stood enchanted under the glow of His personality. He could explain it to himself no more than could any one else—unless, perhaps, it were Mabel. The others had been as he had been: awed and overcome, yet at the same time kindled in the very depths of their souls. They had come out—Snowford, Cartwright, Pemberton, and the rest—on to the steps of Paul's House, following that strange figure. They had intended to say something, but they were dumb as they saw the sea of white faces, heard the groan and the silence, and experienced that compelling wave of magnetism that surged up like something physical, as the volor rose and started on that indescribable progress.

Once more he had seen Him, as he and Mabel stood together on the deck of the electric boat that carried them south. The white ship had passed along overhead, smooth and steady, above the heads of that vast multitude, bearing Him who, if any had the right to that title, was indeed the Saviour of the world. Then they had come home, and found the priest.

That, too, had been a shock to him; for, at first sight, it seemed that this priest was the very man he had seen ascend the rostrum two hours before. It was an extraordinary likeness—the same young face and white hair. Mabel, of course, had not noticed it; for she had only seen Felsenburgh at a great distance; and he himself had soon been reassured. And as for his mother—it was terrible enough; if it had not been for Mabel there would have

been violence done last night. How collected and reasonable she had been! And, as for his mother—he must leave
her alone for the present. By and bye, perhaps, something
might be done. The future! It was that which engrossed
him—the future, and the absorbing power of the personality under whose dominion he had fallen last night. All else
seemed insignificant now—even his mother's defection,
her illness—all paled before this new dawn of an unknown
sun. And in an hour he would know more; he was summoned to Westminster to a meeting of the whole House;
their proposals to Felsenburgh were to be formulated; it
was intended to offer him a great position.

Yes, as Mabel had said; this was now their work—to
carry into effect the new principle that had suddenly become
incarnate in this grey-haired young American—the principle of Universal Brotherhood. It would mean enormous
labour; all foreign relations would have to be readjusted—
trade, policy, methods of government—all demanded re-
statement. Europe was already organised internally on a
basis of mutual protection: that basis was now gone. There
was no more any protection, because there was no more any
menace. Enormous labour, too, awaited the Government in
other directions. A Blue-book must be prepared, containing
a complete report of the proceedings in the East, together
with the text of the Treaty which had been laid before them
in Paris, signed by the Eastern Emperor, the feudal kings,
the Turkish Republic, and countersigned by the American
plenipotentiaries.... Finally, even home politics required
reform: the friction of old strife between centre and extremes
must cease forthwith—there must be but one party now,
and that at the Prophet's disposal.... He grew bewildered as
he regarded the prospect, and saw how the whole plane of

the world was shifted, how the entire foundation of western life required readjustment. It was a Revolution indeed, a cataclysm more stupendous than even invasion itself; but it was the conversion of darkness into light, and chaos into order.

He drew a deep breath, and so sat pondering.

Mabel came down to him half-an-hour later, as he dined early before starting for Whitehall.

"Mother is quieter," she said. "We must be very patient, Oliver. Have you decided yet as to whether the priest is to come again?"

He shook his head.

"I can think of nothing," he said, "but of what I have to do. You decide, my dear; I leave it in your hands."

She nodded.

"I will talk to her again presently. Just now she can understand very little of what has happened…. What time shall you be home?"

"Probably not to-night. We shall sit all night."

"Yes, dear. And what shall I tell Mr. Phillips?"

"I will telephone in the morning…. Mabel, do you remember what I told you about the priest?"

"His likeness to the other?"

"Yes. What do you make of that?"

She smiled.

"I make nothing at all of it. Why should they not be alike?"

He took a fig from the dish, and swallowed it, and stood up.

"It is only very curious," he said. "Now, good-night, my dear."

III

"Oh, mother," said Mabel, kneeling by the bed; "cannot you understand what has happened?"

She had tried desperately to tell the old lady of the extraordinary change that had taken place in the world—and without success. It seemed to her that some great issue depended on it; that it would be piteous if the old woman went out into the dark unconscious of what had come. It was as if a Christian knelt by the death-bed of a Jew on the first Easter Monday. But the old lady lay in her bed, terrified but obdurate.

"Mother," said the girl, "let me tell you again. Do you not understand that all which Jesus Christ promised has come true, though in another way? The reign of God has really begun; but we know now who God is. You said just now you wanted the Forgiveness of Sins; well, you have that; we all have it, because there is no such thing as sin. There is only Crime. And then Communion. You used to believe that that made you a partaker of God; well, we are all partakers of God, because we are human beings. Don't you see that Christianity is only one way of saying all that? I dare say it was the only way, for a time; but that is all over now. Oh! and how much better this is! It is true—true. You can see it to be true!"

She paused a moment, forcing herself to look at that piteous old face, the flushed wrinkled cheeks, the writhing knotted hands on the coverlet.

"Look how Christianity has failed—how it has divided people; think of all the cruelties—the Inquisition, the Religious Wars; the separations between husband and wife and parents and children—the disobedience to the State, the treasons. Oh! you cannot believe that these were right. What kind of a God would that be! And then Hell; how could you ever have believed in that? … Oh! mother, don't believe anything so frightful…. Don't you understand that that God has gone—that He never existed at all—that it was all a hideous nightmare; and that now we all know at last what the truth is…. Mother! think of what happened last night—how He came—the Man of whom you were so frightened. I told you what He was like—so quiet and strong—how every one was silent—of the—the extraordinary atmosphere, and how six millions of people saw Him. And think what He has done—how He has healed all the old wounds—how the whole world is at peace at last—and of what is going to happen. Oh! mother, give up those horrible old lies; give them up; be brave."

"The priest, the priest!" moaned the old woman at last.

"Oh! no, no, no—not the priest; he can do nothing. He knows it's all lies, too!"

"The priest! the priest!" moaned the other again. "He can tell you; he knows the answer."

Her face was convulsed with effort, and her old fingers fumbled and twisted with the rosary. Mabel grew suddenly frightened, and stood up.

"Oh! mother!" She stooped and kissed her. "There! I won't say any more now. But just think about it quietly. Don't be in the least afraid; it is all perfectly right."

She stood a moment, still looking compassionately down; torn by sympathy and desire. No! it was no use now; she must wait till the next day.

"I'll look in again presently," she said, "when you have had dinner. Mother! don't look like that! Kiss me!"

It was astonishing, she told herself that evening, how any one could be so blind. And what a confession of weakness, too, to call only for the priest! It was ludicrous, absurd!

She herself was filled with an extraordinary peace. Even death itself seemed now no longer terrible, for was not death swallowed up in victory? She contrasted the selfish individualism of the Christian, who sobbed and shrank from death, or, at the best, thought of it only as the gate to his own eternal life, with the free altruism of the New Believer who asked no more than that Man should live and grow, that the Spirit of the World should triumph and reveal Himself, while he, the unit, was content to sink back into that reservoir of energy from which he drew his life. At this moment she would have suffered anything, faced death cheerfully—she contemplated even the old woman upstairs with pity—for was it not piteous that death should not bring her to herself and reality?

She was in a quiet whirl of intoxication; it was as if the heavy veil of sense had rolled back at last and shown a sweet, eternal landscape behind—a shadowless land of peace where the lion lay down with the lamb, and the leopard with the kid. There should be war no more: that bloody spectre was dead, and with him the brood of evil that lived in his shadow—superstition, conflict, terror, and unreality. The idols were smashed, and rats had run out; Jehovah was fallen; the wild-eyed dreamer of Galilee was in his grave; the reign of priests was ended. And in their place stood a strange, quiet figure of indomitable power and unruffled tenderness.... He whom she had seen—the Son of Man, the Saviour of the world, as she had called Him just now— He who bore these titles was no longer a monstrous figure, half God and half man, claiming both natures and possessing neither; one who was tempted without temptation, and who conquered without merit, as his followers said. Here was one instead whom she could follow, a god indeed and a man as well—a god because human, and a man because so divine.

She said no more that night. She looked into the bedroom for a few minutes, and saw the old woman asleep. Her old hand lay out on the coverlet, and still between the fingers was twisted the silly string of beads. Mabel went softly across in the shaded light, and tried to detach it; but the wrinkled fingers writhed and closed, and a murmur came from the half-open lips. Ah! how piteous it was, thought the girl, how hopeless that a soul should flow out into such darkness, unwilling to make the supreme, generous surrender, and lay down its life because life itself demanded it!

Then she went to her own room.

The clocks were chiming three, and the grey dawn lay on the wall, when she awoke to find by her bed the woman who had sat with the old lady.

"Come at once, madam; Mrs. Brand is dying."

IV

Oliver was with them by six o'clock; he came straight up into his mother's room to find that all was over.

The room was full of the morning light and the clean air, and a bubble of bird-music poured in from the lawn. But his wife knelt by the bed, still holding the wrinkled hands of the old woman, her face buried in her arms. The face of his mother was quieter than he had ever seen it, the lines showed only like the faintest shadows on an alabaster mask; her lips were set in a smile. He looked for a moment, waiting until the spasm that caught his throat had died again. Then he put his hand on his wife's shoulder.

"When?" he said.

Mabel lifted her face.

"Oh! Oliver," she murmured. "It was an hour ago.... Look at this."

She released the dead hands and showed the rosary still twisted there; it had snapped in the last struggle, and a brown bead lay beneath the fingers.

"I did what I could," sobbed Mabel. "I was not hard with her. But she would not listen. She kept on crying out for the priest as long as she could speak."

"My dear ..." began the man. Then he, too, went down on his knees by his wife, leaned forward and kissed the rosary, while tears blinded him.

"Yes, yes," he said. "Leave her in peace. I would not move it for the world: it was her toy, was it not?"

The girl stared at him, astonished.

"We can be generous, too," he said. "We have all the world at last. And she—she has lost nothing: it was too late."

"I did what I could."

"Yes, my darling, and you were right. But she was too old; she could not understand."

He paused.

"Euthanasia?" he whispered with something very like tenderness.

She nodded.

"Yes," she said; "just as the last agony began. She resisted, but I knew you would wish it."

They talked together for an hour in the garden before Oliver went to his room; and he began to tell her presently of all that had passed.

"He has refused," he said. "We offered to create an office for Him; He was to have been called Consultor, and he refused it two hours ago. But He has promised to be at our service.... No, I must not tell you where He is.... He will return to America soon, we think; but He will not leave us. We have drawn up a programme, and it is to be sent to Him presently.... Yes, we were unanimous."

"And the programme?"

"It concerns the Franchise, the Poor Laws and Trade. I can tell you no more than that. It was He who suggested the points. But we are not sure if we understand Him yet."

"But, my dear——"

"Yes; it is quite extraordinary. I have never seen such things. There was practically no argument."

"Do the people understand?"

"I think so. We shall have to guard against a reaction. They say that the Catholics will be in danger. There is an article this morning in the *Era*. The proofs were sent to us for sanction. It suggests that means must be taken to protect the Catholics."

Mabel smiled.

"It is a strange irony," he said. "But they have a right to exist. How far they have a right to share in the government is another matter. That will come before us, I think, in a week or two."

"Tell me more about Him."

"There is really nothing to tell; we know nothing, except that He is the supreme force in the world. France is in a ferment, and has offered him Dictatorship. That, too, He has refused. Germany has made the same proposal as ourselves; Italy, the same as France, with the title of Perpetual Tribune. America has done nothing yet, and Spain is divided."

"And the East?"

"The Emperor thanked Him; no more than that."

Mabel drew a long breath, and stood looking out across the heat haze that was beginning to rise from the town beneath. These were matters so vast that she could not take them in. But to her imagination Europe lay like a busy hive, moving to and fro in the sunshine. She saw the blue distance of France, the towns of Germany, the Alps, and beyond them the Pyrenees and sun-baked Spain; and all were intent on the same business, to capture if they could this astonishing figure that had risen over the world. Sober England, too, was alight with zeal. Each country desired nothing better than that this man should rule over them; and He had refused them all.

"He has refused them all!" she repeated breathlessly.

"Yes, all. We think He may be waiting to hear from America. He still holds office there, you know."

"How old is He?"

"Not more than thirty-two or three. He has only been in office a few months. Before that He lived alone in Vermont. Then He stood for the Senate; then He made a speech or two; then He was appointed delegate, though no one seems to have realised His power. And the rest we know."

Mabel shook her head meditatively.

"We know nothing," she said. "Nothing; nothing! Where did He learn His languages?"

"It is supposed that He travelled for many years. But no one knows. He has said nothing."

She turned swiftly to her husband.

"But what does it all mean? What is His power? Tell me, Oliver?"

He smiled back, shaking his head.

"Well, Markham said that it was his incorruption—that and his oratory; but that explains nothing."

"No, it explains nothing," said the girl.

"It is just personality," went on Oliver, "at least, that's the label to use. But that, too, is only a label."

"Yes, just a label. But it is that. They all felt it in Paul's House, and in the streets afterwards. Did you not feel it?"

"Feel it!" cried the man, with shining eyes. "Why, I would die for Him!"

They went back to the house presently, and it was not till they reached the door that either said a word about the dead old woman who lay upstairs.

"They are with her now," said Mabel softly. "I will communicate with the people."

He nodded gravely.

"It had better be this afternoon," he said. "I have a spare hour at fourteen o'clock. Oh! by the way, Mabel, do you know who took the message to the priest?"

"I think so."

"Yes, it was Phillips. I saw him last night. He will not come here again."

"Did he confess it?"

"He did. He was most offensive."

But Oliver's face softened again as he nodded to his wife at the foot of the stairs, and turned to go up once more to his mother's room.

CHAPTER II

I

IT SEEMED to Percy Franklin as he drew near Rome, sliding five hundred feet high through the summer dawn, that he was approaching the very gates of heaven, or, still better, he was a child coming home. For what he had left behind him ten hours before in London was not a bad specimen, he thought, of the superior mansions of hell. It was a world whence God seemed to have withdrawn Himself, leaving it indeed in a state of profound complacency—a state without hope or faith, but a condition in which, although life continued, there was absent the one essential to well-being. It was not that there was not expectation—for London was on tip-toe with excitement. There were rumours of all kinds: Felsenburgh was coming back; he was back; he had never gone. He was to be President of the Council, Prime Minister, Tribune, with full capacities of democratic government and personal sacro-sanctity, even King—if not Emperor of the West. The entire constitution was to be remodelled, there was to be a complete rearrangement of the pieces; crime was to be abolished by the mysterious power that had killed war; there was to be free food—the secret of life was discovered, there was to be no more death—so the rumours ran.... Yet that was lacking, to the priest's mind, which made life worth living....

In Paris, while the volor waited at the great station at Montmartre, once known as the Church of the Sacred Heart, he had heard the roaring of the mob in love with life at last, and seen the banners go past. As it rose again over the suburbs he had seen the long lines of trains streaming in, visible as bright serpents in the brilliant glory of the electric globes, bringing the country folk up to the Council of the Nation which the legislators, mad with drama, had summoned to decide the great question. At Lyons it had been the same. The night was as clear as the day, and as full of sound. Mid France was arriving to register its votes.

He had fallen asleep as the cold air of the Alps began to envelop the car, and had caught but glimpses of the solemn moonlit peaks below him, the black profundities of the gulfs, the silver glint of the shield-like lakes, and the soft glow of Interlaken and the towns in the Rhone Valley. Once he had been moved in spite of himself, as one of the huge German volors had passed in the night, a blaze of ghostly lights and gilding, resembling a huge moth with antennae of electric light, and the two ships had saluted one another through half a league of silent air, with a pathetic cry as of two strange night-birds who have no leisure to pause. Milan and Turin had been quiet, for Italy was organised on other principles than France, and Florence was not yet half awake. And now the Campagna was slipping past like a grey-green rug, wrinkled and tumbled, five hundred feet beneath, and Rome was all but in sight. The indicator above his seat moved its finger from one hundred to ninety miles.

He shook off the doze at last, and drew out his office book; but as he pronounced the words his attention was elsewhere, and, when Prime was said, he closed the book once more, propped himself more comfortably, drawing the furs

round him, and stretching his feet on the empty seat opposite. He was alone in his compartment; the three men who
had come in at Paris had descended at Turin.

He had been remarkably relieved when the message had
come three days before from the Cardinal-Protector, bidding
him make arrangements for a long absence from England,
and, as soon as that was done, to come to Rome. He understood that the ecclesiastical authorities were really disturbed
at last.

He reviewed the last day or two, considering the report he
would have to present. Since his last letter, three days before,
seven notable apostasies had taken place in Westminster diocese alone, two priests and five important laymen. There was
talk of revolt on all sides; he had seen a threatening document,
called a "petition," demanding the right to dispense with all
ecclesiastical vestments, signed by one hundred and twenty
priests from England and Wales. The "petitioners" pointed
out that persecution was coming swiftly at the hands of the
mob; that the Government was not sincere in the promises
of protection; they hinted that religious loyalty was already
strained to breaking-point even in the case of the most faithful, and that with all but those it had already broken.

And as to his comments Percy was clear. He would tell
the authorities, as he had already told them fifty times, that it
was not persecution that mattered; it was this new outburst of
enthusiasm for Humanity—an enthusiasm which had waxed
a hundredfold more hot since the coming of Felsenburgh and
the publication of the Eastern news—which was melting the
hearts of all but the very few. Man had suddenly fallen in
love with man. The conventional were rubbing their eyes and
wondering why they had ever believed, or even dreamed, that
there was a God to love, asking one another what was the

secret of the spell that had held them so long. Christianity and Theism were passing together from the world's mind as a morning mist passes when the sun comes up. His recommendations—? Yes, he had those clear, and ran them over in his mind with a sense of despair.

For himself, he scarcely knew if he believed what he professed. His emotions seemed to have been finally extinguished in the vision of the white car and the silence of the crowd that evening three weeks before. It had been so horribly real and positive; the delicate aspirations and hopes of the soul appeared so shadowy when compared with that burning, heart-shaking passion of the people. He had never seen anything like it; no congregation under the spell of the most kindling preacher alive had ever responded with one-tenth of the fervour with which that irreligious crowd, standing in the cold dawn of the London streets, had greeted the coming of their saviour. And as for the man himself—Percy could not analyse what it was that possessed him as he had stared, muttering the name of Jesus, on that quiet figure in black with features and hair so like his own. He only knew that a hand had gripped his heart—a hand warm, not cold—and had quenched, it seemed, all sense of religious conviction. It had only been with an effort that sickened him to remember, that he had refrained from that interior act of capitulation that is so familiar to all who have cultivated an inner life and understand what failure means. There had been one citadel that had not flung wide its gates—all else had yielded. His emotions had been stormed, his intellect silenced, his memory of grace obscured, a spiritual nausea had sickened his soul, yet the secret fortress of the will had, in an agony, held fast the doors and refused to cry out and call Felsenburgh king.

Ah! how he had prayed during those three weeks! It appeared to him that he had done little else; there had been no peace. Lances of doubt thrust again and again through door and window; masses of argument had crashed from above; he had been on the alert day and night, repelling this, blindly, and denying that, endeavouring to keep his foothold on the slippery plane of the supernatural, sending up cry after cry to the Lord Who hid Himself. He had slept with his crucifix in his hand, he had awakened himself by kissing it; while he wrote, talked, ate, walked, and sat in cars, the inner life had been busy—making frantic speechless acts of faith in a religion which his intellect denied and from which his emotions shrank. There had been moments of ecstasy—now in a crowded street, when he recognised that God was all, that the Creator was the key to the creature's life, that a humble act of adoration was transcendently greater than the most noble natural act, that the Supernatural was the origin and end of existence—there had come to him such moments in the night, in the silence of the Cathedral, when the lamp flickered, and a soundless air had breathed from the iron door of the tabernacle. Then again passion ebbed, and left him stranded on misery, but set with a determination (which might equally be that of pride or faith) that no power in earth or hell should hinder him from professing Christianity even if he could not realise it. It was Christianity alone that made life tolerable.

Percy drew a long vibrating breath, and changed his position; for far away his unseeing eyes had descried a dome, like a blue bubble set on a carpet of green; and his brain had interrupted itself to tell him that this was Rome.

He got up presently, passed out of his compartment, and moved forward up the central gangway, seeing, as he went, through the glass doors to right and left his fellow-passengers, some still asleep, some staring out at the view, some reading. He put his eye to the glass square in the door, and for a minute or two watched, fascinated, the steady figure of the steerer at his post. There he stood motionless, his hands on the steel circle that directed the vast wings, his eyes on the wind-gauge that revealed to him as on the face of a clock both the force and the direction of the high gusts; now and again his hands moved slightly, and the huge fans responded, now lifting, now lowering. Beneath him and in front, fixed on a circular table, were the glass domes of various indicators—Percy did not know the meaning of half—one seemed a kind of barometer, intended, he guessed, to declare the height at which they were traveling, another a compass. And beyond, through the curved windows, lay the enormous sky. Well, it was all very wonderful, thought the priest, and it was with the force of which all this was but one symptom that the supernatural had to compete.

He sighed, turned, and went back to his compartment.

It was an astonishing vision that began presently to open before him—scarcely beautiful except for its strangeness, and as unreal as a raised map. Far to his right, as he could see through the glass doors, lay the grey line of the sea against the luminous sky, rising and falling ever so slightly as the car, apparently motionless, tilted imperceptibly against the western breeze; the only other movement was the faint pulsation of the huge throbbing screw in the rear. To the left stretched the limitless country, flitting beneath, in glimpses seen between the motionless wings, with here and there the streak of a village, flattened out of recognition, or the flash of water, and bounded far away by the low masses of the Umbrian hills; while in front, seen and gone again as the car veered, lay the confused line of Rome and the huge new suburbs, all crowned by the great dome growing every instant. Around, above and beneath, his eyes were conscious of wide air-spaces, overhead deepening into lapis-lazuli down to horizons of pale turquoise. The only sound, of which he had long ceased to be directly conscious, was that of the steady rush of air, less shrill now as the speed began to drop down—down—to forty miles an hour. There was a clang of a bell, and immediately he was aware of a sense of faint sickness as the car dropped in a glorious swoop, and he staggered a little as he grasped his rugs together. When he looked again the motion seemed to have ceased; he could see towers ahead, a line of houseroofs, and beneath he caught a glimpse of a road and more roofs with patches of green between. A bell clanged again, and a long sweet cry followed. On all sides he could hear the movement of feet; a guard in uniform passed swiftly along the glazed corridor; again came the faint nausea; and as he looked up once more from his luggage for an instant he saw the dome, grey now and lined, almost on level with his own eyes, huge against the vivid sky. The world span round for a moment; he shut his eyes, and when he looked again walls seemed to heave up past him and stop, swaying. There was the last bell, a faint vibration as the car grounded in the steel-netted dock; a line of faces rocked and grew still outside the windows, and Percy passed out towards the doors, carrying his bags.

II

He still felt a sense of insecure motion as he sat alone over coffee an hour later in one of the remote rooms of the Vatican; but there was a sense of exhilaration as well, as his tired brain realised where he was. It had been strange to drive over the rattling stones in the weedy little cab, such as he remembered

ten years ago when he had left Rome, newly ordained. While
the world had moved on, Rome had stood still; she had other
affairs to think of than physical improvements, now that the
spiritual weight of the earth rested entirely upon her shoulders.
All had seemed unchanged—or rather it had reverted to the
condition of nearly one hundred and fifty years ago. Histories
related how the improvements of the Italian government had
gradually dropped out of use as soon as the city, eighty years
before, had been given her independence; the trams ceased to
run; volors were not allowed to enter the walls; the new buildings, permitted to remain, had been converted to ecclesiastical use; the Quirinal became the offices of the "Red Pope";
the embassies, huge seminaries; even the Vatican itself, with
the exception of the upper floor, had become the abode of the
Sacred College, who surrounded the Supreme Pontiff as stars
their sun.

It was an extraordinary city, said antiquarians—the one
living example of the old days. Here were to be seen the
ancient inconveniences, the insanitary horrors, the incarnation of a world given over to dreaming. The old Church
pomp was back, too; the cardinals drove again in gilt coaches;
the Pope rode on his white mule; the Blessed Sacrament went
through the ill-smelling streets with the sound of bells and the
light of lanterns. A brilliant description of it had interested
the civilised world immensely for about forty-eight hours; the
appalling retrogression was still used occasionally as the text
for violent denunciations by the poorly educated; the well-
educated had ceased to do anything but take for granted that
superstition and progress were irreconcilable enemies.

Yet Percy, even in the glimpses he had had in the streets,
as he drove from the volor station outside the People's Gate,
of the old peasant dresses, the blue and red-fringed wine

carts, the cabbage-strewn gutters, the wet clothes flapping on strings, the mules and horses—strange though these were, he had found them a refreshment. It had seemed to remind him that man was human, and not divine as the rest of the world proclaimed—human, and therefore careless and individualistic; human, and therefore occupied with interests other than those of speed, cleanliness, and precision.

The room in which he sat now by the window with shading blinds, for the sun was already hot, seemed to revert back even further than to a century-and-a-half. The old damask and gilding that he had expected was gone, and its absence gave the impression of great severity. There was a wide deal table running the length of the room, with upright wooden arm chairs set against it; the floor was red-tiled, with strips of matting for the feet, the white, distempered walls had only a couple of old pictures hung upon them, and a large crucifix flanked by candles stood on a little altar by the further door. There was no more furniture than that, with the exception of a writing-desk between the windows, on which stood a typewriter. That jarred somehow on his sense of fitness, and he wondered at it.

He finished the last drop of coffee in the thick-rimmed white cup, and sat back in his chair.

Already the burden was lighter, and he was astonished at the swiftness with which it had become so. Life looked simpler here; the interior world was taken more for granted; it was not even a matter of debate. There it was, imperious and objective, and through it glimmered to the eyes of the soul the old Figures that had become shrouded behind the rush of worldly circumstance. The very shadow of God appeared to rest here; it was no longer impossible to realise that the saints watched and interceded, that Mary sat on her throne, that the white disc on the altar was Jesus Christ. Percy was not yet at peace—after all, he had been but an hour in Rome; and air, charged with never so much grace, could scarcely do more than it had done. But he felt more at ease, less desperately anxious, more childlike, more content to rest on the authority that claimed without explanation, and asserted that the world, as a matter of fact, proved by evidences without and within, was made this way and not that, for this purpose and not the other. Yet he had used the conveniences which he hated; he had left London a bare twelve hours before, and now here he sat in a place which was either a stagnant backwater of life, or else the very mid-current of it; he was not yet sure which.

There was a step outside, a handle was turned; and the Cardinal-Protector came through.

Percy had not seen him for four years, and for a moment scarcely recognised him.

It was a very old man that he saw now, bent and feeble, his face covered with wrinkles, crowned by very thin, white hair, and the little scarlet cap on top; he was in his black Benedictine habit with a plain abbatial cross on his breast, and walked hesitatingly, with a black stick. The only sign of vigour was in the narrow bright slit of his eyes showing beneath drooping lids. He held out his hand, smiling, and Percy, remembering in time that he was in the Vatican, bowed low only as he kissed the amethyst.

"Welcome to Rome, father," said the old man, speaking with an unexpected briskness. "They told me you were here half-an-hour ago; I thought I would leave you to wash and have your coffee."

Percy murmured something.

"Yes; you are tired, no doubt," said the Cardinal, pulling out a chair.

"Indeed not, your Eminence. I slept excellently."

The Cardinal made a little gesture to a chair.

"But I must have a word with you. The Holy Father wishes to see you at eleven o'clock."

Percy started a little.

"We move quickly in these days, father.... There is no time to dawdle. You understand that you are to remain in Rome for the present?"

"I have made all arrangements for that, your Eminence."

"That is very well.... We are pleased with you here, Father Franklin. The Holy Father has been greatly impressed by your comments. You have foreseen things in a very remarkable manner."

Percy flushed with pleasure, it was almost the first hint of encouragement he had had. Cardinal Martin went on.

"I may say that you are considered our most valuable correspondent—certainly in England. That is why you are summoned. You are to help us here in future—a kind of consultor: any one can relate facts; not every one can understand them.... You look very young, father. How old are you?"

"I am thirty-three, your Eminence."

"Ah! your white hair helps you.... Now, father, will you come with me into my room? It is now eight o'clock. I will keep you till nine—no longer. Then you shall have some rest, and at eleven I shall take you up to his Holiness."

Percy rose with a strange sense of elation, and ran to open the door for the Cardinal to go through.

III

At a few minutes before eleven Percy came out of his little white-washed room in his new ferraiuola, soutane and buckle shoes, and tapped at the door of the Cardinal's room.

He felt a great deal more self-possessed now. He had talked to the Cardinal freely and strongly, had described the effect that Felsenburgh had had upon London, and even the paralysis that had seized upon himself. He had stated his belief that they were on the edge of a movement unparalleled in history: he related little scenes that he had witnessed—a group kneeling before a picture of Felsenburgh, a dying man calling him by name, the aspect of the crowd that had waited in Westminster to hear the result of the offer made to the stranger. He showed him half-a-dozen cuttings from newspapers, pointing out their hysterical enthusiasm; he even went so far as to venture upon prophecy, and to declare his belief that persecution was within reasonable distance.

"The world seems very oddly alive," he said; "it is as if the whole thing was flushed and nervous."

The Cardinal nodded.

"We, too," he said, "even we feel it."

For the rest the Cardinal had sat watching him out of his narrow eyes, nodding from time to time, putting an occasional question, but listening throughout with great attention.

"And your recommendations, father—" he had said, and then interrupted himself. "No, that is too much to ask. The Holy Father will speak of that."

He had congratulated him upon his Latin then—for they had spoken in that language throughout this second interview; and Percy had explained how loyal Catholic England had been in obeying the order, given ten years before, that

Latin should become to the Church what Esperanto was becoming to the world.

"That is very well," said the old man. "His Holiness will be pleased at that."

At his second tap the door opened and the Cardinal came out, taking him by the arm without a word; and together they turned to the lift entrance.

Percy ventured to make a remark as they slid noiselessly up towards the papal apartment.

"I am surprised at the lift, your Eminence, and the typewriter in the audience-room,"

"Why, father?"

"Why, all the rest of Rome is back in the old days."

The Cardinal looked at him, puzzled.

"Is it? I suppose it is. I never thought of that."

A Swiss guard flung back the door of the lift, saluted and went before them along the plain flagged passage to where his comrade stood. Then he saluted again and went back. A Pontifical chamberlain, in all the sombre glory of purple, black, and a Spanish ruff, peeped from the door, and made haste to open it. It really seemed almost incredible that such things still existed.

"In a moment, your Eminence," he said in Latin. "Will your Eminence wait here?"

It was a little square room, with half-a-dozen doors, plainly contrived out of one of the huge old halls, for it was immensely high, and the tarnished gilt cornice vanished directly in two places into the white walls. The partitions, too, seemed thin; for as the two men sat down there was a murmur of voices faintly audible, the shuffling of footsteps, and the old eternal click of the typewriter from which Percy hoped he had escaped. They were alone in the room, which was furnished with the same simplicity as the Cardinal's— giving the impression of a curious mingling of ascetic poverty and dignity by its red-tiled floor, its white walls, its altar and two vast bronze candlesticks of incalculable value that stood on the dais. The shutters here, too, were drawn; and there was nothing to distract Percy from the excitement that surged up now tenfold in heart and brain.

It was *Papa Angelicus* whom he was about to see; that amazing old man who had been appointed Secretary of State just fifty years ago, at the age of thirty, and Pope nine years previously. It was he who carried out the extraordinary policy of yielding the churches throughout the whole of Italy to the Government, in exchange for the temporal lordship of Rome, and who had since set himself to make it a city of saints. He had cared, it appeared, nothing whatever for the world's opinion; his policy, so far as it could be called one, consisted in a very simple thing; he had declared in Epistle after Epistle that the object of the Church was to do glory to God by producing supernatural virtues in man, and that nothing at all was of any significance or importance except so far as it effected this object. He had further maintained that since Peter was the Rock, the City of Peter was the Capital of the world, and should set an example to its dependency: this could not be done unless Peter ruled his City, and therefore he had sacrificed every church and ecclesiastical building in the country for that one end. Then he had set about ruling his city: he had said that on the whole the latter-day discoveries of man tended to distract immortal souls from a contemplation of eternal verities—not that these discoveries could be anything but good in themselves, since after all they gave insight into the wonderful laws of God—but that at present they were too exciting to the imagination. So he had removed the trams, the volors, the laboratories, the manufactories—saying that there was plenty of room for them outside Rome—and had allowed them to be planted in the suburbs: in their place he had raised shrines, religious houses and Calvaries. Then he had attended further to the souls of his subjects. Since Rome was of limited area, and, still more because the world corrupted without its proper salt, he allowed no man under the age of fifty to live within its walls for more than one month in each year, except those who received his permit. They might live, of course, immediately outside the city (and they did, by tens of thousands), but they were to understand that by doing so they sinned against the spirit, though not the letter, of their Father's wishes. Then he had divided the city into national quarters, saying that as each nation had its peculiar virtues, each was to let its light shine steadily in its proper place. Rents had instantly begun to rise, so he had legislated against that by reserving in each quarter a number of streets at fixed prices, and had issued an *ipso facto* excommunication against all who erred in this respect. The rest were abandoned to the millionaires. He had retained the Leonine City entirely at his own disposal. Then he had restored Capital Punishment, with as much serene gravity as that with which he had made himself the derision of the civilised world in other matters, saying that though human life was holy, human virtue was more holy still; and he had added to the crime of murder, the crimes of adultery, idolatry and apostasy, for which this punishment was theoretically sanctioned. There had not been, however, more than two such executions in the eight years of his reign, since criminals, of course, with the exception of devoted believers, instantly made their way to the suburbs, where they were no longer under his jurisdiction.

But he had not stayed here. He had sent once more ambassadors to every country in the world, informing the Government of each of their arrival. No attention was paid to this, beyond that of laughter; but he had continued, undisturbed, to claim his rights, and, meanwhile, used his legates for the important work of disseminating his views. Epistles appeared from time to time in every town, laying down the principles of the papal claims with as much tranquility as if they were everywhere acknowledged. Freemasonry was steadily denounced, as well as democratic ideas of every kind; men were urged to remember their immortal souls and the Majesty of God, and to reflect upon the fact that in a few years all would be called to give their account to Him Who was Creator and Ruler of the world, Whose Vicar was John XXIV, P.P., whose name and seal were appended.

That was a line of action that took the world completely by surprise. People had expected hysteria, argument, and passionate exhortation; disguised emissaries, plots, and protests. There were none of these. It was as if progress had not yet begun, and volors were uninvented, as if the entire universe had not come to disbelieve in God, and to discover that itself was God. Here was this silly old man, talking in his sleep, babbling of the Cross, and the inner life and the forgiveness of sins, exactly as his predecessors had talked two thousand years before. Well, it was only one sign more that Rome had lost not only its power, but its common sense as well. It was really time that something should be done.

And this was the man, thought Percy, *Papa Angelicus*, whom he was to see in a minute or two.

The Cardinal put his hand on the priest's knee as the door opened, and a purple prelate appeared, bowing.

"Only this," he said. "Be absolutely frank."

Percy stood up, trembling. Then he followed his patron towards the inner door.

IV

A white figure sat in the green gloom, beside a great writing-table, three or four yards away, but with the chair wheeled round to face the door by which the two entered. So much Percy saw as he performed the first genuflection. Then he dropped his eyes, advanced, genuflected again, advanced once more, and for the third time genuflected, lifting the thin white hand, stretched out, to his lips. He heard the door close as he stood up.

"Father Franklin, Holiness," said the Cardinal's voice at his ear.

A white-sleeved arm waved to a couple of chairs set a yard away, and the two sat down.

While the Cardinal, talking in slow Latin, said a few sentences, explaining that this was the English priest whose correspondence had been found so useful, Percy began to look with all his eyes.

He knew the Pope's face well, from a hundred photographs and moving pictures; even his gestures were familiar to him, the slight bowing of the head in assent, the tiny eloquent movement of the hands; but Percy, with a sense of being platitudinal, told himself that the living presence was very different.

It was a very upright old man that he saw in the chair before him, of medium height and girth, with hands clasping the bosses of his chair-arms, and an appearance of great and deliberate dignity. But it was at the face chiefly that he looked, dropping his gaze three or four times, as the Pope's blue eyes turned on him. They were extraordinary eyes, reminding him of what historians said of Pius X.; the lids drew straight lines across them, giving him the look of a hawk, but the rest of the face contradicted them. There was no sharpness in that. It was neither thin nor fat, but beautifully modelled in an oval outline: the lips were were clean-cut, with a look of passion in their curves; the nose came down in an aquiline sweep, ending in chiselled nostrils; the chin was firm and cloven, and the poise of the whole head was strangely youthful. It was a face of great generosity and sweetness, set at an angle between defiance and humility, but ecclesiastical from ear to ear and brow to chin; the forehead was slightly compressed at the temples, and beneath the white cap lay white hair. It had been the subject of laughter at the music-halls nine years before, when the composite face of well-known priests had been thrown on a screen, side by side with the new Pope's, for the two were almost indistinguishable.

Percy found himself trying to sum it up, but nothing came to him except the word "priest." It was that, and that was all. *Ecce sacerdos magnus*! He was astonished at the look of youth, for the Pope was eighty-eight this year; yet his figure was as upright as that of a man of fifty, his shoulders unbowed, his head set on them like an athlete's, and his wrinkles scarcely perceptible in the half light. *Papa Angelicus*! reflected Percy.

The Cardinal ceased his explanations, and made a little gesture. Percy drew up all his faculties tense and tight to answer the questions that he knew were coming.

"I welcome you, my son," said a very soft, resonant voice.

Percy bowed, desperately, from the waist.

The Pope dropped his eyes again, lifted a paper-weight with his left hand, and began to play with it gently as he talked.

"Now, my son, deliver a little discourse. I suggest to you three heads—what has happened, what is happening, what will happen, with a peroration as to what should happen."

Percy drew a long breath, settled himself back, clasped the fingers of his left hand in the fingers of his right, fixed his eyes firmly upon the cross-embroidered red shoe opposite, and began. (Had he not rehearsed this a hundred times!)

He first stated his theme; to the effect that all the forces of the civilised world were concentrating into two camps—the world and God. Up to the present time the forces of the world had been incoherent and spasmodic, breaking out in various ways—revolutions and wars had been like the movements of a mob, undisciplined, unskilled, and unrestrained. To meet this, the Church, too, had acted through her Catholicity—dispersion rather than concentration: *franc-tireurs* had been opposed to *franc-tireurs*. But during the last hundred years there had been indications that the method of warfare was to change. Europe, at any rate, had grown weary of internal strife; the unions first of Labour, then of Capital, then of Labour and Capital combined, illustrated this in the economic sphere; the peaceful partition of Africa in the political sphere; the spread of Humanitarian religion in the spiritual sphere. Over against this must be placed the increased centralisation of the Church. By the wisdom of her pontiffs, over-ruled by God Almighty, the lines had been drawing tighter every year. He instanced the abolition of all local usages, including those so long cherished by the East, the establishment of the Cardinal-Protectorates in Rome, the enforced merging of all friars into one Order, though retaining their familiar names, under the authority of the supreme General; all monks, with the exception of the Carthusians, the Carmelites and the Trappists, into another; of the three excepted into a third; and the classification of nuns after the same plan. Further, he remarked on the more recent decrees, establishing the sense of the Vatican decision on infallibility, the new version of Canon Law, the immense simplification that had taken place in ecclesiastical government, the hierarchy, rubrics and the affairs of missionary countries, with the new and extraordinary privileges granted to mission priests. At this point he became aware that his self-consciousness had left him, and he began, even with little gestures, and a slightly raised voice, to enlarge on the significance of the last month's events.

All that had gone before, he said, pointed to what had now actually taken place—namely, the reconciliation of the world on a basis other than that of Divine Truth. It was the intention of God and His Vicars to reconcile all men in Christ Jesus; but the corner-stone had once more been rejected, and instead of the chaos that the pious had prophesied, there was coming into existence a unity unlike anything known in history. This was the more deadly from the fact that it contained so many elements of indubitable good. War, apparently, was now extinct, and it was not Christianity that had done it; union was now seen to be better than disunion, and the lesson had been learned apart from the Church. In fact, natural virtues had suddenly waxed luxuriant, and supernatural virtues were despised. Friendliness took the place of charity, contentment the place of hope, and knowledge the place of faith.

Percy stopped, he had become conscious that he was preaching a kind of sermon.

"Yes, my son," said the kind voice. "What else?"

What else? ... Very well, continued Percy, movements such as these brought forth men, and the Man of this movement was Julian Felsenburgh. He had accomplished a work that—apart from God—seemed miraculous. He had broken down the eternal division between East and West, coming himself from the continent that alone could produce such powers; he had prevailed by sheer force of personality over the two supreme tyrants of life—religious fanaticism and party government. His influence over the impassive English was another miracle, yet he had also set on fire France, Germany, and Spain. Percy here described one or two of his little scenes, saying that it was like the vision of a god: and he quoted freely some of the titles given to the Man by sober, unhysterical newspapers. Felsenburgh was called the Son of Man, because he was so pure-bred a cosmopolitan; the Saviour of the World, because he had slain war and himself survived— even—even—here Percy's voice faltered—even Incarnate God, because he was the perfect representative of divine man.

The quiet, priestly face watching opposite never winced or moved; and he went on.

Persecution, he said, was coming. There had been a riot or two already. But persecution was not to be feared. It would no doubt cause apostasies, as it had always done, but these were deplorable only on account of the individual apostates. On the other hand, it would reassure the faithful, and purge out the half-hearted. Once, in the early ages, Satan's attack had been made on the bodily side, with whips and fire and beasts; in the sixteenth century it had been on the intellectual side; in the twentieth century on the springs of moral and spiritual life. Now it seemed as if the assault was on all three planes at once. But what was chiefly to be feared was the positive influence of Humanitarianism: it was coming, like the kingdom of God, with power; it was crushing the imaginative and the romantic, it was assuming rather than asserting its own truth; it was smothering with bolsters instead of wounding and stimulating with steel or controversy. It seemed to be forcing its way, almost objectively, into the inner world. Persons who had scarcely heard its name were professing its tenets; priests absorbed it, as they absorbed God in Communion—he mentioned the names of the recent apostates—children drank it in like Christianity itself. The soul "naturally Christian" seemed to be becoming "the soul naturally infidel." Persecution, cried the priest, was to be welcomed like salvation, prayed for, and grasped; but he feared that the authorities were too shrewd, and knew the antidote and the poison apart. There might be individual martyrdoms—in fact there would be, and very many—but they would be in spite of secular government, not because of it. Finally, he expected, Humanitarianism would presently put on the dress of liturgy and sacrifice, and when that was done, the Church's cause, unless God intervened, would be over.

Percy sat back, trembling.

"Yes, my son. And what do you think should be done?"

Percy flung out his hands.

"Holy Father—the Mass, prayer, the rosary. These first and last. The world denies their power: it is on their power that Christians must throw all their weight. All things in Jesus Christ—in Jesus Christ, first and last. Nothing else can avail. He must do all, for we can do nothing."

The white head bowed. Then it rose erect.

"Yes, my son…. But so long as Jesus Christ deigns to use us, we must be used. He is Prophet and King as well as Priest. We then, too, must be prophet and king as well as priest. What of Prophecy and Royalty?"

The voice thrilled Percy like a trumpet.

"Yes, Holiness.... For prophecy, then, let us preach charity; for Royalty, let us reign on crosses. We must love and suffer...." (He drew one sobbing breath.) "Your Holiness has preached charity always. Let charity then issue in good deeds. Let us be foremost in them; let us engage in trade honestly, in family life chastely, in government uprightly. And as for suffering—ah! Holiness!"

His old scheme leaped back to his mind, and stood poised there convincing and imperious.

"Yes, my son, speak plainly."

"Your Holiness—it is old—old as Rome—every fool has desired it: a new Order, Holiness—a new Order," he stammered.

The white hand dropped the paper-weight; the Pope leaned forward, looking intently at the priest.

"Yes, my son?"

Percy threw himself on his knees.

"A new Order, Holiness—no habit or badge—subject to your Holiness only—freer than Jesuits, poorer than Franciscans, more mortified than Carthusians: men and women alike—the three vows with the intention of martyrdom; the Pantheon for their Church; each bishop responsible for their sustenance; a lieutenant in each country.... (Holiness, it is the thought of a fool.) ... And Christ Crucified for their patron."

The Pope stood up abruptly—so abruptly that Cardinal Martin sprang up too, apprehensive and terrified. It seemed that this young man had gone too far.

Then the Pope sat down again, extending his hand.

"God bless you, my son. You have leave to go.... Will your Eminence stay for a few minutes?"

CHAPTER III

I

THE CARDINAL said very little to Percy when they met again that evening, beyond congratulating him on the way he had borne himself with the Pope. It seemed that the priest had done right by his extreme frankness. Then he told him of his duties.

Percy was to retain the couple of rooms that had been put at his disposal: he was to say Mass, as a rule, in the Cardinal's oratory; and after that, at nine, he was to present himself for instructions: he was to dine at noon with the Cardinal, after which he was to consider himself at liberty till *Ave Maria*: then, once more he was to be at his master's disposal until supper. The work he would principally have to do would be the reading of all English correspondence, and the drawing up of a report upon it.

Percy found it a very pleasant and serene life, and the sense of home deepened every day. He had an abundance of time to himself, which he occupied resolutely in relaxation. From eight to nine he usually walked abroad, going sedately through the streets with his senses passive, looking into churches, watching the people, and gradually absorbing the strange naturalness of life under ancient conditions. At times it appeared to him like an historical dream; at times it seemed that there was no other reality; that the silent, tense world of modern civilisation was itself a phantom, and that here was the simple naturalness of the soul's childhood back again. Even the reading of the English correspondence did not greatly affect him, for the stream of his mind was beginning to run clear again in this sweet old channel; and he read, dissected, analysed and diagnosed with a deepening tranquillity.

There was not, after all, a great deal of news. It was a kind of lull after storm. Felsenburgh was still in retirement; he had refused the offers made to him by France and Italy, as that of England; and, although nothing definite was announced, it seemed that he was confining himself at present to an unofficial attitude. Meanwhile the Parliaments of Europe were busy in the preliminary stages of code-revision. Nothing would be done, it was understood, until the autumn sessions.

Life in Rome was very strange. The city had now become not only the centre of faith but, in a sense, a microcosm of it. It was divided into four huge quarters—Anglo-Saxon, Latin, Teutonic and Eastern—besides Trastevere, which was occupied almost entirely by Papal offices, seminaries, and schools. Anglo-Saxondom occupied the southwestern quarter, now entirely covered with houses, including the Aventine, the Celian and Testaccio. The Latins inhabited old Rome, between the Course and the river; the Teutons the northeastern quarter, bounded on the south by St. Laurence's Street; and the Easterns the remaining quarter, of which the centre was the Lateran. In this manner the true Romans were scarcely conscious of intrusion; they possessed a multitude of their own churches, they were allowed to revel in narrow, dark streets and hold their markets; and it was here that Percy usually walked, in a passion of historical retrospect. But the other quarters were strange enough, too. It was curious to see how a progeny of Gothic churches, served by northern priests, had grown up naturally in the Anglo-Saxon and Teutonic districts, and how the wide, grey streets, the neat pavements, the severe houses, showed how the northerns had not yet realised the requirements of southern life. The Easterns, on the other hand, resembled the Latins; their streets were as narrow and dark, their smells as overwhelming, their churches as dirty and as homely, and their colours even more brilliant.

Outside the walls the confusion was indescribable. If the city represented a carved miniature of the world, the suburbs represented the same model broken into a thousand pieces, tumbled in a bag and shot out at random. So far as the eye could see, on all sides from the roof of the Vatican, there stretched an endless plain of house-roofs, broken by spires, towers, domes and chimneys, under which lived human beings of every race beneath the sun. Here were the great manufactories, the monster buildings of the new world, the stations, the schools, the offices, all under secular dominion, yet surrounded by six millions of souls who lived here for love of religion. It was these who had despaired of modern life, tired out with change and effort, who had fled from the new system for refuge to the Church, but who could not obtain leave to live in the city itself. New houses were continually springing up in all directions. A gigantic compass, fixed by one leg in Rome, and with a span of five miles, would, if twirled, revolve through packed streets through its entire circle. Beyond that too houses stretched into the indefinite distance.

But Percy did not realise the significance of all that he saw, until the occasion of the Pope's name-day towards the end of August.

It was yet cool and early, when he followed his patron, whom he was to serve as chaplain, along the broad passages of the Vatican towards the room where the Pope and Cardinals were to assemble. Through a window, as he looked out into the Piazza, the crowd was yet more dense, if that were possible, than it had been an hour before. The huge oval square was cobbled with heads, through which ran a broad road, kept by papal troops for the passage of the carriages; and up the broad ribbon, white in the eastern light, came monstrous vehicles, a blaze of gilding and colour and cream tint; slow cheers swelled up and died, and through all came the rush and patter of wheels over the stones, like the sound of a tide-swept pebbly beach.

As they waited in an ante-chamber, halted by the pressure in front and behind—a pack of scarlet and white and purple—he looked out again, and realised what he had known only intellectually before, that here before his eyes was the royalty of the old world assembled—and he began to perceive its significance.

Round the steps of the basilica spread a great fan of coaches, each yoked to eight horses—the white of France and Spain, the black of Germany, Italy and Russia, and the cream-coloured of England. Those stood out in the near half-circle, and beyond was the sweep of the lesser powers: Greece, Norway, Sweden, Roumania and the Balkan States. One, the Turk, was alone wanting, he reminded himself. The emblems of some were visible—eagles, lions, leopards—guarding the royal crown above the roof of each. From the foot of the steps to the head ran a broad scarlet carpet, lined with soldiers.

Percy leaned against the shutter, and began to meditate.

Here was all that was left of Royalty. He had seen their palaces before, here and there in the various quarters, with standards flying, and scarlet-liveried men lounging on the steps. He had raised his hat a dozen times as a landau thundered past him up the Course; he had even seen the lilies of France and the leopards of England pass together in the solemn parade of the Pincian Hill. He had read in the papers every now and again during the last five years that family after family had made its way to Rome, after papal recognition had been granted; he had been told by the Cardinal on the previous evening that William of England, with his Consort, had landed at Ostia in the morning and that the tale of the Powers was complete. But he had never before realised the stupendous, overwhelming fact of the assembly of the world's royalty under the shadow of Peter's Throne, nor the appalling danger that its presence constituted in the midst of a democratic world. That world, he knew, affected to laugh at the folly and the childishness of it all—at the desperate play-acting of Divine Right on the part of fallen and despised families; but the same world, he knew very well, had not yet lost quite all its sentiment; and if that sentiment should happen to become resentful——

The pressure relaxed; Percy slipped out of the recess, and followed in the slow-moving stream.

Half-an-hour later he was in his place among the ecclesiastics, as the papal procession came out through the glimmering dusk of the chapel of the Blessed Sacrament into the nave of the enormous church; but even before he had entered the chapel he heard the quiet roar of recognition and the cry of the trumpets that greeted the Supreme Pontiff as he came out, a hundred yards ahead, borne on the *sedia gestatoria*, with the fans going behind him. When Percy himself came out, five minutes later, walking in his quaternion, and saw the sight that was waiting, he remembered with a sudden throb at his heart that other sight he had seen in London in a summer dawn three months before....

Far ahead, seeming to cleave its way through the surging heads, like the poop of an ancient ship, moved the canopy beneath which sat the Lord of the world, and between him and the priest, as if it were the wake of that same ship, swayed the gorgeous procession—Protonotaries Apostolic, Generals of Religious Orders and the rest—making its way along with white, gold, scarlet and silver foam between the living banks on either side. Overhead hung the splendid barrel of the roof, and far in front the haven of God's altar reared its monstrous pillars, beneath which burned the seven yellow stars that were the harbour lights of sanctity. It was an astonishing sight, but too vast and bewildering to do anything but oppress the observers with a consciousness of their own futility. The enormous enclosed air, the giant statues, the dim and distant roofs, the indescribable concert of sound—of the movement of feet, the murmur of ten thousand voices, the peal of organs like the crying of gnats, the thin celestial music—the faint suggestive smell of incense and men and bruised bay myrtle—and, supreme above all, the vibrant atmosphere of human emotion, shot with supernatural aspiration, as the Hope of the World, the holder of Divine Vice-Royalty, passed on his way to stand between God and man—this affected the priest as the action of a drug that at once lulls and stimulates, that blinds while it gives new vision, that deafens while it opens stopped ears, that exalts while it plunges into new gulfs of consciousness. Here, then, was the other formulated answer to the problem of life. The two Cities of Augustine lay for him to choose. The one was that of a world self-originated, self-organised and self-sufficient, interpreted by men such as Marx and Hervé, socialists, materialists, and, in the end, hedonists, summed up at last in Felsenburgh. The other lay displayed in the sight he saw before him, telling of a Creator and of a creation, of a Divine purpose, a redemption, and a world transcendent and eternal from which all sprang and to which all moved. One of the two, John and Julian, was the Vicar, and the other the Ape, of God.... And Percy's heart in one more spasm of conviction made its choice....

But the summit was not yet reached.

As Percy came at last out from the nave beneath the dome, on his way to the tribune beyond the papal throne, he became aware of a new element.

A great space was cleared about the altar and confession, extending, as he could see at least on his side, to the point that marked the entrance to the transepts; at this point ran rails straight across from side to side, continuing the lines of the nave. Beyond this red-hung barrier lay a gradual slope of faces, white and motionless; a glimmer of steel bounded it, and above, a third of the distance down the transept, rose in solemn serried array a line of canopies. These were of scarlet, like cardinalitial baldachini, but upon the upright surface of each burned gigantic coats supported by beasts and topped by crowns. Under each was a figure or two—no more—in splendid isolation, and through the interspaces between the thrones showed again a misty slope of faces.

His heart quickened as he saw it—as he swept his eyes round and across to the right and saw as in a mirror the rep- lica of the left in the right transept. It was there then that they sat—those lonely survivors of that strange company of per- sons who, till half-a-century ago, had reigned as God's tempo- ral Vicegerents with the consent of their subjects. They were unrecognised, now, save by Him from whom they drew their sovereignty—pinnacles clustering and hanging from a dome, from which the walls had been withdrawn. These were men and women who had learned at last that power comes from above, and their title to rule came not from their subjects but from the Supreme Ruler of all—shepherds without sheep, captains without soldiers to command. It was piteous—horribly piteous, yet inspiring. The act of faith was so sublime; and Percy's heart quickened as he understood it. These, then, men and women like himself, were not ashamed to appeal from man to God, to assume insignia which the world regarded as playthings, but which to them were emblems of supernatural commission. Was there not mirrored here, he asked himself, some far-off shadow of One Who rode on the colt of an ass amid the sneers of the great and the enthusiasm of children? ...

It was yet more kindling as the Mass went on, and he saw the male sovereigns come down to do their services at the altar, and to go to and fro between it and the Throne. There they went bareheaded, the stately silent figures. The English king, once again *Fidei Defensor*, bore the train in place of the old king of Spain, who, with the Austrian Emperor, alone of all European sovereigns, had preserved the unbroken continuity of faith. The old man leaned over his fald-stool, mumbling and weeping, even crying out now and again in love and devotion, as, like Simeon, he saw his Salvation. The Austrian Emperor twice administered the *Lavabo*; the German sovereign, who had lost his throne and all but his life upon his conversion four years before, by a new privilege placed and withdrew the cushion, as his Lord kneeled before the Lord of them both. So movement by movement the gorgeous drama was enacted; the murmuring of the crowds died to a stillness that was but one wordless prayer as the tiny White Disc rose between the white hands, and the thin angelic music pealed in the dome. For here was the one hope of these thousands, as mighty and as little as once within the Manger. There was none other that fought for them but only God. Surely then, if the blood of men and the tears of women could not avail to move the Judge and Observer of all from His silence, surely at least here the bloodless Death of His only Son, that once on Calvary had darkened heaven and rent the earth, pleaded now with such sorrowful splendour upon this island of faith amid a sea of laughter and hatred—this at least must avail! How could it not?

*   *   *   *   *

Percy had just sat down, tired out with the long ceremonies, when the door opened abruptly, and the Cardinal, still in his robes, came in swiftly, shutting the door behind him.

"Father Franklin," he said, in a strange breathless voice, "there is the worst of news. Felsenburgh is appointed President of Europe."

II

It was late that night before Percy returned, completely exhausted by his labours. For hour after hour he had sat with the Cardinal, opening dispatches that poured into the electric receivers from all over Europe, and were brought in one by one into the quiet sitting-room. Three times in the afternoon the Cardinal had been sent for, once by the Pope and twice to the Quirinal.

There was no doubt at all that the news was true; and it seemed that Felsenburgh must have waited deliberately for the offer. All others he had refused. There had been a Convention of the Powers, each of whom had been anxious to secure him, and each of whom had severally failed; these private claims had been withdrawn, and an united message sent. The new proposal was to the effect that Felsenburgh should assume a position hitherto undreamed of in democracy; that he should receive a House of Government in every capital of Europe; that his veto of any measure should be final for three years; that any measure he chose to introduce three times in three consecutive years should become law; that his title should be that of President of Europe. From his side practically nothing was asked, except that he should refuse any other official position offered him that did not receive the sanction of all the Powers.

And all this, Percy saw very well, involved the danger of an united Europe increased tenfold. It involved all the stupendous force of Socialism directed by a brilliant individual. It was the combination of the strongest characteristics of the two methods of government. The offer had been accepted by Felsenburgh after eight hours' silence.

It was remarkable, too, to observe how the news had been accepted by the two other divisions of the world. The East was enthusiastic; America was divided. But in any case America was powerless: the balance of the world was overwhelmingly against her.

Percy threw himself, as he was, on to his bed, and lay there with drumming pulses, closed eyes and a huge despair at his heart. The world indeed had risen like a giant over the horizons of Rome, and the holy city was no better now than a sand castle before a tide. So much he grasped. As to how ruin would come, in what form and from what direction, he neither knew nor cared. Only he knew now that it would come.

He had learned by now something of his own temperament; and he turned his eyes inwards to observe himself bitterly, as a doctor in mortal disease might with a dreadful complacency diagnose his own symptoms. It was even a relief to turn from the monstrous mechanism of the world to see in miniature one hopeless human heart. For his own religion he no longer feared; he knew, as absolutely as a man may know the colour of his eyes, that it was secure again and beyond shaking. During those weeks in Rome the cloudy deposit had run clear and the channel was once more visible. Or, better still, that vast erection of dogma, ceremony, custom and morals in which he had been educated, and on which he had looked all his life (as a man may stare upon some great set-piece that bewilders him), seeing now one spark of light, now another, flare and wane in the darkness, had little by little kindled and revealed itself in one stupendous blaze of divine fire that explains itself. Huge principles, once bewildering and even repellent, were again luminously self-evident; he saw, for example, that while Humanity-Religion endeavoured to abolish suffering the Divine Religion embraced it, so that the blind pangs even of beasts were within the Father's Will and Scheme; or that while from one angle one colour only of the web of life was visible—material, or intellectual, or artistic— from another the Supernatural was as eminently obvious. Humanity-Religion could only be true if at least half of man's nature, aspirations and sorrows were ignored. Christianity, on the other hand, at least included and accounted for these, even if it did not explain them. This ... and this ... and this ... all made the one and perfect whole. There was the Catholic Faith, more certain to him than the existence of himself: it was true and alive. He might be damned, but God reigned. He might go mad, but Jesus Christ was Incarnate Deity, proving Himself so by death and Resurrection, and John his Vicar. These things were as the bones of the Universe—facts beyond doubting—if they were not true, nothing anywhere was anything but a dream.

Difficulties?—Why, there were ten thousand. He did not in the least understand why God had made the world as it was, nor how Hell could be the creation of Love, nor how bread was transubstantiated into the Body of God—but—well, these things were so. He had travelled far, he began to see, from his old status of faith, when he had believed that divine truth could be demonstrated on intellectual grounds. He had learned now (he knew not how) that the supernatural cried to the supernatural; the Christ without to the Christ within; that pure human reason indeed could not contradict, yet neither could it adequately prove the mysteries of faith, except on premisses visible only to him who receives Revelation as a fact, that it is the moral state, rather than the intellectual, to which the Spirit of God speaks with the greater certitude. That which he had both learned and taught he now knew, that Faith, having, like himself, a body and a spirit—an historical expression and an inner verity—speaks now by one, now by another. This man believes because he sees—accepts the Incarnation or the Church from its credentials; that man, perceiving that these things are spiritual facts, yields himself wholly to the message and authority of her who alone professes them, as well as to the manifestation of them upon the historical plane; and in the darkness leans upon her arm. Or, best of all, because he has believed, now he sees.

So he looked with a kind of interested indolence at other tracts of his nature.

First, there was his intellect, puzzled beyond description, demanding, Why, why, why? Why was it allowed? How was it conceivable that God did not intervene, and that the Father of men could permit His dear world to be so ranged against Him? What did He mean to do? Was this eternal silence never to be broken? It was very well for those that had the Faith, but what of the countless millions who were settling down in contented blasphemy? Were these not, too, His children and the sheep of His pasture? What was the Catholic Church made for if not to convert the world, and why then had Almighty God allowed it, on the one side, to dwindle to a handful, and, on the other, the world to find its peace apart from Him?

He considered his emotions, but there was no comfort there, no stimulus. Oh! yes; he could pray still, by mere cold acts of the will, and his theology told him that God accepted such. He could say *"Adveniat regnum tuum.... Fiat voluntas tua,"* five thousand times a day, if God wanted that; but there was no sting or touch, no sense of vibration through the cords that his will threw up to the Heavenly Throne. What in the world then did God want him to do? Was it just then to repeat formulas, to lie still, to open despatches, to listen through the telephone, and to suffer.

And then the rest of the world—the madness that had seized upon the nations; the amazing stories that had poured in that day of the men in Paris, who, raving like Bacchantes, had stripped themselves naked in the Place de Concorde, and stabbed themselves to the heart, crying out to thunders of applause that life was too enthralling to be endured; of the woman who sang herself mad last night in Spain, and fell laughing and foaming in the concert hall at Seville; of the crucifixion of the Catholics that morning in the Pyrenees, and the apostasy of three bishops in Germany.... And this ... and this ... and a thousand more horrors were permitted, and God made no sign and spoke no word....

There was a tap, and Percy sprang up as the Cardinal came in.

He looked horribly worn; and his eyes had a kind of sunken brilliance that revealed fever. He made a little motion to Percy to sit down, and himself sat in the deep chair, trembling a little, and gathering his buckled feet beneath his red-buttoned cassock.

"You must forgive me, father," he said. "I am anxious for the Bishop's safety. He should be here by now."

This was the Bishop of Southwark, Percy remembered, who left England early that morning.

"He is coming straight through, your Eminence?"

"Yes; he should have been here by twenty-three. It is after midnight, is it not?"

As he spoke, the bells chimed out the half-hour.

It was nearly quiet now. All day the air had been full of sound; mobs had paraded the suburbs; the gates of the City had been barred, yet that was only an earnest of what was to be expected when the world understood itself.

The Cardinal seemed to recover himself after a few minutes' silence.

"You look tired out, father," he said kindly.

Percy smiled.

"And your Eminence?" he said.

The old man smiled too.

"Why, yes," he said. "I shall not last much longer, father. And then it will be you to suffer."

Percy sat up, suddenly, sick at heart.

"Why, yes," said the Cardinal. "The Holy Father has arranged it. You are to succeed me, you know. It need be no secret."

Percy drew a long trembling breath.

"Eminence," he began piteously.

The other lifted a thin old hand.

"I understand all that," he said softly. "You wish to die, is it not so?—and be at peace. There are many who wish that.

But we must suffer first. *Et pati et mori*. Father Franklin, there must be no faltering."

There was a long silence.

The news was too stunning to convey anything to the priest but a sense of horrible shock. The thought had simply never entered his mind that he, a man under forty, should be considered eligible to succeed this wise, patient old prelate. As for the honour—Percy was past that now, even had he thought of it. There was but one view before him—of a long and intolerable journey, on a road that went uphill, to be traversed with a burden on his shoulders that he could not support.

Yet he recognised its inevitability. The fact was announced to him as indisputable; it was to be; there was nothing to be said. But it was as if one more gulf had opened, and he stared into it with a dull, sick horror, incapable of expression.

The Cardinal first broke the silence.

"Father Franklin," he said, "I have seen to-day a picture of Felsenburgh. Do you know whom I at first took it for?"

Percy smiled listlessly.

"Yes, father, I took it for you. Now, what do you make of that?"

"I don't understand, Eminence."

"Why—" He broke off, suddenly changing the subject.

"There was a murder in the City to-day," he said. "A Catholic stabbed a blasphemer."

Percy glanced at him again.

"Oh! yes; he has not attempted to escape," went on the old man. "He is in gaol."

"And——"

"He will be executed. The trial will begin to-morrow.… It is sad enough. It is the first murder for eight months."

The irony of the position was evident enough to Percy as he sat listening to the deepening silence outside in the star-lit night. Here was this poor city pretending that nothing was the matter, quietly administering its derided justice; and there, outside, were the forces gathering that would put an end to all. His enthusiasm seemed dead. There was no thrill from the thought of the splendid disregard of material facts of which this was one tiny instance, none of despairing courage or drunken recklessness. He felt like one who watches a fly washing his face on the cylinder of an engine—the huge steel slides along bearing the tiny life towards enormous death—another moment and it will be over; and yet the watcher cannot interfere. The supernatural thus lay, perfect and alive, but immeasurably tiny; the huge forces were in motion, the world was heaving up, and Percy could do nothing but stare and frown. Yet, as has been said, there was no shadow on his faith; the fly he knew was greater than the engine from the superiority of its order of life; if it were crushed, life would not be the final sufferer; so much he knew, but how it was so, he did not know.

As the two sat there, again came a step and a tap; and a servant's face looked in.

"His Lordship is come, Eminence," he said.

The Cardinal rose painfully, supporting himself by the table. Then he paused, seeming to remember something, and fumbled in his pocket.

"See that, father," he said, and pushed a small silver disc towards the priest. "No; when I am gone."

Percy closed the door and came back, taking up the little round object.

It was a coin, fresh from the mint. On one side was the familiar wreath with the word "fivepence" in the midst, with its Esperanto equivalent beneath, and on the other the profile of a man, with an inscription. Percy turned it to read:

"Julian Felsenburgh, la Prezidante de Uropo."

III

It was at ten o'clock on the following morning that the Cardinals were summoned to the Pope's presence to hear the allocution.

Percy, from his seat among the Consultors, watched them come in, men of every nation and temperament and age—the Italians all together, gesticulating, and flashing teeth; the Anglo-Saxons steady-faced and serious; an old French Cardinal leaning on his stick, walking with the English Benedictine. It was one of the great plain stately rooms of which the Vatican now chiefly consisted, seated lengthwise like a chapel. At the lower end, traversed by the gangway, were the seats of the Consultors; at the upper end, the dais with the papal throne. Three or four benches with desks before them, standing out beyond the Consultors' seats, were reserved for the arrivals of the day before—prelates and priests who had poured into Rome from every European country on the announcement of the amazing news.

Percy had not an idea as to what would be said. It was scarcely possible that nothing but platitudes would be uttered, yet what else could be said in view of the complete doubtfulness of the situation? All that was known even this morning was that the Presidentship of Europe was a fact; the little silver coin he had seen witnessed to that; that there had been an outburst of persecution, repressed sternly by local authorities; and that Felsenburgh was to-day to begin his tour from capital to capital. He was expected in Turin by the end of the week. From every Catholic centre throughout the world had come in messages imploring guidance; it was said that apostacy was rising like a tidal wave, that persecution threatened everywhere, and that even bishops were beginning to yield.

As for the Holy Father, all was doubtful. Those who knew, said nothing; and the only rumour that escaped was to the effect that he had spent all night in prayer at the tomb of the Apostle....

The murmur died suddenly to a rustle and a silence; there was a ripple of sinking heads along the seats as the door beside the canopy opened, and a moment later John, *Pater Patrum*, was on his throne.

At first Percy understood nothing. He stared only, as at a picture, through the dusty sunlight that poured in through the shrouded windows, at the scarlet lines to right and left, up to the huge scarlet canopy, and the white figure that sat there. Certainly, these southerners understood the power of effect. It was as vivid and impressive as a vision of the Host in a jewelled monstrance. Every accessory was gorgeous, the high room, the colour of the robes, the chains and crosses, and as the eye moved along to its climax it was met by a piece of dead white—as if glory was exhausted and declared itself impotent to tell the supreme secret. Scarlet and purple and gold were well enough for those who stood on the steps of the throne—they needed it; but for Him who sat there nothing was needed. Let colours die and sounds faint in the presence of God's Viceroy. Yet what expression was required found itself adequately provided in that beautiful oval face, the poised imperious head, the sweet brilliant eyes and the clean-curved lips that spoke so strongly. There was not a sound in the room, not a rustle, nor a breathing—even without it seemed as if the world were allowing the supernatural to state its defence uninterruptedly, before summing up and clamouring condemnation.

Percy made a violent effort at self-repression, clenched his hands and listened.

"…Since this then is so, sons in Jesus Christ, it is for us to answer. We wrestle not, as the Doctor of the Gentiles teaches us, *against flesh and blood, but against principalities and powers, against the rulers of the world of this darkness, against the spirits of wickedness in the high places. Wherefore,* he continues, *take unto you the armour of God;* and he further declares to us its nature—*the girdle of truth, the breastplate of justice, the shoes of peace, the shield of faith, the helmet of salvation, and the sword of the Spirit.*

"By this, therefore, the Word of God bids us to war, but not with the weapons of this world, for neither is His kingdom of this world; and it is to remind you of the principles of this warfare that we have summoned you to Our Presence."

The voice paused, and there was a rustling sigh along the seats. Then the voice continued on a slightly higher note.

"It has ever been the wisdom of Our predecessors, as is also their duty, while keeping silence at certain seasons, at others to speak freely the whole counsel of God. From this duty We Ourself must not be deterred by the knowledge of Our own weakness and ignorance, but to trust rather that He Who has placed Us on this throne will deign to speak through Our mouth and use Our words to His glory.

"First, then, it is necessary to utter Our sentence as to the new movement, as men call it, which has latterly been inaugurated by the rulers of this world.

"We are not unmindful of the blessings of peace and unity, nor do We forget that the appearance of these things

has been the fruit of much that we have condemned. It is this
appearance of peace that has deceived many, causing them to
doubt the promise of the Prince of Peace that it is through
Him alone that *we have access to the Father.* That true peace,
passing understanding, concerns not only the relations of men
between themselves, but, supremely, the relations of men with
their Maker; and it is in this necessary point that the efforts
of the world are found wanting. It is not indeed to be wondered at that in a world which has rejected God this necessary
matter should be forgotten. Men have thought—led astray by
seducers—that the unity of nations was the greatest prize of
this life, forgetting the words of our Saviour, Who said that
He came to bring not peace but a sword, and that it is *through
many tribulations* that we enter God's Kingdom. First, then,
there should be established the peace of man with God, and
after that the unity of man with man will follow. *Seek ye first,*
said Jesus Christ, *the kingdom of God—and then all these things
shall be added unto you.*

"First, then, We once more condemn and anathematise
the opinions of those who teach and believe the contrary of
this; and we renew once more all the condemnations uttered
by Ourself or Our predecessors against all those societies,
organisations and communities that have been formed for
the furtherance of an unity on another than a divine foundation; and We remind Our children throughout the world
that it is forbidden to them to enter or to aid or to approve
in any manner whatsoever any of those bodies named in such
condemnations."

Percy moved in his seat, conscious of a touch of impatience.... The manner was superb, tranquil and stately as a
river; but the matter a trifle *banal.* Here was this old reproba-
tion of Freemasonry, repeated in unoriginal language.

"Secondly," went on the steady voice, "We wish to make known to you Our desires for the future; and here We tread on what many have considered dangerous ground."

Again came that rustle. Percy saw more than one cardinal lean forward with hand crooked at ear to hear the better. It was evident that something important was coming.

"There are many points," went on the high voice, "of which it is not Our intention to speak at this time, for of their own nature they are secret, and must be treated of on another occasion. But what We say here, We say to the world. Since the assaults of our enemies are both open and secret, so too must be Our defences. This then is Our intention."

The Pope paused again, lifted one hand as if mechanically to his breast, and grasped the cross that hung there.

"While the army of Christ is one, it consists of many divisions, each of which has its proper function and object. In times past God has raised up companies of His servants to do this or that particular work—the sons of St. Francis to preach poverty, those of St. Bernard to labour in prayer with all holy women dedicating themselves to this purpose, the Society of Jesus for the education of youth and the conversion of the heathen—together with all the other Religious Orders whose names are known throughout the world. Each such company was raised up at a particular season of need, and each has corresponded nobly with the divine vocation. It has also been the especial glory of each, for the furtherance of its intention, while pursuing its end, to cut off from itself all such activities (good in themselves) which would hinder that work for which God had called it into being—following in this matter the words of our Redeemer, *Every branch that beareth fruit, He purgeth it that it may bring forth more fruit.* At this present season, then, it appears to Our Humility that all such Orders (which once more We commend and bless) are not perfectly suited by the very conditions of their respective Rules to perform the great work which the time requires. Our warfare lies not with ignorance in particular, whether of the heathens to whom the Gospel has not yet come, or of those whose fathers have rejected it, nor with *the deceitful riches of this world*, nor with *science falsely so-called*, nor indeed with any one of those strongholds of infidelity against whom We have laboured in the past. Rather it appears as if at last the time was come of which the apostle spoke when he said that *that day shall not come, except there come a falling away first, and that Man of Sin be revealed, the Son of Perdition, who opposeth and exalteth himself above all that is called God.*

"It is not with this or that force that we are concerned, but rather with the unveiled immensity of that power whose time was foretold, and whose destruction is prepared."

The voice paused again, and Percy gripped the rail before him to stay the trembling of his hands. There was no rustle now, nothing but a silence that tingled and shook. The Pope drew a long breath, turned his head slowly to right and left, and went on more deliberately than ever.

"It seems good, then, to Our Humility, that the Vicar of Christ should himself invite God's children to this new warfare; and it is Our intention to enroll under the title of the Order of Christ Crucified the names of all who offer themselves to this supreme service. In doing this We are aware of the novelty of Our action, and the disregard of all such precautions as have been necessary in the past. We take counsel in this matter with none save Him Who we believe has inspired it.

"First, then, let us say, that although obedient service will be required from all who shall be admitted to this Order, Our primary intention in instituting it lies in God's regard rather in man's, in appealing to Him Who asks our generosity rather than to those who deny it, and dedicating once more by a formal and deliberate act our souls and bodies to the heavenly Will and service of Him Who alone can rightly claim such offering, and will accept our poverty.

"Briefly, we dictate only the following conditions.

"None shall be capable of entering the Order except such as shall be above the age of seventeen years.

"No badge, habit, nor insignia shall be attached to it.

"The Three Evangelical Counsels shall be the foundation of the Rule, to which we add a fourth intention, namely, that of a desire to receive the crown of martyrdom and a purpose of embracing it.

"The bishop of every diocese, if he himself shall enter the Order, shall be the superior within the limits of his own jurisdiction, and alone shall be exempt from the literal observance of the Vow of Poverty so long as he retains his see. Such bishops as do not feel the vocation to the Order shall retain their sees under the usual conditions, but shall have no Religious claim on the members of the Order.

"Further, We announce Our intention of Ourself entering the Order as its supreme prelate, and of making Our profession within the course of a few days.

"Further, We declare that in Our Own pontificate none shall be elevated to the Sacred College save those who have made their profession in the Order; and We shall dedicate shortly the Basilica of St. Peter and St. Paul as the central church of the Order, in which church We shall raise to the altars without any delay those happy souls who shall lay down their lives in the pursuance of their vocation.

"Of that vocation it is unnecessary to speak beyond

indicating that it may be pursued under any conditions laid down by the Superiors. As regards the novitiate, its conditions and requirements, we shall shortly issue the necessary directions. Each diocesan superior (for it is Our hope that none will hold back) shall have all such rights as usually appertain to Religious Superiors, and shall be empowered to employ his subjects in any work that, in his opinion, shall subserve the glory of God and the salvation of souls. It is Our Own intention to employ in Our service none except those who shall make their profession."

He raised his eyes once more, seemingly without emotion, then he continued:

"So far, then, We have determined. On other matters We shall take counsel immediately; but it is Our wish that these words shall be communicated to all the world, that there may be no delay in making known what it is that Christ through His Vicar asks of all who profess the Divine Name. We offer no rewards except those which God Himself has promised to those that love Him, and lay down their life for Him; no promise of peace, save of that which passeth understanding; no home save that which befits pilgrims and sojourners who seek a City to come; no honour save the world's contempt; no life, save that which is *hid with Christ in God.*"

CHAPTER IV

I

OLIVER BRAND, seated in his little private room at Whitehall, was expecting a visitor. It was already close upon ten o'clock, and at half-past he must be in the House. He had hoped that Mr. Francis, whoever he might be, would not detain him long. Even now, every moment was a respite, for the work had become simply prodigious during the last weeks.

But he was not reprieved for more than a minute, for the last boom from the Victoria Tower had scarcely ceased to throb when the door opened and a clerky voice uttered the name he was expecting.

Oliver shot one quick look at the stranger, at his drooping lids and down-turned mouth, summed him up fairly and accurately in the moments during which they seated themselves, and went briskly to business.

"At twenty-five minutes past, sir, I must leave this room," he said. "Until then—" he made a little gesture.

Mr. Francis reassured him.

"Thank you, Mr. Brand—that is ample time. Then, if you will excuse me—" He groped in his breast-pocket, and drew out a long envelope.

"I will leave this with you," he said, "when I go. It sets out our desires at length and our names. And this is what I have to say, sir."

He sat back, crossed his legs, and went on, with a touch of eagerness in his voice.

"I am a kind of deputation, as you know," he said. "We have something both to ask and to offer. I am chosen because it was my own idea. First, may I ask a question?"

Oliver bowed.

"I wish to ask nothing that I ought not. But I believe it is practically certain, is it not?—that Divine Worship is to be restored throughout the kingdom?"

Oliver smiled.

"I suppose so," he said. "The bill has been read for the third time, and, as you know, the President is to speak upon it this evening."

"He will not veto it?"

"We suppose not. He has assented to it in Germany."

"Just so," said Mr. Francis. "And if he assents here, I suppose it will become law immediately."

Oliver leaned over the table, and drew out the green paper that contained the Bill.

"You have this, of course—" he said. "Well, it becomes law at once; and the first feast will be observed on the first of October. 'Paternity,' is it not? Yes, Paternity."

"There will be something of a rush then," said the other eagerly. "Why, that is only a week hence."

"I have not charge of this department," said Oliver, laying back the Bill. "But I understand that the ritual will be that already in use in Germany. There is no reason why we should be peculiar."

"And the Abbey will be used?"

"Why, yes."

"Well, sir," said Mr. Francis, "of course I know the Government Commission has studied it all very closely, and no doubt has its own plans. But it appears to me that they will want all the experience they can get."

"No doubt."

"Well, Mr. Brand, the society which I represent consists entirely of men who were once Catholic priests. We number about two hundred in London. I will leave a pamphlet with you, if I may, stating our objects, our constitution, and so on. It seemed to us that here was a matter in which our past experience might be of service to the Government. Catholic ceremonies, as you know, are very intricate, and some of us studied them very deeply in the old days. We used to say that Masters of Ceremonies were born, not made, and we have a fair number of those amongst us. But indeed every priest is something of a ceremonialist."

He paused.

"Yes, Mr. Francis?"

"I am sure the Government realises the immense importance of all going smoothly. If Divine Service was at all grotesque or disorderly, it would largely defeat its own object. So I have been deputed to see you, Mr. Brand, and to suggest to you that here is a body of men—reckon it as at least twenty-five—who have had special experience in this kind of thing, and are perfectly ready to put themselves at the disposal of the Government."

Oliver could not resist a faint flicker of a smile at the corner of his mouth. It was a very grim bit of irony, he thought, but it seemed sensible enough.

"I quite understand, Mr. Francis. It seems a very reasonable suggestion. But I do not think I am the proper person. Mr. Snowford—"

"Yes, yes, sir, I know. But your speech the other day inspired us all. You said exactly what was in all our hearts—that the world could not live without worship; and that now that God was found at last——"

Oliver waved his hand. He hated even a touch of flattery.

"It is very good of you, Mr. Francis. I will certainly speak to Mr. Snowford. I understand that you offer yourselves as—as Masters of Ceremonies——?"

"Yes, sir; and sacristans. I have studied the German ritual very carefully; it is more elaborate than I had thought it. It will need a good deal of adroitness. I imagine that you will want at least a dozen *Ceremoniarii* in the Abbey; and a dozen more in the vestries will scarcely be too much."

Oliver nodded abruptly, looking curiously at the eager pathetic face of the man opposite him; yet it had something, too, of that mask-like priestly look that he had seen before in others like him. This was evidently a devotee.

"You are all Masons, of course?" he said.

"Why, of course, Mr. Brand."

"Very good. I will speak to Mr. Snowford to-day if I can catch him."

He glanced at the clock. There were yet three or four minutes.

"You have seen the new appointment in Rome, sir," went on Mr. Francis.

Oliver shook his head. He was not particularly interested in Rome just now.

"Cardinal Martin is dead—he died on Tuesday—and his place is already filled."

"Indeed, sir?"

"Yes—the new man was once a friend of mine—Franklin, his name is—Percy Franklin."

"Eh?"

"What is the matter, Mr. Brand? Did you know him?"

Oliver was eyeing him darkly, a little pale.

"Yes; I knew him," he said quietly. "At least, I think so."

"He was at Westminster until a month or two ago."

"Yes, yes," said Oliver, still looking at him. "And you knew him, Mr. Francis?"

"I knew him—yes."

"Ah!—well, I should like to have a talk some day about him."

He broke off. It yet wanted a minute to his time.

"And that is all?" he asked.

"That is all my actual business, sir," answered the other.

"But I hope you will allow me to say how much we all appreciate what you have done, Mr. Brand. I do not think it is possible for any, except ourselves, to understand what the loss of worship means to us. It was very strange at first——"

His voice trembled a little, and he stopped. Oliver felt interested, and checked himself in his movement to rise.

"Yes, Mr. Francis?"

The melancholy brown eyes turned on him full.

"It was an illusion, of course, sir—we know that. But I, at any rate, dare to hope that it was not all wasted—all our aspirations and penitence and praise. We mistook our God, but none the less it reached Him—it found its way to the Spirit of the World. It taught us that the individual was nothing, and that He was all. And now——"

"Yes, sir," said the other softly. He was really touched.

The sad brown eyes opened full.

"And now Mr. Felsenburgh is come." He swallowed in his throat. "Julian Felsenburgh!" There was a world of sudden passion in his gentle voice, and Oliver's own heart responded.

"I know, sir," he said; "I know all that you mean."

"Oh! to have a Saviour at last!" cried Francis. "One that

can be seen and handled and praised to His Face! It is like a dream—too good to be true!"

Oliver glanced at the clock, and rose abruptly, holding out his hand.

"Forgive me, sir. I must not stay. You have touched me very deeply.... I will speak to Snowford. Your address is here, I understand?"

He pointed to the papers.

"Yes, Mr. Brand. There is one more question."

"I must not stay, sir," said Oliver, shaking his head.

"One instant—is it true that this worship will be compulsory?"

Oliver bowed as he gathered up his papers.

II

Mabel, seated in the gallery that evening behind the President's chair, had already glanced at her watch half-a-dozen times in the last hour, hoping each time that twenty-one o'clock was nearer than she feared. She knew well enough by now that the President of Europe would not be half-a-minute either before or after his time. His supreme punctuality was famous all over the continent. He had said Twenty-One, so it was to be twenty-one.

A sharp bell-note impinged from beneath, and in a moment the drawling voice of the speaker stopped. Once more she lifted her wrist, saw that it wanted five minutes of the hour; then she leaned forward from her corner and stared down into the House.

A great change had passed over it at the metallic noise. All down the long brown seats members were shifting and arranging themselves more decorously, uncrossing their legs, slipping their hats beneath the leather fringes. As she looked, too, she saw the President of the House coming down the three steps from his chair, for Another would need it in a few moments.

The house was full from end to end; a late comer ran in from the twilight of the south door and looked distractedly about him in the full light before he saw his vacant place. The galleries at the lower end were occupied too, down there, where she had failed to obtain a seat. Yet from all the crowded interior there was no sound but a sibilant whispering; from the passages behind she could hear again the quick bell-note repeat itself as the lobbies were cleared; and from Parliament Square outside once more came the heavy murmur of the crowd that had been inaudible for the last twenty minutes. When that ceased she would know that he was come.

How strange and wonderful it was to be here—on this night of all, when the President was to speak! A month ago he had assented to a similar Bill in Germany, and had delivered a speech on the same subject at Turin. To-morrow he was to be in Spain. No one knew where he had been during the past week. A rumour had spread that his volor had been seen passing over Lake Como, and had been instantly contradicted. No one knew either what he would say to-night. It might be three words or twenty thousand. There were a few clauses in the Bill—notably those bearing on the point as to when the new worship was to be made compulsory on all subjects over the age of seven—it might be he would object and veto these. In that case all must be done again, and the Bill re-passed, unless the House accepted his amendment instantly by acclamation.

Mabel herself was inclined to these clauses. They provided that, although worship was to be offered in every parish

church of England on the ensuing first day of October, this
was not to be compulsory on all subjects till the New Year;
whereas, Germany, who had passed the Bill only a month
before, had caused it to come into full force immediately, thus
compelling all her Catholic subjects either to leave the country without delay or suffer the penalties. These penalties were
not vindictive: on a first offence a week's detention only was
to be given; on the second, one month's imprisonment; on
the third, one year's; and on the fourth, perpetual imprisonment until the criminal yielded. These were merciful terms,
it seemed; for even imprisonment itself meant no more than
reasonable confinement and employment on Government
works. There were no mediaeval horrors here; and the act of
worship demanded was so little, too; it consisted of no more
than bodily presence in the church or cathedral on the four
new festivals of Maternity, Life, Sustenance and Paternity, celebrated on the first day of each quarter. Sunday worship was
to be purely voluntary.

She could not understand how any man could refuse this
homage. These four things were facts—they were the manifestations of what she called the Spirit of the World—and if
others called that Power God, yet surely these ought to be
considered as His functions. Where then was the difficulty? It
was not as if Christian worship were not permitted, under the
usual regulations. Catholics could still go to Mass. And yet
appalling things were threatened in Germany: not less than
twelve thousand persons had already left for Rome; and it was
rumoured that forty thousand would refuse this simple act of
homage a few days hence. It bewildered and angered her to
think of it.

For herself the new worship was a crowning sign of the
triumph of Humanity. Her heart had yearned for some such

thing as this—some public corporate profession of what all now believed. She had so resented the dulness of folk who were content with action and never considered its springs. Surely this instinct within her was a true one; she desired to stand with her fellows in some solemn place, consecrated not by priests but by the will of man; to have as her inspirers sweet singing and the peal of organs; to utter her sorrow with thousands beside her at her own feebleness of immolation before the Spirit of all; to sing aloud her praise of the glory of life, and to offer by sacrifice and incense an emblematic homage to That from which she drew her being, and to whom one day she must render it again. Ah! these Christians had understood human nature, she had told herself a hundred times: it was true that they had degraded it, darkened light, poisoned thought, misinterpreted instinct; but they had understood that man must worship—must worship or sink.

For herself she intended to go at least once a week to the little old church half-a-mile away from her home, to kneel there before the sunlit sanctuary, to meditate on sweet mysteries, to present herself to That which she was yearning to love, and to drink, it might be, new draughts of life and power.

Ah! but the Bill must pass first.... She clenched her hands on the rail, and stared steadily before her on the ranks of heads, the open gangways, the great mace on the table, and heard, above the murmur of the crowd outside and the dying whispers within, her own heart beat.

She could not see Him, she knew. He would come in from beneath through the door that none but He might use, straight into the seat beneath the canopy. But she would hear His voice—that must be joy enough for her....

Ah! there was silence now outside; the soft roar had died. He had come then. And through swimming eyes she saw the

long ridges of heads rise beneath her, and through drumming
ears heard the murmur of many feet. All faces looked this
way; and she watched them as a mirror to see the reflected
light of His presence. There was a gentle sobbing somewhere
in the air—was it her own or another's? … the click of a door;
a great mellow booming overhead, shock after shock, as the
huge tenor bells tolled their three strokes; and, in an instant,
over the white faces passed a ripple, as if some breeze of passion shook the souls within; there was a swaying here and
there; and a passionless voice spoke half a dozen words in
Esperanto, out of sight:

"Englishmen, I assent to the Bill of Worship."

III

It was not until mid-day breakfast on the following morning
that husband and wife met again. Oliver had slept in town
and telephoned about eleven o' clock that he would be home
immediately, bringing a guest with him: and shortly before
noon she heard their voices in the hall.

Mr. Francis, who was presently introduced to her, seemed
a harmless kind of man, she thought, not interesting, though
he seemed in earnest about this Bill. It was not until breakfast
was nearly over that she understood who he was.

"Don't go, Mabel," said her husband, as she made a movement to rise. "You will like to hear about this, I expect. My
wife knows all that I know," he added.

Mr. Francis smiled and bowed.

"I may tell her about you, sir?" said Oliver again.

"Why, certainly."

Then she heard that he had been a Catholic priest a few
months before, and that Mr. Snowford was in consultation

with him as to the ceremonies in the Abbey. She was conscious of a sudden interest as she heard this.

"Oh! do talk," she said. "I want to hear everything."

It seemed that Mr. Francis had seen the new Minister of Public Worship that morning, and had received a definite commission from him to take charge of the ceremonies on the first of October. Two dozen of his colleagues, too, were to be enrolled among the *ceremoniarii*, at least temporarily—and after the event they were to be sent on a lecturing tour to organise the national worship throughout the country.

Of course things would be somewhat sloppy at first, said Mr. Francis; but by the New Year it was hoped that all would be in order, at least in the cathedrals and principal towns.

"It is important," he said, "that this should be done as soon as possible. It is very necessary to make a good impression. There are thousands who have the instinct of worship, without knowing how to satisfy it."

"That is perfectly true," said Oliver. "I have felt that for a long time. I suppose it is the deepest instinct in man."

"As to the ceremonies—" went on the other, with a slightly important air. His eyes roved round a moment; then he dived into his breast-pocket, and drew out a thin red-covered book.

"Here is the Order of Worship for the Feast of Paternity," he said. "I have had it interleaved, and have made a few notes."

He began to turn the pages, and Mabel, with considerable excitement, drew her chair a little closer to listen.

"That is right, sir," said the other. "Now give us a little lecture."

Mr. Francis closed the book on his finger, pushed his plate aside, and began to discourse.

"First," he said, "we must remember that this ritual is based almost entirely upon that of the Masons. Three-quarters at least of the entire function will be occupied by that. With that the *ceremoniarii* will not interfere, beyond seeing that the insignia are ready in the vestries and properly put on. The proper officials will conduct the rest.... I need not speak of that then. The difficulties begin with the last quarter."

He paused, and with a glance of apology began arranging forks and glasses before him on the cloth.

"Now here," he said, "we have the old sanctuary of the abbey. In the place of the reredos and Communion table there will be erected the large altar of which the ritual speaks, with the steps leading up to it from the floor. Behind the altar—extending almost to the old shrine of the Confessor—will stand the pedestal with the emblematic figure upon it; and—so far as I understand from the absence of directions—each such figure will remain in place until the eve of the next quarterly feast."

"What kind of figure?" put in the girl.

Francis glanced at her husband.

"I understand that Mr. Markenheim has been consulted," he said. "He will design and execute them. Each is to represent its own feast. This for Paternity——"

He paused again.

"Yes, Mr. Francis?"

"This one, I understand, is to be the naked figure of a man."

"A kind of Apollo—or Jupiter, my dear," put in Oliver.

Yes—that seemed all right, thought Mabel. Mr. Francis's voice moved on hastily.

"A new procession enters at this point, after the discourse," he said. "It is this that will need special marshalling. I suppose no rehearsal will be possible?"

"Scarcely," said Oliver, smiling.

The Master of Ceremonies sighed.

"I feared not. Then we must issue very precise printed instructions. Those who take part will withdraw, I imagine, during the hymn, to the old chapel of St. Faith. That is what seems to me the best."

He indicated the chapel.

"After the entrance of the procession all will take their places on these two sides—here—and here—while the celebrant with the sacred ministers——"

"Eh?"

Mr. Francis permitted a slight grimace to appear on his face; he flushed a little.

"The President of Europe——" He broke off. "Ah! that is the point. Will the President take part? That is not made clear in the ritual."

"We think so," said Oliver. "He is to be approached."

"Well, if not, I suppose the Minister of Public Worship will officiate. He with his supporters pass straight up to the foot of the altar. Remember that the figure is still veiled, and that the candles have been lighted during the approach of the procession. There follow the Aspirations printed in the ritual with the responds. These are sung by the choir, and will be most impressive, I think. Then the officiant ascends the altar alone, and, standing, declaims the Address, as it is called. At the close of it—at the point, that is to say, marked here with a star, the thurifers will leave the chapel, four in number. One ascends the altar, leaving the others swinging their thuribles at its foot—hands his to the officiant and retires. Upon the sounding of a bell the curtains are drawn back, the officiant censes the image in silence with four double swings, and, as he ceases the choir sings the appointed antiphon."

He waved his hands.

"The rest is easy," he said. "We need not discuss that."

To Mabel's mind even the previous ceremonies seemed easy enough. But she was undeceived.

"You have no idea, Mrs. Brand," went on the *ceremoniarius*, "of the difficulties involved even in such a simple matter as this. The stupidity of people is prodigious. I foresee a great deal of hard work for us all.... Who is to deliver the discourse, Mr. Brand?"

Oliver shook his head.

"I have no idea," he said. "I suppose Mr. Snowford will select."

Mr. Francis looked at him doubtfully.

"What is your opinion of the whole affair, sir?" he said.

Oliver paused a moment.

"I think it is necessary," he began. "There would not be such a cry for worship if it was not a real need. I think too—yes, I think that on the whole the ritual is impressive. I do not see how it could be bettered...."

"Yes, Oliver?" put in his wife, questioningly.

"No—there is nothing—except ... except I hope the people will understand it."

Mr. Francis broke in:

"My dear sir, worship involves a touch of mystery. You must remember that. It was the lack of that that made Empire Day fail in the last century. For myself, I think it is admirable. Of course much must depend on the manner in which it is presented. I see many details at present undecided—the colour of the curtains, and so forth. But the main plan is magnificent. It is simple, impressive, and, above all, it is unmistakable in its main lesson——"

"And that you take to be——?"

"I take it that it is homage offered to Life," said the other slowly. "Life under four aspects—Maternity corresponds to Christmas and the Christian fable; it is the feast of home, love, faithfulness. Life itself is approached in spring, teeming, young, passionate. Sustenance in midsummer, abundance, comfort, plenty, and the rest, corresponding somewhat to the Catholic *Corpus Christi*; and Paternity, the protective, generative, masterful idea, as winter draws on.... I understand it was a German thought."

Oliver nodded.

"Yes," he said. "And I suppose it will be the business of the speaker to explain all this."

"I take it so. It appears to me far more suggestive than the alternative plan—Citizenship, Labour, and so forth. These, after all, are subordinate to Life."

Mr. Francis spoke with an extraordinary suppressed enthusiasm, and the priestly look was more evident than ever. It was plain that his heart at least demanded worship.

Mabel clasped her hands suddenly.

"I think it is beautiful," she said softly, "and—and it is so real."

Mr. Francis turned on her with a glow in his brown eyes.

"Ah! yes, madam. That is it. There is no Faith, as we used to call it: it is the vision of Facts that no one can doubt; and the incense declares the sole divinity of Life as well as its mystery."

"What of the figures?" put in Oliver.

"A stone image is impossible, of course. It must be clay for the present. Mr. Markenheim is to set to work immediately. If the figures are approved they can then be executed in marble."

Again Mabel spoke with a soft gravity.

"It seems to me," she said, "that this is the last thing that we needed. It is so hard to keep our principles clear—we must have a body for them—some kind of expression——"

She paused.

"Yes, Mabel?"

"I do not mean," she went on, "that some cannot live without it, but many cannot. The unimaginative need concrete images. There must be some channel for their aspirations to flow through— Ah! I cannot express myself!"

Oliver nodded slowly. He, too, seemed to be in a meditative mood.

"Yes," he said. "And this, I suppose, will mould men's thoughts too: it will keep out all danger of superstition."

Mr. Francis turned on him abruptly.

"What do you think of the Pope's new Religious Order, sir?"

Oliver's face took on it a tinge of grimness.

"I think it is the worst step he ever took—for himself, I mean. Either it is a real effort, in which case it will provoke immense indignation—or it is a sham, and will discredit him. Why do you ask?"

"I was wondering whether any disturbance will be made in the abbey."

"I should be sorry for the brawler."

A bell rang sharply from the row of telephone labels.

Oliver rose and went to it. Mabel watched him as he touched a button—mentioned his name, and put his ear to the opening.

"It is Snowford's secretary," he said abruptly to the two expectant faces. "Snowford wants to—ah!"

Again he mentioned his name and listened. They heard a sentence or two from him that seemed significant.

"Ah! that is certain, is it? I am sorry.... Yes.... Oh! but that is better than nothing .... Yes; he is here.... Indeed. Very well; we will be with you directly."

He looked on the tube, touched the button again, and came back to them.

"I am sorry," he said. "The President will take no part at the Feast. But it is uncertain whether he will not be present. Mr. Snowford wants to see us both at once, Mr. Francis. Markenheim is with him."

But though Mabel was herself disappointed, she thought he looked graver than the disappointment warranted.

CHAPTER V

I

PERCY FRANKLIN, the new Cardinal-Protector of England, came slowly along the passage leading from the Pope's apartments, with Hans Steinmann, Cardinal Protector of Germany, blowing at his side. They entered the lift, still in silence, and passed out, two splendid vivid figures, one erect and virile, the other bent, fat, and very German from spectacles to flat buckled feet.

At the door of Percy's suite, the Englishman paused, made a little gesture of reverence, and went in without a word.

A secretary, young Mr. Brent, lately from England, stood up as his patron came in.

"Eminence," he said, "the English papers are come."

Percy put out a hand, took a paper, passed on into his inner room, and sat down.

There it all was—gigantic headlines, and four columns of print broken by startling title phrases in capital letters, after the fashion set by America a hundred years ago. No better way even yet had been found of misinforming the unintelligent.

He looked at the top. It was the English edition of the *Era*. Then he read the headlines. They ran as follows:

"THE NATIONAL WORSHIP. BEWILDERING SPLENDOUR. RELIGIOUS ENTHUSIASM. THE ABBEY AND GOD. CATHOLIC FANATIC. EX—PRIESTS AS FUNCTIONARIES."

He ran his eyes down the page, reading the vivid little phrases, and drawing from the whole a kind of impressionist view of the scenes in the Abbey on the previous day, of which he had already been informed by the telegraph, and the discussion of which had been the purpose of his interview just now with the Holy Father.

There plainly was no additional news; and he was laying the paper down when his eye caught a name.

"It is understood that Mr. Francis, the *ceremoniarius* (to whom the thanks of all are due for his reverent zeal and skill), will proceed shortly to the northern towns to lecture on the Ritual. It is interesting to reflect that this gentleman only a few months ago was officiating at a Catholic altar. He was assisted in his labours by twenty-four *confreres* with the same experience behind them."

"Good God!" said Percy aloud. Then he laid the paper down.

But his thoughts had soon left this renegade behind, and once more he was running over in his mind the significance of the whole affair, and the advice that he had thought it his duty to give just now upstairs.

Briefly, there was no use in disputing the fact that the inauguration of Pantheistic worship had been as stupendous a success in England as in Germany. France, by the way, was still too busy with the cult of human individuals, to develop larger ideas.

But England was deeper; and, somehow, in spite of prophecy, the affair had taken place without even a touch of bathos or grotesqueness. It had been said that England was too solid and too humorous. Yet there had been extraordinary scenes the day before. A great murmur of enthusiasm had rolled round the Abbey from end to end as the gorgeous curtains ran back, and the huge masculine figure, majestic and over-whelming, coloured with exquisite art, had stood out above the blaze of candles against the tall screen that shrouded the shrine. Markenheim had done his work well; and Mr. Brand's passionate discourse had well prepared the popular mind for the revelation. He had quoted in his peroration passage after passage from the Jewish prophets, telling of the City of Peace whose walls rose now before their eyes.

"*Arise, shine, for thy light is come, and the glory of the Lord is risen upon thee.... For behold I create new heavens and a new earth; and the former shall not be remembered nor come into mind.... Violence shall no more be heard in thy land, wasting nor destruction within thy borders. O thou so long afflicted, tossed with tempest and not comforted; behold I will lay thy stones with fair colours, and thy foundations with sapphires.... I will make thy windows of agates and thy gates of carbuncles, and all thy borders of pleasant stones. Arise, shine, for thy light is come.*"

As the chink of the censer-chains had sounded in the stillness, with one consent the enormous crowd had fallen on its knees, and so remained, as the smoke curled up from the hands of the rebel figure who held the thurible. Then the organ had begun to blow, and from the huge massed chorus in the transepts had rolled out the anthem, broken by one passionate cry, from some mad Catholic. But it had been silenced in an instant....

It was incredible—utterly incredible, Percy had told himself. Yet the incredible had happened; and England had found its worship once more—the necessary culmination of unimpeded subjectivity. From the provinces had come the like news. In cathedral after cathedral had been the same scenes. Markenheim's masterpiece, executed in four days after the passing of the bill, had been reproduced by the ordinary machinery, and

four thousand replicas had been despatched to every important centre. Telegraphic reports had streamed into the London
papers that everywhere the new movement had been received
with acclamation, and that human instincts had found adequate expression at last. If there had not been a God, mused
Percy reminiscently, it would have been necessary to invent
one. He was astonished, too, at the skill with which the new
cult had been framed. It moved round no disputable points;
there was no possibility of divergent political tendencies to mar
its success, no over-insistence on citizenship, labour and the
rest, for those who were secretly individualistic and idle. Life
was the one fount and centre of it all, clad in the gorgeous
robes of ancient worship. Of course the thought had been
Felsenburgh's, though a German name had been mentioned.
It was Positivism of a kind, Catholicism without Christianity,
Humanity worship without its inadequacy. It was not man that
was worshipped but the Idea of man, deprived of his supernatural principle. Sacrifice, too, was recognised—the instinct
of oblation without the demand made by transcendent Holiness upon the blood-guiltiness of man.... In fact,—in fact, said
Percy, it was exactly as clever as the devil, and as old as Cain.

The advice he had given to the Holy Father just now was
a counsel of despair, or of hope; he really did not know which.
He had urged that a stringent decree should be issued, forbidding any acts of violence on the part of Catholics. The faithful were to be encouraged to be patient, to hold utterly aloof
from the worship, to say nothing unless they were questioned,
to suffer bonds gladly. He had suggested, in company with
the German Cardinal, that they two should return to their
respective countries at the close of the year, to encourage the
waverers; but the answer had been that their vocation was to
remain in Rome, unless something unforeseen happened.

As for Felsenburgh, there was little news. It was said that he was in the East; but further details were secret. Percy understood quite well why he had not been present at the worship as had been expected. First, it would have been difficult to decide between the two countries that had established it; and, secondly, he was too brilliant a politician to risk the possible association of failure with his own person; thirdly, there was something the matter with the East.

This last point was difficult to understand; it had not yet become explicit, but it seemed as if the movement of last year had not yet run its course. It was undoubtedly difficult to explain the new President's constant absences from his adopted continent, unless there was something that demanded his presence elsewhere; but the extreme discretion of the East and the stringent precautions taken by the Empire made it impossible to know any details. It was apparently connected with religion; there were rumours, portents, prophets, ecstatics there.

Upon Percy himself had fallen a subtle change which he himself was recognising. He no longer soared to confidence or sank to despair. He said his Mass, read his enormous correspondence, meditated strictly; and, though he felt nothing, he knew everything. There was not a tinge of doubt upon his faith, but neither was there emotion in it. He was as one who laboured in the depths of the earth, crushed even in imagination, yet conscious that somewhere birds sang, and the sun shone, and water ran. He understood his own state well enough, and perceived that he had come to a reality of faith that was new to him, for it was sheer faith—sheer apprehension of the Spiritual—without either the dangers or the joys of imaginative vision. He expressed it to himself by saying that there were three processes through which God led the soul: the first was that of external faith, which assents to all things presented by the accustomed authority, practises religion, and is neither interested nor doubtful; the second follows the quickening of the emotional and perceptive powers of the soul, and is set about with consolations, desires, mystical visions and perils; it is in this plane that resolutions are taken and vocations found and shipwrecks experienced; and the third, mysterious and inexpressible, consists in the re-enactment in the purely spiritual sphere of all that has preceded (as a play follows a rehearsal), in which God is grasped but not experienced, grace is absorbed unconsciously and even distastefully, and little by little the inner spirit is conformed in the depths of its being, far within the spheres of emotion and intellectual perception, to the image and mind of Christ.

So he lay back now, thinking, a long, stately, scarlet figure, in his deep chair, staring out over Holy Rome seen through the misty September haze. How long, he wondered, would there be peace? To his eyes even already the air was black with doom.

He struck his hand-bell at last.

"Bring me Father Blackmore's last report," he said, as his secretary appeared.

II

Percy's intuitive faculties were keen by nature and had been vastly increased by cultivation. He had never forgotten Father Blackmore's shrewd remarks of a year ago; and one of his first acts as Cardinal-Protector had been to appoint that priest on the list of English correspondents. Hitherto he had received some dozen letters, and not one of them had been without its grain of gold. Especially he had noticed that one warning ran through them all, namely, that sooner or later there would be some overt act of provocation on the part of English Catholics; and it was the memory of this that had inspired his vehement entreaties to the Pope this morning. As in the Roman and African persecutions of the first three centuries, so now, the greatest danger to the Catholic community lay not in the unjust measures of the Government but in the indiscreet zeal of the faithful themselves. The world desired nothing better than a handle to its blade. The scabbard was already cast away.

When the young man had brought the four closely written sheets, dated from Westminster, the previous evening, Percy turned at once to the last paragraph before the usual Recommendations.

"Mr. Brand's late secretary, Mr. Phillips, whom your Eminence commended to me, has been to see me two or three times. He is in a curious state. He has no faith; yet, intellectually, he sees no hope anywhere but in the Catholic Church. He has even begged for admission to the Order of Christ Crucified, which of course is impossible. But there is no doubt he is sincere; otherwise he would have professed Catholicism. I have introduced him to many Catholics in the hope that they may help him. I should much wish your Eminence to see him."

Before leaving England, Percy had followed up the acquaintance he had made so strangely over Mrs. Brand's reconciliation to God, and, scarcely knowing why, had commended him to the priest. He had not been particularly impressed by Mr. Phillips; he had thought him a timid, undecided creature, yet he had been struck by the extremely unselfish action by which the man had forfeited his position. There must surely be a good deal behind.

And now the impulse had come to send for him. Perhaps the spiritual atmosphere of Rome would precipitate faith. In any case, the conversation of Mr. Brand's late secretary might be instructive.

He struck the bell again.

"Mr. Brent," he said, "in your next letter to Father Black-more, tell him that I wish to see the man whom he proposed to send—Mr. Phillips."

"Yes, Eminence."

"There is no hurry. He can send him at his leisure."

"Yes, Eminence."

"But he must not come till January. That will be time enough, unless there is urgent reason."

"Yes, Eminence."

The development of the Order of Christ Crucified had gone forward with almost miraculous success. The appeal issued by the Holy Father throughout Christendom had been as fire among stubble. It seemed as if the Christian world had reached exactly that point of tension at which a new organisation of this nature was needed, and the response had startled even the most sanguine. Practically the whole of Rome with its suburbs—three millions in all—had run to the enrolling stations in St. Peter's as starving men run to food, and desperate to the storming of a breach. For day after day the Pope himself had sat enthroned below the altar of the Chair, a glorious, radiant figure, growing ever white and weary towards evening, imparting his Blessing with a silent sign to each individual of the vast crowd that swarmed up between the barriers, fresh from fast and Communion, to kneel before his new Superior and kiss the Pontifical ring. The requirements had been as stringent as circumstances allowed. Each postulant was obliged to go to confession to a specially authorised priest, who examined sharply into motives and sincerity, and only one-third of the applicants had been accepted. This, the authorities pointed out to the scornful, was not an excessive proportion; for it was to be remembered that most of those who had presented themselves had already undergone a sifting fierce as fire. Of the three millions in Rome, two millions at least were exiles for their faith, preferring to live obscure and despised in the shadow of God rather than in the desolate glare of their own infidel countries.

On the fifth evening of the enrolment of novices an astonishing incident had taken place. The old king of Spain (Queen Victoria's second son), already on the edge of the grave, had just risen and tottered before his Ruler; it seemed for an instant as if he would fall, when the Pope himself, by a sudden movement, had risen, caught him in his arms and kissed him; and then, still standing, had spread his arms abroad and delivered a *fervorino* such as never had been heard before in the history of the basilica.

"*Benedictus Dominus!*" he cried, with upraised face and shining eyes. "Blessed be the Lord God of Israel, for he hath visited and redeemed His people. I, John, Vicar of Christ, Servant of Servants, and sinner among sinners, bid you be of good courage in the Name of God. By Him Who hung on the Cross, I promise eternal life to all who persevere in His Order. He Himself has said it. *To him that overcometh I will give a crown of life.*

"Little children; fear not him that killeth the body. There is no more that he can do. God and His Mother are amongst us...."

So his voice had poured on, telling the enormous awestricken crowd of the blood that already had been shed on the place where they stood, of the body of the Apostle that lay scarcely fifty yards away, urging, encouraging, inspiring. They had vowed themselves to death, if that were God's Will; and if not, the intention would be taken for the deed. They were under obedience now; their wills were no longer theirs but God's: under chastity—for their bodies were bought with a price; under poverty, and theirs was the kingdom of heaven.

He had ended by a great silent Benediction of the City and the World: and there were not wanting a half-dozen of the faithful who had seen, they thought, a white shape in the form of a bird that hung in the air while he spoke—white as a mist, translucent as water....

The consequent scenes in the city and suburbs had been unparalleled, for thousands of families had with one consent dissolved human ties. Husbands had found their way to the huge houses on the Quirinal set apart for them; wives to the Aventine; while the children, as confident as their parents, had swarmed over to the Sisters of St. Vincent who had received at the Pope's orders the gift of three streets to shelter them in. Everywhere the smoke of burning went up in the squares where household property, rendered useless by the vows of poverty, were consumed by their late owners; and daily long trains moved out from the station outside the walls carrying jubilant loads of those who were despatched by the Pope's delegates to be the salt of men, consumed in their function, and leaven plunged in the vast measures of the infidel world. And that infidel world welcomed their coming with bitter laughter.

From the rest of Christendom had poured in news of success. The same precautions had been observed as in Rome, for the directions issued were precise and searching; and day after

day came in the long rolls of the new Religious drawn up by
the diocesan superiors.

Within the last few days, too, other lists had arrived, more
glorious than all. Not only did reports stream in that already
the Order was beginning its work and that already broken communications were being re-established, that devoted missioners
were in process of organising themselves, and that hope was
once more rising in the most desperate hearts; but better than
all this was the tidings of victory in another sphere. In Paris
forty of the newborn Order had been burned alive in one day
in the Latin quarter, before the Government intervened. From
Spain, Holland, Russia had come in other names. In Dussel-
dorf eighteen men and boys, surprised at their singing of Prime
in the church of Saint Laurence, had been cast down one by
one into the city-sewer, each chanting as he vanished:

"*Christi Fili Dei vivi miserere nobis,*"

and from the darkness had come up the same broken
song till it was silenced with stones. Meanwhile, the German
prisons were thronged with the first batches of recusants.

The world shrugged its shoulders, and declared that they
had brought it on themselves, while yet it deprecated mob-
violence, and requested the attention of the authorities and
the decisive repression of this new conspiracy of superstition.
And within St. Peter's Church the workmen were busy at the
long rows of new altars, affixing to the stone diptychs the
brass-forged names of those who had already fulfilled their
vows and gained their crowns.

It was the first word of God's reply to the world's challenge.

As Christmas drew on it was announced that the Sovereign Pontiff would sing Mass on the last day of the year, at

the papal altar of Saint Peter's, on behalf of the Order; and preparations began to be made.

It was to be a kind of public inauguration of the new enterprise; and, to the astonishment of all, a special summons was issued to all members of the Sacred College through-out the world to be present, unless hindered by sickness. It seemed as if the Pope were determined that the world should understand that war was declared; for, although the com-mand would not involve the absence of any Cardinal from his province for more that five days, yet many inconveniences must surely result. However, it had been said, and it was to be done.

It was a strange Christmas.

Percy was ordered to attend the Pope at his second Mass, and himself said his three at midnight in his own private ora-tory. For the first time in his life he saw that of which he had heard so often, the wonderful old-world Pontifical procession, lit by torches, going through the streets from the Lateran to St. Anastasia, where the Pope for the last few years had restored the ancient custom discontinued for nearly a century-and-a-half. The little basilica was reserved, of course, in every corner for the peculiarly privileged; but the streets outside along the whole route from the Cathedral to the church—and, indeed, the other two sides of the triangle as well, were one dense mass of silent heads and flaming torches. The Holy Father was attended at the altar by the usual sovereigns; and Percy from his place watched the heavenly drama of Christ's Pas-sion enacted through the veil of His nativity at the hands of His old Angelic Vicar. It was hard to perceive Calvary here; it was surely the air of Bethlehem, the celestial light, not the supernatural darkness, that beamed round the simple altar. It was the Child called Wonderful that lay there beneath the old hands, rather than the stricken man of Sorrows.

Adeste fideles sang the choir from the tribune.—Come, let us adore, rather than weep; let us exult, be content, be ourselves like little children. As He for us became a child, let us become childlike for Him. Let us put on the garments of infancy and the shoes of peace. *For the Lord hath reigned; He is clothed with beauty: the Lord is clothed with strength and hath girded Himself. He hath established the world which shall not be moved: His throne is prepared from of old. He is from everlasting. Rejoice greatly then, O daughter of Zion, shout for joy, O daughter of Jerusalem; behold thy King cometh, to thee, the Holy One, the Saviour of the world.* It will be time, then, to suffer by and bye, when the Prince of this world cometh upon the Prince of Heaven.

So Percy mused, standing apart in his gorgeousness, striving to make himself little and simple. Surely nothing was too hard for God! Might not this mystic Birth once more do what it had done before—bring into subjection through the might of its weakness every proud thing that exalts itself above all that is called God? It had drawn wise Kings once across the desert, as well as shepherds from their flocks. It had kings about it now, kneeling with the poor and foolish, kings who had laid down their crowns, who brought the gold of loyal hearts, the myrrh of desired martyrdom, and the incense of a pure faith. Could not republics, too, lay aside their splendour, mobs be tamed, selfishness deny itself, and wisdom confess its ignorance? …

Then he remembered Felsenburgh; and his heart sickened within him.

III

Six days later, Percy rose as usual, said his Mass, breakfasted, and sat down to say office until his servant should summon him to vest for the Pontifical Mass.

He had learned to expect bad news now so constantly—of apostasies, deaths, losses—that the lull of the previous week had come to him with extraordinary refreshment. It appeared to him as if his musings in St. Anastasia had been truer than he thought, and that the sweetness of the old feast had not yet wholly lost its power even over a world that denied its substance. For nothing at all had happened of importance. A few more martyrdoms had been chronicled, but they had been isolated cases; and of Felsenburgh there had been no tidings at all. Europe confessed its ignorance of his business.

On the other hand, to-morrow, Percy knew very well, would be a day of extraordinary moment in England and Germany at any rate; for in England it was appointed as the first occasion of compulsory worship throughout the country, while it was the second in Germany. Men and women would have to declare themselves now.

He had seen on the previous evening a photograph of the image that was to be worshipped next day in the Abbey; and, in a fit of loathing, had torn it to shreds. It represented a nude woman, huge and majestic, entrancingly lovely, with head and shoulders thrown back, as one who sees a strange and heavenly vision, arms down-stretched and hands a little raised, with wide fingers, as in astonishment—the whole attitude, with feet and knees pressed together, suggestive of expectation, hope and wonder; in devilish mockery her long hair was crowned with twelve stars. This, then, was the spouse of the other, the embodiment of man's ideal maternity, still waiting for her child....

When the white scraps lay like poisonous snow at his feet, he had sprung across the room to his *prie-dieu*, and fallen there in an agony of reparation.

"Oh! Mother, Mother!" he cried to the stately Queen of Heaven who, with Her true Son long ago in Her arms, looked down on him from Her bracket—no more than that.

But he was still again this morning, and celebrated Saint Silvester, Pope and Martyr, the last saint in the procession of the Christian year, with tolerable equanimity. The sights of last night, the throng of officials, the stately scarlet, unfamiliar figures of the Cardinals who had come in from north, south, east and west—these helped to reassure him again—unreasonably, as he knew, yet effectually. The very air was electric with expectation. All night the *piazza* had been crowded by a huge, silent mob waiting till the opening of the doors at seven o' clock. Now the church itself was full, and the *piazza* full again. Far down the street to the river, so far as he could see as he had leaned from his window just now, lay that solemn motionless pavement of heads. The roof of the colonnade showed a fringe of them, the house-tops were black—and this in the bitter cold of a clear, frosty morning, for it was announced that after Mass and the proceeding of the members of the Order past the Pontifical Throne, the Pope would give Apostolic Benediction to the City and the World.

Percy finished Terce, closed his book and lay back; his servant would be here in a minute now.

His mind began to run over the function, and he reflected that the entire Sacred College (with the exception of the Cardinal-Protector of Jerusalem, detained by sickness), numbering sixty-four members, would take part. This would mean an unique sight by and bye. Eight years before, he remembered, after the freedom of Rome, there had been a similar assembly; but the Cardinals at that time amounted to no more than fifty-three all told, and four had been absent.

Then he heard voices in his ante-room, a quick step, and a loud English expostulation. That was curious, and he sat up.

Then he heard a sentence.

"His Eminence must go to vest; it is useless."

There was a sharp answer, a faint scuffle, and a snatch at the handle. This was indecent; so Percy stood up, made three strides of it to the door, and tore it open.

A man stood there, whom at first he did not recognise, pale and disordered.

"Why—" began Percy, and recoiled.

"Mr. Phillips!" he said.

The other threw out his hands.

"It is I, sir—your Eminence—this moment arrived. It is life and death. Your servant tells me——"

"Who sent you?"

"Father Blackmore."

"Good news or bad?"

The man rolled his eyes towards the servant, who still stood erect and offended a yard away; and Percy understood.

He put his hand on the other's arm, drawing him through the doorway.

"Tap upon this door in two minutes, James," he said.

They passed across the polished floor together; Percy went to his usual place in the window, leaned against the shutter, and spoke.

"Tell me in one sentence, sir," he said to the breathless man.

"There is a plot among the Catholics. They intend destroying the Abbey to-morrow with explosives. I knew that the Pope——"

Percy cut him short with a gesture.

CHAPTER VI

I

THE VOLOR-STAGE was comparatively empty this afternoon, as the little party of six stepped out on to it from the lift. There was nothing to distinguish these from ordinary travellers. The two Cardinals of Germany and England were wrapped in plain furs, without insignia of any kind; their chaplains stood near them, while the two men-servants hurried forward with the bags to secure a private compartment.

The four kept complete silence, watching the busy movements of the officials on board, staring unseeingly at the sleek, polished monster that lay netted in steel at their feet, and the great folded fins that would presently be cutting the thin air at a hundred and fifty miles an hour.

Then Percy, by a sudden movement, turned from the others, went to the open window that looked over Rome, and leaned there with his elbows on the sill, looking.

It was a strange view before him.

It was darkening now towards sunset, and the sky, prim-rose-green overhead, deepened to a clear tawny orange above the horizon, with a sanguine line or two at the edge, and beneath that lay the deep evening violet of the city, blotted here and there by the black of cypresses and cut by the thin leafless pinnacles of a poplar grove that aspired without the walls. But right across the picture rose the enormous dome, of an indescribable tint; it was grey, it was violet—it was what the eye chose to make it—and through it, giving its solidity the air of a bubble, shone the southern sky, flushed too with faint orange. It was this that was supreme and dominant; the serrated line of domes, spires and pinnacles, the crowded roofs beneath, in the valley dell' Inferno, the fairy hills far away—all were but the annexe to this mighty tabernacle of God. Already lights were beginning to shine, as for thirty centuries they had shone; thin straight skeins of smoke were ascending against the darkening sky. The hum of this Mother of cities was beginning to be still, for the keen air kept folks indoors; and the evening peace was descending that closed another day and another year. Beneath in the narrow streets Percy could see tiny figures, hurrying like belated ants; the crack of a whip, the cry of a woman, the wail of a child came up to this immense elevation like details of a murmur from another world. They, too, would soon be quiet, and there would be peace.

A heavy bell beat faintly from far away, and the drowsy city turned to murmur its good-night to the Mother of God. From a thousand towers came the tiny melody, floating across the great air spaces, in a thousand accents, the solemn bass of St. Peter's, the mellow tenor of the Lateran, the rough cry from some old slum church, the peevish tinkle of convents and chapels—all softened and made mystical in this grave evening air—it was the wedding of delicate sound and clear light. Above, the liquid orange sky; beneath, this sweet subdued ecstasy of bells.

"*Alma Redemptoris Mater*," whispered Percy, his eyes wet with tears. "Gentle Mother of the Redeemer—the open door of the sky, star of the sea—have mercy on sinners. *The Angel of the Lord announced it to Mary, and she conceived of the Holy Ghost…. Pour, therefore, Lord, Thy grace into our hearts. Let us, who know Christ's incarnation, rise through passion and cross to the glory of Resurrection—through the same Christ our Lord."*

Another bell clanged sharply close at hand, calling him down to earth, and wrong, and labour and grief; and he turned to see the motionless volor itself one blaze of brilliant internal light, and the two priests following the German Cardinal across the gangway.

It was the rear compartment that the men had taken; and when he had seen that the old man was comfortable, still without a word he passed out again into the central passage to see the last of Rome.

The exit-door had now been snapped, and as Percy stood at the opposite window looking out at the high wall that would presently sink beneath him, throughout the whole of the delicate frame began to run the vibration of the electric engine. There was the murmur of talking somewhere, a heavy step shook the floor, a bell clanged again, twice, and a sweet wind-chord sounded. Again it sounded; the vibration ceased, and the edge of the high wall against the tawny sky on which he had fixed his eyes sank suddenly like a dropped bar, and he staggered a little in his place. A moment later the dome rose again, and itself sank, the city, a fringe of towers and a mass of dark roofs, pricked with light, span like a whirlpool; the jewelled stars themselves sprang this way and that; and with one more long cry the marvellous machine righted itself, beat with its wings, and settled down, with the note of the flying air passing through rising shrillness into vibrant silence, to its long voyage to the north.

Further and further sank the city behind; it was a patch now: greyness on black. The sky seemed to grow more huge

and all-containing as the earth relapsed into darkness; it
glowed like a vast dome of wonderful glass, darkening even as
it glowed; and as Percy dropped his eyes once more round the
extreme edge of the car the city was but a line and a bubble—
a line and a swelling—a line, and nothingness.

He drew a long breath, and went back to his friends.

II

"Tell me again," said the old Cardinal, when the two were
settled down opposite to one another, and the chaplains were
gone to another compartment. "Who is this man?"

"This man? He was secretary to Oliver Brand, one of our
politicians. He fetched me to old Mrs. Brand's death-bed, and
lost his place in consequence. He is in journalism now. He is
perfectly honest. No, he is not a Catholic, though he longs to
be one. That is why they confided in him."

"And they?"

"I know nothing of them, except that they are a desperate set. They have enough faith to act, but not enough to
be patient.… I suppose they thought this man would sym-
pathise. But unfortunately he has a conscience, and he also
sees that any attempt of this kind would be the last straw on
the back of toleration. Eminence, do you realise how violent
the feeling is against us?"

The old man shook his head lamentably.

"Do I not?" he murmured. "And my Germans are in it?
Are you sure?"

"Eminence, it is a vast plot. It has been simmering for
months. There have been meetings every week. They have
kept the secret marvellously. Your Germans only delayed that
the blow might be more complete. And now, to-morrow—"

Percy drew back with a despairing gesture.

"And the Holy Father?"

"I went to him as soon as Mass was over. He withdrew all opposition, and sent for you. It is our one chance, Eminence."

"And you think our plan will hinder it?"

"I have no idea, but I can think of nothing else. I shall go straight to the Archbishop and tell him all. We arrive, I believe, at three o'clock, and you in Berlin about seven, I suppose, by German time. The function is fixed for eleven. By eleven, then, we shall have done all that is possible. The Government will know, and they will know, too, that we are innocent in Rome. I imagine they will cause it to be announced that the Cardinal-Protector and the Archbishop, with his coadjutors, will be present in the sacristies. They will double every guard; they will parade volors overhead—and then—well! in God's hands be the rest."

"Do you think the conspirators will attempt it?"

"I have no idea," said Percy shortly.

"I understand they have alternative plans."

"Just so. If all is clear, they intend dropping the explosive from above; if not, at least three men have offered to sacrifice themselves by taking it into the Abbey themselves.... And you, Eminence?"

The old man eyed him steadily.

"My programme is yours," he said. "Eminence, have you considered the effect in either case? If nothing happens——"

"If nothing happens we shall be accused of a fraud, of seeking to advertise ourselves. If anything happens—well, we shall all go before God together. Pray God it may be the second," he added passionately.

"It will be at least easier to bear," observed the old man.

"I beg your pardon, Eminence. I should not have said that."

There fell a silence between the two, in which no sound was heard but the faint untiring vibration of the screw, and the sudden cough of a man in the next compartment. Percy leaned his head wearily on his hand, and stared from the window.

The earth was now dark beneath them—an immense emptiness; above, the huge engulfing sky was still faintly luminous, and through the high frosty mist through which they moved stars glimmered now and again, as the car swayed and tacked across the wind.

"It will be cold among the Alps," murmured Percy. Then he broke off. "And I have not one shred of evidence," he said; "nothing but the word of a man."

"And you are sure?"

"I am sure."

"Eminence," said the German suddenly, staring straight into his face, "the likeness is extraordinary."

Percy smiled listlessly. He was tired of hearing that.

"What do you make of it?" persisted the other.

"I have been asked that before," said Percy. "I have no views."

"It seems to me that God means something," murmured the German heavily, still staring at him.

"Well, Eminence?"

"A kind of antithesis—a reverse of the medal. I do not know."

Again there was silence. A chaplain looked in through the glazed door, a homely, blue-eyed German, and was waved away once more.

"Eminence," said the old man abruptly, "there is surely more to speak of. Plans to be made."

Percy shook his head.

"There are no plans to be made," he said. "We know nothing but the fact—no names—nothing. We—we are like children in a tiger's cage. And one of us has just made a gesture in the tiger's face."

"I suppose we shall communicate with one another?"

"If we are in existence."

It was curious how Percy took the lead. He had worn his scarlet for about three months, and his companion for twelve years; yet it was the younger who dictated plans and arranged. He was scarcely conscious of its strangeness, however. Ever since the shocking news of the morning, when a new mine had been sprung under the shaking Church, and he had watched the stately ceremonial, the gorgeous splendour, the dignified, tranquil movements of the Pope and his court, with a secret that burned his heart and brain—above all, since that quick interview in which old plans had been reversed and a startling decision formed, and a blessing given and received, and a farewell looked not uttered—all done in half-an-hour—his whole nature had concentrated itself into one keen tense force, like a coiled spring. He felt power tingling to his fingertips—power and the dulness of an immense despair. Every prop had been cut, every brace severed; he, the City of Rome, the Catholic Church, the very supernatural itself, seemed to hang now on one single thing—the Finger of God. And if that failed—well, nothing would ever matter any more....

He was going now to one of two things—ignominy or death. There was no third thing—unless, indeed, the conspirators were actually taken with their instruments upon them. But that was impossible. Either they would refrain, knowing that God's ministers would fall with them, and in that case there would be the ignominy of a detected fraud, of a

miserable attempt to win credit. Or they would not refrain;
they would count the death of a Cardinal and a few bishops a
cheap price to pay for revenge—and in that case—well, there
was Death and Judgment. But Percy had ceased to fear. No
ignominy could be greater than that which he already bore—
the ignominy of loneliness and discredit. And death could be
nothing but sweet—it would at least be knowledge and rest.
He was willing to risk all on God.

The other, with a little gesture of apology, took out his
office book presently, and began to read.

Percy looked at him with an immense envy. Ah! if only he
were as old as that! He could bear a year or two more of this
misery, but not fifty years, he thought. It was an almost endless vista that (even if things went well) opened before him,
of continual strife, self-repression, energy, misrepresentation
from his enemies. The Church was sinking further every day.
What if this new spasm of fervour were no more that the
dying flare of faith? How could he bear that? He would have
to see the tide of atheism rise higher and more triumphant
every day; Felsenburgh had given it an impetus of whose end
there was no prophesying. Never before had a single man
wielded the full power of democracy. Then once more he
looked forward to the morrow. Oh! if it could end in death!
… *Beati mortui qui in domino moriuntur!* …

It was no good; it was cowardly to think in this fashion.
After all, God was God—He takes up the isles as a very little
thing.

Percy took out his office book, found Prime and
St. Sylvester, signed himself with the cross, and began to pray.
A minute later the two chaplains slipped in once more and sat
down; and all was silent, save for that throb of the screw, and
the strange whispering rush of air outside.

III

It was about nineteen o'clock that the ruddy English conductor looked in at the doorway, waking Percy from his doze.

"Dinner will be served in half-an-hour, gentlemen," he said (speaking Esperanto, as the rule was on international cars). "We do not stop at Turin to-night."

He shut the door and went out, and the sound of closing doors came down the corridor as he made the same announcement to each compartment.

There were no passengers to descend at Turin, then, reflected Percy; and no doubt a wireless message had been received that there were none to come on board either. That was good news: it would give him more time in London. It might even enable Cardinal Steinmann to catch an earlier volor from Paris to Berlin; but he was not sure how they ran. It was a pity that the German had not been able to catch the thirteen o'clock from Rome to Berlin direct. So he calculated, in a kind of superficial insensibility.

He stood up presently to stretch himself. Then he passed out and along the corridor to the lavatory to wash his hands.

He became fascinated by the view as he stood before the basin at the rear of the car, for even now they were passing over Turin. It was a blur of light, vivid and beautiful, that shone beneath him in the midst of this gulf of darkness, sweeping away southwards into the gloom as the car sped on towards the Alps. How little, he thought, seemed this great city seen from above; and yet, how mighty it was! It was from that glimmer, already five miles behind, that Italy was controlled; in one of these dolls' houses of which he had caught but a glimpse, men sat in council over souls and bodies, and abolished God, and smiled at His Church. And God allowed it all,

and made no sign. It was there that Felsenburgh had been, a
month or two ago—Felsenburgh, his double! And again the
mental sword tore and stabbed at his heart.

A few minutes later, the four ecclesiastics were sitting
at their round table in a little screened compartment of the
dining-room in the bows of the air-ship. It was an excellent
dinner, served, as usual, from the kitchen in the bowels of the
volor, and rose, course by course, with a smooth click, into
the centre of the table. There was a bottle of red wine to each
dinner, and both table and chairs swung easily to the very
slight motion of the ship. But they did not talk much, for
there was only one subject possible to the two cardinals, and
the chaplains had not yet been admitted into the full secret.

It was growing cold now, and even the hot-air footrests
did not quite compensate for the deathly iciness of the breath
that began to stream down from the Alps, which the ship was
now approaching at a slight incline. It was necessary to rise
at least nine thousand feet from the usual level, in order to
pass the frontier of the Mont Cenis at a safe angle; and at the
same time it was necessary to go a little slower over the Alps
themselves, owing to the extreme rarity of the air, and the difficulty in causing the screw to revolve sufficiently quickly to
counteract it.

"There will be clouds to-night," said a voice clear and distinct from the passage, as the door swung slightly to a movement of the car.

Percy got up and closed it.

The German Cardinal began to grow a little fidgety
towards the end of dinner.

"I shall go back," he said at last. "I shall be better in my
fur rug."

His chaplain dutifully went after him, leaving his own dinner unfinished, and Percy was left alone with Father Corkran, his English chaplain lately from Scotland.

He finished his wine, ate a couple of figs, and then sat staring out through the plate-glass window in front.

"Ah!" he said. "Excuse me, father. There are the Alps at last."

The front of the car consisted of three divisions, in the centre of one of which stood the steersman, his eyes looking straight ahead, and his hands upon the wheel. On either side of him, separated from him by aluminium walls, was contrived a narrow slip of a compartment, with a long curved window at the height of a man's eyes, through which a magnificent view could be obtained. It was to one of these that Percy went, passing along the corridor, and seeing through half-opened doors other parties still over their wine. He pushed the spring door on the left and went through.

He had crossed the Alps three times before in his life, and well remembered the extraordinary effect they had had on him, especially as he had once seen them from a great altitude upon a clear day—an eternal, immeasurable sea of white ice, broken by hummocks and wrinkles that from below were soaring peaks named and reverenced; and, beyond, the spherical curve of the earth's edge that dropped in a haze of air into unutterable space. But this time they seemed more amazing than ever, and he looked out on them with the interest of a sick child.

The car was now ascending rapidly towards the pass up across the huge tumbled slopes, ravines, and cliffs that lie like outworks of the enormous wall. Seen from this great height they were in themselves comparatively insignificant, but they at least suggested the vastness of the bastions of which they

were no more that buttresses. As Percy turned, he could see
the moonless sky alight with frosty stars, and the dimness of
the illumination made the scene even more impressive; but as
he turned again, there was a change. The vast air about him
seemed now to be perceived through frosted glass. The velvet
blackness of the pine forests had faded to heavy grey, the pale
glint of water and ice seen and gone again in a moment, the
monstrous nakedness of rock spires and slopes, rising towards
him and sliding away again beneath with a crawling motion—
all these had lost their distinctness of outline, and were veiled
in invisible white. As he looked yet higher to right and left
the sight became terrifying, for the giant walls of rock rushing towards him, the huge grotesque shapes towering on all
sides, ran upward into a curtain of cloud visible only from the
dancing radiance thrown upon it by the brilliantly lighted car.
Even as he looked, two straight fingers of splendour, resembling horns, shot out, as the bow searchlights were turned on;
and the car itself, already travelling at half-speed, dropped to
quarter-speed, and began to sway softly from side to side as
the huge air-planes beat the mist through which they moved,
and the antennae of light pierced it. Still up they went, and
on—yet swift enough to let Percy see one great pinnacle rear
itself, elongate, sink down into a cruel needle, and vanish
into nothingness a thousand feet below. The motion grew yet
more nauseous, as the car moved up at a sharp angle preserv-
ing its level, simultaneously rising, advancing and swaying.
Once, hoarse and sonorous, an unfrozen torrent roared like
a beast, it seemed within twenty yards, and was dumb again
on the instant. Now, too, the horns began to cry, long, lamentable hootings, ringing sadly in that echoing desolation like
the wail of wandering souls; and as Percy, awed beyond feeling, wiped the gathering moisture from the glass, and stared

again, it appeared as if he floated now, motionless except for the slight rocking beneath his feet, in a world of whiteness, as remote from earth as from heaven, poised in hopeless infinite space, blind, alone, frozen, lost in a white hell of desolation.

Once, as he stared, a huge whiteness moved towards him through the veil, slid slowly sideways and down, disclosing, as the car veered, a gigantic slope smooth as oil, with one cluster of black rock cutting it like the fingers of a man's hand groping from a mountainous wave.

Then, as once more the car cried aloud like a lost sheep, there answered it, it seemed scarcely ten yards away, first one windy scream of dismay, another and another; a clang of bells, a chorus broke out; and the air was full of the beating of wings.

IV

There was one horrible instant before a clang of a bell, the answering scream, and a whirling motion showed that the steersman was alert. Then like a stone the car dropped, and Percy clutched at the rail before him to steady the terrible sensation of falling into emptiness. He could hear behind him the crash of crockery, the bumping of heavy bodies, and as the car again checked on its wide wings, a rush of footsteps broke out and a cry or two of dismay. Outside, but high and far away, the hooting went on; the air was full of it; and in a flash he recognised that it could not be one or ten or twenty cars, but at least a hundred that had answered the call, and that somewhere overhead were hooting and flapping. The invisible ravines and cliffs on all sides took up the crying; long wails whooped and moaned and died amid a clash of bells, further and further every instant, but now in every direction, behind, above, in front, and far to right and left. Once more the car began to move, sinking in a long still curve towards the face of the mountain; and as it checked, and began to sway again on its huge wings, he turned to the door, seeing as he did so, through the cloudy windows in the glow of light a spire of rock not thirty feet below rising from the mist, and one smooth shoulder of snow curving away into invisibility.

Within, the car shewed brutal signs of the sudden check: the doors of the dining compartments, as he passed along, were flung wide; glasses, plates, pools of wine and tumbled fruit rolled to and fro on the heaving floors; one man, sitting helplessly on the ground, rolled vacant, terrified eyes upon the priest. He glanced in at the door through which he had come just now, and Father Corkran staggered up from his seat and came towards him, reeling at the motion underfoot; simultaneously there was a rush from the opposite door, where a party of Americans had been dining; and as Percy, beckoning with his head, turned again to go down to the stern-end of the ship, he found the narrow passage blocked with the crowd that had run out. A babble of talking and cries made questions impossible; and Percy, with his chaplain behind him, gripped the aluminium panelling, and step by step began to make his way in search of his friends.

Half-way down the passage, as he pushed and struggled, a voice made itself heard above the din; and in the momentary silence that followed, again sounded the far-away crying of the volors overhead.

"Seats, gentlemen, seats," roared the voice. "We are moving immediately."

Then the crowd melted as the conductor came through, red-faced and determined, and Percy, springing into his wake, found his way clear to the stern.

The Cardinal seemed none the worse. He had been asleep, he explained, and saved himself in time from rolling on to the floor; but his old face twitched as he talked.

"But what is it?" he said. "What is the meaning?"

Father Bechlin related how he had actually seen one of the troop of volors within five yards of the window; it was crowded with faces, he said, from stem to stern. Then it had soared suddenly, and vanished in whorls of mist.

Percy shook his head, saying nothing. He had no explanation.

"They are inquiring, I understand," said Father Bechlin again. "The conductor was at his instrument just now."

There was nothing to be seen from the windows now. Only, as Percy stared out, still dazed with the shock, he saw the cruel needle of rock wavering beneath as if seen through water, and the huge shoulder of snow swaying softly up and down. It was quieter outside. It appeared that the flock had passed, only somewhere from an infinite height still sounded a fitful wailing, as if a lonely bird were wandering, lost in space.

"That is the signalling volor," murmured Percy to himself.

He had no theory—no suggestion. Yet the matter seemed an ominous one. It was unheard of that an encounter with a hundred volors should take place, and he wondered why they were going southwards. Again the name of Felsenburgh came to his mind. What if that sinister man were still somewhere overhead?

"Eminence," began the old man again. But at that instant the car began to move.

A bell clanged, a vibration tingled underfoot, and then, soft as a flake of snow, the great ship began to rise, its movement perceptible only by the sudden drop and vanishing of the spire of rock at which Percy still stared. Slowly the snowfield too began to flit downwards, a black cleft whisked smoothly into sight from above, and disappeared again below, and a moment later once more the car seemed poised in white space as it climbed the slope of air down which it had dropped just now. Again the wind-chord rent the atmosphere; and this time the answer was as faint and distant as a cry from another world. The speed quickened, and the steady throb of the screw began to replace the swaying motion of the wings. Again came the hoot, wild and echoing through the barren wilderness of rock walls beneath, and again with a sudden impulse the car soared. It was going in great circles now, cautious as a cat, climbing, climbing, punctuating the ascent with cry after cry, searching the blind air for dangers. Once again a vast white slope came into sight, illuminated by the glare from the windows, sinking ever more and more swiftly, receding and approaching—until for one instant a jagged line of rocks grinned like teeth through the mist, dropped away and vanished, and with a clash of bells, and a last scream of warning, the throb of the screw passed from a whirr to a rising note, and the note to stillness, as the huge ship, clear at last of the frontier peaks, shook out her wings steady once more, and set out for her humming flight through space.... Whatever it was, was behind them now, vanished into the thick night.

There was a sound of talking from the interior of the car, hasty, breathless voices, questioning, exclaiming, and the authoritative terse answer of the guard. A step came along outside, and Percy sprang to meet it, but, as he laid his hand on the door, it was pushed from without, and to his astonishment the English guard came straight through, closing it behind him.

He stood there, looking strangely at the four priests, with compressed lips and anxious eyes.

"Well?" cried Percy.

"All right, gentlemen. But I'm thinking you'd better descend at Paris. I know who you are, gentlemen—and though I'm not a Catholic——"

He stopped again.

"For God's sake, man—" began Percy.

"Oh! the news, gentlemen. Well, it was two hundred cars going to Rome. There is a Catholic plot, sir, discovered in London——"

"Well?"

"To wipe out the Abbey. So they're going——"

"Ah!"

"Yes, sir—to wipe out Rome."

Then he was gone again.

CHAPTER VII

I

IT WAS nearly sixteen o'clock on the same day, the last day of the year, that Mabel went into the little church that stood in the street beneath her house.

The dark was falling softly layer on layer; across the roofs to westward burned the smouldering fire of the winter sunset, and the interior was full of the dying light.

She had slept a little in her chair that afternoon, and had awakened with that strange cleansed sense of spirit and mind that sometimes follows such sleep. She wondered later how she could have slept at such a time, and above all, how it was that she had perceived nothing of that cloud of fear and fury that even now was falling over town and country alike. She remembered afterwards an unusual busy-ness on the broad tracks beneath her as she had looked out on them from her windows, and an unusual calling of horns and whistles; but she thought nothing of it, and passed down an hour later for a meditation in the church.

She had grown to love the quiet place, and came in often like this to steady her thoughts and concentrate them on the significance that lay beneath the surface of life—the huge principles upon which all lived, and which so plainly were the true realities. Indeed, such devotion was becoming almost recognised among certain classes of people. Addresses were

delivered now and then; little books were being published as
guides to the interior life, curiously resembling the old Catholic books on mental prayer.

She went to-day to her usual seat, sat down, folded her
hands, looked for a minute or two upon the old stone sanctuary, the white image and the darkening window. Then she
closed her eyes and began to think, according to the method
she followed.

First she concentrated her attention on herself, detaching it from all that was merely external and transitory, with-
drawing it inwards ... inwards, until she found that secret
spark which, beneath all frailties and activities, made her a
substantial member of the divine race of human-kind.

This then was the first step.

The second consisted in an act of the intellect, followed
by one of the imagination. All men possessed that spark, she
considered.... Then she sent out her powers, sweeping with
the eyes of her mind the seething world, seeing beneath the
light and dark of the two hemispheres, the countless millions
of mankind—children coming into the world, old men leaving it, the mature rejoicing in it and their own strength. Back
through the ages she looked, through those centuries of crime
and blindness, as the race rose through savagery and superstition to a knowledge of themselves; on through the ages yet
to come, as generation followed generation to some climax
whose perfection, she told herself, she could not fully com-
prehend because she was not of it. Yet, she told herself again,
that climax had already been born; the birthpangs were over;
for had not He come who was the heir of time? ...

Then by a third and vivid act she realised the unity of all,
the central fire of which each spark was but a radiation—that
vast passionless divine being, realising Himself up through

these centuries, one yet many, Him whom men had called God, now no longer unknown, but recognised as the transcendent total of themselves—Him who now, with the coming of the new Saviour, had stirred and awakened and shown Himself as One.

And there she stayed, contemplating the vision of her mind, detaching now this virtue, now that for particular assimilation, dwelling on her deficiencies, seeing in the whole the fulfillment of all aspirations, the sum of all for which men had hoped— that Spirit of Peace, so long hindered yet generated too perpetually by the passions of the world, forced into outline and being by the energy of individual lives, realising itself in pulse after pulse, dominant at last, serene, manifest, and triumphant. There she stayed, losing the sense of individuality, merging it by a long sustained effort of the will, drinking, as she thought, long breaths of the spirit of life and love....

Some sound, she supposed afterwards, disturbed her, and she opened her eyes; and there before her lay the quiet pavement, glimmering through the dusk, the step of the sanctuary, the rostrum on the right, and the peaceful space of darkening air above the white Mother-figure and against the tracery of the old window. It was here that men had worshipped Jesus, that blood-stained Man of Sorrow, who had borne, even on His own confession, not peace but a sword. Yet they had knelt, those blind and hopeless Christians.... Ah! the pathos of it all, the despairing acceptance of any creed that would account for sorrow, the wild worship of any God who had claimed to bear it!

And again came the sound, striking across her peace, though as yet she did not understand why.

It was nearer now; and she turned in astonishment to look down the dusky nave.

It was from without that the sound had come, that strange murmur, that rose and fell again as she listened.

She stood up, her heart quickening a little—only once before had she heard such a sound, once before, in a square, where men raged about a point beneath a platform....

She stepped swiftly out of her seat, passed down the aisle, drew back the curtains beneath the west window, lifted the latch and stepped out.

The street, from where she looked over the railings that barred the entrance to the church, seemed unusually empty and dark. To right and left stretched the houses, overhead the darkening sky was flushed with rose; but it seemed as if the public lights had been forgotten. There was not a living being to be seen.

She had put her hand on the latch of the gate, to open it and go out, when a sudden patter of footsteps made her hesitate; and the next instant a child appeared panting, breathless and terrified, running with her hands before her.

"They're coming, they're coming," sobbed the child, seeing the face looking at her. Then she clung to the bars, staring over her shoulder.

Mabel lifted the latch in an instant; the child sprang in, ran to the door and beat against it, then turning, seized her dress and cowered against her. Mabel shut the gate.

"There, there," she said. "Who is it? Who are coming?"

But the child hid her face, drawing at the kindly skirts; and the next moment came the roar of voices and the trampling of footsteps.

It was not more than a few seconds before the heralds of that grim procession came past. First came a flying squadron of children, laughing, terrified, fascinated, screaming, turning their heads as they ran, with a dog or two yelping among them, and a few women drifting sideways along the pavements. A face of a man, Mabel saw as she glanced in terror upwards, had appeared at the windows opposite, pale and eager—some invalid no doubt dragging himself to see. One group—a well-dressed man in grey, a couple of women carrying babies, a solemn-faced boy—halted immediately before her on the other side of the railings, all talking, none listening, and these too turned their faces to the road on the left, up which every instant the clamour and trampling grew. Yet she could not ask. Her lips moved; but no sound came from them. She was one incarnate apprehension. Across her intense fixity moved pictures of no importance—of Oliver as he had been at breakfast, of her own bedroom with its softened paper, of the dark sanctuary and the white figure on which she had looked just now.

They were coming thicker now; a troop of young men with their arms linked swayed into sight, all talking or crying aloud, none listening—all across the roadway, and behind them surged the crowd, like a wave in a stone-fenced channel, male scarcely distinguishable from female in that pack of faces, and under that sky that grew darker every instant. Except for the noise, which Mabel now hardly noticed, so thick and incessant it was, so complete her concentration in the sense of sight—except for that, it might have been, from its suddenness and overwhelming force, some mob of phantoms trooping on a sudden out of some vista of the spiritual world visible across an open space, and about to vanish again in obscurity. That empty street was full now on this side and that so far as she could see; the young men were gone—running or walking she hardly knew—round the corner to

the right, and the entire space was one stream of heads and
faces, pressing so fiercely that the group at the railings were
detached like weeds and drifted too, sideways, clutching at
the bars, and swept away too and vanished. And all the while
the child tugged and tore at her skirts.

Certain things began to appear now above the heads of
the crowd—objects she could not distinguish in the failing
light—poles, and fantastic shapes, fragments of stuff resembling banners, moving as if alive, turning from side to side,
borne from beneath.

Faces, distorted with passion, looked at her from time to
time as the moving show went past, open mouths cried at
her; but she hardly saw them. She was watching those strange
emblems, straining her eyes through the dusk, striving to distinguish the battered broken shapes, half-guessing, yet afraid
to guess.

Then, on a sudden, from the hidden lamps beneath the
eaves, light leaped into being—that strong, sweet, familiar
light, generated by the great engines underground that, in the
passion of that catastrophic day, all men had forgotten; and
in a moment all changed from a mob of phantoms and shapes
into a pitiless reality of life and death.

Before her moved a great rood, with a figure upon it, of
which one arm hung from the nailed hand, swinging as it
went; an embroidery streamed behind with the swiftness of
the motion.

And next after it came the naked body of a child, impaled,
white and ruddy, the head fallen upon the breast, and the
arms, too, dangling and turning.

And next the figure of a man, hanging by the neck,
dressed it seemed, in a kind of black gown and cape, with its
black capped head twisting from the twisting rope.

II

The same night Oliver Brand came home about an hour before midnight.

For himself, what he had heard and seen that day was still too vivid and too imminent for him to judge of it coolly. He had seen, from his windows in Whitehall, Parliament Square filled with a mob the like of which had not been known in England since the days of Christianity—a mob full of a fury that could scarcely draw its origin except from sources beyond the reach of sense. Thrice during the hours that followed the publication of the Catholic plot and the outbreak of mob-law he had communicated with the Prime Minister asking whether nothing could be done to allay the tumult; and on both occasions he had received the doubtful answer that what could be done would be done, that force was inadmissible at present; but that the police were doing all that was possible.

As regarded the despatch of the volors to Rome, he had assented by silence, as had the rest of the Council. That was, Snowford had said, a judicial punitive act, regrettable but necessary. Peace, in this instance, could not be secured except on terms of war—or rather, since war was obsolete—by the sternness of justice. These Catholics had shown themselves the avowed enemies of society; very well, then society must defend itself, at least this once. Man was still human. And Oliver had listened and said nothing.

As he passed in one of the Government volors over London on his way home, he had caught more than one glimpse of what was proceeding beneath him. The streets were as bright as day, shadowless and clear in the white light, and every roadway was a crawling serpent. From beneath rose up a steady roar of voices, soft and woolly, punctuated by cries.

From here and there ascended the smoke of burning; and once, as he flitted over one of the great squares to the south of Battersea, he had seen as it were a scattered squadron of ants running as if in fear or pursuit…. He knew what was happening…. Well, after all, man was not yet perfectly civilised.

He did not like to think of what awaited him at home. Once, about five hours earlier, he had listened to his wife's voice through the telephone, and what he had heard had nearly caused him to leave all and go to her. Yet he was scarcely prepared for what he found.

As he came into the sitting-room, there was no sound, except that far-away hum from the seething streets below. The room seemed strangely dark and cold; the only light that entered was through one of the windows from which the curtains were withdrawn, and, silhouetted against the luminous sky beyond, was the upright figure of a woman, looking and listening….

He pressed the knob of the electric light; and Mabel turned slowly towards him. She was in her day-dress, with a cloak thrown over her shoulders, and her face was almost as that of a stranger. It was perfectly colourless, her lips were compressed and her eyes full of an emotion which he could not interpret. It might equally have been anger, terror or misery.

She stood there in the steady light, motionless, looking at him.

For a moment he did not trust himself to speak. He passed across to the window, closed it and drew the curtains. Then he took that rigid figure gently by the arm.

"Mabel," he said, "Mabel."

She submitted to be drawn towards the sofa, but there was no response to his touch. He sat down and looked up at her with a kind of despairing apprehension.

"My dear, I am tired out," he said.

Still she looked at him. There was in her pose that rigidity that actors simulate; yet he knew it for the real thing. He had seen that silence once or twice before in the presence of a horror—once at any rate, at the sight of a splash of blood on her shoe.

"Well, my darling, sit down, at least," he said.

She obeyed him mechanically—sat, and still stared at him. In the silence once more that soft roar rose and died from the invisible world of tumult outside the windows. Within here all was quiet. He knew perfectly that two things strove within her, her loyalty to her faith and her hatred of those crimes in the name of justice. As he looked on her he saw that these two were at death grips, that hatred was prevailing, and that she herself was little more than a passive battlefield. Then, as with a long-drawn howl of a wolf, there surged and sank the voices of the mob a mile away, the tension broke.... She threw herself forward towards him, he caught her by the wrists, and so she rested, clasped in his arms, her face and bosom on his knees, and her whole body torn by emotion.

For a full minute neither spoke. Oliver understood well enough, yet at present he had no words. He only drew her a little closer to himself, kissed her hair two or three times, and settled himself to hold her. He began to rehearse what he must say presently.

Then she raised her flushed face for an instant, looked at him passionately, dropped her head again and began to sob out broken words.

He could only catch a sentence here and there, yet he knew what she was saying....

It was the ruin of all her hopes, she sobbed, the end of her religion. Let her die, die and have done with it! It was

all gone, gone, swept away in this murderous passion of the
people of her faith … they were no better than Christians,
after all, as fierce as the men on whom they avenged themselves, as dark as though the Saviour, Julian, had never come;
it was all lost.… War and Passion and Murder had returned to
the body from which she had thought them gone forever.…
The burning churches, the hunted Catholics, the raging of
the streets on which she had looked that day, the bodies of
the child and the priest carried on poles, the burning churches
and convents.… All streamed out, incoherent, broken by
sobs, details of horror, lamentations, reproaches, interpreted
by the writhing of her head and hands upon his knees. The
collapse was complete.

He put his hands again beneath her arms and raised her.
He was worn out by his work, yet he knew he must quiet her.
This was more serious than any previous crisis. Yet he knew
her power of recovery.

"Sit down, my darling," he said. "There … give me your
hands. Now listen to me."

He made really an admirable defence, for it was what he
had been repeating to himself all day.

Men were not yet perfect, he said; there ran in their veins
the blood of men who for twenty centuries had been Christians.… There must be no despair; faith in man was of the
very essence of religion, faith in man's best self, in what he
would become, not in what at present he actually was. They
were at the beginning of the new religion, not in its maturity;
there must be sourness in the young fruit.… Consider, too,
the provocation! Remember the appalling crime that these
Catholics had contemplated; they had set themselves to strike
the new Faith in its very heart.…

"My darling," he said, "men are not changed in an instant. What if those Christians had succeeded! ... I condemn it all as strongly as you. I saw a couple of newspapers this afternoon that are as wicked as anything that the Christians have ever done. They exulted in all these crimes. It will throw the movement back ten years.... Do you think that there are not thousands like yourself who hate and detest this violence? ... But what does faith mean, except that we know that mercy will prevail? Faith, patience and hope—these are our weapons."

He spoke with passionate conviction, his eyes fixed on hers, in a fierce endeavour to give her his own confidence, and to reassure the remnants of his own doubtfulness. It was true that he too hated what she hated, yet he saw things she did not.... Well, well, he told himself, he must remember that she was a woman.

The look of frantic horror passed slowly out of her eyes, giving way to acute misery as he talked, and as his personality once more began to dominate her own. But it was not yet over.

"But the volors," she cried, "the volors! That is deliberate; that is not the work of the mob."

"My darling, it is no more deliberate than the other. We are all human, we are all immature. Yes, the Council permitted it, ... permitted it, remember. The German Government, too, had to yield. We must tame nature slowly, we must not break it."

He talked again for a few minutes, repeating his arguments, soothing, reassuring, encouraging; and he saw that he was beginning to prevail. But she returned to one of his words.

"Permitted it! And you permitted it."

"Dear; I said nothing, either for it or against. I tell you

that if we had forbidden it there would have been yet more murder, and the people would have lost their rulers. We were passive, since we could do nothing."

"Ah! but it would have been better to die…. Oh, Oliver let me die at least! I cannot bear it."

By her hands which he still held he drew her nearer yet to himself.

"Sweetheart," he said gravely, "cannot you trust me a little? If I could tell you all that passed to-day, you would understand. But trust me that I am not heartless. And what of Julian Felsenburgh?"

For a moment he saw hesitation in her eyes; her loyalty to him and her loathing of all that had happened strove within her. Then once again loyalty prevailed, the name of Felsenburgh weighed down the balance, and trust came back with a flood of tears.

"Oh, Oliver," she said, "I know I trust you. But I am so weak, and all is so terrible. And He so strong and merciful. And will He be with us to-morrow?"

It struck midnight from the clock-tower a mile away as they yet sat and talked. She was still tremulous from the struggle; but she looked at him smiling, still holding his hands. He saw that the reaction was upon her in full force at last.

"The New Year, my husband," she said, and rose as she said it, drawing him after her.

"I wish you a happy New Year," she said. "Oh help me, Oliver."

She kissed him, and drew back, still holding his hands looking at him with bright tearful eyes.

"Oliver," she cried again, "I must tell you this…. Do you know what I thought before you came?"

He shook his head, staring at her greedily. How sweet she was! He felt her grip tighten on his hands.

"I thought I could not bear it," she whispered—"that I must end it all—ah! you know what I mean."

His heart flinched as he heard her; and he drew her closer again to himself.

"It is all over! it is all over," she cried. "Ah! do not look like that! I could not tell you if it was not."

As their lips met again there came the vibration of an electric bell from the next room, and Oliver, knowing what it meant, felt even in that instant a tremor shake at his heart. He loosed her hands, and still smiled at her.

"The bell!" she said, with a flash of apprehension.

"But it is all well between us again?"

Her face steadied itself into loyalty and confidence.

"It is all well," she said; and again the impatient bell tingled. "Go, Oliver; I will wait here."

A minute later he was back again, with a strange look on his white face, and his lips compressed. He came straight up to her, taking her once more by the hands, and looking steadily into her steady eyes. In the hearts of both of them resolve and faith were holding down the emotion that was not yet dead. He drew a long breath.

"Yes," he said in an even voice, "it is over."

Her lips moved; and that deadly paleness lay on her cheeks. He gripped her firmly.

"Listen," he said. "You must face it. It is over. Rome is gone. Now we must build something better."

She threw herself sobbing into his arms.

CHAPTER VIII

I

LONG BEFORE dawn on the first morning of the New Year the approaches to the Abbey were already blocked. Victoria Street, Great George Street, Whitehall—even Millbank Street itself—were full and motionless. Broad Sanctuary, divided by the low-walled motor-track, was itself cut into great blocks and wedges of people by the ways which the police kept open for the passage of important personages, and Palace Yard was kept rigidly clear except for one island, occupied by a stand which was itself full from top to bottom and end to end. All roofs and parapets which commanded a view of the Abbey were also one mass of heads. Overhead, like solemn moons, burned the white lights of electric globes.

It was not known at exactly what hour the tumult had steadied itself to definite purpose, except to a few weary controllers of the temporary turnstiles which had been erected the evening before. It had been announced a week previously that, in consideration of the enormous demand for seats, all persons who presented their worship-ticket at an authorised office, and followed the directions issued by the police, would be accounted as having fulfilled the duties of citizenship in that respect, and it was generally made known that it was the Government's intention to toll the great bell of the Abbey at the beginning of the ceremony and at the incensing of the image, during which period silence must be as far as possible preserved by all those within hearing.

London had gone completely mad on the announcement of the Catholic plot on the afternoon before. The secret had leaked out about fourteen o'clock, an hour after the betrayal of the scheme to Mr. Snowford; and practically all commercial activities had ceased on the instant. By fifteen-and-a-half all stores were closed, the Stock Exchange, the City offices, the West End establishments—all had as by irresistible impulse suspended business, and from within two hours after noon until nearly midnight, when the police had been adequately reinforced and enabled to deal with the situation, whole mobs and armies of men, screaming squadrons of women, troops of frantic youths, had paraded the streets, howling, denouncing, and murdering. It was not known how many deaths had taken place, but there was scarcely a street without the signs of outrage. Westminster Cathedral had been sacked, every altar overthrown, indescribable indignities performed there. An unknown priest had scarcely been able to consume the Blessed Sacrament before he was seized and throttled; the Archbishop with eleven priests and two bishops had been hanged at the north end of the church, thirty-five convents had been destroyed, St. George's Cathedral burned to the ground; and it was reported even, by the evening papers, that it was believed that, for the first time since the introduction of Christianity into England, there was not one Tabernacle left within twenty miles of the Abbey. "London," explained the *New People*, in huge headlines, "was cleansed at last of dingy and fantastic nonsense."

It was known at about fifteen-and-a-half o'clock that at least seventy volors had left for Rome, and half-an-hour later that Berlin had reinforced them by sixty more. At midnight,

fortunately at a time when the police had succeeded in shep-
herding the crowds into some kind of order, the news was
flashed on to cloud and placard alike that the grim work was
done, and that Rome had ceased to exist. The early morning
papers added a few details, pointing out, of course, the coincidence of the fall with the close of the year, relating how, by
an astonishing chance, practically all the heads of the hierarchy throughout the world had been assembled in the Vatican
which had been the first object of attack, and how these, in
desperation, it was supposed, had refused to leave the City
when the news came by wireless telegraphy that the punitive force was on its way. There was not a building left in
Rome; the entire place, Leonine City, Trastevere, suburbs—
everything was gone; for the volors, poised at an immense
height, had parcelled out the City beneath them with extreme
care, before beginning to drop the explosives; and five minutes after the first roar from beneath and the first burst of
smoke and flying fragments, the thing was finished. The volors had then dispersed in every direction, pursuing the motor
and rail-tracks along which the population had attempted to
escape so soon as the news was known; and it was supposed
that not less than thirty thousand belated fugitives had been
annihilated by this foresight. It was true, remarked the *Studio*,
that many treasures of incalculable value had been destroyed,
but this was a cheap price to pay for the final and complete
extermination of the Catholic pest. "There comes a point," it
remarked, "when destruction is the only cure for a vermin-
infested house," and it proceeded to observe that now that the
Pope with the entire College of Cardinals, all the ex-Royalties
of Europe, all the most frantic religionists from the inhabited world who had taken up their abode in the "Holy City"
were gone at a stroke, a recrudescence of the superstition was

scarcely to be feared elsewhere. Yet care must even now be taken against any relenting. Catholics (if any were left bold enough to attempt it) must no longer be allowed to take any kind of part in the life of any civilised country. So far as messages had come in from other countries, there was but one chorus of approval at what had been done.

A few papers regretted the incident, or rather the spirit which had lain behind it. It was not seemly, they said, that Humanitarians should have recourse to violence; yet not one pretended that anything could be felt but thanksgiving for the general result. Ireland, too, must be brought into line; they must not dally any longer.

It was now brightening slowly towards dawn, and beyond the river through the faint wintry haze a crimson streak or two began to burn. But all was surprisingly quiet, for this crowd, tired out with an all-night watch, chilled by the bitter cold, and intent on what lay before them, had no energy left for useless effort. Only from packed square and street and lane went up a deep, steady murmur like the sound of the sea a mile away, broken now and again by the hoot and clang of a motor and the rush of its passage as it tore eastwards round the circle through Broad Sanctuary and vanished citywards. And the light broadened and the electric globes sickened and paled, and the haze began to clear a little, showing, not the fresh blue that had been hoped for from the cold of the night, but a high, colourless vault of cloud, washed with grey and faint rose-colour, as the sun came up, a ruddy copper disc, beyond the river.

At nine o'clock the excitement rose a degree higher. The police between Whitehall and the Abbey, looking from their high platforms strung along the route, whence they kept watch and controlled the wire palisadings, showed a certain activity, and a minute later a police-car whirled through the square between the palings, and vanished round the Abbey towers. The crowd murmured and shuffled and began to expect, and a cheer was raised when a moment later four more cars appeared, bearing the Government insignia, and disappeared in the same direction. These were the officials, they said, going to Dean's Yard, where the procession would assemble.

At about a quarter to ten the crowd at the west end of Victoria Street began to raise its voice in a song, and by the time that was over, and the bells had burst out from the Abbey towers, a rumour had somehow made its entrance that Felsenburgh was to be present at the ceremony. There was no assignable reason for this, neither then nor afterwards; in fact, the *Evening Star* declared that it was one more instance of the astonishing instinct of human beings *en masse*; for it was not until an hour later that even the Government were made aware of the facts. Yet the truth remained that at half-past ten one continuous roar went up, drowning even the brazen clamour of the bells, reaching round to Whitehall and the crowded pavements of Westminster Bridge, demanding Julian Felsenburgh. Yet there had been absolutely no news of the President of Europe for the last fortnight, beyond an entirely unsupported report that he was somewhere in the East.

And all the while the motors poured from all directions towards the Abbey and disappeared under the arch into Dean's Yard, bearing those fortunate persons whose tickets actually admitted them to the church itself. Cheers ran and rippled along the lines as the great men were recognised—Lord Pemberton,

Oliver Brand and his wife, Mr. Caldecott, Maxwell, Snow-ford, with the European delegates—even melancholy-faced Mr. Francis himself, the Government *ceremoniarius*, received a greeting. But by a quarter to eleven, when the pealing bells paused, the stream had stopped, the barriers issued out to stop the roads, the wire palisadings vanished, and the crowd for an instant, ceasing its roaring, sighed with relief at the relaxed pressure, and surged out into the roadways. Then once more the roaring began for Julian Felsenburgh.

The sun was now high, still a copper disc, above the Victoria Tower, but paler than an hour ago; the whiteness of the Abbey, the heavy greys of Parliament House, the ten thousand tints of house-roofs, heads, streamers, placards began to disclose themselves.

A single bell tolled five minutes to the hour, and the moments slipped by, until once more the bell stopped, and to the ears of those within hearing of the great west doors came the first blare of the huge organ, reinforced by trumpets. And then, as sudden and profound as the hush of death, there fell an enormous silence.

II

As the five-minutes bell began, sounding like a continuous wind-note in the great vaults overhead, solemn and persistent, Mabel drew a long breath and leaned back in her seat from the rigid position in which for the last half-hour she had been staring out at the wonderful sight. She seemed to herself to have assimilated it at last, to be herself once more, to have drunk her fill of the triumph and the beauty. She was as one who looks upon a summer sea on the morning after a storm. And now the climax was at hand.

From end to end and side to side the interior of the Abbey presented a great broken mosaic of human faces; living slopes, walls, sections and curves. The south transept directly opposite to her, from pavement to rose window, was one sheet of heads; the floor was paved with them, cut in two by the scarlet of the gangway leading from the chapel of St. Faith—on the right, the choir beyond the open space before the sanctuary was a mass of white figures, scarved and surpliced; the high organ gallery, beneath which the screen had been removed, was crowded with them, and, far down beneath, the dim nave stretched the same endless pale living pavement to the shadow beneath the west window. Between every group of columns behind the choir-stalls, before her, to right, left, and behind, were platforms contrived in the masonry; and the exquisite roof, fan-tracery and soaring capital, alone gave the eye an escape from humanity. The whole vast space was full, it seemed, of delicate sunlight that streamed in from the artificial light set outside each window, and poured the ruby and the purple and the blue from the old glass in long shafts of colour across the dusty air, and in broken patches on the faces and dresses behind. The murmur of ten thousand voices filled the place, supplying, it seemed, a solemn accompaniment to that melodious note that now pulsed above it. And finally, more significant than all, was the empty carpeted sanctuary at her feet, the enormous altar with its flight of steps, the gorgeous curtain and the great untenanted sedilia.

Mabel needed some such reassurance, for last night, until the coming of Oliver, had passed for her as a kind of appalling waking dream. From the first shock of what she had seen outside the church, through those hours of waiting, with the knowledge that this was the way in which the Spirit of Peace asserted its superiority, up to that last moment when, in her husband's arms, she had learned of the Fall of Rome, it had appeared to her as if her new world had suddenly corrupted about her. It was incredible, she told herself, that this ravening monster, dripping blood from claws and teeth, that had arisen roaring in the night, could be the Humanity that had become her God. She had thought revenge and cruelty and slaughter to be the brood of Christian superstition, dead and buried under the newborn angel of light, and now it seemed that the monsters yet stirred and lived. All the evening she had sat, walked, lain about her quiet house with the horror heavy about her, flinging open a window now and again in the icy air to listen with clenched hands to the cries and the roarings of the mob that raged in the streets beneath, the clanks, the yells and the hoots of the motor-trains that tore up from the country to swell the frenzy of the city—to watch the red glow of fire, the volumes of smoke that heaved up from the burning chapels and convents.

She had questioned, doubted, resisted her doubts, flung out frantic acts of faith, attempted to renew the confidence that she attained in her meditation, told herself that traditions died slowly; she had knelt, crying out to the spirit of peace that lay, as she knew so well, at the heart of man, though overwhelmed for the moment by evil passion. A line or two ran in her head from one of the old Victorian poets:

You doubt
If any one
Could think or bid it?
How could it come about? …
Who did it?

Not men! Not here!
Oh! not beneath the sun....
... The torch that smouldered till the cup o'er-ran
The wrath of God which is the wrath of Man!

She had even contemplated death, as she had told her husband—the taking of her own life, in a great despair with the world. Seriously she had thought of it; it was an escape perfectly in accord with her morality. The useless and ago-nising were put out of the world by common consent; the Euthanasia houses witnessed to it. Then why not she? ... For she could not bear it! ... Then Oliver had come, she had fought her way back to sanity and confidence; and the phan-tom had gone again.

How sensible and quiet he had been, she was beginning to tell herself now, as the quiet influence of this huge throng in this glorious place of worship possessed her once more—how reasonable in his explanation that man was even now only convalescent and therefore liable to relapse. She had told herself that again and again during the night, but it had been different when he had said so. His personality had once more prevailed; and the name of Felsenburgh had finished the work.

"If He were but here!" she sighed. But she knew He was far away.

It was not until a quarter to eleven that she understood that the crowds outside were clamouring for Him too, and that knowledge reassured her yet further. They knew, then, these wild tigers, where their redemption lay; they under-stood what was their ideal, even if they had not attained to it. Ah! if He were but here, there would be no more question:

the sullen waves would sink beneath His call of peace, the
hazy clouds lift, the rumble die to silence. But He was away—
away on some strange business. Well; He knew His work. He
would surely come soon again to His children who needed
Him so terribly.

   She had the good fortune to be alone in a crowd. Her
neighbour, a grizzled old man with his daughters beyond, was
her only neighbour, and a stranger. At her left rose up the
red-covered barricade over which she could see the sanctuary
and the curtain; and her seat in the tribune, raised some eight
feet above the floor, removed her from any possibility of conversation. She was thankful for that: she did not want to talk;
she wanted only to control her faculties in silence, to reassert
her faith, to look out over this enormous throng gathered to
pay homage to the great Spirit whom they had betrayed, to
renew her own courage and faithfulness. She wondered what
the preacher would say, whether there would be any note of
penitence. Maternity was his subject—that benign aspect of
universal life—tenderness, love, quiet, receptive, protective
passion, the spirit that soothes rather than inspires, that bus-
ies itself with peaceful tasks, that kindles the lights and fires of
home, that gives sleep, food and welcome....
   The bell stopped, and in the instant before the music
began she heard, clear above the murmur within, the roar
of the crowds outside, who still demanded their God. Then,
with a crash, the huge organ awoke, pierced by the cry of the
trumpets and the maddening throb of drums. There was no
delicate prelude here, no slow stirring of life rising through
labyrinths of mystery to the climax of sight—here rather was
full-orbed day, the high noon of knowledge and power, the
dayspring from on high, dawning in mid-heaven. Her heart

quickened to meet it, and her reviving confidence, still convalescent, stirred and smiled, as the tremendous chords blared
overhead, telling of triumph full-armed. God was man, then,
after all—a God who last night had faltered for an hour, but
who rose again on this morning of a new year, scattering
mists, dominant over his own passion, all-compelling and all-
beloved. God was man, and Felsenburgh his Incarnation! Yes,
she must believe that! She did believe that!

Then she saw how already the long procession was wind-
ing up beneath the screen, and by imperceptible art the light
grew yet more acutely beautiful. They were coming, then,
those ministers of a pure worship; grave men who knew in
what they believed, and who, even if they did not at this
moment thrill with feeling (for she knew that in this respect
her husband for one did not), yet believed the principles of
this worship and recognised their need of expression for the
majority of mankind—coming slowly up in fours and pairs
and units, led by robed vergers, rippling over the steps, and
emerging again into the coloured sunlight in all their bravery
of Masonic apron, badge and jewel. Surely here was reassurance enough.

The sanctuary now held a figure or two. Anxious-faced
Mr. Francis, in his robes of office, came gravely down the
steps and stood awaiting the procession, directing with almost
imperceptible motions his satellites who hovered about the
aisles ready to point this way and that to the advancing
stream; and the western-most seats were already beginning
to fill, when on a sudden she recognised that something had
happened.

Just now the roaring of the mob outside had provided a
kind of underbass to the music within, imperceptible except

to sub-consciousness, but clearly discernible in its absence; and this absence was now a fact.

At first she thought that the signal of beginning worship had hushed them; and then, with an indescribable thrill, she remembered that in all her knowledge only one thing had ever availed to quiet a turbulent crowd. Yet she was not sure; it might be an illusion. Even now the mob might be roaring still, and she only deaf to it; but again with an ecstasy that was very near to agony she perceived that the murmur of voices even within the building had ceased, and that some great wave of emotion was stirring the sheets and slopes of faces before her as a wind stirs wheat. A moment later, and she was on her feet, gripping the rail, with her heart like an over-driven engine beating pulses of blood, furious and insistent, through every vein; for with a great rushing surge that sounded like a sigh, heard even above the triumphant tumult overhead, the whole enormous assemblage had risen to its feet.

Confusion seemed to break out in the orderly procession. She saw Mr. Francis run forward quickly, gesticulating like a conductor, and at his signal the long line swayed forward, split, recoiled, and again slid swiftly forward, breaking as it did so into twenty streams that poured along the seats and filled them in a moment. Men ran and pushed, aprons flapped, hands beckoned, all without coherent words.

There was a knocking of feet, the crash of an overturned chair, and then, as if a god had lifted his hand for quiet, the music ceased abruptly, sending a wild echo that swooned and died in a moment; a great sigh filled its place, and, in the coloured sunshine that lay along the immense length of the gangway that ran open now from west to east, far down in the distant nave, a single figure was seen advancing.

III

What Mabel saw and heard and felt from eleven o'clock to half-an-hour after noon on that first morning of the New Year she could never adequately remember. For the time she lost the continuous consciousness of self, the power of reflection, for she was still weak from her struggle; there was no longer in her the process by which events are stored, labelled and recorded; she was no more than a being who observed as it were in one long act, across which considerations played at uncertain intervals. Eyes and ears seemed her sole functions, communicating direct with a burning heart.

She did not even know at what point her senses told her that this was Felsenburgh. She seemed to have known it even before he entered, and she watched Him as in complete silence He came deliberately up the red carpet, superbly alone, rising a step or two at the entrance of the choir, passing on and up before her. He was in his English judicial dress of scarlet and black, but she scarcely noticed it. For her, too, no one else existed but He; this vast assemblage was gone, poised and transfigured in one vibrating atmosphere of an immense human emotion. There was no one, anywhere, but Julian Felsenburgh. Peace and light burned like a glory about Him.

For an instant after passing he disappeared beyond the speaker's tribune, and the instant after reappeared once more, coming up the steps. He reached his place—she could see His profile beneath her and slightly to the left, pure and keen as the blade of a knife, beneath His white hair. He lifted one white-furred sleeve, made a single motion, and with a surge and a rumble, the ten thousand were seated. He motioned again and with a roar they were on their feet.

Again there was a silence. He stood now, perfectly still, His hands laid together on the rail, and His face looking steadily before Him; it seemed as if He who had drawn all eyes and stilled all sounds were waiting until His domination were complete, and there was but one will, one desire, and that beneath His hand. Then He began to speak....

In this again, as Mabel perceived afterwards, there was no precise or verbal record within her of what he said; there was no conscious process by which she received, tested, or approved what she heard. The nearest image under which she could afterwards describe her emotions to herself, was that when He spoke it was she who was speaking. Her own thoughts, her predispositions, her griefs, her disappointment, her passion, her hopes— all these interior acts of the soul known scarcely even to herself, down even, it seemed, to the minutest whorls and eddies of thought, were, by this man, lifted up, cleansed, kindled, satisfied and proclaimed. For the first time in her life she became perfectly aware of what human nature meant; for it was her own heart that passed out upon the air, borne on that immense voice. Again, as once before for a few moments in Paul's House, it seemed that creation, groaning so long, had spoken articulate words at last—had come to growth and coherent thought and perfect speech Yet then He had spoken to men; now it was Man Himself speaking. It was not one man who spoke there, it was Man—Man conscious of his origin, his destiny, and his pilgrimage between, Man sane again after a night of madness— knowing his strength, declaring his law, lamenting in a voice as eloquent as stringed instruments his own failure to correspond. It was a soliloquy rather than an oration. Rome had fallen, English and Italian streets had run with blood, smoke and flame had gone up to heaven, because man had for an instant sunk back to the tiger. Yet it was done, cried the great voice, and there was no repentance; it was done, and ages hence man must still do penance and flush scarlet with shame to remember that once he turned his back on the risen light.

There was no appeal to the lurid, no picture of the tumbling palaces, the running figures, the coughing explosions, the shaking of the earth and the dying of the doomed. It was rather with those hot hearts shouting in the English and German streets, or aloft in the winter air of Italy, the ugly passions that warred there, as the volors rocked at their stations, generating and fulfilling revenge, paying back plot with plot, and violence with violence. For there, cried the voice, was man as he had been, fallen in an instant to the cruel old ages before he had learned what he was and why.

There was no repentance, said the voice again, but there was something better; and as the hard, stinging tones melted, the girl's dry eyes of shame filled in an instant with tears. There was something better—the knowledge of what crimes man was yet capable of, and the will to use that knowledge. Rome was gone, and it was a lamentable shame; Rome was gone, and the air was the sweeter for it; and then in an instant, like the soar of a bird, He was up and away—away from the horrid gulf where He had looked just now, from the fragments of charred bodies, and tumbled houses and all the signs of man's disgrace, to the pure air and sunlight to which man must once more set his face. Yet He bore with Him in that wonderful flight the dew of tears and the aroma of earth. He had not spared words with which to lash and whip the naked human heart, and He did not spare words to lift up the bleeding, shrinking thing, and comfort it with the divine vision of love....

Historically speaking, it was about forty minutes before He turned to the shrouded image behind the altar.

"Oh! Maternity!" he cried. "Mother of us all——"

And then, to those who heard Him, the supreme miracle took place.... For it seemed now in an instant that it was no longer man who spoke, but One who stood upon the stage of the superhuman. The curtain ripped back, as one who stood by it tore, panting, at the strings; and there, it seemed, face to face stood the Mother above the altar, huge, white and protective, and the Child, one passionate incarnation of love, crying to her from the tribune.

"Oh! Mother of us all, and Mother of Me!"

So He praised her to her face, that sublime principle of life, declared her glories and her strength, her Immaculate Motherhood, her seven swords of anguish driven through her heart by the passion and the follies of her Son—He promised her great things, the recognition of her countless children, the love and service of the unborn, the welcome of those yet quickening within the womb. He named her the Wisdom of the Most High, that sweetly orders all things, the Gate of Heaven, House of Ivory, Comforter of the afflicted, Queen of the World; and, to the delirious eyes of those who looked on her it seemed that the grave face smiled to hear Him....

A great panting as of some monstrous life began to fill the air as the mob swayed behind Him, and the torrential voice poured on. Waves of emotion swept up and down; there were cries and sobs, the yelping of a man beside himself at last, from somewhere among the crowded seats, the crash of a bench, and another and another, and the gangways were full, for He no longer held them passive to listen; He was rousing them to some supreme act. The tide crawled nearer, and the faces stared no longer at the Son but the Mother; the girl in the gallery tore at the heavy railing, and sank down sobbing upon her knees. And above all the voice pealed on—and the thin hands blanched to whiteness strained from the wide and sumptuous sleeves as if to reach across the sanctuary itself.

It was a new tale He was telling now, and all to her glory. He was from the East, now they knew, come from some triumph. He had been hailed as King, adored as Divine, as was meet and right—He, the humble superhuman son of a Human Mother—who bore not a sword but peace, not a cross but a crown. So it seemed He was saying; yet no man there knew whether He said it or not—whether the voice proclaimed it, or their hearts asserted it.

He was on the steps of the sanctuary now, still with outstretched hands and pouring words, and the mob rolled after him to the rumble of ten thousand feet and the sighing of ten thousand hearts.... He was at the altar; He was upon it. Again in one last cry, as the crowd broke against the steps beneath, He hailed her Queen and Mother.

The end came in a moment, swift and inevitable. And for an instant, before the girl in the gallery sank down, blind with tears, she saw the tiny figure poised there at the knees of the huge image, beneath the expectant hands, silent and transfigured in the blaze of light. The Mother, it seemed, had found her Son at last.

For an instant she saw it, the soaring columns, the gilding and the colours, the swaying heads, the tossing hands. It was a sea that heaved before her, lights went up and down, the rose window whirled overhead, presences filled the air, heaven flashed away, and the earth shook in ecstasy.

Then in the heavenly light, to the crash of drums, above the screaming of the women and the battering of feet, in one thunder-peal of worship ten thousand voices hailed Him Lord and God.

BOOK III—THE VICTORY

CHAPTER I

I

THE LITTLE room where the new Pope sat reading was a model of simplicity. Its walls were whitewashed, its roof unpolished rafters, and its floor beaten mud. A square table stood in the centre, with a chair beside it; a cold brazier laid for lighting, stood in the wide hearth; a bookshelf against the wall held a dozen volumes. There were three doors, one leading to the private oratory, one to the ante-room, and the third to the little paved court. The south windows were shuttered, but through the ill-fitting hinges streamed knife-blades of fiery light from the hot Eastern day outside.

It was the time of the mid-day siesta, and except for the brisk scything of the *cicade* from the hill-slope behind the house, all was in deep silence.

The Pope, who had dined an hour before, had hardly shifted His attitude in all that time, so intent was He upon His reading. For the while, all was put away, His own memory of those last three months, the bitter anxiety, the intolerable load of responsibility. The book He held was a cheap reprint of the famous biography of Julian Felsenburgh, issued a month before, and He was now drawing to an end.

It was a terse, well-written book, composed by an unknown hand, and some even suspected it to be the disguised work of Felsenburgh himself. More, however, considered that it was written at least with Felsenburgh's consent by one of that small body of intimates whom he had admitted to his society—that body which under him now conducted the affairs of West and East. From certain indications in the book it had been argued that its actual writer was a Westerner.

The main body of the work dealt with his life, or rather with those two or three years known to the world, from his rapid rise in American politics and his mediation in the East down to the event of five months ago, when in swift succession he had been hailed Messiah in Damascus, had been formally adored in London, and finally elected by an extraordinary majority to the Tribuniciate of the two Americas.

The Pope had read rapidly through these objective facts, for He knew them well enough already, and was now studying with close attention the summary of his character, or rather, as the author rather sententiously explained, the summary of his self-manifestation to the world. He read the description of his two main characteristics, his grasp upon words and facts; "words, the daughters of earth, were wedded in this man to facts, the sons of heaven, and Superman was their offspring." His minor characteristics, too were noticed, his appetite for literature, his astonishing memory, his linguistic powers. He possessed, it appeared, both the telescopic and the microscopic eye—he discerned world-wide tendencies and movements on the one hand; he had a passionate capacity for detail on the other. Various anecdotes illustrated these remarks, and a number of terse aphorisms of his were recorded. "No man forgives," he said; "he only understands." "It needs supreme faith to renounce a transcendent God." "A man who believes in himself is almost capable of believing in his neighbour." Here was a sentence that to the Pope's mind was significant of that sublime egotism that is alone capable of confronting the Christian spirit: and again, "To forgive a wrong is to condone a crime," and "The strong man is accessible to no one, but all are accessible to him."

There was a certain pompousness in this array of remarks, but it lay, as the Pope saw very well, not in the speaker but in the scribe. To him who had seen the speaker it was plain how they had been uttered—with no pontifical solemnity, but whirled out in a fiery stream of eloquence, or spoken with that strangely moving simplicity that had constituted his first assault on London. It was possible to hate Felsenburgh, and to fear him; but never to be amused at him.

But plainly the supreme pleasure of the writer was to trace the analogy between his hero and nature. In both there was the same apparent contradictoriness—the combination of utter tenderness and utter ruthlessness. "The power that heals wounds also inflicts them: that clothes the dungheap with sweet growths and grasses, breaks, too, into fire and earth-quake; that causes the partridge to die for her young, also makes the shrike with his living larder." So, too, with Felsen-burgh; He who had wept over the Fall of Rome, a month later had spoken of extermination as an instrument that even now might be judicially used in the service of humanity. Only it must be used with deliberation, not with passion.

The utterance had aroused extraordinary interest, since it seemed so paradoxical from one who preached peace and toleration; and argument had broken out all over the world. But beyond enforcing the dispersal of the Irish Catholics, and the execution of a few individuals, so far that utterance had not been acted upon. Yet the world seemed as a whole to have accepted it, and even now to be waiting for its fulfilment.

As the biographer pointed out, the world enclosed in physical nature should welcome one who followed its precepts, one who was indeed the first to introduce deliberately and confessedly into human affairs such laws as those of the Survival of the Fittest and the immorality of forgiveness. If there was mystery in the one, there was mystery in the other, and both must be accepted if man was to develop.

And the secret of this, it seemed, lay in His personality. To see Him was to believe in Him, or rather to accept Him as inevitably true. "We do not explain nature or escape from it by sentimental regrets: the hare cries like a child, the wounded stag weeps great tears, the robin kills his parents; life exists only on condition of death; and these things happen however we may weave theories that explain nothing. Life must be accepted on those terms; we cannot be wrong if we follow nature; rather to accept them is to find peace—our great mother only reveals her secrets to those who take her as she is." So, too, with Felsenburgh. "It is not for us to discriminate: His personality is of a kind that does not admit it. He is complete and sufficing for those who trust Him and are willing to suffer; an hostile and hateful enigma to those who are not. We must prepare ourselves for the logical outcome of this doctrine. Sentimentality must not be permitted to dominate reason."

Finally, then, the writer showed how to this man belonged properly all those titles hitherto lavished upon imagined Supreme Beings. It was in preparation for Him that these types came into the realms of thought and influenced men's lives.

He was the *Creator*, for it was reserved for him to bring into being the perfect life of union to which all the world had hitherto groaned in vain; it was in His own image and like-ness that He had made man.

Yet He was the *Redeemer* too, for that likeness had in one sense always underlain the tumult of mistake and conflict. He had brought man out of darkness and the shadow of death, guiding their feet into the way of peace. He was the *Saviour* for the same reason—*the Son of Man*, for He alone was per-fectly human; He was the *Absolute*, for He was the content of Ideals; the *Eternal*, for he had lain always in nature's potential-ity and secured by His being the continuity of that order; the *Infinite*, for all finite things fell short of Him who was more than their sum.

He was *Alpha*, then, and *Omega*, the beginning and the end, the first and the last. He was *Dominus et Deus noster* (as Domitian had been, the Pope reflected). He was as simple and as complex as life itself—simple in its essence, complex in its activities.

And last of all, the supreme proof of His mission lay in the immortal nature of His message. There was no more to be added to what He had brought to light—for in Him all diverging lines at last found their origin and their end. As to whether or no He would prove to be personally immortal was an wholly irrelevant thought; it would be indeed fitting if through His means the vital principle should disclose its last secret; but no more than fitting. Already His spirit was in the world; the individual was no more separate from his fellows; death no more than a wrinkle that came and went across the inviolable sea. For man had learned at last that the race was all and self was nothing; the cell had discovered the unity of the body; even, the greatest thinkers declared, the conscious-ness of the individual had yielded the title of Personality to the corporate mass of man—and the restlessness of the unit had sunk into the peace of a common Humanity, for nothing but this could explain the cessation of party strife and national competition—and this, above all, had been the work of Felsenburgh.

"*Behold I am with you always,*" quoted the writer in a passionate peroration, "*even now in the consummation of the world; and the Comforter is come unto you. I am the Door—the Way, the Truth and the Life—the Bread of Life and the Water of Life. My name is Wonderful, the Prince of Peace, the Father Everlasting. It is I who am the Desire of all nations, the fairest among the children of men—and of my Kingdom there shall be no end.*"

The Pope laid down the book, and leaned back, closing his eyes.

II

And as for Himself, what had He to say to all this? A Transcendent God Who hid Himself, a Divine Savior Who delayed to come, a Comforter heard no longer in wind nor seen in fire!

There, in the next room, was a little wooden altar, and above it an iron box, and within that box a silver cup, and within that cup—*Something*. Outside the house, a hundred yards away, lay the domes and plaster roofs of a little village called Nazareth; Carmel was on the right, a mile or two away, Thabor on the left, the plain of Esdraelon in front; and behind, Cana and Galilee, and the quiet lake, and Hermon. And far away to the south lay Jerusalem ....

It was to this tiny strip of holy land that the Pope had come—the land where a Faith had sprouted two thousand years ago, and where, unless God spoke in fire from heaven, it would presently be cut down as a cumberer of the ground. It was here on this material earth that One had walked Whom all men had thought to have been He Who would redeem Israel—in this village that He had fetched water and made boxes and chairs, on that long lake that His Feet had walked, on that high hill that He had flamed in glory, on that smooth, low mountain to the north that He had declared that the meek were blessed and should inherit the earth, that peacemakers were the children of God, that they who hungered and thirsted should be satisfied.

And now it was come to this. Christianity had smouldered away from Europe like a sunset on darkening peaks; Eternal Rome was a heap of ruins; in East and West alike a man had been set upon the throne of God, had been acclaimed as divine. The world had leaped forward; social science was supreme; men had learned consistency; they had learned, too, the social lessons of Christianity apart from a Divine Teacher, or, rather, they said, in spite of Him. There were left, perhaps, three millions, perhaps five, at the utmost ten millions—it was impossible to know—throughout the entire inhabited globe who still worshipped Jesus Christ as God. And the Vicar of Christ sat in a whitewashed room in Nazareth, dressed as simply as His master, waiting for the end.

He had done what He could. There had been a week five months ago when it had been doubtful whether anything at all could be done. There were left three Cardinals alive, Himself, Steinmann, and the Patriarch of Jerusalem; the rest lay mangled somewhere in the ruins of Rome. There was no precedent to follow; so the two Europeans had made their way out to the East, and to the one town in it where quiet

still reigned. With the disappearance of Greek Christianity
there had also vanished the last remnants of internecine war
in Christendom; and by a kind of tacit consent of the world,
Christians were allowed a moderate liberty in Palestine. Russia, which now held the country as a dependency, had sufficient sentiment left to leave it alone; it was true that the holy
places had been desecrated, and remained now only as spots
of antiquarian interest; the altars were gone but the sites were
yet marked, and, although Mass could no longer be said there,
it was understood that private oratories were not forbidden.

It was in this state that the two European Cardinals had
found the Holy City; it was not thought wise to wear insignia of any description in public; and it was practically certain even now that the civilised world was unaware of their
existence; for within three days of their arrival the old Patriarch had died, yet not before Percy Franklin, surely under
the strangest circumstances since those of the first century,
had been elected to the Supreme Pontificate. It had all been
done in a few minutes by the dying man's bedside. The two
old men had insisted. The German had even recurred once
more to the strange resemblance between Percy and Julian
Felsenburgh, and had murmured his old half-heard remarks
about the antithesis, and the Finger of God; and Percy, mar-
velling at his superstition, had accepted, and the election was
recorded. He had taken the name of Silvester, the last saint in
the year, and was the third of that title. He had then retired
to Nazareth with his chaplain; Steinmann had gone back to
Germany, and been hanged in a riot within a fortnight of his
arrival.

The next matter was the creation of new cardinals, and
to twenty persons, with infinite precautions, briefs had been
conveyed. Of these, nine had declined; three more had been

approached, of whom only one had accepted. There were therefore at this moment twelve persons in the world who constituted the Sacred College—two Englishmen, of whom Corkran was one; two Americans, a Frenchman, a German, an Italian, a Spaniard, a Pole, a Chinaman, a Greek, and a Russian. To these were entrusted vast districts over which their control was supreme, subject only to the Holy Father Himself.

As regarded the Pope's own life very little need be said. It resembled, He thought, in its outward circumstances that of such a man as Leo the Great, without His worldly importance or pomp. Theoretically, the Christian world was under His dominion; practically, Christian affairs were administered by local authorities. It was impossible for a hundred reasons for Him to do what He wished with regard to the exchange of communications. An elaborate cypher had been designed, and a private telegraphic station organised on His roof communicating with another in Damascus where Cardinal Corkran had fixed his residence; and from that centre messages occasionally were despatched to ecclesiastical authorities elsewhere; but, for the most part, there was little to be done. The Pope, however, had the satisfaction of knowing that, with incredible difficulty, a little progress had been made towards the reorganisation of the hierarchy in all countries. Bishops were being consecrated freely; there were not less than two thousand of them all told, and of priests an unknown number. The Order of Christ Crucified was doing excellent work, and the tales of not less than four hundred martyrdoms had reached Nazareth during the last two months, accomplished mostly at the hands of the mobs.

In other respects, also, as well as in the primary object of the Order's existence (namely, the affording of an opportunity to all who loved God to dedicate themselves to Him more perfectly), the new Religious were doing good work. The more perilous tasks—the work of communication between prelates, missions to persons of suspected integrity—all the business, in fact, which was carried on now at the vital risk of the agent were entrusted solely to members of the Order. Stringent instructions had been issued from Nazareth that no bishop was to expose himself unnecessarily; each was to regard himself as the heart of his diocese to be protected at all costs save that of Christian honour, and in consequence each had surrounded himself with a group of the new Religious—men and women—who with extraordinary and generous obedience undertook such dangerous tasks as they were capable of performing. It was plain enough by now that had it not been for the Order, the Church would have been little better than paralysed under these new conditions.

Extraordinary facilities were being issued in all directions. Every priest who belonged to the Order received universal jurisdiction subject to the bishop, if any, of the diocese in which he might be; Mass might be said on any day of the year of the Five Wounds, or the Resurrection, or Our Lady; and all had the privilege of the portable altar, now permitted to be wood. Further ritual requirements were relaxed; Mass might be said with any decent vessels of any material capable of destruction, such as glass or china; bread of any description might be used; and no vestments were obligatory except the thin thread that now represented the stole; lights were non-essential; none need wear the clerical habit; and rosary, even without beads, was always permissible instead of the Office.

In this manner priests were rendered capable of giving the sacraments and offering the Holy Sacrifice at the least possible risk to themselves; and these relaxations had already proved of enormous benefit in the European prisons, where by this time many thousands of Catholics were undergoing the penalty of refusing public worship.

The Pope's private life was as simple as His room. He had one Syrian priest for His chaplain, and two Syrian servants. He said His Mass each morning, Himself wearing vestments and His white habit beneath, and heard a Mass after. He then took His coffee, after changing into the tunic and burnous of the country, and spent the morning over business. He dined at noon, slept, and rode out, for the country by reason of its indeterminate position was still in the simplicity of a hundred years ago. He returned at dusk, supped, and worked again till late into the night.

That was all. His chaplain sent what messages were necessary to Damascus; His servants, themselves ignorant of His dignity, dealt with the secular world so far as was required, and the utmost that seemed to be known to His few neighbors was that there lived in the late Sheikh's little house on the hill an eccentric European with a telegraph office. His servants, themselves devout Catholics, knew Him for a bishop, but no more than that. They were told only that there was yet a Pope alive, and with that and the sacraments were content.

To sum up, therefore—the Catholic world knew that their Pope lived under the name of Silvester; and thirteen persons of the entire human race knew that Franklin had been His name, and that the throne of Peter rested for the time in Nazareth.

It was, as a Frenchman had said, just a hundred years ago. Catholicism survived; but no more.

III

And as for His inner life, what can be said of that?

He lay now back in his wooden chair, thinking, with closed eyes.

He could not have described it consistently even to Himself, for indeed He scarcely knew it: He acted rather than indulged in reflex thought. But the centre of His position was simple faith. The Catholic Religion, He knew well enough, gave the only adequate explanation of the universe; it did not unlock all mysteries, but it unlocked more than any other key known to man; He knew, too, perfectly well, that it was the only system of thought that satisfied man as a whole, and accounted for him in his essential nature. Further, He saw well enough that the failure of Christianity to unite all men one to another rested not upon its feebleness but its strength; its lines met in eternity, not in time. Besides, He happened to believe it.

But to this foreground there were other moods whose shifting was out of his control. In His *exalté* moods, which came upon Him like a breeze from Paradise, the background was bright with hope and drama—He saw Himself and His companions as Peter and the Apostles must have regarded themselves, as they proclaimed through the world, in temples, slums, market-places and private houses, the faith that was to shake and transform the world. They had handled the Lord of Life, seen the empty sepulchre, grasped the pierced hands of Him Who was their brother and their God. It was radiantly true, though not a man believed it; the huge superincumbent weight of incredulity could not disturb a fact that was as the sun in heaven. Moreover, the very desperateness of the cause was their inspiration. There was no temptation to lean upon the arm of flesh, for there was none that fought for them but God. Their nakedness was their armour, their slow tongues their persuasiveness, their weakness demanded God's strength, and found it. Yet there was this difference, and it was a significant one. For Peter the spiritual world had an interpretation and a guarantee in the outward events he had witnessed. He had handled the Risen Christ, the external corroborated the internal. But for Silvester it was not so. For Him it was necessary so to grasp spiritual truths in the super-natural sphere that the external events of the Incarnation were proved by rather than proved the certitude of His spiritual apprehension. Certainly, historically speaking, Christianity was true—proved by its records—yet to see that needed illu-mination. He apprehended the power of the Resurrection, therefore Christ was risen.

Therefore in heavier moods it was different with him. There were periods, lasting sometimes for days together, clouding Him when He awoke, stifling Him as He tried to sleep, dulling the very savour of the Sacrament and the thrill of the Precious Blood; times in which the darkness was so intolerable that even the solid objects of faith attenuated themselves to shadow, when half His nature was blind not only to Christ, but to God Himself, and the reality of His own existence—when His own awful dignity seemed as the insignia of a fool. And was it conceivable, His earthly mind demanded, that He and His college of twelve and His few thousands should be right, and the entire consensus of the civilised world wrong? It was not that the world had not heard the message of the Gospel; it had heard little else for two thousand years, and now pronounced it false—false in its external credentials, and false therefore in its spiritual claims. It was a lost cause for which He suffered; He was not the last of an august line, He was the smoking wick of a candle of folly; He was the *reductio ad absurdum* of a ludicrous syllogism based on impossible premises. He was not worth killing, He and His company of the insane—they were no more than the crowned dunces of the world's school. Sanity sat on the solid benches of materialism. And this heaviness waxed so dark sometimes that He almost persuaded Himself that His faith was gone; the clamours of mind so loud that the whisper of the heart was unheard, the desires for earthly peace so fierce that supernatural ambitions were silenced—so dense was the gloom, that, hoping against hope, believing against knowledge, and loving against truth, He cried as One other had cried on another day like this—*Eli, Eli, lama sabachthani!* … But that, at least, He never failed to cry.

One thing alone gave Him power to go on, so far at least as His consciousness was concerned, and that was His meditation. He had travelled far in the mystical life since His agonies of effort. Now He used no deliberate descents into the spiritual world: He threw, as it were, His hands over His head, and dropped into spacelessness. Consciousness would draw Him up, as a cork, to the surface, but He would do no more than repeat His action, until by that cessation of activity, which is the supreme energy, He floated in the twilight realm of transcendence; and there God would deal with Him—now by an articulate sentence, now by a sword of pain, now by an air like the vivifying breath of the sea. Sometimes after Communion He would treat Him so, sometimes as He fell asleep, sometimes in the whirl of work. Yet His consciousness did not seem to retain for long such experiences; five minutes later, it might be, he would be wrestling once more with the all but sensible phantoms of the mind and the heart.

There He lay, then, in the chair, revolving the intolerable

blasphemies that He had read. His white hair was thin upon His browned temples, His hands were as the hands of a spirit, and His young face lined and patched with sorrow. His bare feet protruded from beneath His stained tunic, and His old brown burnous lay on the floor beside Him....

It was an hour before He moved, and the sun had already lost half its fierceness, when the steps of the horses sounded in the paved court outside. Then He sat up, slipped His feet into their shoes, and lifted the burnous from the floor, as the door opened and the lean sunburned priest came through.

"The horses, Holiness," said the man.

The Pope spoke not one word that afternoon, until the two came towards sunset up the bridle-path that leads between Thabor and Nazareth. They had taken their usual round through Cana, mounting a hillock from which the long mirror of Gennesareth could be seen, and passing on, always bearing to the right, under the shadow of Thabor until once more Esdraelon spread itself beneath like a grey-green carpet, a vast circle, twenty miles across, sprinkled sparsely with groups of huts, white walls and roofs, with Nain visible on the other side, Carmel heaving its long form far off on the right, and Nazareth nestling a mile or two away on the plateau on which they had halted.

It was a sight of extraordinary peace, and seemed an extract from some old picture-book designed centuries ago. Here was no crowd of roofs, no pressure of hot humanity, no terrible evidences of civilisation and manufactory and strenuous, fruitless effort. A few tired Jews had come back to this quiet little land, as old people may return to their native place, with no hope of renewing their youth, or refinding their ideals, but with a kind of sentimentality that prevails so often

over more logical motives, and a few more barrack-like houses
had been added here and there to the obscure villages in sight.
But it was very much as it had been a hundred years ago.

The plain was half shadowed by Carmel, and half in dusty
golden light. Overhead the clear Eastern sky was flushed with
rose, as it had flushed for Abraham, Jacob, and the Son of
David. There was no little cloud here, as a man's hand, over
the sea, charged with both promise and terror; no sound of
chariot-wheels from earth or heaven, no vision of heavenly
horses such as a young man had seen thirty centuries ago
in this very sky. Here was the old earth and the old heaven,
unchanged and unchangeable; the patient, returning spring
had starred the thin soil with flowers of Bethlehem, and those
glorious lilies to which Solomon's scarlet garments might
not be compared. There was no whisper from the Throne as
when Gabriel had once stooped through this very air to hail
Her who was blessed among women, no breath of promise or
hope beyond that which God sends through every movement
of His created robe of life.

As the two halted, and the horses looked out with steady,
inquisitive eyes at the immensity of light and air beneath
them, a soft hooting cry broke out, and a shepherd passed
below along the hillside a hundred yards away, trailing his
long shadow behind him, and to the mellow tinkle of bells his
flock came after, a troop of obedient sheep and wilful goats,
cropping and following and cropping again as they went on
to the fold, called by name in that sad minor voice of him
who knew each, and led instead of driving. The soft clank-
ing grew fainter, the shadow of the shepherd shot once to
their very feet, as he topped the rise, and vanished again as he
stepped down once more; and the call grew fainter yet, and
ceased.

The Pope lifted His hand to His eyes for an instant, then smoothed it down his face.

He nodded across to a dim patch of white walls glimmering through the violet haze of the falling twilight.

"That place, father," He said, "what is its name?"

The Syrian priest looked across, back once more at the Pope, and across again.

"That among the palms, Holiness?"

"Yes."

"That is Megiddo," he said. "Some call it Armageddon."

CHAPTER II

I

A T TWENTY-three o'clock that night the Syrian priest went out to watch for the coming of the messenger from Tiberias. Nearly two hours previously he had heard the cry of the Russian volor that plied from Damascus to Tiberias, and Tiberias to Jerusalem, and even as it was the messenger was a little late.

These were very primitive arrangements, but Palestine was out of the world—a slip of useless country—and it was necessary for a man to ride from Tiberias to Nazareth each night with papers from Cardinal Corkran to the Pope, and to return with correspondence. It was a dangerous task, and the members of the New Order who surrounded the Cardinal undertook it by turns. In this manner all matters for which the Pope's personal attention was required, and which were too long and not too urgent, could be dealt with at leisure by him, and an answer returned within the twenty-four hours.

It was a brilliant moonlit night. The great golden shield was riding high above Thabor, shedding its strange metallic light down the long slopes and over the moor-like country that rose up from before the house-door—casting too heavy black shadows that seemed far more concrete and solid than the brilliant pale surfaces of the rock slabs or even than the diamond flashes from the quartz and crystal that here and there sparkled up the stony pathway. Compared with this clear splendour, the yellow light from the shuttered house seemed a hot and tawdry thing; and the priest, leaning against the door-post, his eyes alone alight in his dark face, sank down at last with a kind of Eastern sensuousness to bathe himself in the glory, and to spread his lean, brown hands out to it.

This was a very simple man, in faith as well as in life. For him there were neither the ecstasies nor the desolations of his master. It was an immense and solemn joy to him to live here at the spot of God's Incarnation and in attendance upon His Vicar. As regarded the movements of the world, he observed them as a man in a ship watches the heaving of the waves far beneath. Of course the world was restless, he half perceived, for, as the Latin Doctor had said, all hearts were restless until they found their rest in God. *Quare fremuerunt gentes? … Adversus Dominum, et adversus Christum ejus!* As to the end—he was not greatly concerned. It might well be that the ship would be overwhelmed, but the moment of the catastrophe would be the end of all things earthly. The gates of hell shall not prevail: when Rome falls, the world falls; and when the world falls, Christ is manifest in power. For himself, he imagined that the end was not far away. When he had named Megiddo this afternoon it had been in his mind; to him it seemed natural that at the consummation of all things Christ's Vicar should dwell at Nazareth where His King had come on earth—and that the Armageddon of the Divine John should be within sight of the scene where Christ had first taken His earthly sceptre and should take it again. After all, it would not be the first battle that Megiddo had seen. Israel and Amalek had met here; Israel and Assyria; Sesostris had ridden here and Sennacherib. Christian and Turk had contended here, like Michael and Satan, over the place where God's Body had lain.

As to the exact method of that end, he had no clear views; it would be a battle of some kind, and what field could be found more evidently designed for that than this huge flat circular plain of Esdraelon, twenty miles across, sufficient to hold all the armies of the earth in its embrace? To his view once more, ignorant as he was of present statistics, the world was divided into two large sections, Christians and heathens, and he supposed them very much of a size. Something would happen, troops would land at Khaifa, they would stream southwards from Tiberias, Damascus and remote Asia, northwards from Jerusalem, Egypt and Africa; eastwards from Europe; westwards from Asia again and the far-off Americas. And, surely, the time could not be far away, for here was Christ's Vicar; and, as He Himself had said in His gospel of the Advent, *Ubicumque fuerit corpus, illic congregabuntur et aquilae.*

Of more subtle interpretations of prophecy he had no knowledge. For him words were things, not merely labels upon ideas. What Christ and St. Paul and St. John had said— these things were so. He had escaped, owing chiefly to his isolation from the world, that vast expansion of Ritschlian ideas that during the last century had been responsible for the desertion by so many of any intelligible creed. For others this had been the supreme struggle—the difficulty of decision between the facts that words were not things, and yet that the things they represented were in themselves objective. But to this man, sitting now in the moonlight, listening to the far-off tap of hoofs over the hill as the messenger came up from Cana, faith was as simple as an exact science. Here Gabriel had descended on wide feathered wings from the Throne of God set beyond the stars, the Holy Ghost had breathed in a beam of ineffable light, the Word had become Flesh as Mary folded her arms and bowed her head to the decree of

the Eternal. And here once more, he thought, though it was
no more than a guess—yet he thought that already the running of chariot-wheels was audible — the tumult of the host
of God gathering about the camp of the saints—he thought
that already beyond the bars of the dark Gabriel set to his
lips the trumpet of doom and heaven was astir. He might be
wrong at this time, as others had been wrong at other times,
but neither he nor they could be wrong for ever; there must
some day be an end to the patience of God, even though that
patience sprang from the eternity of His nature.

He stood up, as down the pale moonlit path a hundred
yards away came a pale figure of one who rode, with a leather
bag strapped to his girdle.

II

It would be about three o'clock in the morning that the priest
awoke in his little mud-walled room next to that of the Holy
Father's, and heard a footstep coming up the stairs. Last evening he had left his master as usual beginning to open the pile
of letters arrived from Cardinal Corkran, and himself had gone
straight to his bed and slept. He lay now a moment or two, still
drowsy, listening to the pad of feet, and an instant later sat up
abruptly, for a deliberate tap had sounded on the door. Again it
came; he sprang out of bed in his long night-tunic, drew it up
hastily in his girdle, went to the door and opened it.

The Pope was standing there, with a little lamp in one
hand, for the dawn had scarcely yet begun, and a paper in
the other.

"I beg your pardon, Father; but there is a message I must
have sent at once to his Eminence."

Together they went out through the Pope's room, the priest, still half-blind with sleep, passed up the stairs, and emerged into the clear cold air of the upper roof. The Pope blew out His lamp, and set it on the parapet.

"You will be cold, Father; fetch your cloak."

"And you, Holiness?"

The other made a little gesture of denial, and went across to the tiny temporary shed where the wireless telegraphic instrument stood.

"Fetch your cloak, Father," He said again over His shoulder. "I will ring up meanwhile."

When the priest came back three minutes later, in his slippers and cloak, carrying another cloak also for his master, the Pope was still seated at the table. He did not even move His head as the other came up, but once more pressed on the lever that, communicating with the twelve-foot pole that rose through the pent-house overhead, shot out the quivering energy through the eighty miles of glimmering air that lay between Nazareth and Damascus.

This simple priest had scarcely even by now become accustomed to this extraordinary device invented a century ago and perfected through all those years to this precise exactness—that device by which with the help of a stick, a bundle of wires, and a box of wheels, something, at last established to be at the root of all matter, if not at the very root of physical life, spoke across the spaces of the world to a tiny receiver tuned by a hair's breadth to the vibration with which it was set in relations.

The air was surprisingly cold, considering the heat that had preceded and would follow it, and the priest shivered a little as he stood clear of the roof, and stared, now at the motionless figure in the chair before him, now at the vast vault of the sky

passing, even as he looked, from a cold colourless luminosity to
a tender tint of yellow, as far away beyond Thabor and Moab
the dawn began to deepen. From the village half-a-mile away
arose the crowing of a cock, thin and brazen as a trumpet; a
dog barked once and was silent again; and then, on a sudden,
a single stroke upon a bell hung in the roof recalled him in an
instant, and told him that his work was to begin.

The Pope pressed the lever again at the sound, twice,
and then, after a pause, once more—waited a moment for an
answer, and then when it came, rose and signed to the priest
to take his place.

The Syrian sat down, handing the extra cloak to his master, and waited until the other had settled Himself in a chair
set in such a position at the side of the table that the face
of each was visible to the other. Then he waited, with his
brown fingers poised above the row of keys, looking at the
other's face as He arranged himself to speak. That face, he
thought, looking out from the hood, seemed paler than ever
in this cold light of dawn; the black arched eyebrows accentu-
ated this, and even the steady lips, preparing to speak, seemed
white and bloodless. He had His paper in His hand, and His
eyes were fixed upon this.

"Make sure it is the Cardinal," he said abruptly.

The priest tapped off an enquiry, and, with moving lips,
read off the printed message, as like magic it precipitated itself
on to the tall white sheet of paper that faced him.

"It is his Eminence, Holiness," he said softly. "He is alone
at the instrument."

"Very well. Now then; begin."

"We have received your Eminence's letter, and have noted
the news.... It should have been forwarded by telegraphy—
why was that not done?"

The voice paused, and the priest who had snapped off the message, more quickly than a man could write it, read aloud the answer.

" 'I did not understand that it was urgent. I thought it was but one more assault. I had intended to communicate more so soon as I heard more.' "

"Of course it was urgent," came the voice again in the deliberate intonation that was used between these two in the case of messages for transmission. "Remember that all news of this kind is always urgent."

" 'I will remember,' " read the priest. " 'I regret my mistake.' "

"You tell us," went on the Pope, His eyes still downcast on the paper, "that this measure is decided upon; you name only three authorities. Give me, now, all the authorities you have, if you have more."

There was a moment's pause. Then the priest began to read off the names.

" 'Besides the three Cardinals whose names I sent, the Archbishops of Thibet, Cairo, Calcutta and Sydney have all asked if the news was true, and for directions if it is true; besides others whose names I can communicate if I may leave the table for a moment.' "

"Do so," said the Pope.

Again there was a pause. Then once more the names began.

" 'The Bishops of Bukarest, the Marquesas Islands and Newfoundland. The Franciscans in Japan, the Crutched Friars in Morocco, the Archbishops of Manitoba and Portland, and the Cardinal-Archbishop of Pekin. I have despatched two members of Christ Crucified to England.' "

"Tell us when the news first arrived, and how."

" 'I was called up to the instrument yesterday evening at about twenty o'clock. The Archbishop of Sydney was asking, through our station at Bombay, whether the news was true. I replied I had heard nothing of it. Within ten minutes four more inquiries had come to the same effect and three minutes later Cardinal Ruspoli sent the positive news from Turin. This was accompanied by a similar message from Father Petrovski in Moscow. Then——' "

"Stop. Why did not Cardinal Dolgorovski communicate it?"

" 'He did communicate it three hours later.' "

"Why not at once?"

" 'His Eminence had not heard it.' "

"Find out at what hour the news reached Moscow—not now, but within the day."

" 'I will.' "

"Go on, then."

" 'Cardinal Malpas communicated it within five minutes of Cardinal Ruspoli, and the rest of the inquiries arrived before midnight. China reported it at twenty-three.' "

"Then when do you suppose the news was made public?"

" 'It was decided first at the secret London conference, yesterday, at about sixteen o'clock by our time. The Plenipotentiaries appear to have signed it at that hour. After that it was communicated to the world. It was published here half an hour past midnight.' "

"Then Felsenburgh was in London?"

" 'I am not yet sure. Cardinal Malpas tells me that Felsenburgh gave his provisional consent on the previous day.' "

"Very good. That is all you know, then?"

" 'I was called up an hour ago by Cardinal Ruspoli again. He tells me that he fears a riot in Florence; it will be the first of many revolutions, he says.' "

"Does he ask for anything?"

" 'Only for directions.' "

"Tell him that we send him the Apostolic Benediction, and will forward directions within the course of two hours. Select twelve members of the Order for immediate service."

" 'I will. ' "

"Communicate that message also, as soon as we have finished, to all the Sacred College, and bid them communicate it with all discretion to all metropolitans and bishops, that priests and people may know that We bear them in Our heart."

" 'I will, Holiness.' "

"Tell them, finally, that We had foreseen this long ago; that We commend them to the Eternal Father without Whose Providence no sparrow falls to the ground. Bid them be quiet and confident; to do nothing, save confess their faith when they are questioned. All other directions shall be issued to their pastors immediately!"

" 'I will, Holiness.' "

There was again a pause.

The Pope had been speaking with the utmost tranquillity as one in a dream. His eyes were downcast upon the paper, His whole body as motionless as an image. Yet to the priest who listened, despatching the Latin messages, and reading aloud the replies, it seemed, although so little intelligible news had reached him, as if something very strange and great was impending. There was the sense of a peculiar strain in the air, and although he drew no deductions from the fact that apparently the whole Catholic world was in frantic communications with Damascus, yet he remembered his meditations of the evening before as he had waited for the messenger. It seemed as if the powers of this world were contemplating one more step—with its nature he was not greatly concerned.

The Pope spoke again in His natural voice.

"Father," he said, "what I am about to say now is as if I told it in confession. You understand?—Very well. Now begin."

Then again the intonation began.

"Eminence. We shall say the Mass of the Holy Ghost in one hour from now. At the end of that time, you will cause that all the Sacred College shall be in touch with yourself, and waiting for Our commands. This new decision is unlike any that have preceded it. Surely you understand that now. Two or three plans are in Our mind, yet We are not sure yet which it is that Our Lord intends. After Mass We shall communicate to you that which He shall show Us to be according to His Will. We beg of you to say Mass also, immediately, for Our intention. Whatever must be done must be done quickly. The matter of Cardinal Dolgorovski you may leave until later. But We wish to hear the result of your inquiries, especially in London, before mid-day. *Benedicat te Omnipotens Deus, Pater et Filius et Spiritus Sanctus.*"

" '*Amen!* ' " murmured the priest, reading it from the sheet.

III

The little chapel in the house was scarcely more dignified than the other rooms. Of ornaments, except those absolutely essential to liturgy and devotion, there were none. In the plaster of the walls were indented in slight relief the fourteen stations of the Cross; a small stone image of the Mother of God stood in a corner, with an iron-work candlestick before it, and on the solid uncarved stone altar, raised on a stone step, stood six more iron candlesticks and an iron crucifix. A tabernacle, also of iron, shrouded by linen curtains, stood beneath the cross; a small stone slab projecting from the wall served as a credence. There was but one window, and this looked into the court, so that the eyes of strangers might not penetrate.

It seemed to the Syrian priest as he went about his business—laying out the vestments in the little sacristy that opened out at one side of the altar, preparing the cruets and stripping the covering from the altar-cloth—that even that slight work was wearying. There seemed a certain oppression in the air. As to how far that was the result of his broken rest he did not know, but he feared that it was one more of those scirocco days that threatened. That yellowish tinge of dawn had not passed with the sun-rising; even now, as he went noiselessly on his bare feet between the predella and the *prie-dieu* where the silent white figure was still motionless, he caught now and again, above the roof across the tiny court, a glimpse of that faint sand-tinged sky that was the promise of heat and heaviness.

He finished at last, lighted the candles, genuflected, and stood with bowed head waiting for the Holy Father to rise from His knees. A servant's footstep sounded in the court, coming across to hear Mass, and simultaneously the Pope rose and went towards the sacristy, where the red vestments of God who came by fire were laid ready for the Sacrifice.

Silvester's bearing at Mass was singularly unostentatious. He moved as swiftly as any young priest, His voice was quite even and quite low, and his pace neither rapid nor pompous. According to tradition, He occupied half-an-hour *ab amictu ad amictum*; and even in the tiny empty chapel He observed to keep His eyes always downcast. And yet this Syrian never served His Mass without a thrill of something resembling fear; it was not only his knowledge of the awful dignity of this simple celebrant; but, although he could not have expressed it so, there was an aroma of an emotion about the vestmented figure that affected him almost physically—an entire absence of self-consciousness, and in its place the consciousness of some other Presence, a perfection of manner even in the smallest details that could only arise from absolute recollection. Even in Rome in the old days it had been one of the sights of Rome to see Father Franklin say Mass; seminary students on the eve of ordination were sent to that sight to learn the perfect manner and method.

To-day all was as usual, but at the Communion the priest looked up suddenly at the moment when the Host had been consumed, with a half impression that either a sound or a gesture had invited it; and, as he looked, his heart began to beat thick and convulsive at the base of his throat. Yet to the outward eyes there was nothing unusual. The figure stood there with bowed head, the chin resting on the tips of the long fingers, the body absolutely upright, and standing with that curious light poise as if no weight rested upon the feet. But to the inner sense something was apparent; the Syrian could not in the least formulate it to himself; but afterwards he reflected that he had stared expecting some visible or audible manifestation to take place. It was an impression that might be described under the terms of either light or sound; at any instant that delicate vivid force, that to the eyes of the soul burned beneath the red chasuble and the white alb, might have suddenly welled outwards under the appearance of a gush of radiant light rendering luminous not only the clear brown flesh seen beneath the white hair, but the very texture of the coarse, dead, stained stuffs that swathed the rest of the body. Or it might have shown itself in the strain of a long chord on strings or wind, as if the mystical union of the dedicated soul with the ineffable God-head and Humanity of Jesus Christ generated such a sound as ceaselessly flows out with the river of life from beneath the Throne of the Lamb. Or yet once more it might have declared itself under the guise of a perfume—the very essence of distilled sweetness—such a scent as that which, streaming out through the gross tabernacle of a saint's body, is to those who observe it as the breath of heavenly roses....

The moments passed in that hush of purity and peace; sounds came and went outside, the rattle of a cart far away, the sawing of the first *cicada* in the coarse grass twenty yards away beyond the wall; some one behind the priest was breathing short and thick under the pressure of an intolerable emotion, and yet the figure stood there still, without a movement or sway to break the carved motionlessness of the alb-folds or the perfect poise of the white-shod feet. When He moved at last to uncover the Precious Blood, to lay His hands on the altar and adore, it was as if a statue had stirred into life; to the server it was very nearly as a shock.

Again, when the chalice was empty, that first impression reasserted itself; the human and the external died in the embrace of the Divine and Invisible, and once more silence lived and glowed.... And again as the spiritual energy sank back again into its origin, Silvester stretched out the chalice.

With knees that shook and eyes wide in expectation, the priest rose, adored, and went to the credence.

It was customary after the Pope's Mass that the priest himself should offer the Sacrifice in his presence, but to-day so soon as the vestments had been laid one by one on the rough chest, Silvester turned to the priest.

"Presently," he said softly. "Go up, father, at once to the roof, and tell the Cardinal to be ready. I shall come in five minutes."

It was surely a scirocco-day, thought the priest, as he came up on to the flat roof. Overhead, instead of the clear blue proper to that hour of the morning, lay a pale yellow sky darkening even to brown at the horizon. Thabor, before him, hung distant and sombre seen through the impalpable atmosphere of sand, and across the plain, as he glanced behind him, beyond the white streak of Nain nothing was visible except the pale outline of the tops of the hills against the sky. Even at this morning hour, too, the air was hot and breathless, broken only by the slow-stifling lift of the south-western breeze that, blowing across countless miles of sand beyond far-away Egypt, gathered up the heat of the huge waterless continent and was pouring it, with scarcely a streak of sea to soften its malignity, on this poor strip of land. Carmel, too, as he turned again, was swathed about its base with mist, half dry and half damp, and above showed its long bull-head running out defiantly against the western sky. The very table as he touched it was dry and hot to the hand, by mid-day the steel would be intolerable.

He pressed the lever, and waited; pressed it again, and waited again. There came the answering ring, and he tapped across the eighty miles of air that his Eminence's presence was required at once. A minute or two passed, and then, after another rap of the bell, a line flicked out on the new white sheet.

" 'I am here. Is it his Holiness?' "

He felt a hand upon his shoulder, and turned to see Silvester, hooded and in white, behind his chair.

"Tell him yes. Ask him if there is further news."

The Pope went to the chair once more and sat down, and a minute later the priest, with growing excitement, read out the answer.

" 'Inquiries are pouring in. Many expect your Holiness to issue a challenge. My secretaries have been occupied since four o'clock. The anxiety is indescribable. Some are denying that they have a Pope. Something must be done at once.' "

"Is that all?" asked the Pope.

Again the priest read out the answer. " 'Yes and no. The news is true. It will be enforced immediately. Unless a step is taken immediately there will be widespread and final apostasy.' "

"Very good," murmured the Pope, in his official voice. "Now listen carefully, Eminence." He was silent for a moment, his fingers joined beneath his chin as just now at Mass. Then he spoke.

"We are about to place ourselves unreservedly in the hands of God. Human prudence must no longer restrain us. We command you then, using all discretion that is possible, to communicate these wishes of Ours to the following persons under the strictest secrecy, and to no others whatsoever. And for this service you are to employ messengers, taken from the Order of Christ Crucified, two for each message, which is not to be committed to writing in any form. The members of the Sacred College, numbering twelve; the Metropolitans and Patriarchs through the entire world, numbering twenty-two; the Generals of the Religious Orders: the Society of Jesus, the Friars, the Monks Ordinary, and the Monks Contemplative—four. These persons, thirty-eight in number, with the chaplain of your Eminence, who shall act as notary, and my own who shall assist him, and Ourself—forty-one all told—these persons are to present themselves here at Our palace of Nazareth not later than the Eve of Pentecost. We feel Ourselves unwilling to decide the steps necessary to be taken with reference to the new decree, except we first hear the counsel of our advisers, and give them an opportunity of communicating freely one with another. These words, as we have spoken them, are to be forwarded to all those persons whom we have named; and your Eminence will further inform them that our deliberations will not occupy more than four days.

"As regards the questions of provisioning the council and all matters of that kind, your Eminence will despatch today the chaplain of whom we have spoken, who with my own chaplain will at once set about preparations, and your Eminence will yourself follow, appointing Father Marabout to act in your absence, not later than four days hence.

"Finally, to all who have asked explicit directions in the face of this new decree, communicate this one sentence, and no more.

"*Lose not your confidence which hath a great reward. For yet a little while, and He that is to come will come and will not delay.* —Silvester the Bishop, Servant of the Servants of God."

CHAPTER III

I

OLIVER BRAND stepped out from the Conference Hall in Westminster on Friday evening, so soon as the business was over and the Plenipotentiaries had risen from the table, more concerned as to the effect of the news upon his wife than upon the world.

He traced the beginning of the change to the day five months ago when the President of the World had first declared the development of his policy, and while Oliver himself had yielded to that development, and from defending it in public had gradually convinced himself of its necessity, Mabel, for the first time in her life, had shown herself absolutely obstinate.

The woman to his mind seemed to him to have fallen into some kind of insanity. Felsenburgh's declaration had been made a week or two after his Acclamation at Westminster, and Mabel had received the news of it at first with absolute incredulity.

Then, when there was no longer any doubt that he had declared the extermination of the Supernaturalists to be a possible necessity, there had been a terrible scene between husband and wife. She had said that she had been deceived; that the world's hope was a monstrous mockery; that the reign of universal peace was as far away as ever; that Felsenburgh had betrayed his trust and broken his word. There had been an appalling scene. He did not even now like to recall it to his imagination. She had quieted after a while, but his arguments, delivered with infinite patience, seemed to produce very little effect. She settled down into silence, hardly answering him. One thing only seemed to touch her, and that was when he spoke of the President himself. It was becoming plain to him that she was but a woman after all at the mercy of a strong personality, but utterly beyond the reach of logic. He was very much disappointed. Yet he trusted to time to cure her.

The Government of England had taken swift and skilful steps to reassure those who, like Mabel, recoiled from the inevitable logic of the new policy. An army of speakers traversed the country, defending and explaining; the press was engineered with extraordinary adroitness, and it was possible to say that there was not a person among the millions of England who had not easy access to the Government's defence.

Briefly, shorn of rhetoric, their arguments were as follows, and there was no doubt that, on the whole, they had the effect of quieting the amazed revolt of the more sentimental minds.

Peace, it was pointed out, had for the first time in the world's history become an universal fact. There was no longer one State, however small, whose interests were not identical with those of one of the three divisions of the world of which it was a dependency, and that first stage had been accomplished nearly half-a-century ago. But the second stage—the reunion of these three divisions under a common head—an infinitely greater achievement than the former, since the conflicting interests were incalculably more vast—this had been consummated by a single Person, Who, it appeared, had emerged from humanity at the very instant when such a Character was demanded. It was surely not much to ask that those on whom these benefits had come should assent to the will and judgment of Him through whom they had come. This, then, was an appeal to faith.

The second main argument was addressed to reason. Persecution, as all enlightened persons confessed, was the method of a majority of savages who desired to force a set of opinions upon a minority who did not spontaneously share them. Now the peculiar malevolence of persecution in the past lay, not in the employment of force, but in the abuse of it. That any one kingdom should dictate religious opinions to a minority of its members was an intolerable tyranny, for no one State possessed the right to lay down universal laws, the contrary to which might be held by its neighbour. This, however, disguised, was nothing else than the Individualism of Nations, a heresy even more disastrous to the commonwealth of the world than the Individualism of the Individual. But with the arrival of the universal community of interests the whole situation was changed. The single personality of the human race had succeeded to the incoherence of divided units, and with that consummation—which might be compared to a coming of age, an entirely new set of rights had come into being. The human race was now a single entity with a supreme responsibility towards itself; there were no longer any private rights at all, such as had certainly existed, in the period previous to this. Man now possessed dominion over every cell which composed His Mystical Body, and where any such cell asserted itself to the detriment of the Body, the rights of the whole were unqualified.

And there was no religion but one that claimed the equal rights of universal jurisdiction—and that the Catholic. The sects of the East, while each retained characteristics of its own, had yet found in the New Man the incarnation of their ideals, and had therefore given in their allegiance to the authority of the whole Body of whom He was Head. But the very essence of the Catholic Religion was treason to the very idea of man. Christians directed their homage to a supposed supernatural Being who was not only—so they claimed—outside of the world but positively transcended it. Christians, then—leaving aside the mad fable of the Incarnation, which might very well be suffered to die of its own folly—deliberately severed themselves from that Body of which by human generation they had been made members. They were as mortified limbs yielding themselves to the domination of an outside force other than that which was their only life, and by that very act imperilled the entire Body. This madness, then, was the one crime which still deserved the name. Murder, theft, rape, even anarchy itself, were as trifling faults compared to this monstrous sin, for while these injured indeed the Body they did not strike at its heart—individuals suffered, and therefore those minor criminals deserved restraint; but the very Life was not struck at. But in Christianity there was a poison actually deadly. Every cell that became infected with it was infected in that very fibre that bound it to the spring of life. This, and this alone, was the supreme crime of High Treason against man—and nothing but complete removal from the world could be an adequate remedy.

These, then, were the main arguments addressed to that section of the world which still recoiled from the deliberate utterance of Felsenburgh, and their success had been remarkable. Of course, the logic, in itself indisputable, had been dressed in a variety of costumes gilded with rhetoric, flushed with passion, and it had done its work in such manner that as summer drew on Felsenburgh had announced privately that he proposed to introduce a bill which should carry out to its logical conclusion the policy of which he had spoken.

Now, this too, had been accomplished.

II

Oliver let himself into his house, and went straight upstairs to Mabel's room. It would not do to let her hear the news from any but his own lips. She was not there, and on inquiry he heard that she had gone out an hour before.

He was disconcerted at this. The decree had been signed half-an-hour earlier, and in answer to an inquiry from Lord Pemberton it had been stated that there was no longer any reason for secrecy, and that the decision might be communicated to the press. Oliver had hurried away immediately in order to make sure that Mabel should hear the news from him, and now she was out, and at any moment the placards might tell her of what had been done.

He felt extremely uneasy, but for another hour or so was ashamed to act. Then he went to the tube and asked another question or two, but the servant had no idea of Mabel's movements; it might be she had gone to the church; sometimes she did at this hour. He sent the woman off to see, and himself sat down again in the window-seat of his wife's room, staring out disconsolately at the wide array of roofs in the golden sunset light, that seemed to his eyes to be strangely beautiful this evening. The sky was not that pure gold which it had been every night during this last week; there was a touch of rose in it, and this extended across the entire vault so far as he could see from west to east. He reflected on what he had lately read in an old book to the effect that the abolition of smoke had certainly changed evening colours for the worse.... There had been a couple of severe earthquakes, too, in America—he

wondered whether there was any connection.... Then his
thoughts flew back to Mabel....

It was about ten minutes before he heard her footstep on
the stairs, and as he stood up she came in.

There was something in her face that told him that she
knew everything, and his heart sickened at her pale rigidity. There was no fury there—nothing but white, hopeless
despair, and an immense determination. Her lips showed a
straight line, and her eyes, beneath her white summer hat,
seemed contracted to pinpricks. She stood there, closing the
door mechanically behind her, and made no further movement towards him.

"Is it true?" she said.

Oliver drew one steady breath, and sat down again.

"Is what true, my dear?"

"Is it true," she said again, "that all are to be questioned
as to whether they believe in God, and to be killed if they
confess it?"

Oliver licked his dry lips.

"You put it very harshly," he said. "The question is,
whether the world has a right——"

She made a sharp movement with her head.

"It is true then. And you signed it?"

"My dear, I beg you not to make a scene. I am tired out.
And I will not answer that until you have heard what I have
to say."

"Say it, then."

"Sit down, then."

She shook her head.

"Very well, then.... Well, this is the point. The world
is one now, not many. Individualism is dead. It died when
Felsenburgh became President of the World. You surely see

that absolutely new conditions prevail now—there has never been anything like it before. You know all this as well as I do."

Again came that jerk of impatience.

"You will please to hear me out," he said wearily. "Well, now that this has happened, there is a new morality; it is exactly like a child coming to the age of reason. We are obliged, therefore, to see that this continues—that there is no going back—no mortification—that all the limbs are in good health. 'If thy hand offend thee, cut it off,' said Jesus Christ. Well, that is what we say.... Now, for any one to say that they believe in God—I doubt very much whether there is any one who really does believe, or understands what it means—but for any one even to say so is the very worst crime conceivable: it is high treason. But there is going to be no violence; it will all be quite quiet and merciful. Why, you have always approved of Euthanasia, as we all do. Well, it is that that will be used; and——"

Once more she made a little movement with her hand. The rest of her was like an image.

"Is this any use?" she asked.

Oliver stood up. He could not bear the hardness of her voice.

"Mabel, my darling——"

For an instant her lips shook; then again she looked at him with eyes of ice.

"I don't want that," she said. "It is of no use.... Then you did sign it?"

Oliver had a sense of miserable desperation as he looked back at her. He would infinitely have preferred that she had stormed and wept.

"Mabel——" he cried again.

"Then you did sign it?" ...

"I did sign it," he said at last.

She turned and went towards the door. He sprang after her.

"Mabel, where are you going?"

Then, for the first time in her life, she lied to her husband frankly and fully.

"I am going to rest a little," she said. "I shall see you presently at supper."

He still hesitated, but she met his eyes, pale indeed, but so honest that he fell back.

"Very well, my dear…. Mabel, try to understand."

He came down to supper half-an-hour later, primed with logic, and even kindled with emotion. The argument seemed to him now so utterly convincing; granted the premises that they both accepted and lived by, the conclusion was simply inevitable.

He waited a minute or two, and at last went to the tube that communicated with the servants' quarters.

"Where is Mrs. Brand?" he asked.

There was an instant's silence, and then the answer came:

"She left the house half-an-hour ago, sir. I thought you knew."

III

That same evening Mr. Francis was very busy in his office over the details connected with the festival of Sustenance that was to be celebrated on the first of July. It was the first time that the particular ceremony had taken place, and he was anxious that it should be as successful as its predecessors. There were a few differences between this and the others, and it was necessary that the *ceremoniarii* should be fully instructed.

So, with his model before him—a miniature replica of the interior of the Abbey, with tiny dummy figures on blocks that could be shifted this way and that, he was engaged in adding in a minute ecclesiastical hand rubrical notes to his copy of the Order of Proceedings.

When the porter therefore rang up a little after twenty one o'clock, that a lady wished to see him, he answered rather brusquely down the tube that it was impossible. But the bell rang again, and to his impatient question, the reply came up that it was Mrs. Brand below, and that she did not ask for more than ten minutes' conversation. This was quite another matter. Oliver Brand was an important personage, and his wife therefore had significance, and Mr. Francis apologised, gave directions that she was to come to his ante-room, and rose, sighing, from his dummy Abbey and officials.

She seemed very quiet this evening, he thought, as he shook hands with her a minute later; she wore her veil down, so that he could not see her face very well, but her voice seemed to lack its usual vivacity.

"I am so sorry to interrupt you, Mr. Francis," she said. "I only want to ask you one or two questions."

He smiled at her encouragingly.

"Mr. Brand, no doubt——"

"No," she said, "Mr. Brand has not sent me. It is entirely my own affair. You will see my reasons presently. I will begin at once. I know I must not keep you."

It all seemed rather odd, he thought, but no doubt he would understand soon.

"First," she said, "I think you used to know Father Franklin. He became a Cardinal, didn't he?"

Mr. Francis assented, smiling.

"Do you know if he is alive?"

"No," he said. "He is dead. He was in Rome, you know, at the time of its destruction."

"Ah! You are sure?"

"Quite sure. Only one Cardinal escaped—Steinmann. He was hanged in Berlin; and the Patriarch of Jerusalem died a week or two later."

"Ah! very well. Well, now, here is a very odd question. I ask for a particular reason, which I cannot explain, but you will soon understand.... It is this—Why do Catholics believe in God?"

He was so much taken aback that for a moment he sat staring.

"Yes," she said tranquilly, "it is a very odd question. But—" she hesitated. "Well, I will tell you," she said. "The fact is, that I have a friend who is—is in danger from this new law. I want to be able to argue with her; and I must know her side. You are the only priest—I mean who has been a priest—whom I ever knew, except Father Franklin. So I thought you would not mind telling me."

Her voice was entirely natural; there was not a tremor or a falter in it. Mr. Francis smiled genially, rubbing his hands softly together.

"Ah!" he said. "Yes, I see.... Well, that is a very large question. Would not to-morrow, perhaps——?"

"I only want just the shortest answer," she said. "It is really important for me to know at once. You see, this new law comes into force——"

He nodded.

"Well—very briefly, I should say this: Catholics say that God can be perceived by reason; that from the arrangements of the world they can deduce that there must have been an Arranger—a Mind, you understand. Then they say that they deduce other things about God—that He is Love, for example, because of happiness——"

"And the pain?" she interrupted.

He smiled again.

"Yes. That is the point—that is the weak point."

"But what do they say about that?"

"Well, briefly, they say that pain is the result of sin——"

"And sin? You see, I know nothing at all, Mr. Francis."

"Well, sin is the rebellion of man's will against God's."

"What do they mean by that?"

"Well, you see, they say that God wanted to be loved by His creatures, so He made them free; otherwise they could not really love. But if they were free, it means that they could if they liked refuse to love and obey God; and that is what is called Sin. You see what nonsense——"

She jerked her head a little.

"Yes, yes," she said. "But I really want to get at what they think.... Well, then, that is all?"

Mr. Francis pursed his lips.

"Scarcely," he said; "that is hardly more than what they call Natural Religion. Catholics believe much more than that."

"Well?"

"My dear Mrs. Brand, it is impossible to put it in a few words. But, in brief, they believe that God became man—that Jesus was God, and that He did this in order to save them from sin by dying——"

"By bearing pain, you mean?"

"Yes; by dying. Well, what they call the Incarnation is really the point. Everything else flows from that. And, once

a man believes that, I must confess that all the rest follows—
even down to scapulars and holy water."

"Mr. Francis, I don't understand a word you're saying."

He smiled indulgently.

"Of course not," he said; "it is all incredible nonsense.
But, you know, I did really believe it all once."

"But it's unreasonable," she said.

He made a little demurring sound.

"Yes," he said, "in one sense, of course it is—utterly
unreasonable. But in another sense——"

She leaned forward suddenly, and he could catch the glint
of her eyes beneath her white veil.

"Ah!" she said, almost breathlessly. "That is what I want
to hear. Now, tell me how they justify it."

He paused an instant, considering.

"Well," he said slowly, "as far as I remember, they say that
there are other faculties besides those of reason. They say, for
example, that the heart sometimes finds out things that the
reason cannot—intuitions, you see. For instance, they say that
all things such as self-sacrifice and chivalry and even art—all
come from the heart, that Reason comes with them—in rules
of technique, for instance—but that it cannot prove them;
they are quite apart from that."

"I think I see."

"Well, they say that Religion is like that—in other words,
they practically confess that it is merely a matter of emotion."
He paused again, trying to be fair. "Well, perhaps they would
not say that—although it is true. But briefly——"

"Well?"

"Well, they say there is a thing called Faith—a kind of
deep conviction unlike anything else—supernatural—which
God is supposed to give to people who desire it—to people
who pray for it, and lead good lives, and so on——"

"And this Faith?"

"Well, this Faith, acting upon what they call Evidences— this Faith makes them absolutely certain that there is a God, that He was made man and so on, with the Church and all the rest of it. They say too that this is further proved by the effect that their religion has had in the world, and by the way it explains man's nature to himself You see, it is just a case of self-suggestion."

He heard her sigh, and stopped.

"Is that any clearer, Mrs. Brand?"

"Thank you very much," she said, "it certainly is clearer.... And it is true that Christians have died for this Faith, whatever it is?"

"Oh! yes. Thousands and thousands. Just as Mohammedans have for theirs."

"The Mohammedans believe in God, too, don't they?"

"Well, they did, and I suppose that a few do now. But very few: the rest have become esoteric, as they say."

"And—and which would you say were the most highly evolved people—East or West?"

"Oh! West undoubtedly. The East thinks a good deal, but it doesn't act much. And that always leads to confusion—even to stagnation of thought."

"And Christianity certainly has been the Religion of the West up to a hundred years ago?"

"Oh! yes."

She was silent then, and Mr. Francis had time again to reflect how very odd all this was. She certainly must be very much attached to this Christian friend of hers.

Then she stood up, and he rose with her.

"Thank you so much, Mr. Francis .... Then that is the kind of outline?"

"Well, yes; so far as one can put it in a few words."

"Thank you.... I mustn't keep you."

He went with her towards the door. But within a yard of it she stopped.

"And you, Mr. Francis. You were brought up in all this. Does it ever come back to you?"

He smiled.

"Never," he said, "except as a dream."

"How do you account for that, then? If it is all self-suggestion, you have had thirty years of it."

She paused; and for a moment he hesitated what to answer.

"How would your old fellow-Catholics account for it?"

"They would say that I had forfeited light—that Faith was withdrawn."

"And you?"

Again he paused.

"I should say that I had made a stronger self-suggestion the other way."

"I see.... Good-night, Mr. Francis."

She would not let him come down the lift with her, so when he had seen the smooth box drop noiselessly below the level, he went back again to his model of the Abbey and the little dummy figures. But, before he began to move these about again, he sat for a moment or two with pursed lips, staring.

CHAPTER IV

I

A WEEK later Mabel awoke about dawn; and for a moment or two forgot where she was. She even spoke Oliver's name aloud, staring round the unfamiliar room, wondering what she did here. Then she remembered, and was silent....

It was the eighth day she had spent in this Home; her probation was finished: to-day she was at liberty to do that for which she had come. On the Saturday of the previous week she had gone through her private examination before the magistrate, stating under the usual conditions of secrecy her name, age and home, as well as her reasons for making the application for Euthanasia; and all had passed off well. She had selected Manchester as being sufficiently remote and sufficiently large to secure her freedom from Oliver's molestation; and her secret had been admirably kept. There was not a hint that her husband knew anything of her intentions; for, after all, in these cases the police were bound to assist the fugitive. Individualism was at least so far recognised as to secure to those weary of life the right of relinquishing it. She scarcely knew why she had selected this method, except that any other seemed impossible. The knife required skill and resolution; firearms were unthinkable, and poison, under the new stringent regulations, was hard to obtain. Besides, she seriously wished to test her own intentions, and to be quite sure that there was no other way than this....

Well, she was as certain as ever. The thought had first come to her in the mad misery of the outbreak of violence on the last day of the old year. Then it had gone again, soothed away by the arguments that man was still liable to relapse.

Then once more it had recurred, a cold and convincing phantom, in the plain daylight revealed by Felsenburgh's Declaration. It had taken up its abode with her then, yet she controlled it, hoping against hope that the Declaration would not be carried into action, occasionally revolting against its horror. Yet it had never been far away; and finally when the policy sprouted into deliberate law, she had yielded herself resolutely to its suggestion. That was eight days ago; and she had not had one moment of faltering since that.

Yet she had ceased to condemn. The logic had silenced her. All that she knew was that she could not bear it; that she had misconceived the New Faith; that for her, whatever it was for others, there was no hope.... She had not even a child of her own.

Those eight days, required by law, had passed very peacefully. She had taken with her enough money to enter one of the private homes furnished with sufficient comfort to save from distractions those who had been accustomed to gentle living: the nurses had been pleasant and sympathetic; she had nothing to complain of.

She had suffered, of course, to some degree from reactions. The second night after her arrival had been terrible, when as she lay in bed in the hot darkness, her whole sentient life had protested and struggled against the fate her will ordained. It had demanded the familiar things—the promise of food and breath and human intercourse; it had writhed in horror against the blind dark towards which it moved so inevitably; and, in the agony had been pacified only by the half-hinted promise of some deeper voice suggesting that death was not the end. With morning light sanity had come back; the will had reassumed the mastery, and, with it, had withdrawn explicitly the implied hope of continued existence. She had suffered again for an hour or two from a more concrete fear; the memory came back to her of those shocking revelations that ten years ago had convulsed England and brought about the establishment of these Homes under Government supervision—those evidences that for years in the great vivisection-laboratories human subjects had been practised upon—persons who with the same intentions as herself had cut themselves off from the world in private euthanasia-houses, to whom had been supplied a gas that suspended instead of destroying animation.... But this, too, had passed with the return of light. Such things were impossible now under the new system—at least, in England. She had refrained from making an end upon the Continent for this very reason. There, where sentiment was weaker, and logic more imperious, materialism was more consistent. Since men were but animals—the conclusion was inevitable.

There had been but one physical drawback, the intolerable heat of the days and nights. It seemed, scientists said, that an entirely unexpected heat-wave had been generated; there were a dozen theories, most of which were mutually exclusive one of another. It was humiliating, she thought, that men who professed to have taken the earth under their charge should be so completely baffled. The conditions of the weather had of course been accompanied by disasters; there had been earthquakes of astonishing violence, a ripple had wrecked not less than twenty-five towns in America; an island or two had disappeared, and that bewildering Vesuvius seemed to be working up for a *dénouement*. But no one

knew really the explanation. One man had been wild enough
to say that some cataclysm had taken place in the centre of
the earth.... So she had heard from her nurse; but she was
not greatly interested. It was only tiresome that she could not
walk much in the garden, and had to be content with sitting
in her own cool shaded room on the second floor.

There was only one other matter of which she had asked,
namely, the effect of the new decree; but the nurse did not
seem to know much about that. It appeared that there had
been an outrage or two, but the law had not yet been enforced
to any great extent; a week, after all, was a short time, even
though the decree had taken effect at once, and magistrates
were beginning the prescribed census.

It seemed to her as she lay awake this morning, staring
at the tinted ceiling, and out now and again at the quiet
little room, that the heat was worse than ever. For a minute she thought she must have overslept; but, as she touched
her repeater, it told her that it was scarcely after four o'clock.
Well, well; she would not have to bear it much longer; she
thought that about eight it would be time to make an end.
There was her letter to Oliver yet to be written; and one or
two final arrangements to be made.

As regarded the morality of what she was doing—the
relation, that is to say, which her act bore to the common life
of man—she had no shadow of doubt. It was her belief, as of
the whole Humanitarian world, that just as bodily pain occasionally justified this termination of life, so also did mental
pain. There was a certain pitch of distress at which the individual was no longer necessary to himself or the world; it was
the most charitable act that could be performed. But she had
never thought in old days that that state could ever be hers;

Life had been much too interesting. But it had come to this: there was no question of it.

Perhaps a dozen times in that week she had thought over her conversation with Mr. Francis. Her going to him had been little more than instinctive; she did just wish to hear what the other side was—whether Christianity was as ludicrous as she had always thought. It seemed that it was not ludicrous; it was only terribly pathetic. It was just a lovely dream—an exquisite piece of poetry. It would be heavenly to believe it, but she did not. No—a transcendent God was unthinkable, although not quite so unthinkable as a merely immeasurable Man. And as for the Incarnation—well, well!

There seemed no way out of it. The Humanity Religion was the only one. Man was God, or at least His highest manifestations; and He was a God with which she did not wish to have anything more to do. These faint new instincts after something other than intellect and emotion were, she knew perfectly well, nothing but refined emotion itself.

She had thought a great deal of Felsenburgh, however, and was astonished at her own feeling. He was certainly the most impressive man she had ever seen; it did seem very probable indeed that He was what He claimed to be—the Incarnation of the ideal Man, the first perfect product of humanity. But the logic of his position was too much for her. She saw now that He was perfectly logical—that He had not been inconsistent in denouncing the destruction of Rome and a week later making His declaration. It was the passion of one man against another that He denounced—of kingdom against kingdom, and sect against sect—for this was suicidal for the race. He denounced passion, too, not judicial action. Therefore, this new decree was as logical as Himself—it was a judicial act on the part of an united world against a tiny majority that threatened the principle of life and faith: and it was to be carried out with supreme mercy; there was no revenge or passion or partisan spirit in it from beginning to end; no more than a man is revengeful or passionate when he amputates a diseased limb—Oliver had convinced her of that.

Yes, it was logical and sound. And it was because it was so that she could not bear it.... But ah! what a sublime man Felsenburgh was; it was a joy to her even to recall his speeches and his personality. She would have liked to see him again. But it was no good. She had better be done with it as tranquilly as possible. And the world must go forward without her. She was just tired out with Facts.

She dozed off again presently, and it seemed scarcely five minutes before she looked up to see a gentle smiling face of a white-capped nurse bending over her.

"It is nearly six o'clock, my dear—the time you told me. I came to see about breakfast."

Mabel drew a long breath. Then she sat up suddenly, throwing back the sheet.

II

It struck a quarter-past six from the little clock on the mantel-shelf as she laid down her pen. Then she took up the closely written sheets, leaned back in her deep chair, and began to read.

"HOME OF REST,
"NO. 3A MANCHESTER WEST.
"MY DEAR: I am very sorry, but it has come back to me. I really cannot go on any longer, so I am going to escape in

the only way left, as I once told you. I have had a very quiet and happy time here; they have been most kind and considerate. You see, of course, from the heading on this paper, what I mean....

"Well, you have always been very dear to me; you are still, even at this moment. So you have a right to know my reasons so far as I know them myself. It is very difficult to understand myself; but it seems to me that I am not strong enough to live. So long as I was pleased and excited it was all very well—especially when He came. But I think I had expected it to be different; I did not understand as I do now how it must come to this—how it is all quite logical and right. I could bear it, when I thought that they had acted through passion, but this is deliberate. I did not realise that Peace must have its laws, and must protect itself. And, somehow, that Peace is not what I want. It is being alive at all that is wrong.

"Then there is this difficulty. I know how absolutely in agreement you are with this new state of affairs; of course you are, because you are so much stronger and more logical than I am. But if you have a wife she must be of one mind with you. And I am not, any more, at least not with my heart, though I see you are right.... Do you understand, my dear?

"If we had had a child, it might have been different. I might have liked to go on living for his sake. But Humanity, somehow—Oh! Oliver! I can't—I can't.

"I know I am wrong, and that you are right—but there it is; I cannot change myself. So I am quite sure that I must go.

"Then I want to tell you this—that I am not at all frightened. I never can understand why people are—unless, of course, they are Christians. I should be horribly frightened if I was one of them. But, you see, we both *know* that there is nothing beyond. It is life that I am frightened of—not death.

Of course, I should be frightened if there was any pain; but the doctors tell me there is absolutely none. It is simply going to sleep. The nerves are dead before the brain. I am going to do it myself. I don't want any one else in the room. In a few minutes the nurse here—Sister Anne, with whom I have made great friends—will bring in the thing, and then she will leave me.

"As regards what happens afterwards, I do not mind at all. Please do exactly what you wish. The cremation will take place to-morrow morning at noon, so that you can be here if you like. Or you can send directions, and they will send on the urn to you. I know you liked to have your mother's urn in the garden; so perhaps you will like mine. Please do exactly what you like. And with all my things too. Of course I leave them to you.

"Now, my dear, I want to say this—that I am very sorry indeed now that I was so tiresome and stupid. I think I did really believe your arguments all along. But I did not want to believe them. Do you see now why I was so tiresome? ...

"Oliver, my darling, you have been extraordinarily good to me.... Yes, I know I am crying, but I am really very happy. This is such a lovely ending. I wish I hadn't been obliged to make you so anxious during this last week: but I had to—I knew you would persuade me against it, if you found me, and that would have been worse than ever. I am sorry I told you that lie, too. Indeed, it is the first I ever did tell you.

"Well, I don't think there is much more to say. Oliver, my dear, good-bye. I send you my love with all my heart.

"Mabel."

She sat still when she had read it through, and her eyes were still wet with tears. Yet it was all perfectly true. She was far happier than she could be if she had still the prospect of going back. Life seemed entirely blank: death was so obvious an escape; her soul ached for it, as a body for sleep.

She directed the envelope, still with a perfectly steady hand, laid it on the table, and leaned back once more, glancing again at her untasted breakfast.

Then she suddenly began to think of her conversation with Mr. Francis; and, by a strange association of ideas, remembered the fall of the volor in Brighton, the busyness of the priest, and the Euthanasia boxes....

*   *   *   *   *

When Sister Anne came in a few minutes later, she was astonished at what she saw. The girl crouched at the window, her hands on the sill, staring out at the sky in an attitude of unmistakable horror.

Sister Anne came across the room quickly, setting down something on the table as she passed. She touched the girl on the shoulder.

"My dear, what is it?"

There was a long sobbing breath, and Mabel turned, rising as she turned, and clutched the nurse with one shaking hand, pointing out with the other.

"There!" she said. "There—look!"

"Well, my dear, what is it? I see nothing. It is a little dark!"

"Dark!" said the other. "You call that dark! Why, why, it is black—black!"

The nurse drew her softly backwards to the chair, turning her from the window. She recognised nervous fear; but no more than that. But Mabel tore herself free, and wheeled again.

"You call that a little dark," she said. "Why, look, sister, look!"

Yet there was nothing remarkable to be seen. In front rose up the feathery hand of an elm, then the shuttered windows across the court, the roof, and above that the morning sky, a little heavy and dusky as before a storm; but no more than that.

"Well, what is it, my dear? What do you see?"

"Why, why ... look! look!—There, listen to that."

A faint far-away rumble sounded as the rolling of a wagon—so faint that it might almost be an aural delusion. But the girl's hands were at her ears, and her face was one white wide-eyed mask of terror. The nurse threw her arms round her.

"My dear," she said, "you are not yourself. That is nothing but a little heat-thunder. Sit down quietly."

She could feel the girl's body shaking beneath her hands, but there was no resistance as she drew her to the chair.

"The lights! The lights!" sobbed Mabel.

"Will you promise me to sit quietly, then?"

She nodded; and the nurse went across to the door, smiling tenderly; she had seen such things before. A moment later the room was full of exquisite sunlight, as she switched the handle. As she turned, she saw that Mabel had wheeled herself round in the chair, and with clasped hands was still staring out at the sky above the roofs; but she was plainly quieter again now. The nurse came back, and put her hand on her shoulder.

"You are overwrought, my dear.... Now you must believe me. There is nothing to be frightened of. It is just nervous excitement.... Shall I pull down the blind?"

Mabel turned her face.... Yes, certainly the light had reassured her. Her face was still white and bewildered, but the steady look was coming back to her eyes, though, even as she spoke, they wandered back more than once to the window.

"Nurse," she said more quietly, "please look again and tell me if you see nothing. If you say there is nothing I will believe that I am going mad. No; you must not touch the blind."

No; there was nothing. The sky was a little dark, as if a blight were coming on; but there was hardly more than a veil of cloud, and the light was scarcely more than tinged with gloom. It was just such a sky as precedes a spring thunderstorm. She said so, clearly and firmly.

Mabel's face steadied still more.

"Very well, nurse.... Then——"

She turned to the little table by the side on which Sister Anne had set down what she had brought into the room.

"Show me, please."

The nurse still hesitated.

"Are you sure you are not too frightened, my dear? Shall I get you anything?"

"I have no more to say," said Mabel firmly. "Show me, please."

Sister Anne turned resolutely to the table.

There rested upon it a white-enamelled box, delicately painted with flowers. From this box emerged a white flexible tube with a broad mouthpiece, fitted with two leather-covered steel clasps. From the side of the box nearest the chair protruded a little china handle.

"Now, my dear," began the nurse quietly, watching the other's eyes turn once again to the window, and then back—"now, my dear, you sit there, as you are now. Your head right back, please. When you are ready, you put this over your mouth, and clasp the springs behind your head.... So.... it works quite easily. Then you turn this handle, round that way, as far as it will go. And that is all."

Mabel nodded. She had regained her self-command, and understood plainly enough, though even as she spoke once again her eyes strayed away to the window.

"That is all," she said. "And what then?"

The nurse eyed her doubtfully for a moment.

"I understand perfectly," said Mabel. "And what then?"

"There is nothing more. Breathe naturally. You will feel sleepy almost directly. Then you close your eyes, and that is all."

Mabel laid the tube on the table and stood up. She was completely herself now.

"Give me a kiss, sister," she said.

The nurse nodded and smiled to her once more at the door. But Mabel hardly noticed it; again she was looking towards the window.

"I shall come back in half-an-hour," said Sister Anne. Then her eyes caught a square of white upon the centre table. "Ah! that letter!" she said.

"Yes," said the girl absently. "Please take it."

The nurse took it up, glanced at the address, and again at Mabel. Still she hesitated.

"In half-an-hour," she repeated. "There is no hurry at all. It doesn't take five minutes.... Good-bye, my dear."

But Mabel was still looking out of the window, and made no answer.

III

Mabel stood perfectly still until she heard the locking of the door and the withdrawal of the key. Then once more she went to the window and clasped the sill.

From where she stood there was visible to her first the courtyard beneath, with its lawn in the centre, and a couple of trees growing there—all plain in the brilliant light that now streamed from her window; and secondly, above the roofs, a tremendous pall of ruddy black. It was the more terrible from the contrast. Earth, it seemed, was capable of light; heaven had failed.

It appeared, too, that there was a curious stillness. The house was, usually, quiet enough at this hour: the inhabitants of that place were in no mood for bustle: but now it was more than quiet; it was deathly still: it was such a hush as precedes the sudden crash of the sky's artillery. But the moments went by, and there was no such crash: only once again there sounded a solemn rolling, as of some great wain far away; stupendously impressive, for with it to the girl's ears there seemed mingled a murmur of innumerable voices, ghostly crying and applause. Then again the hush settled down like wool.

She had begun to understand now. The darkness and the sounds were not for all eyes and ears. The nurse had seen and heard nothing extraordinary, and the rest of the world of men saw and heard nothing. To them it was no more than the hint of a coming storm.

Mabel did not attempt to distinguish between the subjective and the objective. It was nothing to her as to whether the sights and sounds were generated by her own brain or perceived by some faculty hitherto unknown. She seemed to herself to be standing already apart from the world which she had known; it was receding from her, or, rather, while standing where it had always done, it was melting, transforming itself, passing to some other mode of existence. The strangeness seemed no more strange than anything else—than that … that little painted box upon the table.

Then, hardly knowing what she said, looking steadily upon that appalling sky, she began to speak....

"O God!" she said. "If You are really there—really there——"

Her voice faltered, and she gripped the sill to steady herself. She wondered vaguely why she spoke so; it was neither intellect nor emotion that inspired her. Yet she continued....

"O God, I know You are not there—of course You are not. But if You were there, I know what I would say to You. I would tell You how puzzled and tired I am. No—No—I need not tell You: You would know it. But I would say that I was very sorry for all this. Oh! You would know that too. I need not say anything at all. O God! I don't know what I want to say. I would like You to look after Oliver, of course, and all Your poor Christians. Oh! they will have such a hard time.... God. God—You would understand, wouldn't You?" ...

Again came the heavy rumble and the solemn bass of a myriad voices; it seemed a shade nearer, she thought.... She never liked thunderstorms or shouting crowds. They always gave her a headache....

"Well, well," she said. "Good-bye, everything——"

Then she was in the chair. The mouthpiece—yes; that was it....

She was furious at the trembling of her hands; twice the spring slipped from her polished coils of hair... Then it was fixed ... and as if a breeze fanned her, her sense came back....

She found she could breathe quite easily; there was no resistance—that was a comfort; there would be no suffocation about it.... She put out her left hand and touched the handle, conscious less of its sudden coolness than of the unbearable heat in which the room seemed almost suddenly plunged.

She could hear the drumming pulses in her temples and the roaring of the voices…. She dropped the handle once more, and with both hands tore at the loose white wrapper that she had put on this morning…. Yes, that was a little easier; she could breathe better so. Again her fingers felt for and found the handle, but the sweat streamed from her fingers, and for an instant she could not turn the knob. Then it yielded suddenly….

For one instant the sweet languid smell struck her consciousness like a blow, for she knew it as the scent of death. Then the steady will that had borne her so far asserted itself, and she laid her hands softly in her lap, breathing deeply and easily.

She had closed her eyes at the turning of the handle, but now opened them again, curious to watch the aspect of the fading world. She had determined to do this a week ago: she would at least miss nothing of this unique last experience.

It seemed at first that there was no change. There was the feathery head of the elm, the lead roof opposite, and the terrible sky above. She noticed a pigeon, white against the blackness, soar and swoop again out of sight in an instant….

… Then the following things happened….

There was a sudden sensation of ecstatic lightness in all her limbs; she attempted to lift a hand, and was aware that it was impossible; it was no longer hers. She attempted to lower her eyes from that broad strip of violet sky, and perceived that that too was impossible. Then she understood that the will had already lost touch with the body, that the crumbling world had receded to an infinite distance—that was as she had expected, but what continued to puzzle her was that her

mind was still active. It was true that the world she had known
had withdrawn itself from the dominion of consciousness, as
her body had done, except, that was, in the sense of hearing, which was still strangely alert; yet there was still enough
memory to be aware that there was such a world—that there
were other persons in existence; that men went about their
business, knowing nothing of what had happened; but faces,
names, places had all alike gone. In fact, she was conscious
of herself in such a manner as she had never been before; it
seemed as if she had penetrated at last into some recess of her
being into which hitherto she had only looked as through
clouded glass. This was very strange, and yet it was familiar,
too; she had arrived, it seemed, at a centre, round the circum-
ference of which she had been circling all her life; and it was
more than a mere point: it was a distinct space, walled and
enclosed.... At the same instant she knew that hearing, too,
was gone....

Then an amazing thing happened—yet it appeared to her
that she had always known it would happen, although her
mind had never articulated it. This is what happened.

The enclosure melted, with a sound of breaking, and a
limitless space was about her—limitless, different to everything else, and alive, and astir. It was alive, as a breathing,
panting body is alive—self-evident and overpowering—it was
one, yet it was many; it was immaterial, yet absolutely real—
real in a sense in which she never dreamed of reality....

Yet even this was familiar, as a place often visited in dreams
is familiar; and then, without warning, something resembling
sound or light, something which she knew in an instant to be
unique, tore across it....

Then she saw, and understood....

CHAPTER V

I

OLIVER HAD passed the days since Mabel's disappearance in an indescribable horror. He had done all that was possible: he had traced her to the station and to Victoria, where he lost her clue; he had communicated with the police, and the official answer, telling him nothing, had arrived to the effect that there was no news: and it was not until the Tuesday following her disappearance that Mr. Francis, hearing by chance of his trouble, informed him by telephone that he had spoken with her on the Friday night. But there was no satisfaction to be got from him—indeed, the news was bad rather than good, for Oliver could not but be dismayed at the report of the conversation, in spite of Mr. Francis's assurances that Mrs. Brand had shown no kind of inclination to defend the Christian cause.

Two theories gradually emerged in his mind; either she was gone to the protection of some unknown Catholic, or—and he grew sick at the thought—she had applied somewhere for Euthanasia as she had once threatened, and was now under the care of the Law; such an event was sufficiently common since the passing of the Release Act in 1998. And it was frightful that he could not condemn it.

On the Tuesday evening, as he sat heavily in his room, for the hundredth time attempting to trace out some coherent line through the maze of intercourse he had had with his wife during these past months, his bell suddenly rang. It was the red label of Whitehall that had made its appearance; and for an instant his heart leaped with hope that it was news of her. But at the first words it sank again.

"Brand," came the sharp fairy voice, "is that you? … Yes, I am Snowford. You are wanted at once—at once, you understand. There is an extraordinary meeting of the Council at twenty o'clock. The President will be there. You understand the urgency. No time for more. Come instantly to my room."

Even this message scarcely distracted him. He, with the rest of the world, was no longer surprised at the sudden descents of the President. He came and vanished again without warning, travelling and working with incredible energy, yet always, as it seemed, retaining his personal calm.

It was already after nineteen; Oliver supped immediately, and a quarter-of-an-hour before the hour presented himself in Snowford's room, where half a dozen of his colleagues were assembled.

That minister came forward to meet him, with a strange excitement in his face. He drew him aside by a button.

"See here, Brand, you are wanted to speak first— immediately after the President's Secretary who will open; they are coming from Paris. It is about a new matter altogether. He has had information of the whereabouts of the Pope…. It seems that there is one…. Oh, you will understand presently. Oh, and by the way," he went on, looking curiously at the strained face, "I am sorry to hear of your anxiety. Pemberton told me just now."

Oliver lifted a hand abruptly.

"Tell me," he said. "What am I wanted to say?"

"Well, the President will have a proposal, we imagine. You know our minds well enough. Just explain our attitude towards the Catholics."

Oliver's eyes shrank suddenly to two bright lines beneath the lids. He nodded.

Cartwright came up presently, an immense, bent old man with a face of parchment, as befitted the Lord Chief Justice.

"By the way, Brand, what do you know of a man called Phillips? He seems to have mentioned your name."

"He was my secretary," said Oliver slowly. "What about him?"

"I think he must be mad. He had given himself up to a magistrate, entreating to be examined at once. The magistrate has applied for instructions. You see, the Act has scarcely begun to move yet."

"But what has he done?"

"That's the difficulty. He says he cannot deny God, neither can he affirm Him.—He was your secretary, then?"

"Certainly. I knew he was inclined to Christianity. I had to get rid of him for that."

"Well, he is to be remanded for a week. Perhaps he will be able to make up his mind."

Then the talk shifted off again. Two or three more came up, and all eyed Oliver with a certain curiosity; the story was gone about that his wife had left him. They wished to see how he took it.

At five minutes before the hour a bell ran, and the door into the corridor was thrown open.

"Come, gentlemen," said the Prime Minister.

The Council Chamber was a long high room on the first floor; its walls from floor to ceiling were lined with books. A noiseless rubber carpet was underfoot. There were no windows; the room was lighted artificially. A long table, set round with armed chairs, ran the length of the floor, eight on either side; and the Presidential chair, raised on a dais, stood at the head.

Each man went straight to his chair in silence, and remained there, waiting.

The room was beautifully cool, in spite of the absence of windows, and was a pleasant contrast to the hot evening outside through which most of these men had come. They, too, had wondered at the surprising weather, and had smiled at the conflict of the infallible. But they were not thinking about that now: the coming of the President was a matter which always silenced the most loquacious. Besides, this time, they understood that the affair was more serious than usual.

At one minute before the hour, again a bell sounded, four times, and ceased; and at the signal each man turned instinctively to the high sliding door behind the Presidential chair. There was dead silence within and without: the huge Government offices were luxuriously provided with sound-deadening apparatus, and not even the rolling of the vast motors within a hundred yards was able to send a vibration through the layers of rubber on which the walls rested. There was only one noise that could penetrate, and that the sound of thunder. The experts were at present unable to exclude this.

Again the silence seemed to fall in one yet deeper veil. Then the door opened, and a figure came swiftly through, followed by Another in black and scarlet.

II

He passed straight up to the chair, followed by two secretaries, bowed slightly to this side and that, sat down and made a little gesture. Then they, too, were in their chairs, upright and intent. For perhaps the hundredth time, Oliver, staring upon the President, marvelled at the quietness and the astounding personality of Him. He was in the English judicial dress that had passed down through the centuries—black and scarlet with sleeves of white fur and a crimson sash—and that had lately been adopted as the English presidential costume of him who stood at the head of the legislature. But it was in His personality, in the atmosphere that flowed from Him, that the marvel lay. It was as the scent of the sea to the physical nature—it exhilarated, cleansed, kindled, intoxicated. It was as inexplicably attractive as a cherry orchard in spring, as affecting as the cry of stringed instruments, as compelling as a storm. So writers had said. They compared it to a stream of clear water, to the flash of a gem, to the love of a woman. They lost all decency sometimes; they said it fitted all moods, as the voice of many waters; they called it again and again, as explicitly as possible, the Divine Nature perfectly Incarnate at last....

Then Oliver's reflections dropped from him like a mantle, for the President, with downcast eyes and head thrown back, made a little gesture to the ruddy-faced secretary on His right; and this man, without a movement, began to speak like an impersonal actor repeating his part.

"Gentlemen," he said, in an even, resonant voice, "the President is come direct from Paris. This afternoon His Honour was in Berlin; this morning, early, in Moscow. Yesterday in New York. To-night His Honour must be in Turin; and to-morrow will begin to return through Spain, North Africa, Greece and the southeastern states."

This was the usual formula for such speeches. The President spoke but little himself now; but was careful for the information of his subjects on occasions like this. His secretaries were perfectly trained, and this speaker was no exception. After a slight pause, he continued:

"This is the business, gentlemen.

"Last Thursday, as you are aware, the Plenipotentiaries signed the Test Act in this room, and it was immediately communicated all over the world. At sixteen o'clock His Honour received a message from a man named Dolgorovski—who is, it is understood, one of the Cardinals of the Catholic Church. This he claimed; and on inquiry it was found to be a fact. His information confirmed what was already suspected—namely, that there was a man claiming to be Pope, who had created (so the phrase is) other cardinals, shortly after the destruction of Rome, subsequent to which his own election took place in Jerusalem. It appears that this Pope, with a good deal of statesmanship, has chosen to keep his own name and place of residence a secret from even his own followers, with the exception of the twelve cardinals; that he has done a great deal, through the instrumentality of one of his cardinals in particular, and through his new Order in general, towards the reorganisation of the Catholic Church; and that at this moment he is living, apart from the world, in complete security.

"His Honour blames Himself that He did not do more than suspect something of the kind—misled, He thinks, by a belief that if there had been a Pope, news would have been heard of it from other quarters, for, as is well known, the entire structure of the Christian Church rests upon him as upon a rock. Further, His Honour thinks inquiries should have been made in the very place where now it is understood that this Pope is living.

"The man's name, gentlemen, is Franklin——"

Oliver started uncontrollably, but relapsed again to bright-eyed intelligence as for an instant the President glanced up from his motionlessness.

"Franklin," repeated the secretary, "and he is living in Nazareth, where, it is said, the Founder of Christianity passed His youth.

"Now this, gentlemen, His Honour heard on Thursday in last week. He caused inquiries to be made, and on Friday morning received further intelligence from Dolgorovski that this Pope had summoned to Nazareth a meeting of his cardinals, and certain other officials, from all over the world, to consider what steps should be taken in view of the new Test Act. This His Honour takes to show an extreme want of statesmanship which seems hard to reconcile with his former action. These persons are summoned by special messengers to meet on Saturday next, and will begin their deliberations after some Christian ceremonies on the following morning.

"You wish, gentlemen, no doubt, to know Dolgorovski's motives in making all this known. His Honour is satisfied that they are genuine. The man has been losing belief in his religion; in fact, he has come to see that this religion is the supreme obstacle to the consolidation of the race. He has esteemed it his duty, therefore, to lay this information before His Honour. It is interesting as an historical parallel to reflect that the same kind of incident marked the rise of Christianity as will mark, it is thought, its final extinction—namely, the informing on the part of one of the leaders of the place and method by which the principal personage may be best approached. It is also, surely, very significant that the scene of the extinction of Christianity is identical with that of its inauguration....

"Well, gentlemen, His Honour's proposal is as follows, carrying out the Declaration to which you all acceded. It is that a force should proceed during the night of Saturday next to Palestine, and on the Sunday morning, when these men will be all gathered together, that this force should finish as swiftly and mercifully as possible the work to which the Powers have set their hands. So far, the consent of the Governments which have been consulted has been unanimous, and there is little doubt that the rest will be equally so. His Honour felt that He could not act in so grave a matter on His own responsibility; it is not merely local; it is a catholic administration of justice, and will have results wider than it is safe minutely to prophesy.

"It is not necessary to enter into His Honour's reasons. They are already well known to you; but before asking for your opinion, He desires me to indicate what He thinks, in the event of your approval, should be the method of action.

"Each Government, it is proposed, should take part in the final scene, for it is something of a symbolic action; and for this purpose it is thought well that each of the three Departments of the World should depute volors, to the number of the constituting States, one hundred and twenty-two all told, to set about the business. These volors should have no common meeting-ground, otherwise the news will surely penetrate to Nazareth, for it is understood that this new Order of Christ Crucified has a highly organised system of espionage. The *rendezvous*, then, should be no other than Nazareth itself; and the time of meeting should be, it is thought, not later than nine o'clock according to Palestine reckoning.

These details, however, can be decided and communicated as soon as a determination has been formed as regards the entire scheme.

"With respect to the exact method of carrying out the conclusion, His Honour is inclined to think it will be more merciful to enter into no negotiations with the persons concerned. An opportunity should be given to the inhabitants of the village to make their escape if they so desire it, and then, with the explosives that the force should carry, the end can be practically instantaneous.

"For Himself, His Honour proposes to be there in person, and further that the actual discharge should take place from His own car. It seems but suitable that the world which has done His Honour the goodness to elect Him to its Presidentship should act through His hands; and this would be at least some slight token of respect to a superstition which, however infamous, is yet the one and only force capable of withstanding the true progress of man.

"His Honour promises you, gentlemen, that in the event of this plan being carried out, we shall be no more troubled with Christianity. Already the moral effect of the Test Act has been prodigious. It is understood that, by tens of thousands, Catholics, numbering among them even members of this new fanatical Religious Order, have been renouncing their follies even in these few days; and a final blow struck now at the very heart and head of the Catholic Church, eliminating, as it would do, the actual body on which the entire organisation subsists, would render its resurrection impossible. It is a well-known fact that, granted the extinction of the line of Popes, together with those necessary for its continuance, there could be no longer any question amongst even the most ignorant that the claim of Jesus had ceased to be either reasonable or possible. Even the Order that has provided the sinews for this new movement must cease to exist.

"Dolgorovski, of course, is the difficulty, for it is not certainly known whether one Cardinal would be considered sufficient for the propagation of the line; and, although reluctantly, His Honour feels bound to suggest that at the conclusion of the affair, Dolgorovski, also, who will not, of course, be with his fellows at Nazareth, should be mercifully removed from even the danger of a relapse....

"His Honour, then, asks you, gentlemen, as briefly as possible, to state your views on the points of which I have had the privilege of speaking."

The quiet business-like voice ceased.

He had spoken throughout in the manner with which he had begun; his eyes had been downcast throughout; his voice had been tranquil and restrained. His deportment had been admirable.

There was an instant's silence, and all eyes settled steadily again upon the motionless figure in black and scarlet and the ivory face.

Then Oliver stood up. His face was as white as paper; his eyes bright and dilated.

"Sir," he said, "I have no doubt that we are all of one mind. I need say no more than that, so far as I am a representative of my colleagues, we assent to the proposal, and leave all details in your Honour's hands."

The President lifted his eyes, and ran them swiftly along the rigid faces turned to him.

Then, in the breathless hush, he spoke for the first time in his strange voice, now as passionless as a frozen river.

"Is there any other proposal?"

There was a murmur of assent as the men rose to their feet.

"Thank you, gentlemen," said the secretary.

III

It was a little before seven o'clock on the morning of Saturday that Oliver stepped out of the motor that had carried him to Wimbledon Common, and began to go up the steps of the old volor-stage, abandoned five years ago. It had been thought better, in view of the extreme secrecy that was to be kept, that England's representative in the expedition should start from a comparatively unknown point, and this old stage, in disuse now, except for occasional trials of new Government machines, had been selected. Even the lift had been removed, and it was necessary to climb the hundred and fifty steps on foot.

It was with a certain unwillingness that he had accepted this post among the four delegates, for nothing had been heard of his wife, and it was terrible to him to leave London while her fate was as yet doubtful. On the whole, he was less inclined than ever now to accept the Euthanasia theory; he had spoken to one or two of her friends, all of whom declared that she had never even hinted at such an end. And, again, although he was well aware of the eight-day law in the matter, even if she had determined on such a step there was nothing to show that she was yet in England, and, in fact, it was more than likely that if she were bent on such an act she would go abroad for it, where laxer conditions prevailed. In short, it seemed that he could do no good by remaining in England, and the temptation to be present at the final act of justice in the East by which land, and, in fact, it was more than likely that if she were to be wiped out, and Franklin, too, among them—Franklin, that parody of the Lord of the

World—this, added to the opinion of his colleagues in the Government, and the curious sense, never absent from him now, that Felsenburgh's approval was a thing to die for if necessary—these things had finally prevailed. He left behind him at home his secretary, with instructions that no expense was to be spared in communicating with him should any news of his wife arrive during his absence.

It was terribly hot this morning, and, by the time that he reached the top he noticed that the monster in the net was already fitted into its white aluminum casing, and that the fans within the corridor and saloon were already active. He stepped inside to secure a seat in the saloon, set his bag down, and after a word or two with the guard, who, of course, had not yet been informed of their destination, learning that the others were not yet come, he went out again on to the platform for coolness' sake, and to brood in peace.

London looked strange this morning, he thought. Here beneath him was the common, parched somewhat with the intense heat of the previous week, stretching for perhaps half-a-mile—tumbled ground, smooth stretches of turf, and the heads of heavy trees—up to the first house-roofs, set, too, it seemed, in bowers of foliage. Then beyond that began the serried array, line beyond line, broken in one spot by the gleam of a river-reach, and then on again fading beyond eyesight. But what surprised him was the density of the air; it was now, as old books related it had been in the days of smoke. There was no freshness, no translucence of morning atmosphere; it was impossible to point in any one direction to the source of this veiling gloom, for on all sides it was the same. Even the sky overhead lacked its blue; it appeared painted with a muddy brush, and the sun shewed the same faint tinge of red. Yes, it was like that, he said wearily to himself—like a second-rate sketch; there was no sense of mystery as of a veiled city, but rather unreality. The shadows seemed lacking in definiteness, the outlines and grouping in coherence. A storm was wanted, he reflected; or even, it might be, one more earthquake on the other side of the world would, in wonderful illustration of the globe's unity, relieve the pressure on this side. Well, well; the journey would be worth taking even for the interest of observing climatic changes; but it would be terribly hot, he mused, by the time the south of France was reached.

Then his thoughts leaped back to their own gnawing misery.

It was another ten minutes before he saw the scarlet Government motor, with awnings out, slide up the road from the direction of Fulham; and yet five minutes more before the three men appeared with their servants behind them— Maxwell, Snowford and Cartwright, all alike, as was Oliver, in white duck from head to foot.

They did not speak one word of their business, for the officials were going to and fro, and it was advisable to guard against even the smallest possibility of betrayal. The guard had been told that the volor was required for a three day's journey, that provisions were to be taken in for that period, and that the first point towards which the course was to lie was the centre of the South Downs. There would be no stopping for at least a day and a night.

Further instructions had reached them from the President on the previous morning, by which time He had completed his visitation, and received the assent of the Emergency Councils of the world. This Snowford commented upon in an undertone, and added a word or two as to details, as the four stood together looking out over the city.

Briefly, the plan was as follows, at least so far as it concerned England. The volor was to approach Palestine from
the direction of the Mediterranean, observing to get into
touch with France on her left and Spain on her right within
ten miles of the eastern end of Crete. The approximate hour
was fixed at twenty-three (eastern time). At this point she was
to show her night signal, a scarlet line on a white field; and in
the event of her failing to observe her neighbours was to circle
at that point, at a height of eight hundred feet, until either
the two were sighted or further instructions were received.
For the purpose of dealing with emergencies, the President's
car, which would finally make its entrance from the south,
was to be accompanied by an *aide-de-camp* capable of moving at a very high speed, whose signals were to be taken as
Felsenburgh's own.

So soon as the circle was completed, having Esdraelon
as its centre with a radius of five hundred and forty miles,
the volors were to advance, dropping gradually to within five
hundred feet of sea-level, and diminishing their distance one
from another from the twenty-five miles or so at which they
would first find themselves, until they were as near as safety
allowed. In this manner the advance at a pace of fifty miles
an hour from the moment that the circle was arranged would
bring them within sight of Nazareth at about nine o'clock on
the Sunday morning.

The guard came up to the four as they stood there silent.
"We are ready, gentlemen," he said.
"What do you think of the weather?" asked Snowford
abruptly.
The guard pursed his lips.
"A little thunder, I expect, sir," he said.

Oliver looked at him curiously.

"No more than that?" he asked.

"I should say a storm, sir," observed the guard shortly.

Snowford turned towards the gangway.

"Well, we had best be off: we can lose time further on, if we wish."

It was about five minutes more before all was ready. From the stern of the boat came a faint smell of cooking, for breakfast would be served immediately, and a white-capped cook protruded his head for an instant to question the guard. The four sat down in the gorgeous saloon in the bows; Oliver silent by himself, the other three talking in low voices together. Once more the guard passed through to his compartment at the prow, glancing as he went to see that all were seated; and an instant later came the clang of the signal. Then through all the length of the boat—for she was the fastest ship that England possessed—passed the thrill of the propeller beginning to work up speed; and simultaneously Oliver, staring sideways through the plate-glass window, saw the rail drop away, and the long line of London, pale beneath the tinged sky, surge up suddenly. He caught a glimpse of a little group of persons staring up from below, and they, too, dropped in a great swirl, and vanished. Then, with a flash of dusty green, the Common had vanished, and a pavement of house-roofs began to stream beneath, the long lines of streets on this side and that turning like spokes of a gigantic wheel; once more this pavement thinned, showing green again as between infrequently laid cobble-stones; then they, too, were gone, and the country was open beneath.

Snowford rose, staggering a little.

"I may as well tell the guard now," he said. "Then we need not be interrupted again."

CHAPTER VI

I

THE SYRIAN awoke from a dream that a myriad faces were looking into his own, eager, attentive and horrible, in his corner of the roof-top, and sat up sweating and gasping aloud for breath. For an instant he thought that he was really dying, and that the spiritual world was about him. Then, as he struggled, sense came back, and he stood up, drawing long breaths of the stifling night air.

Above him the sky was as the pit, black and empty; there was not a glimmer of light, though the moon was surely up. He had seen her four hours before, a red sickle, swing slowly out from Thabor. Across the plain, as he looked from the parapet, there was nothing. For a few yards there lay across the broken ground a single crooked lance of light from a half-closed shutter; and beneath that, nothing. To the north again, nothing; to the west a glimmer, pale as a moth's wing, from the house-roofs of Nazareth; to the east, nothing. He might be on a tower-top in space, except for that line of light and that grey glimmer that evaded the eye.

On the roof, however, it was possible to make out at least outlines, for the dormer trap had been left open at the head of the stairs, and from somewhere within the depths of the house there stole up a faint refracted light.

There was a white bundle in that corner; that would be the pillow of the Benedictine abbot. He had seen him lay himself down there some time—was it four hours or four centuries ago? There was a grey shape stretched along that pale wall—the Friar, he thought; there were other irregular outlines breaking the face of the parapet, here and there along the sides.

Very softly, for he knew the caprices of sleep, he stepped across the paved roof to the opposite parapet and looked over, for there yet hung about him a desire for reassurance that he was still in company with flesh and blood. Yes, indeed he was still on earth; for there was a real and distinct light burning among the tumbled rocks, and beside it, delicate as a miniature, the head and shoulders of a man, writing. And in the circle of light were other figures, pale, broken patches on which men lay; a pole or two, erected with the thought of a tent to follow; a little pile of luggage with a rug across it; and beyond the circle other outlines and shapes faded away into the stupendous blackness.

Then the writing man moved his head, and a monstrous shadow fled across the ground; a yelp as of a strangling dog broke out suddenly close behind him, and, as he turned, a moaning figure sat up on the roof, sobbing itself awake. Another moved at the sound, and then as, sighing, the former relapsed heavily against the wall, once more the priest went back to his place, still doubtful as to the reality of all that he saw, and the breathless silence came down again as a pall.

He woke again from dreamless sleep, and there was a change. From his corner, as he raised his heavy eyes, there met them what seemed an unbearable brightness; then, as he looked, it resolved itself into a candle-flame, and beyond it a white sleeve, and higher yet a white face and throat. He understood, and rose reeling; it was the messenger come to fetch him as had been arranged.

As he passed across the space, once he looked round him, and it seemed that the dawn must have come, for that appalling sky overhead was visible at last. An enormous vault, smoke-coloured and opaque, seemed to curve away to the ghostly horizons on either side where the far-away hills raised sharp shapes as if cut in paper. Carmel was before him; at least he thought it was that—a bull head and shoulders thrusting itself forward and ending in an abrupt descent, and beyond that again the glimmering sky. There were no clouds, no outlines to break the huge, smooth, dusky dome beneath the centre of which this house-roof seemed poised. Across the parapet, as he glanced to the right before descending the steps, stretched Esdraelon, sad-coloured and sombre, into the metallic distance. It was all as unreal as some fantastic picture by one who had never looked upon clear sunlight. The silence was complete and profound.

Straight down through the wheeling shadows he went, following the white-hooded head and figure down the stairs, along the tiny passage, stumbling once against the feet of one who slept with limbs tossed loose like a tired dog; the feet drew back mechanically, and a little moan broke from the shadows. Then he went on, passing the servant who stood aside, and entered.

There were half-a-dozen men gathered here, silent, white figures standing apart one from the other, who genuflected as the Pope came in simultaneously through the opposite door, and again stood white-faced and attentive. He ran his eyes over them as he stopped, waiting behind his master's chair—there were two he knew, remembering them from last night—dark-faced Cardinal Ruspoli, and the lean Australian Archbishop, besides Cardinal Corkran, who stood by his chair at the Pope's own table, with papers laid ready.

Silvester sat down, and with a little gesture caused the others to sit too. Then He began at once in that quiet tired voice that his servant knew so well.

"Eminences—we are all here, I think. We need lose no more time, then.... Cardinal Corkran has something to communicate—" He turned a little. "Father, sit down, if you please. This will occupy a little while."

The priest went across to the stone window-seat, whence he could watch the Pope's face in the light of the two candles that now stood on the table between him and the Cardinal-Secretary. Then the Cardinal began, glancing up from his papers.

"Holiness. I had better begin a little way back. Their Eminences have not heard the details properly....

"I received at Damascus, on last Friday week, inquiries from various prelates in different parts of the world, as to the actual measure concerning the new policy of persecution. At first I could tell them nothing positively, for it was not until after twenty o'clock that Cardinal Ruspoli, in Turin, informed me of the facts. Cardinal Malpas confirmed them a few minutes later, and the Cardinal Archbishop of Pekin at twenty-three. Before mid-day on Saturday I received final confirmation from my messengers in London.

"I was at first surprised that Cardinal Dolgorovski did not communicate it; for almost simultaneously with the Turin message I received one from a priest of the Order of Christ Crucified in Moscow, to which, of course, I paid no attention. (It is our rule, Eminences, to treat unauthorised communications in that way.) His Holiness, however, bade me make inquiries, and I learned from Father Petrovoski and others that the Government placards published the news at twenty o'clock—by our time. It was curious, therefore, that the Cardinal had not seen it; if he had seen it, it was, of course, his duty to acquaint me immediately.

"Since that time, however, the following facts have come out. It is established beyond a doubt that Cardinal Dolgorovski received a visitor in the course of the evening. His own chaplain, who, your Eminences are perhaps aware, has been very active in Russia on behalf of the Church, informs me of this privately. Yet the Cardinal asserts, in explanation of his silence, that he was alone during those hours, and had given orders that no one was to be admitted to his presence without urgent cause. This, of course, confirmed His Holiness's opinion, but I received orders from him to act as if nothing had happened, and to command the Cardinal's presence here with the rest of the Sacred College. To this I received an intimation that he would be present. Yesterday, however, a little before mid-day, I received a further message that his Eminency had met with a slight accident, but that he yet hoped to present himself in time for the deliberations. Since then no further news has arrived."

There was a dead silence.

Then the Pope turned to the Syrian priest.

"Father," he said, "it was you who received his Eminency's messages. Have you anything to add to this?"

"No, Holiness."

He turned again.

"My son," he said, "report to Us publicly what you have already reported to Us in private."

A small, bright-eyed man moved out of the shadows.

"Holiness, it was I who conveyed the message to Cardinal

Dolgorovski. He refused at first to receive me. When I reached his presence and communicated the command he was silent; then he smiled; then he told me to carry back the message that he would obey."

Again the Pope was silent.

Then suddenly the tall Australian stood up.

"Holiness," he said, "I was once intimate with that man. It was partly through my means that he sought reception into the Catholic Church. This was not less than fourteen years ago, when the fortunes of the Church seemed about to prosper.... Our friendly relations ceased two years ago, and I may say that, from what I know of him, I find no difficulty in believing——"

As his voice shook with passion and he faltered, Silvester raised his hand.

"We desire no recriminations. Even the evidence is now useless, for what was to be done has been done. For ourselves, we have no doubt as to its nature.... It was to this man that Christ gave the morsel through our hands, saying *Quod facis, fac citius. Cum ergo accepisset ille buccellam, exivit continuo. Erat autem nox.*"

Again fell the silence, and in the pause sounded a long half-vocal sigh from without the door. It came and went as a sleeper turned, for the passage was crowded with exhausted men—as a soul might sigh that passed from light to darkness.

Then Silvester spoke again. And as He spoke He began, as if mechanically, to tear up a long paper, written with lists of names, that lay before Him.

"Eminences, it is three hours after dawn. In two hours more We shall say Mass in your presence, and give Holy Communion. During those two hours We commission you

to communicate this news to all who are assembled here; and
further, We bestow on each and all of you jurisdiction apart
from all previous rules of time and place; we give a Plenary
Indulgence to all who confess and communicate this day.
Father—" he turned to the Syrian— "Father, you will now
expose the Blessed Sacrament in the chapel, after which you
will proceed to the village and inform the inhabitants that if
they wish to save their lives they had best be gone immediately—immediately, you understand."

The Syrian started from his daze.

"Holiness," he stammered, stretching out a hand, "the
lists, the lists!"

(He had seen what these were.)

But Silvester only smiled as He tossed the fragments on to
the table. Then He stood up.

"You need not trouble, my son.... We shall not need
these any more....

"One last word, Eminences.... If there is one heart here
that doubts or is afraid, I have a word to say."

He paused, with an extraordinarily simple deliberateness,
ran the eyes round the tense faces turned to Him.

"I have had a Vision of God," He said softly. "I walk no
more by faith, but by sight."

II

An hour later the priest toiled back in the hot twilight up
the path from the village, followed by half-a-dozen silent
men, twenty yards behind, whose curiosity exceeded their
credulousness. He had left a few more standing bewildered
at the doors of the little mud-houses; and had seen perhaps a
hundred families, weighted with domestic articles, pour like

a stream down the rocky path that led to Khaifa. He had
been cursed by some, even threatened; stared upon by others;
mocked by a few. The fanatical said that the Christians had
brought God's wrath upon the place, and the darkness upon
the sky: the sun was dying, for these hounds were too evil for
him to look upon and live. Others again seemed to see nothing remarkable in the state of the weather....

There was no change in that sky from its state an hour
before, except that perhaps it had lightened a little as the
sun climbed higher behind that impenetrable dusky shroud.
Hills, grass, men's faces—all bore to the priest's eyes the look
of unreality; they were as things seen in a dream by eyes that
roll with sleep through lids weighted with lead. Even to other
physical senses that unreality was present; and once more he
remembered his dream, thankful that that horror at least was
absent. But silence seemed other than a negation of sound, it
was a thing in itself, an affirmation, unruffled by the sound
of footsteps, the thin barking of dogs, the murmur of voices.
It appeared as if the stillness of eternity had descended and
embraced the world's activities, and as if that world, in a desperate attempt to assert its own reality, was braced in a set,
motionless, noiseless, breathless effort to hold itself in being.
What Silvester had said just now was beginning to be true of
this man also. The touch of the powdery soil and the warm
pebbles beneath the priest's bare feet seemed something apart
from the consciousness that usually regards the things of
sense as more real and more intimate than the things of spirit.
Matter still had a reality, still occupied space, but it was of a
subjective nature, the result of internal rather than external
powers. He appeared to himself already to be scarcely more
than a soul, intent and steady, united by a thread only to the

body and the world with which he was yet in relations. He knew that the appalling heat was there; once even, before his eyes a patch of beaten ground cracked and lisped as water that touches hot iron, as he trod upon it. He could feel the heat upon his forehead and hands, his whole body was swathed and soaked in it; yet he regarded it as from an outside stand-point, as a man with neuritis perceives that the pain is no longer in his hand but in the pillow which supports it. So, too, with what his eyes looked upon and his ears heard; so, too, with that faint bitter taste that lay upon his lips and nostrils. There was no longer in him fear or even hope—he regarded himself, the world, and even the enshrouding and awful Presence of spirit as facts with which he had but little to do. He was scarcely even interested; still less was he distressed. There was Thabor before him—at least what once had been Thabor, now it was no more than a huge and dusky dome-shape which impressed itself upon his retina and informed his passive brain of its existence and outline, though that existence seemed no better than that of a dissolving phantom.

It seemed then almost natural—or at least as natural as all else—as he came in through the passage and opened the chapel-door, to see that the floor was crowded with prostrate motionless figures. There they lay, all alike in the white burnous which he had given out last night; and, with forehead on arms, as during the singing of the Litany of the Saints at an ordination, lay the figure he knew best and loved more than all the world, the shoulders and white hair at a slight elevation upon the single altar step. Above the plain altar itself burned the six tall candles; and in the midst, on the mean little throne, stood the white-metal monstrance, with its White Centre....

Then he, too, dropped, and lay as he was....

He did not know how long it was before the circling obser-
vant consciousness, the flow of slow images, the vibration of
particular thoughts, ceased and stilled as a pool rocks quietly to
peace after the dropped stone has long lain still. But it came at
last—that superb tranquillity, possible only when the senses are
physically awake, with which God, perhaps once in a lifetime,
rewards the aspiring and trustful soul—that point of complete
rest in the heart of the Fount of all existence with which one
day He will reward eternally the spirits of His children. There
was no thought in him of articulating this experience, of ana-
lysing its elements, or fingering this or that strain of ecstatic joy.
The time for self-regarding was passed. It was enough that the
experience was there, although he was not even self-reflective
enough to tell himself so. He had passed from that circle whence
the soul looks within, from that circle, too, whence it looks
upon objective glory, to that very centre where it reposes—and
the first sign to him that time had passed was the murmur of
words, heard distinctly and understood, although with that
apartness with which a drowsy man perceives a message from
without—heard as through a veil through which nothing but
thinnest essence could transpire.

*Spiritus Domini replevit orbem terrarum.... The Spirit of
the Lord hath fulfilled all things, alleluia: and that which con-
tains all things hath knowledge of the voice, alleluia, alleluia,
alleluia.*

Exsurgat Deus (and the voice rose ever so slightly). *"Let
God arise and let His enemies be scattered; and let them who hate
Him flee before His face."*

Gloria Patri....

Then he raised his heavy head; and a phantom figure
stood there in red vestments, seeming to float rather than to

stand, with thin hands outstretched, and white cap on white hair seen in the gleam of the steady candle-flames; another, also in white, kneeled on the step....

Kyrie eleison ... Gloria in excelsis Deo ... those things passed like a shadow-show, with movements and rustlings, but he perceived rather the light which cast them. He heard *Deus qui in hodierna die ...* but his passive mind gave no pulse of reflex action, no stir of understanding until these words. *Cum complerentur dies Pentecostes....*

"*When the day of Pentecost was fully come, all the disciples were with one accord in the same place; and there came from heaven suddenly a sound, as of a mighty wind approaching, and it filled the house where they were sitting....*

Then he remembered and understood.... It was Pentecost then! And with memory a shred of reflection came back. Where then was the wind, and the flame, and the earthquake, and the secret voice? Yet the world was silent, rigid in its last effort at self-assertion: there was no tremor to show that God remembered; no actual point of light, yet, breaking the appalling vault of gloom that lay over sea and land to reveal that He burned there in eternity, transcendent and dominant; not even a voice; and at that he understood yet more. He perceived that that world, whose monstrous parody his sleep had presented to him in the night, was other than that he had feared it to be; it was sweet, not terrible; friendly, not hostile; clear, not stifling; and home, not exile. There were presences here, but not those gluttonous, lustful things that had looked on him last night.... He dropped his head again upon his hands, at once ashamed and content; and again he sank down to depths of glimmering inner peace....

Not again, for a while, did he perceive what he did or thought, or what passed there, five yards away on the low step. Once only a ripple passed across that sea of glass, a ripple of fire and sound like a rising star that flicks a line of light across a sleeping lake, like a thin thread of vibration streaming from a quivering string across the stillness of a deep night— and he perceived for an instant as in a formless mirror that a lower nature was struck into existence and into union with the Divine nature at the same moment.... And then no more again but the great encompassing hush, the sense of the inner-most heart of reality, till he found himself kneeling at the rail, and knew that That which alone truly existed on earth approached him with the swiftness of thought and the ardour of Divine Love....

Then, as the Mass ended, and he raised his passive happy soul to receive the last gift of God, there was a cry, a sudden clamour in the passage, and a man stood in the doorway, gab-bling Arabic.

III

Yet even at that sound and sight his soul scarcely tightened the languid threads that united it through every fibre of his body with the world of sense. He saw and heard the tumult in the passage, frantic eyes and mouths crying aloud, and, in strange contrast, the pale ecstatic faces of those princes who turned and looked; even within the tranquil presence-chamber of the spirit where two beings, Incarnate God and all but Discarnate Man, were locked in embrace, a certain mental process went on. Yet all was still as apart from him as a lighted stage and its drama from a self-contained spectator. In the material world, now as attenuated as a mirage, events were at hand; but to his soul, balanced now on reality and awake to facts, these things were but a spectacle....

He turned to the altar again, and there, as he had known it would be, in the midst of clear light, all was at peace: the celebrant, seen as through molten glass, adored as He murmured the mystery of the Word-made-Flesh, and once more passing to the centre, sank upon His knees.

Again the priest understood; for thought was no longer the process of mind, rather it was the glance of a spirit. He knew all now; and, by an inevitable impulse, his throat began to sing aloud words that, as he sang them, opened for the first time as flowers telling their secret to the sun.

O Salutaris hostia
Qui coeli pandis ostium....

They were all singing now; even the Mohammedan catechumen who had burst in a moment ago sang with the rest, his lean head thrust out and his arms tight across his breast; the tiny chapel rang with the forty voices, and the vast world thrilled to hear it....

Still singing, the priest saw the veil laid as by a phantom upon the Pontiff's shoulders; there was a movement, a surge of figures—shadows only in the midst of substance,

... Uni Trinoque Domino....

—and the Pope stood erect, Himself a pallor in the heart of light, with spectral folds of silk dripping from His shoulders, His hands swathed in them, and His down-bent head hidden by the silver-rayed monstrance and That which it bore....

    ... Qui vitam sine termino
    Nobis donet in patria....

    ... They were moving now, and the world of life swung with them; of so much was he aware. He was out in the passage, among the white, frenzied faces that with bared teeth stared up at that sight, silenced at last by the thunder of *Pange Lingua*, and the radiance of those who passed out to eternal life.... At the corner he turned for an instant to see the six pale flames move along a dozen yards behind, as spear-heads about a King, and in the midst the silver rays and the White Heart of God.... Then he was out, and the battle lay in array....

That sky on which he had looked an hour ago had passed from darkness charged with light to light overlaid with darkness—from glimmering night to Wrathful Day—and that light was red....

From behind Thabor on the left to Carmel on the far right, above the hills twenty miles away rested an enormous vault of colour; here were no gradations from zenith to horizon; all was the one deep smoulder of crimson as of the glow of iron. It was such a colour as men have seen at sunsets after rain, while the clouds, more translucent each instant, transmit the glory they cannot contain. Here, too, was the sun, pale as the Host, set like a fragile wafer above the Mount of Transfiguration, and there, far down in the west where men had once cried upon Baal in vain, hung the sickle of the white moon, yet all was no more than stained light that lies broken across carven work of stone....

    ... In suprema nocte coena,

sang the myriad voices,

Recumbens cum fratribus
Observata lege plena
Cibis in legalibus
Cibum turbae duodenae
Se dat suis manibus....

He saw, too, poised as motes in light, that ring of strange fish-creatures, white as milk, except where the angry glory turned their backs to flame, white-winged like floating moths, from the tiny shape far to the south to the monster at hand scarcely five hundred yards away; and even as he looked, singing as he looked, he understood that the circle was nearer, and perceived that these as yet knew nothing....

... Verbum caro, panem verum
Verbo carnem efficit....

... They were nearer still, until now even at his feet there slid along the ground the shadow of a monstrous bird, pale and undefined, as between the wan sun and himself moved out the vast shape that a moment ago hung above the Hill.... Then again it backed across and waited....

... Et si sensus deficit
Ad formandum cor sincerum
Sola fides sufficit....

... He had halted and turned, going in the midst of his fellows, hearing, he thought, the thrill of harping and the throb of heavenly drums; and, across the space, moved now the six flames, steady as if cut of steel in that stupendous poise of heaven and earth; and in their centre the silver-rayed glory and the Whiteness of God made Man....

... Then, with a roar, came the thunder again, pealing in circle beyond circle of those tremendous Presences—Thrones and Powers—who, themselves to the world as substance to shadow, are but shadows again beneath the apex and within the ring of Absolute Deity.... The thunder broke loose, shaking the earth that now cringed on the quivering edge of dissolution....

> Tantum ergo sacramentum
> Veneremur Cernui
> Et antiquum documentum
> Nova Cedat Ritui....

Ah! yes; it was He for whom God waited now—He who far up beneath that trembling shadow of a dome, itself but the piteous core of unimagined splendour, came in His swift chariot, blind to all save that on which He had fixed His eyes so long, unaware that His world corrupted about Him, His shadow moving like a pale cloud across the ghostly plain where Israel had fought and Sennacherib boasted—that plain lighted now with a yet deeper glow, as heaven, kindling to glory beyond glory of yet fiercer spiritual flame, still restrained the power knit at last to the relief of final revelation, and for the last time the voices sang....

> Praestet Fides supplementum
> Sensuum defectui....

... He was coming now, swifter than ever, the heir of temporal ages and the Exile of eternity, the final piteous Prince of rebels, the creature against God, blinder than the sun which paled and the earth that shook; and, as He came, passing even then through the last material stage to the thinness of

a spirit-fabric, the floating circle swirled behind Him, tossing like phantom birds in the wake of a phantom ship.... He
was coming, and the earth, rent once again in its allegiance,
shrank and reeled in the agony of divided homage....

   ... He was coming—and already the shadow swept off
the plain and vanished, and the pale netted wings were rising
to the check; and the great bell clanged, and the long sweet
chord rang out—not more than whispers heard across the
pealing storm of everlasting praise....

> ... GENITORI GENITOQUE
> LAUS ET JUBILATIO
> SALUS HONOR VIRTUS QUOQUE
> SIT ET BENEDICTIO
> PROCEDENTTI AB UTROQUE
> COMPAR SIT LAUDATIO....

and once more

> PROCEDENTI AB UTROQUE
> COMPAR SIT LAUDATIO....

Then this world passed, and the glory of it.

THE END

ABOUT THE AUTHOR

MONSIGNOR ROBERT HUGH BENSON was born in 1871, the son of the Anglican Archbishop of

Monsignor Benson

Canterbury, and himself took Anglican Orders in 1894. After much painful study and soul-searching, he converted and was ordained a Catholic priest in 1904. There followed ten dynamic years of brilliant, buoyant preaching and writing—four books a year: novels, plays, essays, sermons, poems. He was very much in demand for sermons and lectures in England, Rome and even in the United States as can be attested to by Miss Marieli Benziger of Benziger Sisters Publishing: "As a teenager there was no greater hero to all of my family than Monsignor Benson. We were thrilled to learn he was coming for Lent of 1915 to preach in New York. By then the entire family, we three girls and my parents, went nightly to hear him preach.

"When Monsignor Benson died shortly after this we felt as if we had lost a wonderful friend. We had read most of his books and considered him the most outstanding religious we had ever met.

"May his works now being republished bring into the lives of those who get to read and know him, the assurance of his great Faith and understanding of what the real love of God can do to souls that remain loyal to the teachings of the Catholic Church."

Much has been written about Msgr. Benson since his death including a two volume biography by C. C. Martindale, S.J. Of interest to readers might be a few lines taken from the introduction of that biography, *The Life of Monsignor Robert Hugh Benson*: "Finally, while I have most earnestly hoped not to wound the feelings of anyone, Catholic or non-Catholic, of what avail is it to forget that he was … a Catholic priest, passionately eager to spread Roman Catholicism and fiercely antagonistic to alien creeds, even when tenderly devoted to many who might hold them.…"